NEXT TO LAST CHANCE

LOUISA DIXON

GENESIS PRESS, INC.

Columbus, Mississippi

ISBN 1-885478-39-9

Manufactured in the United States of America

Book design by Marie Owen

First Edition

For Jerry and Ben
who give meaning to everything;

And my mother
who has shown me
what perseverance is all about.

AUTHOR'S NOTE

This story is a work of fiction, and every character and every event is fictitious. Any similarity to real persons is absolutely unintentional, including the character of Laura Owen, who bears some resemblance to the author. Official titles and actual positions within state government have often been used, but the characters occupying those positions in the novel originated in the author's imagination. Any resemblance to individuals who hold or have held those positions in real life, is absolutely unintentional and should not be inferred.

I will be forever indebted to Barbara Shor who guided this novel into its final form: In all the learning experiences of my life, I have had few better teachers.

To my friends and my family who helped me along this journey, I give my profound thanks. They endured countless pestering questions and dismal early drafts but gave me candid answers and analyses in return, as well as regular doses of encouragement. Without it, I might not have kept pushing ahead.

Finally, I am especially grateful to Wilbur Colom who saw the possibilities in an early draft and took the chance.

THE CHARACTERS

Alvarez, Olivia—Director of Surveillance, Gulf Goddess casino
Anderson, Jimmie—State Patrol
Britton, Catherine—Director, Crime Laboratory
Campbell, Ted—U.S. Customs Service
Carver, Gibbs—Governor of Mississippi
Coleman, Blake—State Patrol
Coleman, Sally—Wife of Paul Coleman
Collel, Gabriel—State Senator
Cropley, Tim—Reporter
Cummins, Logan—Drug Enforcement Administration
Easterbrook, Hal—FBI Agent
Hemeter, Charlotte—Laura Owen's mother
Hilman, Ann—nee Ruthven, wife of Tom Hilman
Hilman, Carolyn—Mother of Tom Hilman
Hilman, Stephen—Father of Tom Hilman, owner of Hilman Air
Hilman, Tom—Vice President of Hilman Air
Kenner, Bill—State Patrol
Markham, Alex—United States Attorney
Markham, Ford—United States Senator; father of Alex Markham
McNee, Walter—FBI Agent
Owen, Laura—Commissioner of Public Safety for Mississippi
Owen, Semmes—Architect, husband of Laura
Owen, Will—Son of Laura and Semmes Owen
Quinn, Sandy—State Patrol, Mansion Security
Regis, Vic—Chief of Staff to Governor Carver
Rodriguez, Hector—Belize businessman
Salkin, Chris—FBI Agent
Schaeffer , Cleve—Manager, Gulf Goddess casino
Silven, Ginger—Tom Hilman's secretary
Stinley, James—Jackson businessman
Stone, Rachel—Anesthesiologist, wife of Robert Stone
Stone, Robert—State Patrol
Williams, Eddie—Director of Communications, State Patrol

NEXT TO LAST CHANCE

15 YEARS EARLIER

The party had been going for two days at a rambling farmhouse outside
Oxford, Mississippi. Started several years earlier to celebrate the end
of exams at the University, the annual bashes had continued well after
all the original organizers had graduated. No invitations were ever
issued, people just started arriving on the second weekend in May, and
by the time it got really cranked up, two hundred people or more were
drinking and dancing in the old farmhouse. At one o'clock on Monday
morning, the house was still full, although a third of the crowd was
made up of strangers none of the hosts knew.

The center hallway, a wide, high-ceilinged room that ran the length
of the house, was furnished in early barracks style, with three couches,
two daybeds, and an assortment of tattered armchairs. Tom Hilman had
commandeered one of the daybeds and was lying with his head in the
lap of an attractive dark-haired but very young-looking woman who
claimed she was a freshman. The possibility of statutory violations didn't
seem to dampen Tom's enthusiasm in the least. She was tracing Tom's
lips with a long red fingernail while he purred with contentment.

"Hey, Tom," called a familiar voice.

He opened his eyes to see Alex Markham appear at the bottom of the
stairs with his arm around the neck of a luscious but bleary-eyed blonde—
his hand dangling near her impressively large breasts which were barely
restrained by a lime-green halter top.

"Where have you been?" Tom called out.

"One last siesta upstairs," said Alex with a leer.

"Well, it's time to hit the road, Governor."

"Why do people keep calling him Governor?" asked the dark beauty.
"I've been hearing that all weekend."

"That's his life's ambition. It's in the genes, so to speak." Tom sat
up, gesturing toward Alex. "Let me introduce Alex Markham, son of the

2 · LOUISA DIXON

senior senator from the great state of Mississippi, Ford Markham, grandson of the former senior senator, Horace Markham, and great-grandson of Governor Wilton F. Markham."

The young woman reached out to be formally introduced to Alex, but seeing a beer bottle in Alex's left hand and the other grazing the blonde's major assets, she quickly withdrew her hand. "Nice to meet you, Governor," she said in a pert sorority singsong.

"Let's rock and roll, mi amigo," said Alex, unwinding his arm and giving the blonde a quick slap on her rear. "You can get home okay?" he asked her.

The blonde slid onto an empty couch with her head cradled on the armrest. "Don't worry about me, Sweetie," she crooned, dozing off.

With road beers in hand and a six-pack for the ride, Tom and Alex said their good-byes. They were due at work in Jackson, 165 miles south, in less than seven hours. The air was summer thick and low, heavy clouds made it as dark as Mississippi can be. Tom dug his keys out of his jeans pocket, and headed to the driver's side of a mud-splattered dark blue Ford truck with "Hilman Air" in red letters on the doors.

"Hey, I'll drive. You drove up," said Alex.

"Probably shouldn't, Alex, company policy—only employees drive."

"Don't be so damn literal," Alex growled. "Give me the keys."

"You're the lawyer," said Tom, happy for the chance to get in some more sleep. "I trust you'll defend me."

Alex yanked open the door, almost whacking Tom's tall shoulders with the extra-large West Coast rearview mirror. "Watch it, for Christ's sake," Tom said.

"Sorry."

At twenty-three, Alex had just finished his second year of law school and was clerking at a Jackson law firm for the summer. Tom was working as a laborer, learning his father's business—a heating, ventilation, and air-conditioning company—from the ground up. The two had been friends since grade school, although Alex had always dominated, almost like an older brother. Listening to Al Green singing his heart out on WHBQ out of Memphis, they headed south on a two-lane state road through the edge of the hill country to pick up the interstate. Counting on doing 80 mph on I-55, Alex didn't push it past 50 on the two lane.

"Hey, Bozo, this is where you park, not drive," Tom said as Alex wandered onto the shoulder.

Alex straightened the wheel, singing along with the music.

Tom stubbed out his cigarette then leaned through the open window and threw his empty beer can as far into the woods as he could. He pulled a pack of Marlboros from his shirt pocket, but when he saw there was only one left, he put it back. He opened the cooler and pulled out another beer.

"Where did you disappear to last night?"

"I couldn't stand listening to that blonde rattle on and on like she does. I don't see how you put up with it," Tom said.

"Because she puts out like no one I've ever had," Alex replied.

"Really?"

Alex nodded. "You can't even imagine the things she can do."

"But how'd you stand it long enough to find that out?"

"What do you think foreplay is? A discussion of relativity?"

"Hell, no. But your little number's a nitwit," Tom said.

"One of my roommates told me about her. He could only take it for six months, but he said it was worth the effort. Jesus, was he right."

"How about I have a run at her next?" Tom asked.

"Sure thing." Alex crushed his empty with his right hand. "Get me another one, will ya?"

"Don't You Worry 'Bout a Thing" came on the radio as Tom reached toward the cooler. Alex turned up the volume and began imitating Stevie Wonder's swaying rhythms, the car swerving with his movement. Curving down a small hill, the headlights swept across a wide expanse of cotton fields. Up ahead a mile or so where the field roads met the state highway, he could just make out a small group of houses, all dark except for a lone porch light on the last house. Alex chucked the empty can in Tom's corner as Tom handed Alex a fresh beer.

"Jesus!" Alex yelled, dropping the full can and grabbing the wheel. He slammed on the brakes as fast as his beer-soaked reactions allowed. But in the next moment, the right side mirror hit something so hard the truck swerved from the impact. Shards of glass from the mirror flew in toward Tom, and beer sprayed up the inside of the windshield. Alex stopped, threw the truck into reverse and raced backward, looking over his shoulder, searching the darkness for what he'd hit, cursing all the way.

"What in hell happened, Alex?"

"I don't know, I never saw anything until the last second."

"Well, what was it?"

"I don't know, I told you," Alex spat back.

The backup lights illuminated a motionless form lying on the shoulder of the road. Alex jammed on the brakes again and put the truck in park. "Oh, goddammit!"

Tom put what was left of his beer on the dashboard, grabbed a flashlight from the glove box and got out, shaking broken glass onto the road. "Markham, what is it?" Tom said.

Alex didn't move. He just sat there frozen, staring at the houses up ahead.

Tom turned on his light and the beam outlined the bloodied body of a young black man dressed in dark clothing. His head had been nearly severed by the impact. Tom immediately vomited all the beer in him. Wiping his sleeve across his mouth, he knelt by the body, reaching out as if to find a pulse. But the man was completely motionless, his body so devastated that Tom quickly pulled his hand away.

He looked up at Alex who'd gotten out of the car but was still refusing to look in the dead man's direction.

"Christ, you killed the guy, Markham. Look." Tom pointed the flashlight at the man's head and then crawled away, starting to heave again.

Alex closed his eyes and took repeated deep breaths to hold his stomach down. Swearing with every exhale, he shook his head as if that would make it all go away. "Goddamn, why me?"

There was silence. Then Alex extended his foot to nudge the body with his shoe as if he didn't want to touch it. The man wasn't as heavy as he expected, but Alex couldn't move him without using his arms so he bent down and pushed. The young man flopped on his back, revealing a completely mangled face covered in blood. On the verge of throwing up, Alex breathed deeply again and rolled the body two more times away from the roadway, leaving a trail of blood from where the man had first come to rest.

Tom stared at him in horror. "What the hell are you doing?"

"Moving him out of the way."

"You can't just leave him here," Tom objected.

"The hell we can't," Alex said. "We're going to Jackson. He's dead. It was an accident. Get in the truck."

"That's right. It was an accident. We'll tell the police it was an accident."

"Get in the truck before someone comes and finds us," Alex ordered, wiping his hands on his jeans. "We'll talk about this on the road."

They locked stares. Tom didn't move. Alex reached for his arm. Tom jerked away from him, still staring. Alex sprinted around to the driver's side, put the truck in reverse, and backed up until he was even with Tom.

"Get in, goddammit."

Tom stood there, looking toward the body. "You're wrong about this, Alex. Completely wrong."

"No. I'm not. I'm the one who was driving. Get in, I told you." Alex paused a moment and then added with a snarl, "Now."

Tom opened the door and saw Alex's can, crushed and empty, on the floor. He looked at Alex, looked at the can another time, then picked it up by the rim, and aimed for a spot in front of the body. It landed six inches from the man's feet. Tom shoved the broken mirror away from his window, and gingerly inched onto the seat. Alex roared off.

"Slow down, you fool," Tom shouted. "We'll get stopped for speeding."

As they passed the houses, the curtains were all closed and still. Not a light anywhere, save on the furthest porch. Alex hid his face nevertheless, looking toward the fields on the opposite side of the road. They didn't pass another vehicle until they turned onto the interstate.

In Grenada, they hosed down the truck in the stall of a coin-operated all-night car wash. The mirror hadn't broken off, but the door was caved in slightly where each of the three supports were mounted. Alex scraped hair out of the crevices while Tom cleaned up the cab of truck, searching for slivers of glass and wiping up the beer and blood with one of his T-shirts. He carefully inspected every inch of the right side before he took the wheel.

"Tell 'em you misjudged a gatepost out on my farm," Alex said.

Tom didn't respond.

"Look, we were drinking, that makes it vehicular manslaughter, homicide maybe," Alex said. "You know and I know it was an accident, but that doesn't mean we could prove it." Alex paused for a second, checking the road behind them in the remaining sliver of mirror. "And I'm not spending an hour in jail for his accidentally dead black ass."

Tom pulled out his last cigarette and lit it, leaning against the door frame, silent.

Alex started in again. "It would be the end of law school, the end of politics, the end of life as I know it."

"What about my life as I know it? I don't speak up and I'm an accessory— that's the correct term, isn't it, Governor?"

"Yes, but no one will ever know," Alex scolded.

Tom stared ahead at the interstate—not a car or truck in sight for the moment.

"They'd better not, Markham. They sure as hell better not."

1

Laura Owen savored the warm sweet exhaustion after their lovemaking, not daring to move a muscle lest she disturb their perfect position. Semmes lay behind her, enveloping her with his arms and legs. She was small enough to fit neatly into the curve of his long, lean body.

Bliss. Nothing to prove, no one to impress, just warm safety—the only truly safe harbor she knew. If only she could bottle this.

"When do you have to go back to Connor County?" Semmes asked softly.

Laura turned toward him, "I've got to be on the road early, seven at the latest."

"How'd we get so lucky to have you home before the trial was over?" he said, brushing her short brown curls off her forehead.

"The guy from the Attorney General's office had some appointment down here, so I left, too. The show can't go on without him."

"I'll thank the man..." Semmes began, kissing her neck as he nestled in closer, "next time I have the chance. Do I know this guy?"

"You'd know him if you saw him—he was at Ole Miss with us. But he's wound real tight, and he's a little too proud of the title assistant attorney general."

"But is he going to win?"

"I don't know—I wouldn't have tried it the way he has. But I'm not in charge."

"Which must be driving you nuts."

"At first it did, but when the defense started making headway, hometowning us to death, I kinda liked having someone else to hang it on. I wish I'd done the closing argument though."

Semmes propped his blonde head on his right hand, massaging her tummy with his left.

"Mmm," Laura said, rolling away from him. "How about a back

rub?"

"Certainly," Semmes said. He knelt over her and worked his large hands into the muscles of her tiny back. "Did he botch it?"

" 'Botch' might be a little strong, but it could have been so much better."

"He wouldn't let you do it?"

"Nah. This guy was strutting around for a week, getting his pacing correct for the argument. I couldn't have wrestled the moment away for all the tea in China."

"So what's left?"

"The jury gets their charge at ten. Then we wait."

"How long will the jury be out?"

"The longer the better since all the ways the defendant was stealing money from the county makes it pretty complicated. But who knows—they might be too scared to convict him and won't be out more than ten minutes."

"Couldn't someone watch this nice little backside of yours tomorrow?"

"Already took care of that. The State Patrol was there today and they're supposed to be back for the verdict."

"Who arranged for that?"

"I did. Even I admit this creep of a supervisor can be crazy."

"Sweetheart, these people aren't just crazy, they're vicious. You lack that quality, so you've never understood the difference."

"Maybe I'm learning," she said, flashing her blue eyes back toward him.

"That makes me feel a hundred times better." Semmes gave one more deep massage to her shoulders, then he sank back beside her, enveloping her once again in his arms. "Just be careful. Will needs a mom, and God knows, I need a wife."

"I need a wife," Laura murmured.

■ ■ ■ ■

In the dim morning light, Laura slipped into Will's room. Her five-year-old son was sleeping soundly on the upper bunk, arms flung to the sides, covers askew, his stuffed tyrannosaurus abandoned and teetering on the edge. She pulled the sheet snug under his chin and kissed his smooth forehead. Carefully sidestepping the Lego table, the cardboard box castle, and a pile of toy cars, she quietly pulled his door shut.

In the kitchen, she scribbled a note for Will—"We have a date as soon as I get home. You, me, and the next chapter of *Redwall*, XXXOOOXXX, Momma." Then she filled her thermos full of coffee and milk, grabbed a couple of bagels, and headed north.

As the sun rose, the rolling kudzu-covered hills fell away, row after row, from the highway. National Public Radio news analyzed the most recent mindless slaughter in yet another war, more family killing family. Having heard enough, Laura pushed in a cassette, preferring to watch the slow illumination of the landscape to classical melodies and a steaming cup of coffee.

Within an hour, the view was all too clear. Laura passed a row of narrow shotgun shacks almost flush with the road. A skinny little boy, perched in a tire swing, watched her go by. A lone dog wandered toward the road, too old and slow to chase cars anymore. A few chickens scratched the ground in front of the houses, and a brindled cat didn't budge from her spot on the hood of the broken-down car by the ditch. Behind the tiny shacks, huge cotton-picking machines finished gathering the last of the crop, while cultivators moved relentlessly through other fields, turning over the fertile black earth, getting ready for the next planting.

A big house, white-columned and copper-roofed, sat back in the distance on meticulously groomed grounds. The Yazoo Delta boasted the richest farmland in the world, and the hills and sandy southern counties grew pine trees faster and straighter than anywhere, but the state still couldn't feed all of her people.

Not far past the Connor County line, Laura turned east off the highway onto a narrower county road, passing a pickup stopped at the intersection. For a split second, she and the driver were looking straight at each other, his leer pulling the sallow skin and thin lips away to reveal a nearly toothless grin. Laura accelerated, relieved to see through her rearview mirror that the truck had turned north.

The white concrete sidewalk encircling the Connor County courthouse shimmered in the sun as Laura looked for an empty space. She'd never seen the square so full of cars, but she'd been arriving early and leaving late all during the trial. The drivers of the cars had to be in the courthouse because long before WalMart and McDonald's tightened their grip on the local economy, the square had already lost its draw. Teenagers had quit congregating at the cafe, the hardware store stocked fewer items, and one by one, the businesses were closing. These days, everyone traveled thirty miles to shop at the nearest mall.

Three elderly black men were sitting on a bench under the tree outside the front door, enjoying the unusually warm day and watching cars, most of which entered the square on one side and exited on the other, headed elsewhere. The old men perked up when Laura approached. They eyed her warily, watching every step she took up the walk and through the courthouse doors.

The dingy rooms and hallways badly needed repainting. The words *Colored* and *White*, carved above the two marble hallway drinking fountains and, for years, marginally disguised with layers of paint, were quite obvious. On a warm day like this one, the air hung still and close, making closed-door private conferences insufferable. Mismanagement of the county tax dollars meant that, among other things, Connor County couldn't afford to replace the ancient heating and air-conditioning system. Opening the windows hardly changed the temperature, only improved the light.

Court was already in session when Laura reached the swinging doors. Besides the judge, jury, counsel, and the defendant, the gallery was packed—the trial had become quite an event. She tiptoed down the center aisle to the first row, sitting directly behind counsel table for the State, where a very well-dressed black man she hadn't seen before was seated. He looked up and smiled as if he recognized her, then moved over to make room. As she settled onto the bench, the defendant turned her way and gave her one of the dirtiest looks she'd ever received.

The black man leaned over and whispered, "It just got started. You didn't miss much."

The assistant attorney general turned around, motioning for her to move up to the chair beside him. Laura smiled and shook her head.

The instructions took nearly an hour. After the judge dismissed the jury to deliberate, he announced, "Court is dismissed until at least 2:00 P.M.," banged his gavel, and disappeared into his chambers before the bailiff could call out, "All rise."

The county supervisor glared at Laura as he passed by her row, and then spoke to the man beside her. "What's your black ass doing here, Stone? Is the State Patrol part of this witch-hunt, too?"

"We're always on duty," Major Robert Stone said evenly, obviously familiar with the man. "You know that."

Forty-five but in top physical shape without being a muscle man, Robert Stone could take the aging, overweight county supervisor and both men knew it. The defendant's lawyer pulled at his sleeve. "Come along, now."

Laura turned to Robert. "Are you assigned to be here?"

Robert nodded, extending his hand. "Major Robert Stone, ma'am."

"I was expecting someone in uniform like yesterday."

"Your request came to my office, and I decided to handle it myself today."

"I hope this isn't taking you away from important cases," Laura said. "A regular trooper is all I asked for from your commissioner."

"Majors get to pick their assignments. And this one's plenty important. I can't wait to see that dismal excuse for a human being lose this case. We've been chasing him for one thing or another for years."

"Don't count on it yet," Laura said.

"Laura," the assistant attorney general interrupted. "I can't have lunch today. I've got to handle something that came up last night."

"Not to worry," she said.

Laura collected her briefcase and stepped out into the aisle.

"Would you like a cup of coffee or an early lunch?" Robert asked.

"I'd love some lunch. I didn't eat much breakfast," Laura replied. "But could we go somewhere other than the Square Meal? I've had about all of their food I can take."

"How 'bout Dell's Eat Shop in Sibley?" Robert asked.

Laura didn't know the place.

"Not really a white folks' spot, but I'll be your escort. There isn't any better food this side of New Orleans."

■ ■ ■ ■

"If you don't mind my asking a rather tired old question, how'd a nice person like you get mixed up with scumbag supervisors?" Robert asked once they'd ordered two daily specials—barbecue beef, black-eyed peas, turnip greens, and corn bread. The restaurant was a rundown hole-in-the-wall that Laura had passed every time she'd been through the town. But it was the sort of place folks didn't pay much attention to unless they knew what was inside or happened to be photographers searching for the real America.

"It beat practicing criminal law, that's how," Laura answered, reaching for a small glass bowl with packets of sugar.

"You're a lawyer?" Robert asked, looking directly at her as he spoke, soaking in the details of her face.

Laura nodded as she tore off the packet's corner and poured half its contents into her tea, trying her best to ignore Robert's scrutiny. "But I got tired of all the sad stories, con artists, and condescending jerks I had to deal with."

"Why'd you pick criminal law in the first place?" Robert inquired.

"Are we playing twenty questions?" Laura asked.

"Sorry," Robert said, squirming a little, worried he'd pried too far, too quickly. "I just get curious when people show up in unlikely situations. Goes with my job, I guess."

"Well, someone had to make the world safe for democracy," Laura said, smiling. "Why'd you become a cop? You don't look the part either—preppy clothes, tassel loafers."

"Thought I could save Mississippi by joining the very thin ranks of black state troopers," Robert said, smiling broadly to cover his self-consciousness at her remark. "That, plus I was trying to impress the girl next door."

"Did you?"

"She married me, if that's any indication," Robert answered.

"Then you got more out of your career move than I did," Laura said. "I almost lost my husband."

The waitress reappeared with their plates, heaped with meat, steaming vegetables, and corn bread.

"You were saying?" Robert prompted her.

"Where was I?" Laura mumbled, savoring the aromas of their food.

"You almost lost your husband."

"He wasn't leaving me, really. But he was worrying all the time.

And the phone calls in the middle of the night from lowlifes needing to make bail weren't a thrill either."

"Hot sauce, please, ma'am," Robert said, pointing to a small unlabeled bottle.

"My stories always made great dinner-table conversation, but it got old pretty fast. And I wasn't too good at collecting my fees—most of my clients didn't respond to invoices very promptly."

Silence descended over the table while they gobbled down their lunch.

"I did have a string of interesting victories when I was pregnant though," Laura said, taking a sip of water.

"You have a child?" Robert asked, filling his fork with a mouthful of greens and peas.

"Five years old," Laura said, smiling at the memory of her sleeping son. "He's the light of my life."

"Tell me about these victories," Robert asked.

"Well, I gained twice as much weight as I was supposed to. At about six months, I was enormous—almost wider than I am tall. But I was perfectly capable of working—so I'd come waddling in with my client. It was very effective. I think the judges ruled in my favor just to get me out of there before anything happened."

Robert smiled. "You didn't take unfair advantage of them now, did you?"

Laura smiled back. "Every chance I could."

"So, why didn't you switch to one of the big firms and practice some other kind of law?"

"Might have if this job hadn't come up," Laura said.

"And doesn't your husband still worry?" Robert asked, popping a bit of corn bread in his mouth.

"He does, but he's gotten used to it. Are you still married?"

"Yes."

"Children?"

"No."

"Is that all I get? One word answers?"

Robert smiled. "My wife's a doctor."

"Ahhhh, the plot thickens," Laura said, looking askance at Robert. "A cop who shops at trendy men's stores, married to a doc. Bet you have a portfolio, too."

"My wife handles the investments," Robert explained, suddenly shy. "Where'd your accent come from?" he asked, shifting the focus away again.

"You're not from here, are ya little lady," Laura mimicked with a distinct redneck twang. "My dad took a job in New York when I was a baby, so we all went to grade school and high school up North. They moved back after I graduated, and I went to Ole Miss. Then I left again for law school and a couple of clerkships, plus a job in DC."

"And now you're chasing crooked county supervisors?" Robert asked.

"I prefer to think of it as protecting our hard-earned tax dollars," Laura said, gathering up another forkful of peas.

"Tough cases to make?"

"Actually, it's been a lot like shooting ducks in a barrel. Some of these people haven't ever been audited, and they didn't bother to cover their tracks very well. But I don't tell that to just anyone or people will figure out we're not as clever as we seem."

"I think you're being modest," said Robert, sopping up the last bit of sauce with his remaining corn bread. "In addition to crazy."

"How so?" Laura said.

"Anyone who gets up in these supervisors' faces like you've been doing is either crazy or just doesn't know the real score."

"So, what is the real score?"

"Some of them, this one included," he said, jerking his thumb back in the general direction of the Connor County courthouse, "are lawless sons of bitches, excuse my French. They don't stop at anything—even murder."

"We'll see about that," Laura said.

"Like I said, you're crazy."

"Maybe, but I'm still smarter than most of them."

"These people don't play with brains—it's brawn all the way."

"Time'll tell," Laura said. "Someone has to step out there or these pirates will trample all of us."

"They always have and they always will," Robert said. "Don't get me wrong, I've been messin' with these folk for ten years. I just want you to know what kind of scum you're dealing with."

"Don't tell me too much," Laura said. "I might lose my nerve."

■ ■ ■ ■

By four o'clock, Laura could hardly contain her hopes—every passing hour increased the chances for a verdict in the State's favor. She distracted herself with work on another audit report and, for lack of anywhere else to go, used the counsel table to spread out her papers.

From time to time, people wandered in but rarely stayed to chat, even though she'd tried as hard as possible to put them at ease. The fact that they had the guts to approach her was an accomplishment since everyone within fifty miles was under the defendant's thumb in one way or another. One man passed her table, dropped a paper, and as he leaned over to pick it up, spoke so quietly she could hardly hear him. "Lots of us are with you. Don't give up." Then he walked on.

The bailiff was telling Robert that the judge was about to dismiss the jury for the day when the judge's secretary, a rather plump matron with a helmet of silvery hair, motioned to him from across the courtroom. The bailiff hurried away.

Moments later he reappeared and called out: "Court will reconvene in five minutes." Then he went out through the double doors into the hall, repeating, "Five minutes! Court reconvenes in five minutes."

People streamed in. As the supervisor and his lawyer appeared, the crowd parted for them to pass. This time, the defendant totally ignored Laura as he took his seat. Robert sat on the aisle, directly behind the assistant attorney general.

Laura leaned over the railing and whispered, "I hope you have some reinforcements."

"Taken care of," Robert assured her.

The judge entered with the bailiff behind him, announcing: "All rise."

As the judge sat down, he banged his gavel. "Court is now in session. Bailiff, bring in the jury."

The jury—mostly older, black and female—filed in, their faces serious and fearful. Laura looked carefully at each one, but only one older woman returned her look, and she didn't give away their vote.

"Have you reached a verdict?"

The supervisor smiled as the one prosperous-looking white man stood up.

"We have, your Honor," the foreman said stiffly, holding out a piece of paper.

The bailiff handed the jury's verdict to the judge. He opened and read it and looked slowly at the supervisor. When he sent it back to the foreman, Laura's eyes went from the judge back to the jury.

"And how do you find?"

Looking down at the paper, the foreman slowly read, "We find for the State in the amount of one hundred ten thou-"

"You dirty little bitch!" the supervisor yelled, shoving his lawyer aside and heading for Laura. The assistant attorney general stepped out of the way, but Robert moved in from behind and stopped him.

"Don't move," Robert said in his deep, commanding voice, grabbing the supervisor's arm and holding him back.

The judge pounded his gavel as the audience buzzed. "Order, order. Counsel, restrain your client."

The supervisor glared at Laura as Robert, with a lock on the man's shoulders, kept him away. "You'll pay for this, you little..."

"Are you threatening her?" Robert asked.

The man scowled at Robert. "Get out of my way, nigger."

"Excuse me?" Robert said, gripping the man more securely, and filling the man's entire field of vision with his dark face.

"Get out of my way," the man snarled again, then added, slowly, "Major Stone."

The judge pounded his gavel again. "Counsel, inform your client that no such outbursts will be tolerated or he'll be in contempt of this court."

2

By 7:30 P.M., few, except the evening shift radio operators and the cleaning crew, were still at State Patrol Headquarters, but Robert was fairly certain he'd find Lt. Colonel Blake Coleman at his desk. Blake was the assistant chief for Criminal Investigations, Robert's next in command, mentor, and closest confidant. He'd been the district lieutenant over investigations when Robert transferred to move up and out of uniform, twelve years before. Blake had taken an instant liking to Robert and they'd worked together ever since—a talented, relentless team.

"Busy?" Robert asked.

"Not enough to turn you away," Blake said. Eight years Robert's senior, and a full head of gray hair to show for it, Blake sat with his feet propped up on the desk, his reading glasses perched on his long nose, working through reports that sat in two piles beside him. He scrawled his initials on the one he had in his hand and dropped it in the far pile, automatically pulling another toward him. "Where in the devil have you been for the past two days?"

"I had to check on my parents," Robert said, grabbing a small pillow and stretching out on the bright green couch. "I told you that."

"Guess I forgot," Blake said. "They okay?"

"Just old and persnickety. Wish they'd let Rachel and me get them a better car—they're still driving a '56 Chevy pickup that Daddy bought new. But they won't hear of it."

"License plates are free by now."

"Have been for years, and that's why they won't trade. But those two are a hazard, driving ten miles an hour down the road to the store."

"New car wouldn't change that."

"'Spect you're right," Robert said, adjusting his pillow. "I stopped by the Sheriff's office to talk to the new guy."

"What's he like?"

"Not a bright light. The closest he's been to cops is changing the oil in their cars."

"What?" Blake said.

"He worked at a gas station before the Board of Supervisors appointed him to fill out the unexpired term."

"When will those guys learn they can't appoint total incompetents?"

"Never. Maybe someone better will win the election," Robert said. "I took the liberty of rescuing some of their case files from the garbage," he added.

"Why the hell were they in the garbage?" Blake asked.

"The chief deputy told me the guy is a neatness freak. He's throwing out everything."

"What kind of cases?"

"Open, unsolved homicides. A couple of strangulations that looked connected, bunch of gunshot cases, and three vehicular homicides. One was a Vietnam vet left for dead on the side of the road about fifteen years ago. Caused quite a stir back then, but they never solved it."

"Any evidence in the files?"

"Some of them have bits and pieces, fingerprint cards, reports."

"Where are you gonna put this stuff?" Blake asked.

"In the file room," said Robert.

"No, you aren't. I just got rid of half the junk in there."

"Then I'll keep 'em in my office. And give 'em back if someone decent takes over. Obviously, they won't miss them."

"Suit yourself," Blake said.

"Anything come up around here?" Robert asked.

"The Commissioner called me into his office this morning."

Robert's eyes narrowed. "What'd he want?"

"Asked me why we weren't doing more to get the drug problem under control," Blake said, putting down the report and bringing his hands up behind his head.

"You're kidding."

"Nope."

"What brought this on?"

"He'd been called down to the Governor's Mansion to talk about crime and drugs and didn't have any good answers. I knew it was coming—the guys from Mansion security had warned me."

"I remember when they mentioned it in staff meeting two weeks ago."

"That's right, and I passed it on to the chief, but no one did anything to get ready," Blake said, his chiseled features marking his disdain for the commissioner and the chief of patrol. "I guess they figured with the campaign and all, it would go away."

"So what happened?"

"I'm supposed to wave my magic wand and solve the problem," Blake said.

"Did you wave it already?" Robert asked.

Blake jerked his hand through the air. "They wouldn't reassign any more troopers to me, gave me no additional funding, and don't want checkpoint roadblocks. We just have to keep on like we are, hoping the leaders of the drug cartels will stop by to be arrested."

"Spineless...," Robert muttered.

Blake gazed at his wall of plaques, not focusing on any particular one.

"While we're on the subject of spines, I met someone who has plenty of backbone today." Robert propped the pillow up so his head was a little higher. "Laura Owen versus the good ol' boys. It made for a pretty interesting confrontation."

"The woman from the State Auditor's office?"

Robert nodded. "One of the supervisors in Connor County was found liable for a hundred and ten thousand."

"A Connor County jury did that?" Blake asked, astonished.

Robert nodded.

"Did she try the case?"

"No, some knucklehead from the Attorney General's office tried it. But she did all the work."

"Why wasn't it in federal court?"

"Ms. Owen told me the United States Attorney flatly refused to take the case."

"Alex Markham—now there's a really spineless bastard for you," said Blake with a sigh. "His backbone was probably missing at birth."

"Be careful now, you're talking about Mr. Wonder Boy."

"Wonder boy, my ass. Mr. Senator's son. He's a goddamn politician with less guts than a worm."

"What did he do to cross you?"

"That's who the Commissioner kept throwing in my face today. Markham told him he'd prosecute any case we brought him, but we'd never brought him anything."

"That's a lie," Robert said, sitting up straight. "He won't touch our cases."

"I know that, but the Commissioner doesn't," Blake said. "What kind of confrontation did Owen have?"

"That fat bastard supervisor came across the room after Owen when they read the verdict. Had some choice words for me, too, when I stopped him."

"Serious?"

"Serious as a heart attack. She's one tough little woman—literally and figuratively."

"She's small?"

"Little over five feet—relatively attractive, too. She's sure got nerve, though. You'd like her."

■ ■ ■ ■

"Translate this stuff," demanded Governor Gibbs Carver waving a half-inch thick plastic-bound report as Vic Regis, his chief of staff, stepped into the office. At 59, Carver was relatively trim and fit—his six feet two inches making him a commanding presence in most crowds. He was proud of his first term in office, and rightfully so. They'd engineered the passage of several historic pieces of progressive legislation.

The thick report carried the results of a recent poll in Carver's campaign for reelection. It had arrived earlier that morning and showed that his initially wide margin had closed to an uncomfortably tight eight percentage points. There were only twenty days left before the election, but his lead was holding.

Vic Regis was the brains behind Carver's campaigns and administration. As tall as Carver but slim and wiry, he was loaded with political savvy, yet didn't have a scintilla of interest in being the glad-hander himself. He'd come back to Mississippi from a stint in Washington, DC., when four years before, Carver, a successful entrepreneur and venture capitalist, threw his hat in the ring for governor.

Carver sat back with his long legs up on the desk, while Vic took a seat on the couch, spreading his papers on the glass coffee table. All of Carver's campaign stops for the day were in the Jackson area, so he was enjoying a rare break from nonstop traveling.

Vic began running through the high points. "People generally like you. Voters think you're doing a good job in most areas. Strong father figure component with younger voters," Vic said carefully, knowing any mention of Carver's advancing age was always delicate.

"Gray hair must be worth more than I thought," Carver growled. "Just not quite enough."

"Crime is the problem."

"Is that why the point spread's closing?"

"Looks that way," said Vic, pushing his wire-rim glasses back up his aquiline nose. "At least that's what we're getting from the focus groups."

"What the hell can you do about it?" Carver asked.

Vic didn't answer immediately, irked that Carver, who'd steadfastly refused to do anything more for the cops than basic window dressing, now acted as though it were Vic's problem to solve.

"At this point, it's too late to do anything substantive. We're left with drumming up support for a bold crime initiative as the cornerstone of the next four years, and trying to get more endorsements from police chiefs and sheriffs based on that."

"That shouldn't be so hard," Carver said, turning around to look out at the spire of the cathedral and the surrounding office buildings.

"It hasn't been going all that well lately," Vic replied. "Our opponent's been lining up cop endorsements for months. I hear you can't go to a fish fry without seeing him there. He's been working the locals day and night."

"Can't we embarrass this guy?" Carver insisted, swinging back toward Vic. "Finally find the closet where the skeleton is?"

"I'm working on it, but we haven't turned up anything yet."

"Get the State Patrol involved," Carver said.

Vic sat back, his hands behind his head. "That's pretty tricky. The Commissioner hasn't been very successful at galvanizing support. He's just not up to that."

"What do you mean not 'up to that'? What's the guy got to do except talk to his people?"

"As I said, it's tricky—always is with the Patrol. Right now, you don't have a lot of support."

"At the Patrol? They work for me, the ungrateful bastards," Carver muttered.

"And to add to it, the Commissioner told me last evening that he's resigning as soon as the election is over. His health has been poor for some time."

"He's not going to announce this anytime soon, is he?"

"Considering all you've done for him, he said he owed it to you not to upset the apple cart in the middle of the campaign."

"Remind me to thank him," Carver said sarcastically. "What would really have been wonderful is if the bastard had resigned when there was still time for a new appointee to step in and help me out."

"But getting to make that new appointment will be a wonderful opportunity."

"You feel confident enough to talk about the next term?"

"Yup. It'll be tight, but you'll make it," said Vic. "It'll fit right in with where we've been talking about going with the drug problem."

"Do you have anyone in mind? Clearly, you've been thinking about it."

"I'm studying the angles with your long-range plans in mind. You've got to start fighting crime, hard. But you can also use the opportunity to score some political points."

"Exactly," said Carver, pointing at Vic. "Let's find a prosecutor or a judge. But he has to be black—with the right law enforcement pedigree. That would increase the number of my minority appointments and shake up the Patrol, too. They might be integrated, but they still act mighty white."

"What about a woman instead? Laura Owen, for instance."

"Who?" Carver asked, clearly skeptical about Vic's proposal of a woman.

"Laura Owen—over at the State Auditor's office. Proven crime fighter. Great record busting corruption—and she'd shake up the Patrol something awful."

"Are you serious?"

Vic nodded. "Blacks have done better by you than women overall, as far as appointments are concerned—if you're counting heads, that is. I've known her since college. She and her family moved back here after she graduated from high school."

"So she's not from here?"

"She can claim Mississippi all right. Her people arrived way back, First Families and all that. But her father took a job in New York for several years. She knocked the top out at Ole Miss, then went to law school at the University of Virginia. We were classmates, both places. Considering how well she's done with her auditor's investigations, she's got tremendous credibility. And the Connor County case sealed her reputation. Not many have challenged the good ol' boys quite so directly—and won."

"All this stuff with the supervisors adds up to too much baggage."

Vic shook his head. "It's the right kind of baggage. Sends the right signal."

"I think it's going too far. The Patrol will toss her out on her ear. And then I'll have to deal with the aftermath of a bad appointment, the wasted time, as well as a new appointment."

"And why would they toss her out?"

"Well, they may not like blacks, but they sure won't take orders from women."

"I disagree. Some of the older troopers will have trouble with it, but the majority won't—not once they see how hard she fights."

Carver peered over his glasses still looking skeptical. "Would she be interested?"

"Packaged the right way, it could really appeal to Laura's sense of adventure. The only female commissioner in the country, I'll bet."

He shook his head again. "I wouldn't survive it."

"Sure you would. In light of what she's done for the state, how loudly could anyone complain?"

"Very loudly and very clearly. Half, if not most, of the legislature would be against her, and many of my supporters aren't quite ready for something that radical."

"Look," said Vic, "you've got to start thinking beyond these borders if you want to be in the loop for a vice presidential bid."

Carver gazed at a colorful Theora Hamblett painting on the opposite wall, silent for a moment. Vic's last words had struck a responsive chord. "I want to be in that loop more than anything—you're absolutely right about that. But I'm not sure about this Owen thing."

Seeing his uneasiness, Vic added, "We don't have to decide today."

"Good."

"But trust me. She can survive the Patrol, and she can rev up one helluva war on drugs. Just let her loose and stay out of the way, that's all we have to do. Think of the press you can get."

"Let's win this election first," Carver said. "Then I'll test the waters."

3

Tom Hilman awoke before his alarm clock went off to hear the rhythmic squeak of bedsprings from the next room. The sun was up, slipping in through the thick slats of the wooden blinds that covered each window.

"Goddammit to hell, Markham," he muttered. "You and your unquenchable prick." He grabbed a spare pillow and crushed it against his ear. But not only was the squeaking still audible, it had grown louder and more frenzied.

He pressed the pillow down harder and suddenly there was silence.

But now he was wide awake. Too much to do to stay in bed.

Fifteen minutes later, Tom headed down the steps to a dock in Monkey River, Belize. Filtered by banana and palm trees, the sun barely managed to illuminate the showy red and orange bougainvillea blossoms that grew everywhere. The water in the bay shone crystal clear, displaying a shifting palette of blues and greens depending on its depth. There was no doubt about it—this was where he'd come to live permanently, as soon as he could. And this is how he'd dress for the rest of his life— khaki shorts, T-shirt, boat shoes, and a baseball cap to cover his fair head. With weather like this, and money in the bank, life would be infinitely better.

Checking the sky for clouds, he reached the dock where his dinghy was tied up, and rowed out to the *Last Chance,* at anchor in the harbor. The boat, a Morgan Islander sloop, fifty feet long with roomy accommodations below, had carried him all over the Caribbean. It wasn't simply his home away from home, it was his real home as far as he was concerned. On his boat, away from shore, Tom Hilman found the only peace he'd ever known.

He tied the dinghy to the buoy, climbed aboard the sloop and cranked her inboard engine and headed down the coast. A half mile south, in a completely deserted cove, a large cabin cruiser drifted. A man stepped back from the cockpit and watched Tom draw closer, not waving until he was certain it was him. Tom steered his sloop within a few feet of the cabin cruiser.

"Good morning," said Hector Rodriguez, his dark luminous eyes dancing with anticipation. "Everything go well?"

"Perfect."

"Where's your friend, Alex?"

"Getting his money's worth from that young lady you supplied."

"Why did you bring him along? Who is this guy?"

"My insurance policy," Tom answered simply.

"If you say so," said Hector, skeptical.

"Can we get started?"

Hector scanned the shoreline with binoculars. When he spotted the lookout he'd posted earlier, he got a positive wave.

"It's all clear."

Tom dropped anchor and Hector's boat pulled alongside and tied up to *Last Chance*. Pressing hard against the cabin cruiser's floorboard, Hector popped a concealed hatch in the front hull and began lifting out large black plastic bags. He was strong and well muscled, and tirelessly hoisted the 20 kilo bags onto the deck of Tom's boat, counting out loud with each one.

Tom shifted the bags toward the cabin door and when there was no more room, went below. He removed the doors from the hatch behind his bunk, pulled out the lines and equipment stored there, and stashed the bags carefully in the space. When it was nearly full, Tom replaced the lines and equipment. Next, he lifted off the mattress and unscrewed the board for the bunk bed, and filled the space below with more. He then moved to the front of the boat and stowed the remaining bags in the bilge.

After an hour, the 500 kilos of 98 percent pure cocaine were securely stowed, completely hidden from sight. Depending upon how many times it would be "stepped on," the cargo's American street value probably exceeded $30 million.

"It's a little early for a drink, but this calls for a celebration," said

Tom, popping the tops on two cans of beer and handing one to Hector as they settled into seats in the cockpit.

Hector raised his can in a toast. "To a perfect sail."

Tom met his can in the air.

"Does this make you nervous?" Hector said.

"Yes. I'd be a fool if it didn't," Tom answered. "But it's worth the risk. Ten trips—invested—and I'm set for life."

"When do you leave?" Hector said.

"As soon as I get Markham out of bed. Can you watch the boat for me?"

Hector nodded.

"I'll get to Mississippi late Sunday afternoon—unless the weather turns bad. If I don't see you at the Ocean Springs inlet, I won't unload."

"I'll be there—just look for a baby blue Mercedes."

"Isn't that a little flashy?"

"My lawyer drives one just like it."

"Could you get a camcorder that stamps the date and time on the film?"

"Probably."

"Then video as much as you can of our arrival."

"Why do you want this, may I ask?"

"Alex and I go way back, and I've covered his ass more than once. He owes me so much that I'm sure he'll help if I ever get caught. But just in case our history together isn't enough, I plan to make him so nervous he won't hesitate."

"Get him out on deck when you pass me."

"And I'll have a bag somewhere in sight," Tom added, sipping his beer.

"What do you want me to do with your money?"

"Wire two hundred thousand to the Hilman Development account in the Caymans, and leave fifty grand in cash. I'll call you when I'm done. I may not get it there until the next morning, though, if Alex doesn't head north immediately. Unloading is gonna be a real hassle."

"You want help?"

"No. Remember, I see no one but you, and no one else sees me."

"Understood." Hector reached in his pocket and handed Tom two keys. "These are for the hangar—the larger one opens the door, the small one opens the lockers. The cash will be in the locker nearest the door."

Without a hint of nervousness, Tom pulled out a large ring of keys and added the two.

Hector tipped the beer can up for one last swallow. "I'd better be going. Have a safe trip."

They shook hands, and Hector jumped to his boat, cranked the engine and headed toward the shore. The lookout walked out of the trees, onto the beach, and waded toward the cruiser.

Around noon, after Alex had finally disengaged from his lovely companion, showered, and packed his things, the two men loaded their food and supplies, and puttered out of the bay. As they passed Hector's cabin cruiser, Tom gave a small friendly wave to the men on deck, no more than the standard seafaring greeting.

"I like this place," Alex said.

"You like the pussy," Tom smiled.

"No," Alex said, "I mean, that was nice—very nice—but I really like this place. It may be the best spot you've found."

"That's why I took a long lease on the house."

"Can't you buy it?" Alex asked.

"I'm gonna build," Tom said. "Besides, the owner won't sell."

"How'd you meet this guy?"

"Stayed at one of his hotels in the Bahamas. He works for some international outfit in Belize City that exports orange juice," Tom said. "That's why he's in and out of the United States so much. And he owns a lot of real estate."

Sailing the Caribbean Sea north up the coast of Belize and Mexico, heading for the tip of the Yucatan Peninsula, Tom and Alex kept land in sight most of the way, but stayed far enough out so only a few pleasure boats passed by. The weather was perfect, the winds strong enough to make very good time under sail, with a few exhilarating moments now and then. Past Isla Mujeres and Isla Contoy, Tom headed into the Gulf of Mexico. Ocean Springs, Mississippi, lay straight across. If the good weather continued, they might be there with a day to spare.

They had company from time to time. A school of dolphins, leaping in and out of the water, followed them from Cozumel clear into the Gulf before turning back. And they passed oil tankers at a safe distance, some loaded and riding low, others empty and high in the water. Although Tom's cargo didn't make much difference to his draft, he felt a certain kinship with the giant transports.

Even with the monotony of the Gulf, finishing the day with a glowing red sunset, Lyle Lovett on the tape deck, and a beer in hand, came as close to perfection as either man had ever known. Alex loved every minute of the sail, wishing he could extend it, not looking forward to returning to Jackson.

On the second night, Tom prepared red snapper they'd caught, while Alex drank a bourbon at the helm. Before calling him down to eat, Tom switched on a voice-activated recorder hidden in one of the many little storage crannies built into the teak paneling near the table. He was still hoping to pick up some tantalizing admission from Alex, even though he'd ventured nothing interesting the night before.

By 9:30, they were polishing off the second bottle of wine.

"Tell me again, Markham, why in the hell you want to be governor? Working with those Neanderthals in the legislature will numb your brain."

"It's a step, that's the only reason."

"Step to where?"

"On the road to Washington."

"Why didn't you run this time?"

"My father's advice," Alex said. "I've only been United States Attorney for three years, and he thought Carver would beat me. He was right as usual. Who would vote for a young upstart against a robust incumbent grandfather figure?"

"But isn't the experience important—a trial run, so to speak?"

"Losing first time out may be good for the character, but it can be fatal for a political career."

"I can't feature it," Tom said. "I guess I don't have the same kind of drive."

"Probably not, since you seem content to work for Dad."

Tom bristled. "Not if I can find an alternative that supports me in the manner to which I've become accustomed," Tom said, mimicking a haughty, upper-crust accent. He took another big swig of wine. "Do you know what that bastard did?"

"Your dad?"

Tom nodded his head. "Two years ago, he reorganized—called it estate-tax planning—and tied up the company so tight that I won't get a single share of stock if I don't keep working for him. And even then I won't get anything till he dies."

"You're getting paid enough to buy this," Alex said, sweeping his hand around the boat.

"Yeah, but my brother Stephen would have been a full partner by now," Tom said.

"Stop that," Alex said impatiently. "Don't waste your life worrying about a dead older brother,"

"My father never fails to remind me," Tom spat back. " 'Stephen, Jr., would have...'" he said, dropping his voice an octave to sound like his father.

"Look, Hilman," Alex said, leaning on the table and drawing closer to him. "We've been friends for how long? Twenty years?"

"Closer to thirty," Tom corrected him.

"Through all kinds of hell," Alex said.

Tom nodded.

"Drop this shit about your brother once and for all. Forget him. It wasn't your fault he drowned."

"But maybe I could have saved him...."

"Maybe, maybe," Alex said. "But that's over. Move on. This sort of crap won't bring him back."

"Tell my father that," Tom said, shaking his head. "There has to be a better way to make a living than working for him and strangling, little by little."

"Strangled by your dad? Or the memory of your brother?"

"Both," Tom scoffed.

"You ought to run drugs," Alex laughed, trying to lighten things up. "It's very profitable, and if you did it right, it wouldn't be that risky. You can't believe how much money those guys make. It's sickening."

Tom snapped out of his desolate mood and leaned back, his hands behind his head, smiling at his good luck. "The thought had crossed my mind. But I wouldn't want to do it without your help."

Alex stared back at him, silent for a moment. "You're kidding, aren't you?"

Tom hesitated, sizing up Alex's reaction. "Of course I am. But it's mighty attractive to make that much money so fast. I'd be able to quit and enjoy myself now and for the rest of my life."

"Can't disagree with that."

Late Sunday afternoon, Tom approached the inlet to the back bay at Ocean Springs and its deep corridors through the high marsh grasses. He pulled down the sails to run under power only, and turned the helm over to Alex while he went below to pack up. Filling a couple of black plastic bags with trash, he lifted them up on deck just as they reached the Yacht Club. A baby blue Mercedes SL was parked close to the water.

"Now that's a nice car."

Alex looked that way. "I'd consider one if I didn't have to act like a candidate."

"Is that why you go all the way to Belize to get laid?"

Alex shrugged his shoulders.

"We all make our choices," Tom said.

Nearing his own dock, Tom took over and eased *Last Chance* in. His house was set back from the water at the base of a U-shaped piece of property with the dock situated so that he had nearly complete privacy. Building it there had required dredging the cove, an expense no one could understand, particularly not his father, but Tom had insisted. They tied up the sloop and unloaded the clothes and supplies, carrying everything up to the house.

"Much as I'd like to stay away one more night, if you don't need me, I think I'll head north."

Tom held out his hand. "Markham, it's been a pleasure."

"Call me when you've got another one planned. I'm ready."

"You're on."

After Alex left, Tom went directly to the garage and changed the license plates on an older beige van. He backed it out, and drove across the lawn to the dock, parking close to *Last Chance*. Jumping on board, he unloaded his cargo and loaded the van as quickly as he could. He stopped at the garage again on his way out, donned a black wig, baseball cap, and sunglasses, and drove off into the night.

Cameron Airfield, a small private airstrip ten miles away, could be reached staying on city and county roads. He parked in front of an unmarked hangar at the end of the field, unlocked the overhead doors at the back, and drove in. The hangar was big enough for two planes, but only one was kept there now, leaving more room for Tom to maneuver. He unlocked one of the large metal storage lockers that lined the back wall of the hangar and took out a small navy gym bag with a New Orleans Saints' logo. Removing three stacks of hundred-dollar bills, he riffled through them, checking the denominations, then stuffed the money under the front seat of the van.

Unloading took twice as long as he'd expected, but when the five lockers were filled, he locked everything up and took off, dialing Hector's cellular as he drove away.

"You're all set to go."

"I got the video, clear as day."

"Terrific. Leave it at the house in Belize. I'll pick it up next time."

"Which is when?"

"Three months or so."

■ ■ ■ ■

Laura slid into a comfortable upholstered armchair in front of Vic Regis's desk at the Capitol. As usual, Vic was on the phone, gently but firmly twisting some legislator's arm about a bill. He signaled that he'd only be a minute and wound up the conversation directly.

Hanging up, he smiled. "Ready for Christmas?"

"Will's been counting the days on three Advent calendars."

"What's Santa Claus bringing him?"

"I'd guess a new bike, some story tapes, and a huge Lego creation."

"And Semmes? What's going to be in his stocking?"

"A fabulous sauté pan, new herbs and spices, and a gas grill."

"There's a theme to this, I think."

Laura smiled. "Are you going home?"

"Christmas Eve."

"Give your parents my best."

"I will. Everyone's going to make it back this year so Mom's in a state," Vic said. "By the way, congratulations on Connor County. That was a good whack."

"Thank you. I must admit that nothing has ever been quite as bizarre as waiting for that verdict. They couldn't decide whether it was safe to talk to me because if I lost, there'd be hell to pay, but if I won, there might be hell to pay, too."

"I heard he tried to strangle you when the foreman announced their decision."

"Who told you that? He headed my way, but a State Patrol officer stepped in. And that was it. I wish Semmes had never heard about it."

"You had the Patrol there?"

"Yes...I've learned my lessons the hard way."

"The phones were ringing off the hooks around here the day after the decision—10-1 in favor."

"That's nice to hear. The one face I would have paid to see was Alex Markham's when he heard the news. He refused to take the case, you know. And it would have been easy for him with the federal pattern-of-corruption statute to go under. Could have gotten treble damages."

"Bad move for Alex. He's already talking up his campaign for the next race. Even asked the Governor for his endorsement." Vic looked out the window at the bare limbs of the towering white oaks lining the entrance walk. "Mississippi deserves a better governor than him. Too bad so many voters take to his kind—slick, big name, all hat, no cattle."

"It shouldn't be hard to find someone if the only requirement is being better than Alex. I don't care what they say, he's too slimy for me—and for a lot of other people, too."

"Why don't you take him on, Laura?"

She smiled. "If I run for public office, I'm starting out a little more modestly, thank you. Besides, you gotta be nice to people you despise, I'm not certain I can swallow that."

"You'd be a perfect candidate—and there's no reason not to start at Governor. The voters are throwing career people out all over the place."

"Not that many women on the horizon, in case you haven't noticed. We lose as much ground as we gain, it seems," Laura said.

"That's why you should make your move now. A new day is dawning. You've got some name recognition and we can give you more. In fact, to get you on the way, I want to recommend you for commissioner of Public Safety. You'd get all the press you'd need to defeat Alex."

"You mean me as head of the State Patrol?" Laura looked at Vic, flabbergasted. "Are you nuts? The troopers would mutiny."

Vic watched carefully as her expression changed from disbelief to skepticism to interest. "I don't think so. They're not all good ol' boys, you know. Take the trooper who handles Mansion security, Sandy Quinn—a terrific guy. Times are changing."

"We'd have to drag them kicking and screaming into the twentieth century."

"Nah. That job could be very high profile, very challenging. We've mapped out the next major reform: drugs. The Governor has sat by too long on this one."

"Why hasn't the Patrol been more active before this?"

"Never been able to motivate the Commissioner. He's a hail-fellow-well-met sort, but that's been it. The guy liked the title but never got involved, never saw the political potential. It's really a pity though. With all the staff's energy directed toward the Governor's education initiatives, there wasn't anyone or any time to push him into action. So nothing happened—status quo all the way. If he hadn't been so popular, we wouldn't have left him there."

"Where's he going?"

"Retiring. But his departure gives us a golden opportunity to marshal some new forces in this drug war. The Feds shouldn't do it for us."

"Or won't."

"You've heard it all. Hell, you were a criminal defense lawyer."

Laura nodded.

"So you've defended dealers. Drug use is ruining lives by the thousands—and ruining everything else. It's driving up the crime rate, driving up health costs, lowering productivity. I bet you can't name one thing that isn't affected."

"Sort of what you've been saying in your campaign to improve education?"

Vic nodded his head. "Same book, second chapter."

Laura shook her head. "I don't know about running the Patrol. That would be a sea change from what I'm doing now, and I'm just getting going."

"Let the auditor find someone else. You charted the course, now it's time to move on."

Laura paused for a moment, thinking. "So what's the real reason? What do you get out of it?"

"Damn good government."

"Pardon the vernacular, but that's bullshit."

Vic smiled. "We need a full-scale war on drugs, and it would be nice if the Governor won the war or could claim he was winning. I can't think of anyone who would do a better job than you."

"Thanks, I think." She smiled when she looked at Vic, who for all his smoothness, couldn't hide the wheels when they were turning in his head. "What would this be paving the Governor's way to? A U.S. Senate seat?"

Vic shrugged a maybe.

"Vice president, too, I'd bet."

Laura didn't know Governor Carver very well, but she generally liked what he'd said and done in office. She'd glimpsed the unfiltered side of him through Semmes when he'd worked on the renovation of the Governor's Mansion. Semmes had liked him, said the Governor was easygoing but direct. And Carver had entrusted his life to Vic, a move that spoke volumes. She'd known Vic as long as she'd known Semmes— Vic was one of the smartest, most ambitious, yet principled people Laura had ever met.

If she hung around with these two, she might go places.

Places she'd only dreamed about.

She could make a real impact not just one shot here, one shot there.

"And you've got to court the woman's vote, too, huh?" Laura asked.

"I've never been opposed to killing several birds with one stone," Vic replied.

"Is that what I am? A stone?"

"Hell, no. You're a damn heat-seeking missile," Vic said with a broad smile.

Laura walked over to the window and watched a gold Infiniti sedan approach the New Capitol portico and park. Two obviously successful businessmen got out, straightened their ties, fastened the buttons on their suit coats, and put on their game faces. They headed for the entrance, leather writing cases under their arms.

One day, it could be her making decisions—important enough for lobbyists to come courting her.

She snapped back to the real world. "So this would be a two-year appointment if Carver won the Senate seat," Laura said, leaning against the windowsill.

"Maybe, maybe not. The Lieutenant Governor impresses me as the type who might keep the staff just the way it is if he was only going to be there a short while."

"You know better than that," Laura scoffed. "He'd pay off everybody he owed if he had power over the appointments."

Vic shrugged.

"Will you keep your staff out of my way?"

"Yes."

"And if I ever decide to run for office—unlikely as that might be— will you share your hottest tips?"

"Absolutely," Vic said. "Might even sign on for the campaign, if you'd have me."

A vision of the county supervisor's angry, alcoholic face lunging at her in that shabby courtroom came flying back. She was tired of his grubby kind having power.

"Let me think about it."

■ ■ ■ ■

"Hop in, my man," said Blake Coleman as he pulled up alongside Robert Stone who was flipping up his jacket collar for the chilly walk to his car. An icy wind whipped through the tunnel between the old and new buildings at State Patrol headquarters and swirled about the parking lot. "There's something we need to talk about, if you've got the time."

"I've got exactly one hour," Robert answered. "Is that enough?"

"Plenty."

"I can't be late, now," said Robert, sliding into the other seat and rubbing his hands in front of the car heater. "It's Rachel's birthday and she made reservations at Nick's."

"I'll have you back in plenty of time," Blake said, stepping on the gas and turning away from the building.

"What's up?"

"Laura Owen is up."

"She's got another case and needs security?

"Not this time," said Blake. He watched the traffic as he waited to cross the two busy lanes of the boulevard, before entering the interstate. Out on the highway, he looked at Robert, his dark eyes serious, almost forbidding. "Just how smart is she?"

"Real smart," Robert said. "I've told you that."

"Sandy Quinn says she might be the next commissioner."

"Holy shit. Why does he think that?"

"He overheard Vic Regis and the Governor talking about it this morning on the way out to the car," Blake said. "They cut the conversation off when they realized Sandy could hear them. Put that in your pipe and smoke it."

Robert watched the traffic passing them on both sides while Blake held his speed to the limit.

"Cat got your tongue?" Blake asked.

"Kinda takes my breath away," Robert said. "Never in a million years did I consider that a possibility."

"Sandy doesn't think they've made a final offer from what was said," Blake added.

"You'd be chief under her," Robert said with total confidence.

"What makes you think that?"

"Our good Chief Higgs won't work for a woman, that's for certain," Robert said. "So he'll say adios and you'll be it. Who else is there?"

"Kenner for one," Blake said. "He's already pulling in all his chits in case there's a change in the chief's slot. Makin' all kinda promises to anyone who can help him."

Robert shook his head smiling. "Not a chance. This woman doesn't suffer fools. It would be you, I'm telling you."

"What about you?" Blake said. "She's gotten to know you."

Robert shook his head. "If the Governor appoints a woman commissioner, that'll be enough history for one day. The place would implode if she promoted a black to be chief."

"I wouldn't be too sure," Blake said. "There's a strong tendency to appoint people you have some experience with."

"She'll pick a white male—and you deserve it, Coleman. I'll tell her so if I have the chance. Me, I'll take your job."

Blake didn't smile, just kept his eyes on the road, sizing up the possibilities.

■ ■ ■ ■

Will was singing along with "When You Wish Upon a Star." His squeaky young voice drifted from his room where he was busy building Legos. With only a week until Christmas, the house was more than decorated for the season. After they'd covered every square inch of the eleven-foot Christmas tree with colored lights, Semmes and Will had kept going, stringing lights everywhere power would reach. The branches of an old dogwood not far from the front door had been wrapped with steady white lights, and inside, Will had insisted on trimming nearly every window in the living room with twinkling strands.

While they cooked dinner, Semmes regaled Laura with the trials and tribulations of his latest architectural renovation—transforming an antebellum mansion into a bed-and-breakfast. His client was threatening to halt the enormous project in midstream because of marital problems.

It was Laura's night to handle the main course and fix Will's vegetables since he refused to eat anything green except jelly beans. She tenderized three chicken breasts with a metal mallet and dredged them in flour, salt, and pepper, while Semmes washed the romaine lettuce leaves, and then turned his attention to the chopped walnuts and Ramen noodles toasting in butter on the stove.

Laura opened the freezer to get a bag of cut corn. "More wine?"

"A little."

She pulled out the open bottle of Chardonnay and refilled their glasses, raising hers in a toast, "To really great Christmas lights."

Semmes acknowledged the accolade with a smile and a sip, and then went back to stirring the noodles.

"I met with Vic Regis today," Laura said.

"How is Vic? We need to have him over for dinner again."

"Fine," Laura said, taking a deep breath. Semmes wouldn't want her to take the offer, she knew it.

He'd be scared for her.

But it was now or never.

She took another breath and jumped in. "He asked me to consider being commissioner of Public Safety."

"You're kidding," said Semmes without taking his eyes off the saucepan.

"Hardly. The Governor's got to replace the fellow who just retired. Sounds kinda interesting actually."

Semmes moved the saucepan off the heat and stared at her. "Have you lost your mind?"

"I don't think so," Laura answered, reaching for a serving dish and avoiding his eyes. "Don't you think I could do it?"

"Sure you could do it," Semmes said, "but that's not the question."

"What is the question?"

"Whether you'd want to. I thought you were trying to move away from criminal stuff and police work. "

"Yes and no. I mean these audit investigations aren't exactly tea parties."

"Don't I know it! Backwoods lunatics threatening you."

"It wasn't as bad as you think. I wish you'd never heard about that."

"Well, I did," said Semmes, chopping viciously at an innocent bunch of broccoli.

"That's why I had the Patrol there. And that knight in shining armor would be working for me full time."

"You'd have a bodyguard?"

"Heavens no. But there'd be plenty of people around if something went wrong."

Semmes stopped chopping and turned toward her. "What about all those leftist lawyer groups you belonged to? Someone's sure to find out about those."

"I doubt it," Laura said, pouring olive oil into a well-worn aluminum frying pan.

"Don't be too sure."

"It probably wouldn't matter, this is an administrative job. I wouldn't be out there wrestling with bad guys and criminals, I'd be down at the Legislature."

"With 'bad guys and criminals,'" said Semmes, chuckling.

"Vic does it all day long."

"He's a masochist," Semmes said. "We've known that for years."

"What are y'all talking about?" piped up Will's small voice from the other side of the counter.

"Who's there?" Laura said.

"It's me," replied her son, popping into view, smiling at his trick.

"Oh, I didn't recognize the voice," Laura teased him.

"What are y'all talking about?" Will asked again, more insistently.

Semmes drew his finger across his neck and then placed it to his lips. "Momma and I are having an adult conversation."

"I want you to be a state patrolman, Momma," Will said, crawling up on the bar stool.

Laura looked at Will, incredulous. "How do you know about that?"

"I heard you talking on the phone."

Semmes shook his head. "Outnumbered, outmaneuvered, out-flanked."

Laura smiled. "I'll follow your advice, Darlin', I always have."

"Then you do what your heart tells you," Semmes said, softening. "I won't stand in the way if you're determined. Just don't fool yourself into thinking it'll be a cake walk." He turned back to his broccoli.

"Hooray! Momma's going to be a policeman!" Will shouted, dashing out of the kitchen, roaring his version of a police car siren.

Laura walked over to Semmes and wrapped her arms around him from the back, nuzzling into his cashmere sweater. He swung his arm around her, drawing her even closer.

"Just you be careful," he said, planting a kiss on her forehead and lingering there. "I need you too much."

"I promise. I need you too—more than you can imagine."

"I doubt that."

■ ■ ■ ■

Captain Sandy Quinn made certain he was at the door to greet Laura when she appeared for her meeting with the Governor. He wanted to get a good look at her after all he'd heard.

"Ms. Owen?" he asked.

"Yes," Laura said. "I'm here to see Vic Regis and the Governor."

"I'm Captain Sandy Quinn, State Patrol. Can I take your things?"

Laura nodded, pulling off her black wool coat and stuffing the scarf in the sleeve. "I hope I'm not late."

"Hardly, ma'am. They're running a little behind schedule. Would you like some coffee?" Sandy asked, directing her toward a small couch in the entry hallway."

"Please," Laura said. "With milk."

She was looking up at the ceiling lights and their etched glass encasements when Sandy returned. "Have you been here before?"

"My husband's an architect. He was involved in the renovation. I came for the reception when it was finished, but I didn't stay long. It was way too crowded and noisy."

A tray with coffee and cream materialized on the side table, presented by a thin white man in dark pants and a white jacket who departed as silently as he'd appeared.

"I think I know your husband," Sandy said. "Tall, blonde hair?"

Laura nodded and smiled.

"Do you have children?" Sandy asked, making polite conversation.

"One, a five-year-old boy," Laura said. "Almost six."

"My favorite age," Sandy said. "Got two myself, but they're teenagers. Real fistfuls."

"The darkest hour, so I hear."

"That's no exaggeration."

With a quick tap of footsteps in the hallway, Vic Regis appeared.

"Sorry we're running late, Laura," Vic said. "Did you get some coffee?"

"Yes, thank you."

"If you're not in too much of a hurry, the Governor has to make a couple more calls before we meet," Vic said.

"I've got nothing until eleven," Laura replied.

"Some coffee, Mr. Regis?" Sandy asked.

"Don't believe so," Vic said. "Had my quota already."

When they entered his office, Governor Carver stood up and extended both hands to greet Laura.

"Laura, so good of you to come by today."

"I'm honored that you want to talk with me."

"You know," Carver said with a broad smile, "I don't think I've talked to your husband since they finished the renovation here, but not a day goes by that I don't admire the beautiful work he did. How is Semmes doing?"

"Busier than ever," Laura said as she took the seat he offered.

"Does he ever take his nose off the drawing board?"

Laura nodded. "He always finds time to spend with Will. They're the best of friends."

"That's marvelous, marvelous," Governor Carver said. "My children were little so long ago. Now we're waiting for grandchildren to teach us how to have fun all over again."

"Will is the joy of our lives," Laura answered. "I don't know what we did all those years before he was born."

That awkward moment between greetings and the meat of the matter stretched longer than usual as the Governor looked keenly at Laura. "I've heard a lot of good things about you since the Connor County case. You should be very proud."

"Thank you, sir, I am. The audit was actually easy. But wending my way through Connor County politics was the trick."

"I'm familiar with those briar patches. It took guts to hang in there."

"Guts or certifiable looniness."

The Governor smiled. "You've got more backbone than most people are accustomed to—particularly when it's wrapped in such a small package."

The attention sent an embarrassed pink up her neck toward her cheeks. "I've always been underestimated. It's my best weapon."

"Do you need to use it often?" Carver said.

"When the arsenal is limited, you use what you've got."

The two men exchanged quick glances. Vic could see that Carver was pleased.

"How about working for me?" Carver said. "As commissioner of Public Safety."

Laura had expected a get-to-know-me session, not an offer. She looked over at Vic who just smiled. "I'm honored that you'd consider me, Governor, but I wasn't expecting to be offered a position today."

"Take a few days to think about it, if you want. Talk to that good husband of yours."

"I already have. Semmes isn't wild about it—I can say that safely. But he's said the decision is up to me. I think one of his concerns is that I'd be working even more than I already do."

"Probably less once you get going," Vic interjected. "The Patrol has a built-in structure. You'll have a whole roomful of people to delegate almost everything to."

"But how do I figure out whom to trust?"

"It'll be clearer than you think," Carver said.

"I'm tempted, very tempted," Laura responded. "I must say, this is one job in state government I never gave two thoughts about. That must make me as much a creature of stereotypes as I figure the Patrol is. That's what makes it so intriguing."

"Thank your friend Vic, here. He proposed it to me."

"Are you certain you want to put a woman at the Patrol, Governor?"

Carver hesitated, noticeably, and then began. "I wasn't until you walked in here."

Laura felt the flush of self-consciousness rise again.

The Governor looked her straight in the eyes, his directness almost uncomfortable for Laura. "More than an historic appointment—and it would be historic—I want a war on drugs. A hardhitting, take-no-prisoners war. I think you're a great person for the job."

She looked back and forth from one to the other and then locked eyes with the Governor again.

"I'll do it if you promise me one thing. No politics, no pressure about promotions. I get to run it straight—no interference."

"You have our word," Carver said.

"Then you're on."

4

As the Governor and Laura, with Semmes and Will in tow, entered the long meeting room, the hot TV camera lights came on and shutters clicked. The Governor approached the lectern, scanning the faces to see which reporters had been assigned from the papers and TV stations.

"Good morning," Carver said.

Murmurs of "Good morning, Governor," were drowned out by the strong but smooth voice of Tim Cropley, one of the anchors for WTBC. "Good to see you again, sir," Tim said.

Governor Carver cleared his throat to start. "I'm pleased to announce the appointment of Laura Owen as commissioner of Public Safety and head of the Mississippi State Patrol, effective Inauguration Day.   Ms. Owen is no stranger to you. She has led a tireless fight against fraud and misuse of state funds these last four years. She has successfully brought case after case to trial, recovering nearly two million dollars from corrupt officials and contractors. On the heels of her success, I want her to lead the Patrol in another very important campaign, the fight against drug and alcohol abuse." He turned, motioning to Laura.

She squeezed Will's hand one more time, and smiled at Semmes who gave her a warm, encouraging look as she stepped forward.

The podium was normal height for the Governor and Laura was dwarfed—her line of vision obliterated by the mass of microphones. She tried to peer between them, then began moving them aside, creating rumbles and squeaks of feedback.

The Governor's press secretary materialized out of nowhere to help. "Sorry."

"No one mentioned the height requirement," she murmured.

Several of the reporters up front caught her remark and smiled. One woman laughed outright.

Laura smiled back.

This might be okay.

She stood up on tiptoe and began. "I want to thank Governor Carver for having confidence in me. I hope I can live up to his expectations." Laura turned and smiled back at Semmes. "I want especially to thank my husband, Semmes Owen, for supporting me in my decision. Without his encouragement, I could never have accomplished what I have so far.

"It's for the children, mine and yours, that I'll be working," Laura said. "Substance abuse is a raging disease that I believe must be attacked on several different fronts at once. While my main focus will be police enforcement, I will also be working closely with the other state agencies—health, mental health, and education, as well as the Governor's Forum on Children—to do everything I can to help to remove alcohol and narcotics abuse, and all the horrors they bring, from our lives."

The Governor stepped back to her side. "Are there any questions?"

An eager new female TV reporter, far more fashionably dressed and made up than Laura, raised her hand. "Are you the first woman to command the State Patrol?"

"Yes."

"She's the first woman to command any state patrol," Governor Carver added with a broad, proud smile.

Another reporter raised his hand, pencil poised. "How do you think the troopers will take your appointment?"

"Fine," said Laura. "I expect they'll respond like the professionals they are. I'm not a sworn officer, in fact, only one commissioner has ever been sworn. I don't plan to try to be one. I'll manage the agency as an administrator."

From the back came, "Do you have any specific plans?"

"I'm going after drunk drivers and drug smugglers, and I won't fix traffic tickets. Other than that, I don't know yet. I'll wait until I've been in office and seen what needs to be done—and what can be done."

Laura looked around for a moment, enjoying the event.

She liked this and it was going well—at least she thought it was.

"There's one rumor that I want to dispel as quickly as possible," Laura added. "I will not change the Patrol car and uniform colors from blue and gray to pink."

The reporters all laughed. Tim Cropley, the overbearing TV anchor had waited as long as he could. He stepped forward, ignoring Laura's signal to another person. "I understand that several command-level people at the Patrol resigned this morning. Do you have any comment?"

"Retirements are part of the natural course of things in any organization. I'll be filling any vacancies before I take over on January twelfth."

"Are you running for governor?" Cropley asked.

"Not at the moment, but I never rule out anything, Mr. Cropley. I will say this, however: I won't stand a chance in any political race if I don't do a great job as Commissioner. And right now, that's the only thing on my mind."

■ ■ ■ ■

"I'm as proud as a mother could be," Charlotte Hemeter said. "If only your father could have seen this. He'd be bursting."

"Thanks, Mom," Laura replied. She had the phone tucked between her shoulder and ear, pulling off her tight panty hose as fast as possible.

"And Will looked so serious."

"Where did you see him?"

"It was on the noon news. I'm going to tape it at six."

"How did it look?" Laura asked, sitting on the side of the bed and pulling up her blue jeans.

"Well, aside from your not being much taller than the podium..."

"Was it bad?"

"No, but I'd suggest something lower for your next press conference. At least have a step stool handy."

"I'll make a note of that."

"When do you start?"

"I've got to clear up some case files at the State Auditor's office first, and then start interviews to select a new chief."

"There isn't one already?"

"Several people retired this morning, including the chief."

"Because of you?"

"Looks that way."

"I'm not surprised," Charlotte said, "but they should have at least given you a chance."

"It's better this way, Mom. Everyone'll be my appointee, not beholden to someone else."

"Guess you're right. I just think it's rather rude and tacky."

"Rude and tacky don't figure in this business, I'm afraid."

"Well, I hope you're never rude or tacky, young lady."

"I'll try my best, Mom," Laura said, with a tiny grimace. Deciding this was a good stopping place before she actually did say something rude or tacky, she told her mother, "Gotta go get dinner started."

"Well, okay. Love you lots," Charlotte said.

"Me, too, Mom."

She hung up the phone, and sighed as she pulled on her favorite soft, red sweater. She'd be her mother's child forever. No matter how old, or how self-sufficient she might be, her mother would always find room for a midcourse correction.

If only she could avoid being that way with Will.

■ ■ ■ ■

On the twentieth floor of the Sillers State Office Building, Major Jimmie Anderson, looking his usual crisp self, even after an entire day in uniform, closed the door behind him and saw Blake Coleman, waiting.

"You next?"

"I was told to be here at four o'clock," Blake said, looking at his watch.

"Sorry. She's been running late. I think you're the last one," Jimmie said. "What's the deal?"

"She's talking to everyone before making a decision," Blake said. "That's all I know. Didn't you ask for an interview?"

"No, I didn't figure I should bother," Jimmie said. "Everyone knows I backed Carver's opponent—he's my wife's cousin."

"Maybe she doesn't care," Blake answered. "How'd the interview go?"

"Fine, I guess," Jimmie said. "She asked me a lot about the roadmen—training and troop strength."

The door opened behind Jimmie and Laura stepped out. "Lieutenant Colonel Coleman?"

"Yes, ma'am," Blake said, surprised that she was smaller and looked younger than he'd figured from her photographs in the newspaper.

"Whenever you're ready," Laura said, disappearing back into the room.

"Good luck," Jimmie said as Blake stepped forward.

"Please have a seat," said Laura, motioning toward the only other chair in the small room. The walls were lined with document storage cases, stacked haphazardly. She'd been offered an office at State Patrol Headquarters but had preferred to stay on her own turf. This was the only room available in the Governor's staff offices.

Blake smiled politely, enough to show the outlines of long dimples that would appear if he ever really grinned. He was a tall man, thinner now than he'd been when he'd joined the Patrol, but formidable. His long face and deep-set dark eyes made him appear more severe than he actually was. He seemed more ill at ease than most of the others.

"I understand you direct Criminal Investigations."

"Yes, ma'am."

"Then Robert Stone must work for you," Laura said.

"That's right."

"I appreciated his help in Connor County."

"I would have given anything to see that supervisor lose the case," Blake said. "He's been a thorn in my side—in everyone's side, I dare say—for years."

"So Robert told me."

"But I never seem to get out of my office in Jackson," Blake said, his dark eyes taking in every facial and body movement she made.

"Tell me about your career with the Patrol," Laura said.

"Came on straight off a military hitch, then switched to investigations in the seventies, and I've been there ever since, working my way up, slowly but surely."

"So what would you do for the roadmen if you were chief?"

Based on what Sandy Quinn had told him about the Governor's conversations, Blake had expected questions about narcotics—supposedly that's all the Governor and Vic ever discussed. "They're underutilized, undermotivated, and underpaid. I'd try to fix all three as fast as I could."

"How?"

"The solution for the money is the easiest," Blake said, watching Laura scribble notes. "Pay increases, realignment, and rescheduling so they can work second jobs. Motivation will come with some creative job assignments and training. As for utilization, with that many eyes and ears out there, we ought to be gathering a lot more information than we are."

"What kind of information?" Laura asked, noting that Blake was no longer ill at ease. He looked straight at her when he talked, totally involved in the questions and equally certain about the answers.

"About drug couriers," Blake said. "About private planes landing here in the dead of night—all manner of things."

Laura smiled. "Why hasn't it been done before?"

"Forget 'Courtesy, Service and Safety', 'Don't rock the boat' has been the real Patrol motto," Blake said. "Or 'Fly low and fly undetected.'"

"And you would fly higher?"

"Absolutely. From Day One."

"Robert told me I'd like you," Laura said with a smile. "What else have you been dreaming about doing on the day you become chief?"

Blake's long cheeks colored slightly with self-consciousness. "I don't know where to start. There's so much that could be better—petty stuff, from the way equipment is handled, to big-ticket items like car purchasing and repairs. You name it, and it can be improved."

"Is anything working right?"

Blake hesitated.

"This isn't the time for modesty."

Blake took a deep breath. "The Criminal Investigations Bureau is in pretty decent shape."

"Under your brilliant stewardship?"

"I didn't mean to brag," Blake said.

"One of my teachers used to say you shouldn't wait for someone else to toot your horn, because chances are, they won't."

Blake smiled diffidently. "We cut out a lot of the paperwork so we could keep the guys out in the field rather than in the office. And everyone's happier, there's no doubt about it."

"Robert thinks a lot of you."

"And I think a lot of him. Some days I wish we were working cases again instead of managing. We had fun."

"You know what he said about you?" Laura asked.

"I'd hate to think, ma'am."

"That if you told him to jump off the side of the building, he'd do it in a heartbeat because you would have made arrangements for him to land safely."

Blake shifted in his chair, clearly uncomfortable with the praise. "We've been friends a long time—we know each other inside and out."

"So, if you were chief, who would you choose to head investigations?"

"Robert."

"And who would be in charge of uniforms?"

"Jimmie Anderson, the guy who just left."

"Why?"

"Cuz he's honest, he's smart, and he's loyal."

"What about Bill Kenner?"

Blake closed his eyes and shook his head.

"He's got friends in high places," Laura said.

"So do window-washers," Blake said.

Laura chuckled. "So explain loyalty in the Patrol. For instance, Jimmie Anderson backed Carver's opponent when, by statute, the Patrol's not supposed to get involved."

"It's impossible for the Patrol not to be involved—it's in their blood. Some just hide it better than others. And in Jimmie's case, the opponent happened to be his wife's cousin."

"Ahhh," Laura said. "That explains a lot. What about you?"

"I sat this one out."

"Why?"

"Didn't know who'd be better—Carver, who'd done nothing for law enforcement, or a new guy who might make changes I didn't like," Blake said.

"He would have made Jimmie Anderson chief," Laura said.

"That's true, but he also would have forced Jimmie to make Bill Kenner assistant chief. There's a load of ass-kissers..." Blake stopped, blanching at his language.

Laura smiled. "I'm familiar with the term. Use it myself on occasion."

Blake nodded meekly. "Bill Kenner's one of the best...."

"Ass-kissers. So who do I trust?"

"Don't get me wrong. There are plenty of men here with principles."

Laura looked at her watch and sat up straight in her chair. "I've got to cut this short, Mr. Coleman, I'm sorry."

"I appreciate the chance to talk," Blake said, standing quickly and extending his hand across the desk. "It'll be a pleasure working with you, Ms. Owen, in whatever capacity."

"You aren't bothered by the possibility of working for a woman?"

"Not from what Robert's told me."

"I'll let you know my decision before the twelfth," Laura said.

"Thanks for the interview," said Blake, moving toward the door.

"Thank you, Colonel Coleman."

■ ■ ■ ■

If ever there were a monument to power, State Patrol Headquarters was it. Built when nary a thought of energy conservation crossed the architect's mind, the glass and stone structure stood at the windy edge of the interstate and one of its major arteries with cars and trucks steadily whizzing by. Each of the five stories had twelve-foot floor-to-ceiling windows on all sides, and the first floor was a single open space—a fifteen-thousand-square-foot entryway.

The fifth floor, where the commissioner, chief, and other administrative staff had their offices, was a feared and distant sanctum. Usually only command-level troopers crossed that threshold, and then only when summoned for meetings in the conference room. The scale of the huge conference room was straight out of the Pentagon, with glass on two sides. A permanent U-shaped table ran the length of the room, specially built of the same dark wood that paneled the walls, with thirty-four dark swivel chairs placed around the perimeter, and room for forty more. A single desk was at the top of the U.

Nearly every seat was filled with captains, majors, and colonels, all male, and only three out of the twenty-two were black. When Laura opened the door, the talking stopped immediately, and everyone jumped up and stood at attention. She looked at the lone desk and chair at the other end of the room, a pitcher of water and a glass ready, and then turned back to the bottom of the table, closest to her. Seeing a folding chair next to the cabinet behind her, she reached for it and two troopers stumbled over each other to help her.

"I think I'll sit here," she said as they moved to make room. "And please sit down. I appreciate the sentiment, but standing at attention is not necessary. I'm not an Army general and never have been, as I'm sure you know."

A sigh of relief and a cheerful buzz spread around the room as everyone took their places. As she settled herself, it quieted down.

"I want to introduce myself to you today so that you'll get to know me better, and I also want to tell you where I'm headed. But before I start, I'd appreciate it if you'd go around the room and tell me your name and your position. Except for the majors and colonels whom I've interviewed, you're all just a big sea of blue and gray at this point."

One by one, each officer said his name, rank, and what district or department he was from. No one volunteered any extra information.

"As you know, both the chief and the assistant chief for Enforcement have retired, effective today. Many officers, from all ranks, applied for the positions, but I believe in a strong promotional structure. I think it's only proper to choose the chiefs and assistant chiefs from the ranks of major or higher," Laura said. She paused deliberately before adding, "...without regard to political affiliation."

No one in the room moved. She'd sworn everyone to secrecy about her choices, and it was clear they'd kept their word.

"Lt. Colonel Blake Coleman will be the new chief..." Laura said.

A murmur of congratulations began. Laura looked up the table at Bill Kenner who was staring back in disbelief.

"And Major Jimmie Anderson will be assistant chief for Enforcement."

The murmur built to applause. Kenner's face fell even farther.

One look around the room from Blake's serious dark eyes and the buzz ended.

"With Colonel Coleman's promotion," Laura continued, "the position of assistant chief for Criminal Investigations opened up. Major Robert Stone will assume that command."

A new, louder buzz developed at this announcement. The State Patrol was still a bastion of white males and this appointment had broad implications.

"The two positions left vacant by these promotions, Southern

Enforcement and Northern Investigations, will be filled according to promotional competition."

Laura paused, studying their faces. "I know some of you aren't too pleased about my own appointment, but I want us to work together to make the State of Mississippi a safer and better place to live for all its citizens. I'll do my very best at what a commissioner ought to do—finding the resources you need to do your jobs."

Most of the faces remained impassive. They'd heard exactly the same words many times before.

"I want to focus on drunk driving and narcotics interdiction—police work, not politics."

Still no change in expression. Laura decided to throw in some sports lingo.

"The Patrol has been a political football for too long. It's high time we ended the punt, pass, and kick competition."

A couple of smiles appeared and a few arms unfolded. She was making a little headway but not much.

"And I might as well get this out of the way now: I will not tolerate ticket fixing."

A few officers leaned over to consult with neighbors.

"I'll never ask you to help one of my friends or relatives, nor will I tolerate requests from anyone else. If you write a ticket, it stays a ticket. Your discretion comes before the pen hits the paper."

A few heads bobbed in agreement. Some progress.

"You're the troopers, not me. You know how to do your jobs. I expect you to speak up and tell me your needs so you can do your jobs more effectively. I promise I'll listen, and I promise I'll do everything I can to get what you require."

Laura looked around the room again. Big men, all of them. The sort few people messed with, let alone little women.

"One more thing," Laura said. "I will never—I repeat, never—tell you I'll do something unless I'm going to do it."

There were a few snorts, as though this, too, was something they'd heard before.

Laura mustered her strongest, sternest voice. "But if I say I'll do something, you can bet the farm I will."

She stopped talking, having run through the short list of points she wanted to make, upset with herself that she hadn't been more creative about it.

A young officer hesitantly raised his hand. "Commissioner, the papers say you're running for governor. Won't we be a political football again, just a different game?"

"The papers will always say exactly what they want," Laura said, relaxing a bit. "I've got one job, and one job only—this one—and I intend to give the Patrol my full attention."

A groan came from Bill Kenner. Laura was surprised he hadn't hidden his feelings better. She looked toward him as she finished her remarks.

"My background is no different than most previous commissioners—I'm a lawyer. I chased white-collar criminals around Mississippi for four years. I practiced criminal law for six years before that, and I know most of the tricks in the legal defense book. All of this taught me one thing: This country is facing a disastrous future if we don't address narcotics—all forms of substance abuse for that matter—right now. And what better place to start than right here on the Gulf? Mississippi is close enough to be a premier landing strip for South American drug runners. But I'm a newcomer in your world, and I'd appreciate all the advice and criticism—constructive, of course—that you can give me."

Laura looked at the faces again, not certain she'd made any impact at all. "Are there any more questions before I turn this meeting over to Colonel Coleman?"

No one moved. "Thank you, gentlemen. I need to see Colonels Coleman, Anderson, and Stone after you're finished."

As Laura stood to leave, everyone jumped to attention. She shook her head, and obediently they all sat back down. The door had hardly closed when Kenner started in.

"I will not work for a woman."

"Well, what are you going to do about it?" came a question from the other side of the room.

"Don't know, but that woman has no business being commissioner. Women were never intended for this."

Blake Coleman jumped in. "You're way out of line, Kenner. Owen is the Governor's choice, and the Patrol will respect it. Period, the end."

"At least she talks to your face, not behind your back," Jimmie Anderson added. "And Kenner, if she's so unacceptable, why'd you try so hard to get appointed chief?"

Kenner's face grew even redder than usual as a buzz started around the room.

"She's a damn sight better than some of them we've had," came a voice from the back. "Or that idiot, Dearborn."

"That's a goddamned backhanded compliment if I ever heard one," came another.

Nervous laughter was building up.

"Well, I don't plan to sit still for it," Kenner said, folding his arms across his chest and glaring, challenging Blake.

Laura had dawdled long enough to hear Kenner's outburst. It made her mad, but she certainly wasn't surprised, not in this citadel of masculinity. She'd struggled against male power structures for so long that she was used to the tiresome reaction. At least when she'd worked at the State Auditor's office, the other staff members were reasonably progressive thinkers, a welcome respite from this sort of thing.

But there would be few breaks here for her.

Why had she ever let Vic talk her into this?

▪ ▪ ▪ ▪

In case there was any question about who was in charge, the commissioner's corner office was three times bigger than any other office in the building and twice as big as the governor's office at the Capitol. It included a private bath, and two enormous closets, one containing a large safe, and the other, a refrigerator. It was distinctly utilitarian and masculine—brown carpeting, brown walls, brown furniture. When Semmes had first entered the room, he'd suggested moving next door and converting the place into a handball court.

A large, gaily-wrapped box sat on the coffee table, having arrived while she was in the meeting. The card was in Will's scrawl: "To Momma from Daddy and Will." With three rips of the paper, she unwrapped a small cassette player and radio receiver with speakers. She set it up immediately and tuned in Public Radio of Mississippi. A Bach Prelude filled the huge space—a start toward making the room habitable. She traded the enormous high-backed desk chair for a straight chair her size, and began reading through the correspondence and accompanying draft responses that had built up since her predecessor's retirement. She winced at the wordy military-style prose, and reached for a red pen.

An hour later, after the officer's meeting broke up, the three colonels arrived at her office and took places around the coffee table. Laura watched Robert survey it as if he'd never been in the room before that day.

"Ridiculous, isn't it?" Laura said.

"Well, that wasn't the adjective I had in mind," Robert said, "but it fits."

"How bad was it after I left?" Laura asked.

Blake piped up immediately. "Not too bad. Nothing we can't handle. There's always a commotion at the change of an administration—this really isn't much different."

Laura let the obvious lie pass, appreciating his courtesy. "Except I'm a lot different. What's the deal with Major Kenner?"

Jimmie was quick to answer. "He's a jerk and always has been. The Lord told him that a woman's place is in the home. Plus, he was after the chief's job and this was probably his last chance before retirement."

"I'll bet the Lord also told him he should be chief," Robert added. "If it makes you feel any better, Commissioner, he doesn't like blacks either. And thanks to you, I outrank him."

Laura dismissed the subject with a shake of her head. "Let's talk about what we're going to do," she said, leaning forward, her piercing blue eyes moving from man to man. "I'm not a cop, so I'll leave the protocol up to you. But I want to hit dope smugglers and drunk drivers as hard as the Patrol can hit them. I want a coordinated, relentless effort. Blake..." Laura paused. "May I call you Blake?"

"You can call me whatever you want, Commissioner," Blake replied, her politeness a welcome change.

"What do you need to start a full-scale assault using all the Patrol—roadmen, investigators, and agents?" Laura asked.

"Hmm, I'll have to think," Blake mumbled, his eyes lighting up. "No one's ever asked me that question. What are the limits?"

"Only that we have to be able to afford it—my main job will be to find the money. And we have to meet all our other obligations. Other than that, none."

"Off the top, we'll need some specialized training right away and some new equipment." Blake looked at Jimmie and Robert. "Think we could come up with a plan?"

They nodded, smiling.

"There is one thing, though," Laura said.

"Yes, ma'am?"

"We have to get started right away, say, tomorrow. This afternoon would be better. We need to do something immediately to make it crystal clear where we're headed."

Half an hour later as Blake, Robert, and Jimmie headed down the hall toward their offices, Blake turned back to Robert. "Gather up the majors and captains and let's go to lunch. We've got work to do."

Robert nodded. "I'm not going out of my way to find Kenner, if that's okay with you."

"Fine by me," Blake said, "Just cover me, will ya?"

▪ ▪ ▪ ▪

By six-thirty that evening, sitting around the desk in Blake's new and very bare office, they'd mapped out two plans of attack—an expensive pipe dream and the bare bones version. Either was acceptable, but the former would definitely be more fun. They planned to present it to Laura the next day, allowing themselves a night to mull it over.

"When are you gonna move your stuff in here, so I can move into my office?" Robert asked.

"Tonight," said Blake, scanning the space. It was the first moment he'd had to think about arranging his collection of photographs and cop memorabilia. Robert's pager started beeping, a jarring sound in the now-quiet offices. He glanced down, mumbled, "Rachel," and picked up the phone.

"The Commissioner'll be okay, don't you think?" Blake said after Robert hung up.

"I told you that already," Robert answered, standing up and stretching. "Why didn't you believe me?"

Blake shrugged his shoulders. "I guess I couldn't bring myself to hope for too much. She heard every word Kenner said today and didn't make a big deal about it. I like that."

"This could be a helluva ride," Robert said. "Well, gotta go... celebration dinner waiting for me. What's on tap for you?"

"We don't eat until eight at the earliest these days," Blake answered. "Sally gets her mother fed and in bed first."

"Shouldn't your mother-in-law be in a nursing home?"

"She should, but Sally can't bring herself to do it," Blake said. "If it weren't for that extra room I added when we built the garage, we'd have no choice—can't get the wheelchair through our narrow halls."

"Well, don't stay too late," Robert said. "Sets a bad precedent."

"Long enough to pack the rest of the boxes."

Robert stepped toward the door, "Later, man."

"Tomorrow, let's have a cold one to celebrate," Blake called out.

"Book it," called Robert, disappearing into the hallway.

▪ ▪ ▪ ▪

Rachel Stone slashed a sharp knife across a flank steak before dropping the meat into the hot buttered pan while Robert tore up lettuce for the salad. His angelfish wandered to and fro among the plants in the fifty-gallon aquarium sitting on the end of the counter. The huge kitchen was the center of the house they'd built when they'd moved out of the city three years earlier. With no children and with two salaries—compared to what Rachel earned as an anesthesiologist, Robert's paycheck was chump change—they enjoyed comforts neither ever imagined growing up.

"What's Laura Owen really like?" Rachel asked. A small, intense woman, Rachel Stone wore her tightly curled hair cut close to her delicately shaped skull which made her taste in extravagant earrings quite apparent.

"Direct, ambitious, but decent," Robert said, reaching for an avocado. "A lot like you, my dear."

Rachel smiled. "You aren't a token, are you?"

Robert shook his head as he sliced a quarter out of the fruit. "Don't think so. Certainly hope not. I knew her from her days at the State Auditor's office. But I got the promotion because of Blake—he put in the word. She asked him who he felt most comfortable working with and that was it."

Rachel raised her wineglass in a toast. "To Robert Stone, Assistant Chief for Criminal Investigations extraordinaire—and someday Chief of Patrol."

Robert found his own glass amid the vegetables on the counter and clicked it against hers. "Don't get ahead of yourself, Baby," he said, taking a sip and returning to his avocado.

"Why not? It's what you dream about, isn't it?"

"Dreamin' and bein' are different things."

"You never honestly believed they'd let you get this far, did you?"

"No, I didn't."

"Then think positive."

"I just can't believe this state will keep putting people in charge who'll do right. The pendulum always swings back with a vengeance, as you know."

Rachel raised her glass again. "Then, to four great years."

■ ■ ■ ■

The lights were still on in his mother-in-law's room when Blake drove in at 8:30, which meant there might not be any dinner ready. Usually by this time, if the day was going smoothly, there was only the blue glow from her television with his wife, Sally, busy in the kitchen fixing their own dinner. At the back door, ten boxes of Christmas decorations were stacked up, waiting to be hoisted into the crawl space for another year. With the boys no longer home except for three or four days during the holidays, he wasn't entirely certain why his wife persisted in her frenzied preparations each December.

But the kitchen smelled wonderful, making him suddenly hungry, and the table was set, a good sign they'd have a quiet dinner.

Blake pulled off his boots and tie in the bedroom and put them away in the closet. He wandered back into the kitchen and had just popped the top of a beer when the door opened.

"Hi, Honey," said Sally, brightening when she saw him.

"How's your Mom?" Blake asked, leaning down to give her a quick kiss.

"Not too good tonight. She can hardly walk, her feet are so swollen."

"We can afford to move her to Magnolia Hall now," Blake said. "The pay raise will give us enough."

"I know, and I appreciate that. But not quite yet, things are working out pretty well." Despite her protestations, Sally was looking pale and more tired every day. A deep fatigue was eroding her broad, pretty smile. Between her job at the bank and taking care of her mother, she'd given up her evening walks, and fell into bed as soon as they cleaned up the kitchen.

"Just don't wear yourself out."

"Promise," Sally smiled. She was five foot nine and too thin, everyone said. Her once blonde hair, now streaked with gray, was usually pulled back from her face with tortoiseshell headband, accentuating her high cheekbones. "Our dinner's all ready."

"I smelled it," Blake said.

"I felt like we should celebrate tonight," Sally said. "So what happened today?"

"Bill Kenner made a fool of himself, the Commissioner ignored it, thank goodness, and we're off and running."

"Where to?" Sally asked as she pulled a homemade chicken pot pie from the oven and carried it to the eating alcove at the end of the counter.

"She's taking aim at drug dealers, right between the eyes," Blake said, reaching out to massage Sally's shoulders.

"Already?"

Blake nodded, clearly pleased.

"Sounds like your kind of commissioner. A busy four years is in store."

"I'll try my best not to be a total stranger," Blake said, working his thumbs into her tight muscles.

"That feels wonderful," Sally cooed, remaining very still to make it easy for Blake to continue.

"So we'll see you when we see you?" Sally asked after they'd sat down to eat.

Blake nodded.

"Just keep your check on automatic deposit, okay?"

▪ ▪ ▪ ▪

Laura slipped onto a bar stool across the counter from where Semmes was loading the dishwasher.

"Is Will down for the count?" Semmes asked.

"I think so," she said, reaching for her unfinished glass of wine. "But it wasn't easy. The *Redwall* books are too exciting for bedtime reading, but that's all he wants to hear."

"Maybe we need to change the routine—a chapter or two of something exciting in the big chair and then something quieter."

"I'll try anything," Laura said.

"So what was today really like?" Semmes asked as he filled the basket of the coffeemaker, getting set for the morning.

"Bizarre. Unlike anything I've ever experienced," said Laura, finishing off her glass of wine. "Where'd the bottle get to?"

Semmes handed it to her. "Save enough for me, I want to hear this."

She picked up the wine and their two glasses, and headed for the couch and easy chairs in front of their massive stone fireplace, the focal point of the large living room. Stretching out, Laura realized how tired she really was. She'd been running on adrenaline all day, and finally her system was beginning to show the wear and tear.

"Start from the top," said Semmes, sitting down beside her.

"I already told you about the staff meeting...."

"You can skip that. What's it really like up there?"

"Deferential, first off."

"Ass-kissing is what it's really called."

"That too. I'll give you an example. I decided I didn't want that huge high-backed desk chair. I would have looked like little Orphan Annie in it. So I pushed it out of the way and moved a different chair in. When I came back from lunch, the guy who's in charge of property, was there with a transfer form for me to sign about the old chair, and furniture catalogues and two sample chairs to try out. I hadn't said anything except to comment in passing. And boom, it happens."

"That's the military for you, always looking out for the boss."

"Then I get a visit from the armorer. He wanted me to choose my weapon."

"Your weapon?"

"Yes, which kind of pistol I wanted to carry."

"What did you say?"

"Thank you, but no thank you. Of course, I'm sure they think I'm scared of guns."

"I am, if you aren't. But shouldn't you have one?"

"No need. It looks like I'll always have a trail of guys with guns behind me."

"That's reassuring," said Semmes sarcastically.

"I must admit the squeak of leather gun belts is a little disorienting. I did get congratulatory phone calls and requests for lunch dates for next week."

"From whom?

"FBI, Drug Enforcement—cop types wanting to line up early."

"Alex Markham?"

"No."

"Are you going to be able to work with him?"

"If he works with me but I can't be both sides of the equation. It's like he's angry that I even exist."

"You're competition, my dear. Always have been. And he always lost when you were in the game—at Ole Miss, last year in Connor County. He's got to know he made a mistake refusing to go after that supervisor."

Laura took another sip of wine and sighed, "And then there's the legislature."

"Were you down there today?"

"Nope, but I'm going tomorrow. Bright and early, to meet with the House Appropriations chairman about the budget."

"Have you ever met him?"

Laura shook her head. "Vic's escorting me."

"That should help. I get the feeling Vic's pretty well regarded—even by people who don't like Carver."

"I think you're right."

Laura turned away from Semmes to stare into the fire.

"Are you still glad you took the job?"

"Not sure yet. It's a kick, all this 'yes, ma'am, no, ma'am, anything you say, ma'am.' But I'm certain that will wear off."

Semmes stroked her cheek with his finger. "Maybe not, you're the boss man now."

She shut her eyes to savor Semmes' touch.

"I just don't want to make a complete fool of myself."

"You never have. I bet you'll do fine."

"You realize I've really stuck myself out there this time," Laura said, opening her eyes wide and looking at him. "There's no way to go down in flames without a whole lot of people saying, 'I told you so.' "

"I thought of that when you first started talking about it. But that's not your style. You always work so hard to do things right, and this won't be any different."

5

Ann Ruthven sipped a cup of coffee, waiting for Laura at the window table at one of Jackson's newest restaurants. She was already regretting that she'd picked such a popular place. Half of Jackson would wander in and Ann knew they wouldn't have enough time to talk between interruptions. She toyed with the idea of paging Laura and asking her to meet somewhere else when Laura stepped through the door.

"Hi. Long time no see." Laura gave Ann a hug. They'd been college roommates for two years and stayed friends ever since. They were as compatible as two women could be, yet different enough so they never competed for anything—men, activities, or careers. Ann was taller and outdoorsy, yet elegant in her expensively tailored suits. She paid much more attention to her appearance than Laura ever had, selecting colors carefully to complement her long dark hair and brown eyes.

Just as Laura was settling into her seat, a waiter appeared. "Let's eat, I'm starved," Laura said.

"Glad I'm not the only one," Ann said. They quickly looked over the menu and ordered.

"I'm sorry I chose this spot," Ann said. "I've already seen four people I know."

"It'll be fine. If we act like we're in deep conversation, no one will disturb us. Have you been here long?"

"Not very. I came right after I called you. There wasn't enough time to bother going back to the office. How's the State Patrol?"

"I love it, and I never thought I'd say that. It's phenomenal, all the different things I deal with in one day—from new roofs to wiretaps. You get sucked in immediately. And almost everyone has been more than willing to work with me. That alone is amazing."

"Are you wearing a gun?"

"Hell, no. I'm not a cop. Unfortunately though, they think I won't carry one because I'm some kind of pacifist or sissy."

"So what's it like?"

"Exciting and downright frightening at the same time. I'm suddenly in charge of an army that goes where I tell it to go. I'm scared to death I'll suggest something really stupid and no one will speak up to correct me."

"But how do you even know what to do?"

"That takes care of itself. It's a huge operation that moves along under its own steam. With a thousand employees, there's someone already assigned to handle each detail. The heat goes off? That's a job for maintenance. The Legislature needs more information on the budget? Call the comptroller. I just look for ways to make things work better." Laura sipped her water. "So what's up with you?"

Ann took a deep breath and moved a bit closer so she wouldn't be overheard. "I'm pregnant."

"Ann..." Laura breathed in surprise. She didn't have a clue about the appropriate response. "How do you feel about it?"

"I want the baby—no matter what. Being around Will sealed that deal."

"Then it's wonderful."

"Do you really think so? What am I going to do?"

"First, you're going to eat right, starting now." Laura pulled away Ann's coffee. "Then you're going to do whatever you want—marry the dad, go it alone. It's Tom's baby, isn't it?"

"Yes," said Ann. "I haven't seen anyone else in months. But he doesn't know yet... I'm working up to telling him. I'll bet good money he'll be mad as hell."

"Do you want to marry him?" Laura asked, trying to hide her misgivings. Ann Ruthven and Tom Hilman seemed worlds apart, sharing only expensive habits and a love of sailing as far as Laura could tell.

"I'm not sure, but that's probably a moot point. He doesn't want to marry anyone, let alone me." Ann looked out the window, her eyes filling with tears. She picked up her napkin and dabbed at her eyes, trying not to ruin her makeup.

Ann was hardly Tom's usual fare—he usually preferred big tits, no brains. They'd met each other through work. Hilman Air was a big client of the accounting firm where Ann worked as a certified public accountant. But they'd never dated until an Ole Miss football weekend party when Ann's dark eyes touched his fancy—along with a goodly quantity of beer mixed with some very nice cocaine that a few of the boys were partaking of on the side. As far as Ann was concerned, even though Tom was clearly not interested in long-term relationships—those cards were on the table from the start—his good points were that he had plenty of money, a sailboat, and sooner or later, had to settle down a bit. Tom liked Ann's independence. She created no obligations, and he wanted none.

"Oh, Laura, I don't know," Ann said. "We've had such an easy relationship. But that's because he's away so much, or because he's rich, or both. I love the freedom, his freedom, but there's an edge, an uncertainty to him that worries me."

"Talk to him. Then you'll know. Follow your gut."

"I know one thing. I don't want to be a single mother, scraping for money, working all day with a latchkey kid. I want to be home—at least until this child goes off to school."

"I can't disagree," Laura said rather wistfully. "I often wish I hadn't worked these past few years since Will was born. You and the baby can survive working if you have to—the baby'll thrive regardless. But they're only little once. I'm sort of envious."

"I sure can't stay home if there isn't any money coming in the door. I've only got one sister left, and she's in Oregon."

"Whatever happens, Tom owes you support for the child, and I'd bet he makes good money working for his dad."

"I know exactly what he makes, and it's plenty. Don't forget, I do the taxes for his father's corporation."

The waiter arrived with their sandwiches.

"He's gonna say the baby is my fault," Ann added.

"Hey, last time it happened to me I distinctly remember two people being in the room." Laura looked approvingly at Ann's chicken on black bread with a green salad. "That's exactly what you and what's-its-name needs."

Ann, still skeptical, began eating for two.

▪▪▪▪

"You're pregnant?" Tom exploded. "How in the hell did that happen?"

"You know, boy meets girl," Ann said, trying desperately to lighten his anger.

"Don't joke with me, Ann," Tom said, the muscles in his tanned cheeks taut across his jaw. "What about the birth control you said you were using?"

"Nothing's one hundred percent effective except abstinence," Ann replied.

"Or did you do this on purpose?" Tom accused her. "To trap me and my money?"

"I did no such thing," Ann said. "I could make it without you if I had to. I've got some money of my own."

"Then you can pay for the abortion," Tom said.

Ann turned away from him long enough to gather her courage. "I'm not having an abortion, I want this child."

"No abortion? Don't I get to say something about this?

"Say what you like, ignore me and the child if you like, but I'm not having an abortion."

"Just like that?" Tom asked. "You won't even talk about it?"

"No," Ann said. "The only thing to talk about is whether you have something to do with our lives."

"You sure like the sound of the word *our*, I can see," Tom said.

"I do," Ann said. "Ever since Will Owen was born, I've been think-ing about children of my own. And I'm running out of time."

"So you did do this on purpose," Tom said.

"No," Ann snapped back. "If it had been on purpose, I would have picked a better set of genes."

Tom glared at her. "Thanks for the compliment."

"I didn't mean it like that," said Ann, regretting her sharp retort. "I don't want to do this alone, Tom," she pleaded, "I want a father for this child. But I will go it alone if I must."

"Well, I've got to think about that," Tom growled, grabbing his jacket and walking out of her house without another word.

Tom drove north up the Natchez Trace, a dark and lonely road at night, the closest he could come on land to the peace he felt on his boat.

Marriage.

It would disrupt everything, especially the cocaine. No more coming and going whenever he felt like it.

Another baby-hungry bimbo just like the rest of them.

Once his parents found out, they'd claim the baby whether he did or not. Second fiddle to a dead brother, and now second fiddle to a child. And if he refused to acknowledge their grandchild, God only knew what his father would do.

Tom cranked open the sunroof and drove on in silence, not even thinking. When he passed the Beaver Dam nature trail, he pulled off the road onto the grass, and cut his lights. The moon was new and clouds obscured most of the stars so there was an inky blackness all around him. As his eyes slowly adjusted to the darkness, he could make out a large herd of white-tailed deer moving into the meadow.

Damn, how had he let this happen? Escaping from all of it had been so close. Walk into Dad's office, tell him off, quit, and sail away—no strings, no ties, no obligations, and plenty of money.

A child ruined the safety, the simplicity of it all. If only Ann would have an abortion.

As he watched the deer graze, a big buck came out of the woods and wandered among his flock.

What would his father do when he found out? Maybe there'd be some lavish wedding present to proclaim his "joy." Good ol' Dad, the man who measures everyone by their net worth and everything by its price tag.

Money or something that could be converted to money—now that had some possibilities. He could buy a bigger boat with it. More cocaine. Or fewer trips.

Then divorce Ann, give her all his U.S. assets so she wouldn't squawk, and sail into the setting sun.

Tom cranked the engine, catching the eyes of the buck as his headlights flicked on. The huge animal stood there stunned.

That's me.

The herd bolted into the woods. Tom turned around in the empty road and headed back to Jackson.

▪ ▪ ▪ ▪

Only thirty feet off a narrow county road outside of Natchez, past a small and barely readable "Atenas" sign tacked to a tree on the fence row, Semmes was jolted back a hundred years. Enormous pecan trees dripped with Spanish moss. Green shoots and leaves of spring bulbs dotted the shady grassy areas beneath the canopy. The wheel ruts were deep from long use without the benefit of a grader to shave off the mound that built up in between. In places, it scraped the pan of Semmes' new Acura, the weeds and grass obscuring its height.

"Should have brought the Jeep," Semmes muttered. He was considering moving to one side and trying to straddle a wheel rut when the house appeared fifty yards ahead, so he took his chances and stayed where he was, wincing repeatedly as the sounds of earth meeting metal grew more insistent.

The house distracted him—a country house from the 1850s, disheveled and broken down. But it was a gem, and if the client had enough money, it could shine again.

A tallish man with short-cropped gray-blonde hair came round the far side of the house, and waited on the steps up to the gallery. His head was bent slightly forward as he peered over half glasses perched low on his nose, watching Semmes park behind his green Ford pickup.

"Any trouble finding the place?" he called.

"Took a little longer than I planned, but the directions were perfect," Semmes answered. He thrust his hand forward, "Semmes Owen."

"Lamar Bagley, Semmes," the man replied, his smile tentative, matching his let-me-size-you-up-first look from over his readers. "Sorry I didn't warn you about the lane. Never think about it myself with the truck and all."

"More noise than anything," Semmes said. With a nod, Semmes' eyes moved to the house, taking in the details of the leaded glass transom over the front door. "Thank you for letting me look at your house."

"I heard you were the best, and I want the best—if I can afford it."

"Not sure that's true but thank you, " Semmes said, taking two steps up and stopping. "Are the stairs and floors safe?"

"Believe it or not, yes. The only thing we've been able to afford over the years is to keep a roof on her and the steps sturdy."

"A wise choice," Semmes said, mounting a few steps and stopping to look down at the bricks of the curtain wall, then turning to scan the site. "Was this house built at this location or moved here?"

"Moved," Bagley said, clearly impressed. "How'd you know?"

"Foundation and the curtain wall are considerably more recent. Twenties or thirties?"

"Late twenties, I think. The house used to be somewhere on the Creek and my great uncle had it moved up here."

"Bet the creek had moved a little too close."

Semmes walked up and down the gallery, feeling solid oak planks beneath him. He stopped and peered in the double-hung windows, ten feet high at least, looking from side to side at the glass. "Original glass?"

"I can't imagine that would have survived moving."

"Did they take the house apart?"

"That I don't know," Bagley said.

"Excellent work, either way."

Semmes hesitated at the door and Bagley pulled it open. They entered a spacious, cool hall that ran the length of the house to an identical door at the other end. There were six doors, three down each wall, opening into rooms along the sides.

"This hallway was always the living room, though I think the room to the left," Bagley motioned in that direction, "was intended to be the sitting room. But as long as I can remember, it was a bedroom."

"Very little seems to be changed," Semmes said, stepping closer to the tongue-and-groove walls. Bagley rocked back on his heels, his arms crossing his chest, inspecting Semmes.

"This wasn't unusual back then—tongue-and-groove. I love it. Wonderful."

Bagley followed Semmes through the door to the left. Semmes looked slowly around the room.

"I heard you did the renovations at the Governor's Mansion."

"Yes, that was a fun project. Have you seen it?"

"No," Bagley said curtly. "I'm not one of Carver's big supporters. He's gotten a little too big for his britches, I'd say. Never did like his platform to begin with."

Semmes avoided responding by reaching to open a door, then turning to Bagley, "May I?"

"You have the run of the place."

"Thank you," said Semmes, pulling back a door to a cedar-lined closet.

"No matter what Carver says, he's making it harder for businessmen in this state to get ahead, not easier."

Semmes bit his tongue, lifting his arm to feel above a doorway, assiduously avoiding responding. "I try and stay as far away from politics as I can."

"It's just a damn shame, appointing all these women and blacks to government jobs just to have them there. Don't get me wrong, I think the coloreds..." He cast a sly sideways look at Semmes to see how he'd reacted but Semmes had walked across the room to inspect the fireplace. He began again, rephrasing just to be safe. "I think Blacks should have a chance, but not a better chance just because they're black."

"Is there an attic?"

"Yes, but you can only get up there through a trapdoor in the back room and I don't have a ladder with me."

"Do you know if it's floored?"

"Oh, yes. We used to play up there until the day we found a milk snake curled around a rafter. Why?"

"Thinking about heating and cooling possibilities."

Bagley nodded. As Semmes headed for the far door, Bagley launched back into his diatribe.

"I've got nothing against these people, if they're qualified, of course."

Semmes turned and held his hands up for the man to stop. "I need to tell you before this goes any further, that Laura Owen, who runs the State Patrol, is my wife."

Bagley was dumbfounded.

"If that's a problem for you," Semmes continued, "I'll understand. I think owners should have confidence in the architect on a project like this. Any project really. There's a lot of money involved, and designs that you'll live with for a long time."

Semmes stood still, not taking his eyes off Bagley. He needed this sort of thing out of the way at the beginning.

Bagley peered over his glasses at Semmes. "Didn't she do something before she was commissioner?"

"Laura recovered a lot of misspent money for the State Auditor's office and made a lot of people mad along the way."

"And you let her do this?"

"Between Laura and me it's not a matter of letting each other do things. Besides, when she's determined about something, it's hard to stop her."

Bagley hadn't taken his eyes off Semmes. He shook his head slowly. "I'd like to meet your wife someday."

"She loves seeing before and afters."

"Then bring her with you next time."

Semmes breathed a little easier—the first hurdle was crossed.

"Bet you don't get any speeding tickets," Bagley added.

Semmes smiled. "Not lately."

▪▪▪▪

"Welcome to the heartbeat, Robert," said Logan Cummins, Resident Agent in Charge of the Drug Enforcement Administration. "Let me show you around before we leave for lunch. It takes about thirty-five seconds, without introductions."

"I don't think I've ever been up here," said Robert.

"I haven't been much of a host," Logan replied. "There's hardly room to turn around."

Since its inception, the Jackson DEA office had been a tiny operation. Cummins, five handpicked agents, and a secretary, along with conference room, equipment locker and vault, were all crammed into a warren of upholstery-covered partitions and government-issued furniture on the sixth floor of the Federal Building—in the shadow of the FBI. For a group tasked with primary responsibility for narcotics enforcement, the DEA cowboys hadn't been accorded nearly the resources they needed.

But all that was changing, albeit slowly. Several years back, Congress had authorized police agencies to share the assets seized from drug dealers, a move designed to revitalize enforcement efforts. Since Mississippi was a fertile field for drug running, Logan's bottom line had begun improving. But so had interagency rivalry as the different ranks of cops fought for credit on a bust and a share in the spoils—an unintended effect of the legislation.

"The more dopers we catch, the more agents I hire," Logan said, "but there isn't any more space in the building. The life of a redheaded stepchild."

"Maybe we'll be able to help," Robert smiled.

Logan's left eyebrow rose, cocking at a jaunty angle above his green eyes. "You and Blake getting organized?" Logan and Blake had been professional friends for years, working closely and trading information whenever the occasion was right.

"The Commissioner insists on it," said Robert, as he and Logan headed out to the central hallway and the elevators.

"That's what she's said, but talk is easy," Logan answered, punching the call button.

"It's more than talk. You'll start seeing the results soon, I hope."

"Give me a hint," begged Logan. The elevator doors opened and Alex Markham and Special Agent Hal Easterbrook of the FBI were staring out at them. "Later," Logan said to Robert as they stepped in. "Good morning, Hal, Alex."

Easterbrook, permanently detailed from the FBI as an aide to Markham, was as politically ambitious as Alex, and, of late, he'd developed an arrogance that few could tolerate. He nodded, hardly acknowledging Logan.

"Hi, Logan," said Alex, then smiled at Robert in the slightly vague way reserved for newcomers, not certain whether he was a colleague, friend, or target.

"Do you know Lt. Col. Robert Stone of the State Patrol?" Logan asked. "This is Alex Markham, United States Attorney. I think you've already met Hal."

Robert extended his hand immediately. "Nice to meet you, Mr. Markham. Good to see you, Hal."

"You took Blake Coleman's spot when he became chief?" Alex asked.

"Yes, sir," Robert answered. "I was in charge of Northern Investigations before that."

"I see. How do you like working for Ms. Owen?" Alex added with an extra hiss on the Ms.

"Couldn't ask for a better boss, actually."

"Probably not spending much time at the office, then," Alex said.

"On the contrary," Robert said. "She's getting up to speed as fast as can be expected."

The doors opened at the first floor.

"Nice to meet you, Robert," Alex said with a perfunctory nod.

Hal and Alex turned toward the garage, and Robert followed Logan out the front door toward the Mayflower Grill. "Is he always that chilly?"

"He is with me," Logan said. "I didn't go along with all his buddy-buddy stuff with the agents when he was first appointed. You know the type—a lawyer, suddenly fascinated with guns and radios and wanting to be on the scene at a bust."

Robert nodded.

"Owen isn't like that, is she?" Logan said.

"Hardly," Robert said. "She's got good instincts, usually decent ideas—some are a little off the wall. But she stays out of our way, really. Blake's supposed to get the Patrol moving again, I've got narcotics and criminal investigations, and she finds the money to do what we want to do. As close as it gets to perfect, in my book."

"Markham even insisted on going to the Caribbean one time," Logan said, holding the door to the restaurant. A pungent tang of Worcestershire and garlic filled their nostrils. "He's got his pilot's license and wanted to show off."

"Then why haven't there been more convictions?"

"There've been plenty. But they're all slam-dunk nickel and dime cases. He won't go for the riskier stuff unless he has no choice. I bet he puts up a stink when I suggest adding the Patrol to the task force."

"Don't go too far out on a limb," Robert said.

"We need you," Logan said. "In fact, I doubt you'll get as much out of it as we will."

"Why will he gripe?"

"Y'all aren't under his thumb," Logan said, looking down at the menu. "He likes to be in control."

▪ ▪ ▪

"This is a very happy day, son," Stephen Hilman said as he and Tom strolled across the lawn after dinner. At Ann's suggestion, Tom had invited his parents to the Ocean Springs house to tell them the news. Water lapped quietly at the shore, the only steady sound in the quiet cove. The *Last Chance* was tied up at the dock rather than out on its mooring in the cove since Tom was leaving for a sail the next day.

"I'm glad you and Mother approve," Tom said.

"Approve? We're ecstatic," Stephen said. "Ann's a great girl, not..."

"Not like the others?" Tom said, trying to provoke his father.

Stephen Hilman was too content to take the bait. "Frankly, your mother and I had given up hope of your settling down and having a family."

"I can't say I planned it exactly," Tom said.

"But I'm proud that you're sticking by her," Stephen said. "Not only is it the right thing to do, but she's a fine girl. She's smart, she's got good business experience and plenty of horse sense about money. A strong companion can make the rough spots of life much easier to bear, I know that for a fact."

"I know you do, sir," Tom said, hoping his father wouldn't lapse into something about his older brother's death.

"Your mother thinks Ann's wonderful, you know."

"So I gathered at dinner tonight."

"Does she really like to sail?" his father asked. "I mean, is she helpful on board or just a pretty passenger?"

"Ann's as good a crew as I could ask for," Tom said, maneuvering his father toward the dock. "I think she could handle *Last Chance* by herself if she had to. She loves the open seas."

"Is this thing big enough for a family?"

"I guess so," Tom said, not wanting to sound too eager. "I'll have to make some changes here and there, but assuming the baby isn't a sickly sort, we'll start back sailing as soon as we can."

"You're not doing any sailing now?"

"Ann's had morning sickness. She's not interested in sailing till that passes."

Stephen turned toward Tom. "I want to do something grand for you two, Tom. I want to buy you a new boat if you'll let me."

"Dad, that's a wonderful offer, but a new boat is expensive," Tom said.

"I figure it would cost as much as a house," Stephen said.

"A very nice house, sir," Tom said.

"If that would be fitting for Ann, I want to do it," Stephen said. "You've worked hard, and you've done quite well. I'd say you deserve it."

"I don't know about that."

"No, Tom, you do," Stephen said. "I regret we haven't been closer all these years. Let me at least try to mend those fences."

"I don't know what to say."

"Don't say anything, son. And not a word to Ann," Stephen added. "It could be a surprise for her, couldn't it?"

"Easily."

6

Flashing neon lights bathed the area in a bizarre glow as Tom pulled his Jaguar up to the valet parking sign at the Gulf Goddess Casino. He looked about in a proprietary way, handing the attendant, a casually dressed, eager young man, a couple of bucks as he turned over the keys.

"Thank you, Mr. Hilman. Good to see you this evening."

"Nice to be here."

On the adjacent piece of property, banks of ballpark lights flooded another construction site, allowing for round-the-clock shifts. The Goddess had been built on much the same schedule. Hilman Air had the heating, ventilation, and air-conditioning subcontract on both. Since the legalization of dockside gaming in the state, gambling had become big business. Investors were paying premium prices to build, equip, and staff casinos as fast as possible. Dockside had been intended to confine gambling to the sides of "navigable" waters—the banks of the Mississippi River and the ninety miles of Gulf Coast. But with the popularity and financial success of the first casinos, everyone was trying to define a stream or pond near them as navigable, hoping to get in on the action while it was hot.

Building contractors and subcontractors were making out like bandits. Huge boats—actually enormous barges hinged together, allegedly able to float—were going up everywhere. They offered not only gambling but restaurants, entertainment, and child-care facilities, so parents wouldn't have any impediment. Most owners were doing quite well, and the state was raking in unexpected tax revenues.

But there were also losers. And with time, there would be more and more of them. Besides the 97 percent of the people who never won, and the children who oftentimes went without the bare essentials while their parents fed dollars into slot machines, the tawdriness that came with gambling was closing in on the permanent residents of the Coast—both the people and the wildlife.

For centuries, the Mississippi Gulf Coast had survived one storm or invasion after another, bowing, bending, and sometimes breaking under the force of the winds and the whims of the new arrivals. Yet ancient live oaks still spread their boughs over gracious lawns and avenues, a testament to the Coast's ultimate staying power. This latest onslaught might prove no different—but the outlook was bleak.

Gamblers filled up hotels to the exclusion of tourists and visitors, spending little time anywhere except the casinos, deeply cutting into the tourist trade of local businesses. Restaurants on shore were barely hanging on, and sales in specialty shops were dwindling. Unless a business supplied the casinos in some way, it was bound to suffer. What little the "Redneck Riviera" had to offer was in danger.

Tom stepped past a busload of senior citizens, all dressed in comfortable shoes and golf clothes, and entered the lobby, nodding to the imposing but fashionably dressed security guard. "Mr. Schaeffer's expecting me for dinner, I believe."

"Good evening, Mr. Hilman," the guard said. "He's upstairs. You're to go right up." He nodded to a uniformed man who beckoned Tom toward the elevator where he signaled the third floor with a key. As the doors were closing, a noisy foursome of drunken cowboys stepped in, punching two for the restaurant. By the time they fell out, one floor above, the elevator stank of cigarettes and booze.

Cleve Schaeffer was waiting in the low-lit, elegant foyer of the third floor, a well-tailored, expensive but not-too-flashy sport coat and slacks disguised his portly frame. He'd been manager of a casino in Las Vegas, and having done well there, had been promoted to open and run the Goddess. Much preferring the Gulf Coast to the desert, he planned to keep his tables full and profitable, guaranteeing his remaining.

The Goddess was the first casino that Schaeffer had "built," having been present from the start of construction. It was also Hilman Air's first casino, and Tom had been the project manager, taking great pains to make certain the job was done right. During construction and the endless change orders, Tom and Cleve had become very good friends.

"Ahhh, Tom, so glad you could join me."

"My pleasure entirely," Tom said. "I've been on the boat for more than a week, and I'm ready for finer food, prepared by someone other than myself."

Cleve swept him into his corner office, closing the double doors behind him. Long windows filled two walls, the twinkle of lights on the dark Gulf waters barely perceptible. A handsome table for two had been set in front of the windows.

"I see business is booming," Tom said, settling into a comfortable armchair to enjoy the view.

"At least so far, but competition's coming up fast. You know that better than anyone. Hilman Air signs are plastered all up and down the Coast at every other construction site."

"We just won the bid on another job and we're working overtime next door. Things look good, but no one knows how long it will last."

"Glad to hear someone's happy," Cleve said. "It's good news for you but not for me. A drink?"

"Bourbon would be nice. Just rocks."

Tom took a sizeable package of cocaine out of his inside coat pocket and handed it to Cleve in exchange for his glass.

"Thanks very much." Cleve walked to a bookshelf behind his desk and moved several books, revealing a wall safe. Over his shoulder as he dialed the combination, he asked, "Shall I call for dinner?"

"Let's finish this drink first," Tom said. "When I sail, I don't eat much. Dinner will be a treat."

"If you don't mind my asking," Cleve said, "why do you mess with narcotics?"

Cleve's nosiness annoyed Tom. "If I remember correctly, you were the one who first offered me a line or two of coke, not the other way around," Tom said.

Cleve started to protest but Tom went on, a little angrier. "I appreciate your willingness to convert my excess cash to checks, but if you don't want anymore of my private stash, you don't need to do me that favor and I won't keep you supplied."

"No, no, you misunderstand. I'm not critical just curious."

"I don't mess with narcotics except to have plenty for personal use. My cash flow has nothing to do with cocaine, if that's what you're wondering." Tom stood up. "I figured you didn't want to know where the cash comes from."

"You're absolutely right.

Tom walked close to the windows, past the glare. Running lights on three power boats appeared to the right and passed slowly, close to the Goddess. In the distance, what looked like a sailboat rocked in the water.

Cleve joined him, trying to smooth things over with Tom. "Ready for the big day?"

"What big day?"

"Your wedding, of course," Cleve said. "By the way, Georgina and I are looking forward to coming."

"Great," Tom replied, distinctly disinterested. "Ann's handling it all."

"Do I detect last minute jitters?"

"If Ann hadn't gotten pregnant, this wouldn't be happening," Tom said bluntly, turning back to the Gulf.

The silence was long and awkward, but Cleve didn't dare chance trying to clear the air.

"What are the odds that Florida or Alabama will pass casino gambling?" Tom finally asked.

"I was talking to Las Vegas about that this afternoon," Cleve replied, relieved. "With luck, Disney will keep it out of Florida. We don't know about Alabama yet."

■ ■ ■ ■

"Repeat after me...." the Episcopal priest said to Tom.

Tom nodded solemnly, looking down at his and Ann's hands and only glancing up at Ann occasionally as he said his vows. Laura, Ann's matron of honor stood at Ann's left, watching him, perplexed but not surprised. Alex Markham, his best man, stood beside him, arrogant as ever, refusing to look Laura's way.

Ann searched Tom's face for a glimmer of warmth but found instead something resigned and businesslike, vaguely reminiscent of negotiations at a construction project settlement conference. She had staked all her hopes on the fact that Tom hadn't walked out. Considering the trail of women he'd left behind him over the years, this seemed to confirm some feeling for her. But that was small comfort now as she faced a man who wouldn't even look her in the eye when he said his marriage vows.

The priest turned to Ann, "And do you take this man to be your lawfully wedded husband?"

Ann's voice trembled, but she pulled herself together to repeat quietly, but firmly. "In the name of God, I, Ann, take you, Tom, to be my husband; to have and to hold, from this day forward, for better, for worse, for richer, for poorer, in sickness and in health, to love and to cherish," and bucking up for the final bit, "till death do us part."

"I now pronounce you husband and wife," said the priest. "Those whom God has joined together, let no man put asunder."

They exchanged only a perfunctory kiss, before Tom turned toward the hundred or so well-dressed guests gathered on the shady lawn to witness the event. A fifty-two foot sailboat, its name hidden by a sail draped over the stern, was tied up at the dock, with a gaily colored "JUST MARRIED" sign, written and decorated in a childish scrawl, hanging from the boom. The *Last Chance* drifted at anchor in the cove.

Champagne corks popped, and the chamber music trio immediately began playing Handel's "Water Music" as people moved about, relieved to be unchained from the awkward event. Half of them headed toward the couple, the other half toward a table overflowing with tempting southern delicacies. Servants in black-and-white uniforms circulated with trays of filled champagne glasses. Tom took both his glass and Ann's and after a quick toast to her, handed one to Alex and clicked glasses with him.

In the doorway of the bathroom off the master bedroom, Laura looked on, not knowing what to do or say. Music and gay conversations from the reception continued unabated but Ann, overcome with morning sickness and nervousness, was vomiting.

"How long does the doctor think the nausea will last?" Laura asked. "I was over it by this stage, I think."

"I don't know, but I can't keep anything down," Ann said. "If it doesn't stop soon, I'll have to take something. This baby isn't getting much in the way of vitamins and minerals, that's for sure."

"It'll stop...one day soon," Laura said.

Ann looked out the window at the children playing. "All this throwing up is probably the curse of old equipment. Tom's truly pissed that I'm too sick to sail away in the new boat that Daddy gave him. He..."

Fairly certain the wave of nausea had passed, she began reapplying her makeup. "Tom wanted it to be his grand exit, the bastard." Ann's voice trembled as it had during the ceremony, and her eyes began to tear up again.

"What's wrong, Ann?" Laura asked. "This isn't like you. I thought you were about to break down out there."

"Marrying Tom is the biggest mistake of my life, I just know it. Did you hear how he said his vows? Did you see it? He wouldn't even look at me when he said 'to love and to cherish.' He's not marrying me out of love. This is strictly business. I almost backed out right there in the middle of the ceremony but another wave of nausea came over me and I lost my courage. I'm too damned scared to go it alone."

"Maybe you're overreacting. Not every man handles the prospect of a child in his life very well."

"He doesn't give two twits about this baby—or me. He did it for Daddy and Mummy, and it paid off right away. Do you see that boat? Probably cost a quarter of a million."

Laura was awestruck. Knowing little about sailing or sailboats, it had never occurred to her that the boat had cost so much. "Maybe it'll be all right. You'll be a single mother while he sails around the world."

"Or a divorced one with a huge settlement, by God," Ann said with renewed determination.

Laura tried to calm her. "You won't be alone. You'll have the baby, and you'll always have us. When do you get the amnio results?"

"Any day now, I hope."

"Are you going to find out the sex?"

"Nope," Ann said, smiling for the first time, her deep-blue eyes regaining some of their sparkle. "This may be the last surprise in my life. Just so it's healthy."

Laura looked around the Hilman's opulent summer cottage. "At least you'll never have to worry about money."

"No, money won't be a problem, that's for sure." She put the finishing touches on her lips, smoothed her hand over her stomach, looking sideways in the mirror.

Laura rubbed her shoulders. "We'd better get back. Chin up, vomit down, stomach in."

Ann nodded and took her arm.

Laura and Ann strolled out, arm in arm. As the guests flocked toward Ann, Laura watched her friend's smile brighten, ever the easygoing pleaser in the crowd.

Ann would give it her best—Laura was certain of that. But she doubted Ann's best would be sufficient.

Laura slipped away to look for Semmes. She found him in the middle of all the children, playing something akin to touch football. With a soft neon orange football tucked under his arm, he was running from one side of the lawn to the other, weaving in and out of a wild band of little boys. The girls, ignoring their party dresses and patent leather shoes, were chasing him, too. When he made a touchdown, he held the ball high, doing a dance to the delight of everyone.

Laura filled a plate with hors d'oeuvres and surveyed the crowd for someone she knew. Most of the guests were friends of Tom's parents—including Vic Regis who, though he'd known Tom since high school, was now closer to Stephen Hilman, a major contributor to Carver's campaigns. Many of Tom's old crowd—half of them friends from high school—had come. With the passing years and the changes in personalities and tastes, the social circle had become more and more diverse. An event like this was a rare opportunity to bring the motley crew together.

Vic caught her eye and signaled, using her appearance as an excuse to escape Stephen Hilman and several friends who had him besieged. No doubt they were lobbying him about an issue that was still alive in the waning days of the legislative session. Laura polished off another mushroom stuffed with crab, and watched Alex working the crowd with his flashy smile.

"I can't act that enthusiastic all day long," Laura said when Vic appeared at her side.

"It'll come with time," Vic said. "Practice makes perfect."

"Actually, that kinda worries me. I might turn out like Alex."

Semmes formed his toddling defensive line. He was about to snap the ball to Will when a dog ran through the game and grabbed the ball.

Football disintegrated into chase. He left the children and ambled over, panting. "Man, I'm out of shape. I need to work out more often."

Vic crunched the ice from his club soda. "Come work out at the gym in the morning—run, lift weights, whatever. Get there at 6:30 and you can be dressed and at the office by 7:45."

Will and two little girls ran right through them, everyone lifting their plates to avoid a collision. Laura caught him by his collar and whispered in his ear before he pulled away in hot pursuit.

"He's a great little kid," said Vic wistfully. For all his power and persuasiveness, Vic was terminally shy around women and claimed he never had time for anything other than work. Laura and Semmes had set him up with dates on countless occasions. The evenings seemed to go well, but Vic never followed up on his own. "How old is he now?"

"Six," Laura said, watching her son race across the lawn.

"I want to put a brick on his head to stop him growing up so fast," Semmes said.

"His birthday was last weekend," Laura added. "Remember?"

Vic looked at her confused.

"You didn't make it to the cookout because the Senate was debating some bill. Does that ring any bells?"

"Oh, yes," Vic said, knocking his fist against his forehead. "I'm so sorry I couldn't come. Forgive me, I must sound like a complete idiot."

"No," Semmes said, "just overworked. I'm surprised to see you here today."

"Stephen was insistent. Wanted Carver here but he's in Washington. I'd actually sent my regrets, but it turned out that I needed to make one final plea to one of the Coast reps. That's where I'm headed after I leave here."

A photographer with two cameras around his neck walked up. "Commissioner, could you come for a photo with your Ole Miss class?"

Laura nodded to the young man. "Of course, I'd be delighted."

Semmes looked at Vic, feigning hurt feelings. "If I'm not mistaken, we were both in that class, too, weren't we?"

"Oh...you can come, too," the photographer said, embarrassed.

"Why, thank you so much," Semmes said, ever the ignored courtier.

The photographer quickly replied, "I didn't mean it that way. What

I..."

Vic and Semmes smiled. "We're just teasing," Semmes said. "I love being the appendage of the most powerful woman in the state."

The group of nearly twenty clowned around, driving the photographer to distraction. Alex put his fingers V-shaped behind Tom's head, one woman pulled up her dress to display her knees, while Laura stood at attention, saluting, and Semmes toasted the groom with champagne. Vic, congenitally unable to joke—verbally or physically—stood self-consciously at the edge, hands deep in his pants' pockets. Ann watched from the side, laughing.

Laura called to her. "Come on Ann, get in the picture."

"I wasn't in your class," Ann said.

Laura stepped forward, steering Ann in. "You were dying to be—we had more fun."

Tom, now relaxed from all the champagne, took Ann's hand and added, "Vic can get Governor Carver to make it official. Politicians have to be good for something."

The photographer took as many pictures as he could before the group broke up. Alex made a beeline for Vic, nodding to Semmes and Laura as he approached. Vic stiffened as Alex stepped up, his hand out.

"Vic, how's it going?" Alex said.

"Good, Alex," Vic answered. "The session's almost over—more wins than losses."

"Can I help with the crime bill?" Alex asked. "It's a great bill, by the way."

"Laura did all the rewriting once it was in Committee," Vic said, enjoying the sight of Alex's smile disintegrating. "Unfortunately, I don't think we're going to get much out of them this year. But there's always that big push at the end to lay the ground work for the next effort. If you could throw your weight in, we'd appreciate it."

Alex bowed his head deferentially to Laura and, with ice in his voice, muttered, "Let me know if I can help in any way."

"Consider yourself asked," said Laura, barely able to form a smile.

The guests assembled on the dock around the new boat, a Cheoy Lee. Ann's estimate had been a little low. All the optional equipment and appointments brought the final ticket to just more than three hundred thousand dollars. With great flourish and pomp, Stephen uncovered the name, *Next to Last Chance,* as the chamber trio improvised a string fanfare and everyone applauded.

Tom held out a hand for Ann, but she hesitated. "Don't worry—we're only going to go a few feet," Tom said. "Feel free to throw up over the side or in the head. It's an unbelievably nice head, even for a boat."

Taking his hand, Ann stepped aboard in a shower of rice and birdseed from the children. Alex untied the lines, and Tom cranked the quiet engine. As they waved to the guests, the photographer dashed madly about to get pictures. Laura put one arm around Semmes' waist and leaned close as she waved to Ann.

"Better gather up Will," Semmes said, giving her a soft kiss on the forehead. "It's getting late and we've got a long drive ahead. Tomorrow's a school day."

▪▪▪▪

A beautiful starry night spread before them as Semmes drove north, the sunroof open, holding Laura's hand and talking quietly. A Louis Armstrong tape added to the serenity. Will was sleeping soundly in the backseat, exhausted from his efforts to tackle as many little girls as possible. He'd grown so much in the last few months that, stretched out, his feet nearly touched the driver's side door. He was going to be tall, like his dad.

The two-lane road was busy with cars, half of them headed south to casinos. Laura wondered why they hadn't seen a single patrol car, and since Semmes had refused to install patrol radios in his Acura, she couldn't listen to the chatter over the air.

Suddenly, a beat-up Toyota pickup truck, moving toward them several car lengths ahead, wandered into Semmes' path and kept on coming. Semmes swerved as far to the side as possible, but the driver hit Semmes' door with full force and sent the car spinning, its horn blaring. When they finally came to an abrupt stop, Semmes was slumped to the side of the wheel, his side of the car crushed toward him, the windows smashed. The horn cut off, leaving an eerie silence. Then more glass fell and shattered.

Unhurt except for scratches, Laura screamed when she looked at Semmes' motionless body. There was no bleeding that she could see.

"Momma! Momma!" Will called out.

Laura looked back and saw Will, covered in broken glass and bleeding profusely near his feet. She opened her door, jumped out and yanked open Will's door, screaming, "Help me, please help me," to no one in particular.

The driver of the pickup, apparently uninjured, emerged from his vehicle several feet away. He was very young, maybe nineteen, shoulder-length dirty blonde hair with a wisp of a mustache, blue jeans and a T-shirt. He seemed innocent and out of it, staring, without a clue to what he'd done or what to do about it.

Motorists blocked by the accident leaped out of their cars and ran to Laura, paying little attention to the pickup driver. Someone called an ambulance on a cell phone. Laura quickly but gently got Will out of the car, yanking off her jacket to absorb the blood.

A man approached Laura. "Lady, I saw everything. Entirely that pickup's fault. Here's my card."

Laura didn't even look up. "My God, not now," she snapped. The man looked vaguely annoyed and stuffed his card back in his pocket as a woman motorist, an older, kindly looking motherly type, appeared and crouched down to help with Will.

"Wait and tell the police," the woman said directly. "I just called them. Help us, for Christ's sake." The woman looked up at a teenager who had appeared by her side. "Get me the towels from our trunk. Fast as you can."

Looking straight at Will, and smiling as best she could, Laura said quietly, "Will, stay right here with this nice lady. I have to check on Daddy."

Will nodded obediently. Laura and the woman didn't need to exchange a word before Laura flew back to the door, pushing a man aside who was peering in at Semmes but doing nothing. Getting in, Laura felt for Semmes' pulse and found it, faint as it was. His side of the car was so crushed that she couldn't move him. Laura sat on the edge of the seat, rocking slightly, holding Semmes' right hand in both of hers, terrified. The man with the card had started tugging on Semmes' door with no success.

"Oh, God, Semmes. Hold on, Semmes, please." she begged.

Nervously, Laura jumped out of the car and raced around to Semmes' door, pushing the man away and tugging at the crumpled metal herself. It didn't move. She got back in the car, taking Semmes' hand again.

After what seemed like an eternity, police and State Patrol cars began arriving, blue lights flashing. A local officer stopped the traffic completely since impatient drivers were already trying to move through the wreckage. He directed the ambulances in by radio.

The trooper began working to free Semmes. The red lights of a fire truck appeared out of nowhere and three firemen leaped out and assisted the trooper. By the time the ambulance arrived, the door was open, falling off its hinges.

The medics quickly moved Semmes to the ambulance, hollering questions about his medical history at Laura as they worked. Then they departed, sirens wailing, leaving her with Will. A fireman helped bandage Will's leg while they waited for the second ambulance. When it came, Will was lifted onto a stretcher and the ambulance sped away with both Will and Laura. The trooper retrieved Laura's purse from her car, dropped in the witness' card, loaded the pickup driver into his patrol car, and followed.

The emergency room of the county hospital had been quiet all night. When they got word that two ambulances were on the way with serious injuries, the lone doctor on duty phoned one of his partners and nurses hurried in to prepare.

Semmes was rushed to a bay not far from the operating room and an endotracheal breathing tube was immediately inserted, along with an IV in his left arm forcing fluids into him, while another IV was pumping in blood. Semmes seemed to be responding, but was having tremendous trouble breathing.

Will was placed in a bay across the room and pronounced not in danger. Laura held his hand, talking in a soothing voice, trying not to show her fear about Semmes. Will was very frightened but being very brave. Hearing a new set of muffled voices and commands from Semmes' bay, she told Will, "I'll be right back, Sweetheart. I've got to see how Daddy is. This nice nurse will take good care of you while I'm gone."

Will nodded silently as Laura kissed him, then disappeared through the curtain. She pushed her way in among the doctors and nurses. Semmes was motionless, and when she reached for his hand, the doctor next to her quickly took her by the shoulders and directed her out beyond the curtains.

"Mrs. Owen, we're getting your husband ready for surgery. The surgeon's already on his way."

"What's wrong?"

"Most likely his liver and spleen have been badly damaged. We can't be certain until we get in there. A nurse will keep you informed." He turned and hurried back.

Laura stared at the flowing white curtains, listening to the activity when all at once the alarms went off. Semmes' electrocardiogram had gone flat. The bells were cut off and everyone seemed to be talking at once.

"I need an amp of epinephrine," demanded the doctor.

"Still got a flat line," a nurse said.

"Give him another amp of epinephrine," the doctor said again.

"He's responding," said the nurse.

"We'll do CPR," ordered the doctor.

"Everybody off."

There was the unmistakable *thunk* that she'd heard on countless TV doctor shows when they tried to revive a patient's heart. The doctors and nurses worked hard, the tension broken only by the words "everybody off" just before they used the defibrillator again and again.

Laura moved from her post only once to check on Will. No longer in acute pain, he was intrigued by everything that was happening to him, smiling at her as he was wheeled down to the x-ray room.

After nearly half an hour, the doctor appeared at Laura's side.

"I'm sorry, Mrs. Owen," the man said. "He didn't have a chance. We tried everything we could."

Shock pulsed through Laura. She was unable to respond with anything but a lost, pained expression. Forgetting about the doctor entirely, she stared forlornly ahead, too scared to think about what lay beyond the curtain and that moment.

Still looking at the curtain, she murmured, "I know you did," and slipped through. Tears streamed down her face as she stared at Semmes's lifeless body. Motioning to be alone, the nurses and doctors left. She drew close to Semmes, cradling his face gently in her hands, looking closely to memorize every line, every curve of his features. Putting her head down, she pounded the side of the bed in grief, sobbing.

Laura walked slowly toward the front desk, wiping tears away. When she saw the trooper standing near the pickup driver, she lost every bit of self-control and leapt at the driver, screaming, "You killed my husband, you little bastard. You killed him."

The trooper intervened immediately and a nurse took Laura by the shoulders. "Commissioner, he's high as a kite on some kind of drugs. They're waiting to do a blood test in a minute."

Laura took a good look at the young man for the first time. "You're just a kid aren't you? You don't even know what you've done."

He looked back, blankly.

"Where'd you get the drugs?" Laura said. "Who gave you that crap?"

The trooper moved the driver away as the nurse steered Laura toward Will's bay, her eyes never leaving the young man as long as he was in sight. She forced away her grief, but when she pulled back the curtain and saw her son, who looked so much like Semmes, the resemblance brought new tears to her eyes.

"Is Daddy dead?" Will asked, his lip quivering with every word.

Laura somehow held back the sobs that were about to erupt within her but as she told him, tears quietly streamed down both their faces. They hugged each other, holding on tighter than ever before.

■ ■ ■ ■

Mourners packed St. Andrew's Cathedral until it was standing room only. Friends came from everywhere, family, the Governor and Mrs. Carver, Vic Regis, a small complement of troopers led by Blake and Robert. Semmes had been loved by all, and the outpouring was a testament to the goodness of his life. Semmes' partner, and his brother and his sister spoke, each telling humorous tales from his life, leaving everyone with happy and memorable stories. Laura was thankful she'd heard them all the night before when everyone had gathered at the house, because she didn't think she would have been able to maintain any composure otherwise.

But grief is the other side of love, and moments later, her game face dissolved in the midst of the priest's eulogy when he read not from a gospel but from *Romeo and Juliet.*

And when he shall die,
Take him and cut him out in little stars
And he will make the face of heaven so fine
That all the world will be in love with night
And pay no worship to the garish sun.

The tender words, the vision, was too much for her. Everyone heard her futile attempts to stifle her anguish. Blake and Robert both winced. By now, they knew her well enough to understand how devastating Semmes' death was to her.

The priest struggled on, now hurrying. Even in his Lord's economy where nothing was ever lost, it was impossible for the priest to make sense of Semmes' death. He finished with words for Laura, Will, and Semmes' family.

"I ask all of you not to forget Semmes' family in their saddest time. Semmes already rests in peace. Help each of them find theirs."

The pallbearers stepped forward and lifted the wooden casket as the organist played lighter music. As everyone stood up, Charlotte Hemeter hugged her daughter, giving Laura a moment to regain her composure before she faced the crowd. Laura wasn't certain she could hold back her tears but as she stepped out of her pew, she saw the agony on her mother-in-law's face—the agony of a mother losing a child—and her own grief seemed to diminish. Mr. Owen put his arm around her, and in his strong but sad embrace, she found solace. She turned back to Will.

Laura helped him hobble down the aisle on his tiny crutches with her mother on the other side of her. Semmes' parents, sister, and brother were right behind her, followed by her own two brothers and their families. In the portico, with State Patrol honor guards at each side, Will looked solemnly on, starting to wave and then holding his hand back, as the casket was lifted into the hearse.

Laura watched the procession blankly, her heart breaking.

The one man who had never failed her, never held her back and always pointed her ahead, her own fountain of hope and laughter and strength was gone.

She looked at the tears streaming down Will's face and leaned over to give him a hug. A moment later, Laura could feel the gentle touch of her own mother's hand. She turned to see the familiar sweet smile and burst into tears again. She buried her face in her mother's shoulder and wept.

"A day never goes by that I don't miss your father," Charlotte said. "But you'll have to be strong for Will."

"I know," Laura sobbed, "I just don't know how."

"You've always found a way to get through, no matter what was facing you. I've never known you to give up."

Laura turned back to her son, trying to look brave. They slowly struggled down the stairs to a limousine, solicitous funeral directors in their gray suits waiting beside it.

7

After endless meetings with lawyers, accountants, and Semmes' partner, going back to work was a welcome relief. Everyone at headquarters was quietly attentive, scared of saying the wrong thing but eager to help. The mail and message lists were piled high on her desk and as she closed the door to the huge room, she felt both comfortable in its sameness and sad in the emptiness. Tuning in the second movement of Dvorak's "New World Symphony" on her stereo receiver, she flipped through the correspondence and call lists. She was looking for items that were substantive not consoling, desperate to concentrate on something other than Semmes.

The first call came from some minion at Finance and Administration who needed background numbers for the proposed pay raise. It made her feel a little better, as though she was starting to swim toward the distant shore of a lake. The rhythm—stroke, stroke, breathe—would get her to the other side, get her through it. And she had no other choice.

After an hour or so of perfunctory tasks, she went to find Blake Coleman. The door to the Chief of Patrol's office, at the opposite end of the hall, was ajar. Laura knocked as she peeked in and, seeing Blake with Robert Stone, didn't wait for a reply and entered. Blake's feet were up on his credenza and Robert was sprawled on the couch, but they straightened up when they saw her.

"Don't get uncomfortable on my account," she said.

Laura picked up an autographed Casey Stengel baseball from Blake's desk as she sat down. "You like the Mets?" Laura asked suddenly realizing that she really didn't know much about either Blake or Robert except what was in the department personnel files or displayed on the walls of their offices, the latter a truly limited source. Blake's office was filled with the best of his collection of police memorabilia—plaques, certificates, diplomas, photographs. But there was only one family photograph of him with Sally and their two sons, and that picture was already seven years old. Both boys were long gone from home—one at college and the other working. Robert hadn't taken the time to put anything up at all, save a photo of Rachel and their dog.

Blake nodded. "Their farm team used to be here. But I've only seen 'em twice. I was in New York in '64 and had some spare time. Sat through the entire doubleheader with the Giants—twenty-three innings in the second game. Been a fan of theirs ever since."

"Orioles for me," Laura said. "Went to Baltimore every chance I could when I worked in Washington."

"Been to Camden Yards yet?" Blake asked.

"Nope, but I've heard it's great," Laura answered. "I just can't imagine any place being better than the old Memorial Stadium."

Robert tipped his Saints' cap. "Spare me from baseball trivia." He looked at Laura and spoke with true empathy in his voice. "We're all very sorry."

Troopers worked so many wrecks and saw so many mangled and dead bodies that people thought they were completely insensitive to death. But when it struck one of their own, they summoned feelings normally locked away.

"Thank you," was all Laura could muster.

"You shouldn't have come back so soon," Robert added.

"And you needn't have worried about the Patrol," Blake added. "It's run itself for years."

Laura smiled for the first time. "That's exactly why I came back."

At her retort, Blake smiled, too. "You'll ask if you need anything, won't you?"

"Of course I will. I'm not shy about that sort of thing. But working seems to help. It keeps my mind occupied."

An awkward silence fell among them as Laura gazed out at the traffic zooming past on the interstate. "You know, I never thought twice about leaving everything up to you two," she said, looking at Blake then Robert.

"'Preciate the confidence," Blake said.

"But I can't decide whether you both are terrific con artists, anticipating every move I make, or whether we just work well together."

"We work well together," Robert said quietly.

"Hope that's it," Laura said.

"I assure you it is. Most commissioners don't bother to learn as much as you have. They rarely get so involved," Blake said.

Laura smiled, then her look sharpened. "That kid, the pickup driver, was on something," she said.

"Crack cocaine," Robert responded. "I've found out since then that he was a small-time dealer selling a few ounces here and there, but mostly he was using it himself. His daddy is a lawyer, and they got the charge knocked down from possession with intent, to possession. He's still facing vehicular manslaughter."

"I want to know where he got it."

"We're working on it," Blake said.

"And then I want to know who supplied the dealer who sold it to him. And who was his supplier—as far up as you can go. All the way to Colombia would be nice."

Blake looked puzzled. "Commissioner, you practiced criminal law, you know we won't be able to make any charges stick even if we do find out who's in the chain."

"I know that. But I also know that there'll be a next time for each of them." Laura looked from Blake to Robert. "And you'll be waiting for that next time, won't you?"

Practically in unison, they answered, "Yes, ma'am."

Laura smiled faintly as she got up to leave. Both Blake and Robert had to squelch the urge to jump up.

"Thanks for all you did while I was out," Laura said.

Blake and Robert both nodded silently, not speaking until she was out of earshot.

"You think she'll make it?" Blake asked.

"Lookin' pretty shaky, but she's tough," Robert assured him.

Based on what he'd learned and observed since January, Blake doubted she'd quit, but he couldn't help but worry. His appointment was tied to Laura's, and if she left, he might not survive. With all the monthly bills and Sally's mother to worry about, he couldn't afford a pay cut.

"I've got more riding on her success than anyone except the

Governor," Blake said, acutely aware of his vulnerability. He'd been busily making his mark as chief from the first day, and plenty of the disgruntled troopers were gunning for him. Although everything he'd done could be laid off as following Laura's orders, he'd participated in every decision, and he'd never be able to swallow his own words even if given the opportunity. "She's gotta make it."

"You're not alone," Robert said. "They might not be able to fire me, but think how pitiful my life would be if someone like Bill Kenner got to be chief. My ass would be grass. I might just as well go to the house if that happened."

"You gotta nice house to go to—and someone else's paycheck. For me, this bit of sugar can't turn to shit—not if I can help it. Some of the guys may not know it yet, but this is the best thing we've had going for us in a long time."

■ ■ ■ ■

Within a couple of weeks, Laura was back in the swing, and the more disturbing matters that Blake had ordered the staff to postpone had begun making their way onto her schedule.

Waiting outside her door when she'd arrived that morning, was a terrified young trooper assigned to the driver's license bureau, escorted by the captain of his district who'd filed charges against him. The trooper's bank deposits hadn't tallied with the license receipts. All the money was getting to the bank, but as much as two weeks late. Internal Affairs concluded the trooper had been borrowing to pay bills, and the spot audits Laura had instituted had caught him.

Much as she wanted to give him a second chance, she decided not to, and by the end of the meeting, the trooper had waived his disciplinary interview and resigned. Laura promised to talk to the prosecutor on his behalf. She was greatly relieved when they finally left her office.

She'd hardly closed the door when her secretary, Deborah, called on the intercom. "Your mother's on line one, Commissioner, and the Chief and Colonel Stone are waiting."

"Tell them I won't be but a minute," Laura said, punching down the other button. "Hi, Mom. Where are you?"

"Still in Sea Island. I'm staying over a couple more nights to get in a few more rounds of golf. So I won't be coming in tonight."

"Could you change your plane tickets?"

"It cost me extra, but it's too beautiful to leave. How are you and Will doing?"

"Fine. It's good to get back to the office."

"Do you want me to stay with you a few days when I get back?"

"That's always nice, but we're doing okay. Really."

"Then I'll see you Friday. Same plane."

"Okay. We'll be there."

"Give my little man a kiss."

"I will."

"Chin up, dear," her mother said. "I love you."

"It's up. Love you, too, Mom."

Robert knocked on her door and stuck his head in. "Ready?"

"As ready as I'll ever be," Laura said, stashing some papers in her satchel. "Sorry for the delay, but my mother was checking in between the front and back nine."

"Mothers can't be kept on hold," Robert said with a smile. "Blake's waiting downstairs with the car."

A huge Department of Justice seal nearly covered one wall of the United States Attorney's conference room. Alex Markham held forth from the head of the table, standing next to an easel holding an enormous plastic-coated map displaying the countries surrounding the Gulf of Mexico. Several areas in Central and South America had been circled, and arrows from each were pointing to southern Mississippi.

Seated in sinfully comfortable chairs for a government office were the members of Alex's drug task force—Hal Easterbrook, FBI; Logan Cummins, DEA; Ted Campbell, U.S. Customs Service; plus Robert, Blake, and, unexpectedly, Laura, whom Alex had been perturbed to see.

"The last three major air loads intercepted, were headed for Mississippi and Alabama," Alex said.

"Excuse me, Alex," Laura interrupted, "but if so much dope is coming in by plane, why haven't we been intercepting couriers on the ground?"

Annoyed by the interruption, Alex replied gruffly, "That's now your bailiwick. And you'll find out that it takes incredible manpower and training to be effective. But we welcome your assistance." Returning to his easel, he pointed to a new location.

Laura piped up again, "We can start tomorrow."

Alex looked at Laura as if she were some petty annoyance. "Say what?"

"Twenty men just got back from a smuggling apprehension training program with the Louisiana State Police," Laura said. "We've got a team of two in each district and two trainers at the academy who start next week on another group."

Everyone at the table was dumbfounded, including Logan who hadn't heard a word about it from Blake, Robert, or the ever-rumbling law enforcement grapevine. Logan, if not Alex, was genuinely pleased.

"Commissioner, thank you for your interest," Logan said. "I'd heard you were planning to pursue smugglers, but I didn't know you were willing to commit resources so fast. It's a breath of fresh air. DEA has never been able to count on help from the Patrol be..."

Alex cut off Logan's effusion. "I'd want to coordinate this so that we're prepared to assist. We don't want your people stumbling into undercover operations."

"Why don't you tell me where you're going to be, and we'll avoid you," Laura countered.

Shifting his weight and putting his pointer down on the table with a small slap, Alex addressed Blake and Robert, his voice very firm. "You work up a list of dates and places, and we'll clear them."

Laura jumped back in. "Maybe you don't get my drift, Alex. We'll be working drugs every day, in every district. We've got four-hundred and ninety-two pairs of eyes and ears in the Patrol, and I plan to find out what they can see and hear. If you've got a deal going down, find Blake or Robert."

Logan smiled, enjoying the way Alex squirmed. Too many times, Alex had taken all the credit for someone else's hard work. It was an interesting change to watching him fight for center stage.

"Don't you think you need a little more background in these operations before you dive in?" snapped Alex, trying to regain control of the meeting.

"I thought our job was to catch as many bad guys as fast as possible,"

Laura said. "Did I miss something?"

Logan and Ted nodded their heads agreeing with Laura, skillfully hiding their amusement. Hal took his cue from Alex and scowled.

The meeting broke up an hour or so later with Laura holding her ground, never agreeing to Alex's coordination of State Patrol smuggling details. She chatted with Logan and Ted, and then followed Blake and Robert out past the wall of photographs of current state, local, and federal officials—strategically positioned should any of them visit. Alex caught up with Laura to talk privately.

"Is this a crusade to avenge Semmes' death because a doper killed him?" Alex said.

Laura's eyes flashed. "So what if it is?"

"I don't want you going off half-cocked," Alex said. "We've been building up our cases for some time now. You could ruin all my work."

"What do you mean 'my' work?" Laura said. "You prosecute. You don't investigate. In fact, you don't get involved at all until cases are made, then you 'adopt' the ones you like the best, reject the ones you don't, and play the high-profile stuff to the press."

Alex was too angry to reply so Laura pushed on. "This is about turf, isn't it, Alex? You've never had any competition. Scared the TV cameras might focus on someone else?"

He wheeled around and stalked off.

A Jackson General's baseball schedule was taped to the front of the sun visor for ready consultation, but the papers stuffed behind it seemed perilously close to spilling out. Blake drove back to the office, instinctively keeping track of every car behind them. The police radios squawked their usual gibberish, some of which Laura still couldn't understand. The current joke around the Patrol was that Laura—call name A-Adam—couldn't drive and talk on the radio at the same time but she had to pull off the road and stop the car before she keyed the mike.

Blake turned down the volume and looked at Laura in the rearview mirror. "Why doesn't Markham like you?"

"Never has," Laura said. "We were rivals at Ole Miss. Strike that. We were classmates, but he was too damn lazy to compete. Thought he had some birthright to what I had to earn through blood and sweat. Alex was a hot dog, big man on campus. I was Miss Studious. I guess he never expected to see me playing on his turf. He's clearly not pleased."

"Not pleased," Robert said. "Jesus, that's an understatement, wouldn't you say Blake?"

"I'd say," Blake agreed.

"He's never liked anyone else calling the shots," Laura said.

"Logan told me he's been playing it really safe ever since he lost a corruption case a couple of years back when he moved in too soon," Robert added.

"You want the real story?" Laura said.

Robert turned around, interested. "You know it?"

"Alex built up a case with the press to such a point that when he didn't get indictments, he had to either admit his own miscalculations or blame it on someone else," Laura said. "Naturally, he laid it off on some poor low-level government agent who didn't have the ability to defend himself."

"Well, today he was a control freak losing control," Robert said.

"He's bureau of standards for control freak," Laura said. "With his father being a U.S. Senator, his grandfather the senator before him, and his great-grandfather a governor, why the Markhams have run everything around here for generations." Laura looked at the row of enormous mansions on State Street, Jackson's main thoroughfare, where only a few of the grand historic homes remained, the others replaced or absorbed by the neighboring college, the hospital, or businesses.

"He was raised in one of these places," Laura said. "His mother didn't want to be a little fish in a big pond, so she never moved to Washington. She raised Alex here where she'd be hotsy-totsy. I guess he figured he was stepping right up to the governor's plate when suddenly I appeared, blocking his view of the field."

"You sure must be a mighty big threat to him, given how nervous he was today." Blake pulled into his parking space in front of headquarters. "Mind if we check into Mr. Markham a little?"

"Fine by me," she added, "but be quiet about it. Very, very quiet."

"Are we ever anything else?" Robert asked.

▪ ▪ ▪ ▪

"It'll sure be nice when you can make follow-up calls, Alex," Senator

Markham chided. "They're the most crucial part of the effort."

Senator Ford Markham and his son sat at a glass-topped wrought iron table on a wide second-floor gallery at Dinsmor. The family's huge three-story Delta plantation mansion was set well back off the road and surrounded by ancient oaks, and to the south and west, pecan groves. Ceiling fans slowly cooled the area, and the silver pitcher of iced tea on the sideboard sweated profusely. An elderly servant silently cleared the luncheon dishes from the table and refilled their glasses. The men concentrated on their papers, barely noticing and never acknowledging her presence, or even the food.

The Senator leaned back and looked out over the fields where huge machines were planting and fertilizing the cotton crop. It had been a wet spring, and the operators were pushing hard to finish as soon as possible. As the years had passed, the Senator looked forward more and more to his trips home. Unlike Washington, Dinsmor moved at his pace which, except for planting and harvesting, was becoming increasingly stately.

Ford Markham had grown up at Dinsmor, roamed every square inch of the place as a boy, ignoring the poverty of the black sharecroppers who lived on Dinsmor's outer reaches. He was confident of his station in life as the son of Horace W. Markham, Mississippi's senior U.S. Senator. Ford's mother had despised Washington, as did his own wife when he married. A lucky turn of fate for his father, who much preferred the rarefied airs of the seat of power as well as its amenities—not the least of which was the diversity, charm, and beauty of its younger women.

Trapped in a marriage of convenience, his mother had devoted her considerable energy and intelligence to raising her only child, and doing good works in the Delta. She proved to be a key political asset through her highly visible participation in civic, historic, and charitable projects, all of which served to keep her husband's name and face alive back home.

But by the time Ford was in his teens, he was spending more and more time in Washington, fascinated by his father's life. He returned home for college and law school, where he excelled. Eyes always on the prize, Ford joined an established and influential Jackson law firm, spending his weekends at Dinsmor until his father, in the midst of expounding on states' rights, the issue nearest and dearest to his heart, keeled over on the Senate chamber floor and died from a massive stroke.

Ford willingly agreed to step into his father's shoes and easily won the special election. He'd been there ever since, filling the remainder of his father's term, and several full terms of his own, living in his father's Washington town house.

"You know I'd be doing it if I weren't hamstrung by Justice's regulations, sir," Alex said.

"I know. Didn't mean to sound critical, son," Markham said.

"How much do we have so far?"

"A hundred thousand in commitments, thirty thousand in cash. But there's one guy who won't even talk about giving me a dime till you call him. By the way, thank your friend Tom Hilman for his ten thousand. Very generous indeed."

"It sure would be nice to run unopposed—the way you have," Alex said.

"'Fraid that's out of the question. Is Little Miss Trooper still dealing you fits?"

"She's covering an incredible amount of territory. Every time I look up she's been speaking to another Rotary Club somewhere, riding her high horse in the fight against drugs."

"She's a twit," the Senator said. "We can demolish her."

"Well, being a 'widow lady' has boosted her appeal."

"People don't like women neglecting their children, widow or not."

"Unfortunately, when school isn't in session, Ms. Motherhood has her son with her, sitting in the back of the room, coloring."

"Nice touch. She's still not saying what she'll do?"

Alex shook his head. "Governor Carver's the only one who says anything about the race, always pointing out that he won't be there to kick around again—the one benefit of being a lame duck."

"Carver can't afford to be a player in this race for long. He's got his own fish to fry. Life after the governor's office must be looking pretty uncertain when the party's in turmoil here and nationally. Can't count on anything," the Senator said.

"He's got to back her, don't you think?"

"If he's not touting her now, maybe not. And, if he's smart, only enough to court the women's vote."

The Senator peered over his glasses at the machinery and then smiled at Alex. "He could use my support, don't you think? Risky to pick the wrong horse, very risky."

"I couldn't agree more, sir."

"Twit or not, never underestimate the enemy, son. Never. And don't just bat them down a time or two. You have to crush them like cockroaches. Only way you can be sure they're dead."

Footsteps clicked on the upstairs hallway and the Senator motioned to the servant to step to the door and open it. State Senator Gabriel Collel from Fenwick, walked out onto the gallery, a man in his late sixties with waves of silvery gray hair and straight posture. The Markhams stood to greet him.

Gabriel Collel owned a significant amount of Delta farmland, but not a grand house like Dinsmor. His father had started out as a small farmer, squirreling away every cent he could in glass jars under the house. When the banks failed and the Depression set in, he'd bought property all over the county, letting the families stay in their houses and maintain their gardens. That land leveraged his purchase of a farm implement business and, perfectly positioned, he made an absolute killing.

Gabriel took it over from his father, buying a second dealership near the river. Incensed by the Civil Rights Movement and President Johnson's War on Poverty, Gabriel began speaking up. He ran for the State Senate, was elected with hardly any opposition, and in all his subsequent terms, never had a challenger to speak of.

"Ahhh, Gabriel. So glad you could join us," Ford Markham said. "You know Alex."

Alex extended his hand.

Collel boomed, "You're doing a fine job for us."

Alex nodded, "Thank you, sir."

"It's good to see you, Markham, ol' man," Collel continued. "You need to do more constituent work down here, play a round of golf or two." He turned to Alex, "How's your game?"

"It's suffering, sir. Don't get out enough."

"Well, make some time for that. We can have a twosome one day soon since your father's always in Washington."

"I'd like that, sir."

"Coffee, tea? Something stronger?" Senator Markham gestured toward the servant who was standing by, ready.

Collel glanced at the woman without seeing her. "Tea, for me, please."

"I think I'll have a cup of coffee," said the elder Markham.

Collel was a strong force in the Senate. He'd always sat in the back left corner at a desk by himself, so he could keep an eye on all the action. The Lieutenant Governor and the President Pro Tem looked his way before doing anything.

"I hope the word on the street is true," Collel observed, "we need you to run for governor."

"That's my intention, sir," said Alex. "But it's a long time until the election, and I need to remain United States Attorney until the last possible minute. Unfortunately, Justice regulations don't allow campaigning while in office."

Collel grunted. "The rumors emerging about Laura Owen are enough to make me switch parties."

"Don't be rash Gabriel," Senator Markham leaned back. "We've just been discussing what we can do. We need your help."

"Anything, anything." Collel raised his finger, jabbing the air toward Senator Markham. "When that little shrew was auditing state funds, she wanted me to repay travel expenses—said they weren't properly documented. I hope she rots in hell."

"Did you repay it?" Ford Markham asked.

"Hell, no, and since she left, no one's had the balls to ask for it again. The auditor developed enough sense not to push it."

"Then we've got a proposition for you," said the Senator, lowering his voice. He glanced toward the elderly servant standing at the ready near the serving buffet. "We're fine, Nettie. We'll take care of ourselves, now."

"Yes, sir, Senator," the woman said, disappearing into the hallway.

8

The Police Chief's conference had ground along since they'd reconvened after lunch. Laura was on the agenda, ahead of the business meeting, to present an overview of Public Safety operations and to remind them of what the department could do for them. Then the directors of the different divisions—State Patrol, Medical Examiner, Crime Lab, Training Academy, Federal Programs—all were scheduled to make separate presentations. "Chilly" aptly described her reception.

Not unexpected. She'd gotten used to the cold shoulder from most everyone other than the Patrol.

No point in staying to mingle. She doubted there were any allies worth cultivating. Besides, it was a good afternoon to get home early and practice a little baseball in the yard with Will.

Just as she reached the door at the back of the conference room, one of the newer police chiefs, a youngish man from a town of 10,000 with half the budget he needed, caught up with her. Laura listened to his problems and made suggestions about how the department could help and who to call on each specific issue. A couple of other men joined them, and as the group expanded, they moved out in the hall so they wouldn't disturb the business meeting.

Why hadn't they asked her questions during her remarks?

Pride, stupid macho pride. But if she could help, they might remember. Not a certainty, but maybe.

But begging people to let her help—it was pitiful.

■ ■ ■ ■

It was after four when she finally slipped away, but with the longer evenings of late spring, there was still plenty of time for baseball before the mosquitoes drove them inside. Laura would never be a substitute for Semmes—he'd known all about proper batting stances and different catching techniques. But her skills were strong enough to be helpful, throwing endless grounders, pop flies, and some decent pitches. Will would have stayed out until he was covered with insect bites, but Laura called a halt when she started dropping balls to slap at the invaders.

A perfect antidote to the afternoon.

"And then I started a train with two of my friends," Will recounted, in between bites of SpaghettiOs, "and the whole playground was following us, and I was the leader!"

"You're kidding," Laura said. "The whole playground?"

Will smiled, proudly. As Laura picked up her glass, the phone rang. She reached across the counter and hit the speakerphone button.

"Hello?"

"Bitches like you..." came the deep, gravelly voice.

Laura snatched up the handset so Will couldn't hear more.

"...should keep better track of their children."

"Who is this?" Laura insisted, her face flushed with anger.

"I like Will's red-striped shirt—makes him stand out in the crowd."

"How did you get this number?" Laura demanded.

The phone went dead. She hung up and sat back down.

"Who was it, Momma?" Will asked.

"Someone selling something," she said curtly but caught herself as she looked at Will, his normally innocent little face puzzled. "So where did this train of yours go?" she asked him, changing the subject.

"All the way to the North Pole," Will said, smiling again.

"And who did you see there?"

"Some Eskimos."

"Any polar bears?"

Will nodded. "But I was hoping to find Daddy."

Hearing "Daddy" made Laura wince, but seeing Will's carefree expression, she calmed down.

"But you won't find him," Laura said, "at least not really find him."

"I know, but I like to look," Will said.

"Why don't you tell me your favorite thing about Daddy and I'll tell you mine."

Will's eyes lit up. "He could throw footballs!"

"He could cook dinner!" Laura chimed in.

"He could talk like Mickey and Goofy!"

"He liked to go camping!"

Behind his smile, Will dissolved into tears and Laura opened her arms to him. He hopped down from his seat and crawled into her lap, his long legs nearly reaching the floor. Laura hugged him tightly.

"Let's read some more of *Martin The Warrior*, Mom," Will said, in between sobs.

"What a good idea," Laura said. "I was just wondering what those abbey dwellers were up to." She wiped her eyes on her shoulder without loosening her firm hold on Will.

How could she be everything this little boy needed?

Laura didn't think it was possible to fill Semmes' shoes all by herself, to give Will all the variety and stimulation he needed

And who would fend off creeps like that caller for her?

▪ ▪ ▪ ▪

By 8:30 the next morning, the Patrol communications shop was bustling—enjoying Christmas several months early. Eddie Williams, the head of communications, had begun updating the whole radio system—after Laura figured out how to pay for it—distributing new digital radio units to the roadmen. And trickle down had stopped. Higher ranking officers were no longer getting new cars, with younger troopers stuck with hand-me-downs. New cars were now rolling out with young guys behind the wheels keying up brand new radios. Within a matter of months, nearly everyone had been issued some piece of new equipment.

If she couldn't win the troopers' hearts and minds through sound reasoning, Laura was willing to bribe them.

Entering the repair area, Laura stopped to chat with two young troopers waiting for their cars, then flashed her half salute to a technician. "Seen Robert?"

"He's in Eddie's office," the man replied, looking out from under a hood. "How 'bout you build him his own place out here?"

Except for a few square feet in the center, Eddie Williams' office was crammed with electronic paraphernalia, repair manuals, and spare parts. Eddie was holding a metal plate by the far wall while Robert beamed a laser measuring gun at it, comparing the readout to the distance on a measuring tape.

"Have you got a minute?" Laura asked when they'd finished.

Robert looked around, recognizing her voice. "For you? Always."

Eddie put down the plate and moved around the desk. "I'll step out."

"No, stay," said Laura. "You can help, too."

Eddie nodded respectfully. He'd been with the department for nearly his entire life, starting as a radio operator and working his way up to director of communications.

"I think I need some of your gizmos," Laura said. "Some nasty guy has gotten my unlisted number at home. He seems to know my son's whereabouts."

Robert put down the laser device and focused on Laura. "What's he saying?"

"Last night, he called at dinnertime and said something like 'Bitches like me should keep better track of their children.' He went on to say that he liked Will's red-striped shirt, it made him stand out in the crowd."

"Damn," said Robert, stretching the word to two syllables.

"He's watching Will, and he wants me to know it," Laura said, "Wish I had him on tape."

"Lowlifes who play mind games like these are among the scum of the Earth," said Robert, angrily.

"He's probably smart enough not to call from home or work," Eddie said. "Even if he's in a phone booth, we can find the booth but he won't be there."

"Cellular's worse," Robert added. "It's tough to pinpoint the phone— not always impossible, but very tough. We'll get the phone company to do a 'trap and trace.'"

"You definitely need recorders on all lines, both here and at your house," Eddie said, eager to help any way he could. His job was so much better with Laura in charge, he needed to ensure she would stay. "I'll install those today. I can get you set up on Caller ID also if you don't already have it."

"I don't."

"That may or may not tell us anything. They don't display the phone number for pay phones and cellular yet.

"Thanks," said Laura, picking up a new portable radio from a stack of twelve on the desk. "Are we all set for the roadblock next week?"

"Rarin' to go," Robert said.

■ ■ ■ ■

"Here's where I'll be in Ocean Springs," Laura said, handing Blake a sheet of paper. "I leave in the morning, and I'm planning on coming back midday on Monday."

"Does the Governor's office have this?"

Laura nodded.

"Taking Will with you?" Blake asked, standing at the end of her desk, reading her itinerary.

"He's with Semmes' parents this weekend, and I bet his grandmother is already well on her way to spoiling him to death," Laura said. She looked tired and pale.

"Are you okay?" Blake asked, concern clearly in his voice.

Laura smiled bravely to dispel his worry. "I'm fine."

"You don't sound it," he said, taking a seat and looking at her more closely.

"Memorial Day weekend used to be a big deal for us. We always rented a cabin in the Smokies, hiked. Will followed Semmes around like a shadow while I lay about in a hammock and read. As close to heaven as I'll ever know."

Blake nodded, letting a small sympathetic smile show. "And what are you going to do in Ocean Springs?"

"My friend Ann Hilman is driving us down to her husband's house—he's out sailing somewhere," Laura said. "Three days of reading, good food, and sunshine."

"That's definitely what you need."

"It was the last place Semmes and I were together before the accident," she added, her voice cracking with emotion.

"Don't worry about this place," Blake said confidently.

"What are your plans?"

"I'll be hanging around the house, but monitoring what's happening around the state."

"Is everyone scheduled to work?"

Blake nodded. "Near as can be. This is a big weekend for wrecks—we're trying to keep the fatalities down to zero."

"I'll keep my beeper on."

"I suggest you turn that thing off and keep it off," Blake said. "We can find you if something comes up."

"I told Vic I'd have it on."

"Well, tell him differently. The world's not going to come to an end if you aren't in touch for a few nights. You deserve a break."

His deeply solicitous tone was something Laura hadn't heard from a man in a long time. Almost embarrassed by the attention, Laura quickly turned her face away and looked out the window at the traffic. "You're probably right," she said, trying to appear interested in Jackson's version of the rush hour on the Interstate.

Blake had rarely seen her look so fragile. He looked down at her schedule again so she wouldn't see him looking at her.

After an awkward moment, Blake said, "Just in case you need a State Patrol fix, page me over the weekend and I'll give you a rundown on what's happened."

Still looking out the window, Laura took a deep breath before turning to face Blake. "I might have to take you up on that. Without Will or the Patrol, I might not know what to do with myself."

"When do you leave?"

"In the morning," Laura said.

"So what are you doing tonight?" Blake asked.

"I'm going to the movies," Laura said, looking up at the clock.

"By yourself?"

"No, my mother's been here for a few days before she leaves for North Carolina."

"She seems to do a lot of traveling," Blake said.

"Have wheels, will travel. She's going to my brother's this time to take care of his kids while they're away. And he happens to live near a very nice golf course," Laura smiled, bucking up a bit. "But I don't mind going to the movies alone—once the lights go out, I'm lost in the story almost immediately."

"Hardly ever get there myself."

"You should try it. A good one can take you a million miles away from all of this."

▪▪▪▪

Laura and Ann lay on the deck of the *Last Chance* as it rocked in the water, tied to its mooring in the back bay. They'd rowed out in the dinghy, moved bunk cushions up from below, and were soaking up afternoon sun.

"I haven't sunbathed like this in I don't know how long," Laura said. "Fifteen years maybe. And never on a boat."

"That's fairly obvious," Ann said.

"How so?"

"Don't be angry with me, but your farmer's tan always gives you away."

"But there's never any time," Laura pleaded.

"You don't have to justify it. I'm your friend."

"Is it that bad?"

"I wouldn't choose anything sleeveless if I were you."

Laura was silent. Her favorite piece of clothing was a light blue sleeveless summer dress.

"So where did Tom go this time?" Laura asked.

"East, I believe."

"Just East?"

"That's what he said," Ann answered, turning over on her side to face Laura, too pregnant to lay on her stomach. "My guess is the Florida Keys or the Bahamas. A test sail before he heads across the Gulf. Belize is currently his favorite destination."

"You've never been there?"

"Couldn't make the trip in December. And definitely not the one in March. Kinda chapped me that he disappeared right in the middle of all that needed to be done, getting ready for the wedding and all. But maybe it was better that way."

"How does he get the time off?"

"Just takes it."

"Doesn't his father object?"

"I'd think he would. But they have such a strained relationship, maybe the breaks help."

"Are you going to stay down to be here when he gets back?"

"I don't know when he's coming in and I need to get back to work. Anyway, he was in such a foul humor when he docked in March that I don't ever want to experience that again."

"I thought sailing relaxed him?"

"It usually does but not that time."

"Maybe it was just pre-wedding jitters."

"That's what I tried to tell myself."

"Is it getting better between you two?"

"A little. Particularly now that I'm not throwing up anymore."

"Could you sail?"

"I'm dying to, but Tom refuses. Doesn't want something to happen out there."

"I can't exactly blame him."

"I don't argue much."

A large motorboat passed them going faster than the posted speed, rocking *Last Chance* and disturbing their tranquillity. As the water calmed, Laura repositioned herself to maximize the sun on her upper arms and neckline.

"How are you doing?" Ann asked.

"Right now, okay," Laura said. "This was a great idea."

"And Will?"

"He's doing better. Kids are amazingly resilient. But I'll never be a substitute for Semmes and it breaks my heart...." Laura suddenly sat up, massaging her forehead, trying to hold back the emotions what were welling up in her. "He's not going to have a dad to play ball with," she said, erupting in sobs.

Ann moved to her side, putting her arm around her shoulders. "I'm so sorry I said anything," she whispered.

"I've got to get it under control," Laura sobbed. "I can't do this every day."

"You won't, it'll get better with time."

"But never to hear all that whooping and hollering when they were playing outside, I don't know," she moaned.

"I'll get some Kleenex," Ann said. "Sit tight."

By the time she returned with a box, Laura seemed to have calmed down. "I feel so stupid when I do this," she said, wiping her eyes. "It comes on like a faucet."

"It's hardly stupid. I envy you for what you had with Semmes. It's more than I'll ever have, no matter how long I live."

Laura looked out over the marshes at a squadron of brown pelicans circling low, trolling for their dinner. "He should be here to see this, goddammit."

Then in a whisper, "I want him back so badly."

9

Three weeks later, Laura was riding south in the Patrol's Bell Jet Ranger helicopter to the roadblock on Interstate 10 which ran along the Gulf Coast. Minutes away from landing, troopers on the ground requested assistance trailing a car that had run a smaller block on a side road. The copilot operated the searchlight, straining to see the ground, as they combed the dense pine forest for a dark blue car with a peeling red vinyl roof. The din of the motor and blades was too loud to carry on a conversation so they talked over headsets.

"If we had the infrared sensors, Commissioner," the copilot said, "we could tell which of these cars was hot from operating recently. Dark blue ones melt into the blackness."

Laura followed the searchlight's beam, chuckling. "Was this all a setup to demonstrate the need for an infrared?"

"Absolutely not, ma'am," said the pilot.

"In all my life, I've never known people to go to such lengths to talk me into buying something."

"Honest, Commissioner, this just happened, no plan to it," the copilot said. "But now that you mention it, we should have thought of it."

After ten more minutes, they abandoned the search long enough to drop Laura off, landing in a clear space beyond the picnic tables at the rest area. Blake, in uniform, ran up beneath the blades, and opened the back door for her. As soon as they were far enough away, the pilot spun the engine up from ground idle to flight and lifted off, disappearing into the black sky.

"They're still searching for that guy who ran the roadblock," Laura said, fanning her face with the papers in her hand. "Didn't it cool off after dark?"

"Not enough," Blake said. "We're moving the cars through as fast as possible to keep tempers under control."

"How's it going otherwise?"

"Couldn't ask for better," Blake said, smiling. "Catching lots of drunks, two major dopers, three fugitives. And the night is still young."

Laura stepped back to look at Blake. She'd never seen him in uniform before. He'd even trimmed his gray hair so it didn't hang too far over his collar. The hat, set low on his brow, made his long face seem sterner than usual.

"Very impressive," she said.

Blake squirmed self-consciously. "I haven't had a uniform on in years. I'd forgotten what it felt like. You have to suck in your stomach all the time or you'll look like that Master Sergeant over there," pointing to a good-size gut hanging over a gun belt.

For a man who'd spent every waking hour of the past twenty years in plain clothes, Blake was having remarkable success rallying the enforcement troopers. Properly organized and motivated, there was no telling what they could do, but motivation was an enormous hurdle. Take-home pay for a trooper—a tedious job sprinkled with periodic terror— was so crummy that a man or woman with four kids, was eligible for welfare.

Laura was fighting for salary increases, while Blake rearranged the work schedules so troopers could take on second and third jobs. But mostly, he tried to make the work more interesting, and the roadblock was part of the scheme. Troopers from all over had volunteered for the extra duty. It was a change of pace from patrolling, not to mention a chance to see friends assigned to other districts.

Logan Cummins from DEA was at the coffeepot. He'd been there from the beginning, intensely interested in what an operation like this could yield.

"You don't waste any time, do you?" smiled Logan.

"Not if I can help it," Laura said. "Looks like quite a party."

"You just missed the TV cameras. They've been here for hours."

"Did they get any good footage?" Laura asked.

"One guy was driving in the nude. Took him in for indecent exposure."

Laura's eyes widened. "Actually naked?"

"Stark," Blake said. "Not a stitch on him. Liked to flaunt it, too.

Jumped out to protest this flagrant violation of his civil rights. Cameras whirred away through the whole thing."

"Blake engineered this perfectly. There was almost no warning. Troopers appeared out of nowhere. They got two dopers right off the bat, separate cars, a hundred pounds of coke in a hidden compartment." Motioning with his thumb back to the trailer, "Robert's talking to the guy right now to see if we can do a controlled delivery to catch who he's working for."

"How'd they find it?"

"He made a mistake on the name on the registration. He signed the search consent, no hesitation. There was an extra compartment under the spare tire. Pretty nice job actually. They almost missed it."

"The other guy had three nine thousand dollar checks from the Gulf Goddess Casino and five thousand in cash," Blake said. "Says he won it all, but your dogs went nuts on his car. Luckily for us, he had a sawed-off shotgun buried under a blanket in the trunk. He still protested every step of the way to jail."

"How long are you planning to keep the blocks up?" asked Laura.

"We got shifts scheduled all night," Blake said. "But the word's out. The secondary roads are getting people avoiding I-10 and I'm sending more troopers over to them. A few people are pissed, but most of them say they appreciate us getting the drunks off the highway."

A converted school bus painted dull gray, half full of drunk drivers slouching in their seats, was waiting for a full load before leaving for the county lockup. Some sheriffs resented the Patrol's presence in their counties, but not here. The Patrol had been welcomed with open arms: The revenue from the tickets issued went into the sheriff's budget, so he gladly made space in his drunk tank and helped any way he could. Fifty dozen donuts and gallons of coffee and iced tea—his treat—arrived shortly after they set up.

Blake looked over at the group on break, joking with each other. "The troopers are having a ball. All except Bill Kenner, of course."

In fact, Kenner looked absolutely miserable as he took orders from a colonel brimming with ideas. He'd vehemently protested an interstate block as too disruptive and too dangerous, implying that Blake didn't have sufficient experience with traffic to understand the implications.

And of course Kenner had been wrong.

"Can't stand success, can he," Laura observed.

"The Lord didn't intend for life to be fun, you know," Blake said.

"Well, keep everyone out as long as you want," Laura said. "May not get any more couriers, but we might as well lock up as many drunks as possible. Too bad if people get mad."

Hal Easterbrook from the FBI, drove in, his blue light still flashing on the dash as he pulled up and parked near them. He was bent out of shape from having to show his ID to troopers all along the way from I-10. Brushing off his suit pants as he stepped out of the car, he remarked, "Nice operation, Commissioner. Very effective force."

"Glad you could make it, Hal."

Easterbrook looked around in his usual officious manner. He'd risen more quickly than most in the FBI, a function of strategic ass-kissing. He'd instantly appreciated Alex's potential, and itching to hitch his wagon to a star, stopped by to see Alex whenever the occasion presented itself. Within a few months, Alex requested that the FBI permanently detail Hal to his office as his day-to-day liaison, a request quickly granted in light of Senator Markham's position on the Senate Appropriations Committee.

"We were surprised you could set it up so quickly," Hal said.

Logan couldn't tolerate high-handed FBI types, and Hal was particularly offensive, always jumping in late, stealing stats, and taking much more than his share of the credit. "It was brilliant," Logan said, "you should have been here at the start."

Blake stepped forward. "We're trying to utilize the manpower more effectively. It's a specialty we can really develop," he said with an icy edge to the word *manpower*.

"Well, we stand ready to help if you need it," Hal said.

"Are you speaking for the FBI, or the United States Attorney?" Laura asked, eyeing Hal cautiously.

"Ummm," Hal hesitated at the unexpected question, "both."

"Surprising," Laura said.

Robert Stone, dressed in black fatigues except for his Saints' cap, crossed the parking lot toward them while the most recent detainee, a sharply dressed, well-mannered young Hispanic-American, stood at the camper window, watching. Robert nodded to everyone, tipping his hat to Laura. "Good evening, Commissioner. You picked a real good one."

"There wasn't much science to it."

"I know. Proves the stuff is moving all the time."

Blake signaled to the suspect with a nod of his head. "What's his deal?"

"He says he moves about one hundred and fifty kilos a month from places all along the coast to Atlanta and St. Louis, sometimes to Kansas City and Chicago. He doesn't know where the stuff comes in. He gets a call at his home from a man—doesn't know his name—and they tell him to check into a certain hotel by a certain date and time. In this case it was a place in Pascagoula, some We-Don't-Tell-Motel."

Logan interrupted. "That close?"

Robert nodded. "Says he goes there all the time. When he gets to his room, he waits. The guy calls, asks for his room number and some time later, an envelope with two-thousand dollars and car keys is slipped under the door. He waits some more. They call, tell him where the car is, and give him a destination and a time to be there. At the other end, he checks into another hotel and his payment gets slipped under the door. If he's late, no payment. Never sees the guys. He flies home to New Orleans. After expenses, he's clearing twenty grand a month. He says someone follows him all the way, but I don't believe him. If he's been doing this as long as he says, I bet they quit tailing him long ago."

"Where was this load headed?" Laura asked.

"St. Louis," Robert answered.

Logan looked back at the trailer. "How about you introduce me and I'll take a run at him. A controlled delivery would be very nice."

"Fine by me."

They had only taken a few steps when Logan turned back and pointed toward the FBI agent. "Easterbrook, I realize you were present for this conversation, but do me a favor, don't open up a case file on this deal. Okay?"

Blake swallowed a smirk, and Laura looked away to hide her grin.

Hal got huffy instantly. "Listen, Cummins, don't get into that crap here, please. I've had enough."

"You've had enough?" Logan had stopped, glaring at Hal, looking as if he were going back.

Robert pulled on Logan's arm. "Later, guys."

The number of cars coming through slowed down dramatically after midnight. At 2:30 A.M., Blake, Robert, and Laura were sitting around the camper's built-in table talking about the operation.

"We need to beef up the airport details and concentrate on these little strips, not just the big ones. For all of Markham's fancy talk, the feds aren't doing squat," Robert said, leaning back. "It's a matter of manpower. We've got it, they don't."

"I talked to those customs agents for a long time tonight about Gulf operations and air traffic," Laura said. "I'm getting a tour of the surveillance center when I come back down for a speech next month."

"There's so much those guys could do, if they wanted to," Blake said.

"What about that guy you stopped tonight with the casino checks?" Laura asked. "You think he just stopped by to double his money after he got paid?"

"Could be. I'm hoping he tells us a little more in the morning," Robert answered. "But there's all sorts of stuff going on at those places. The FBI agent down here is hot to trot—an ex-agent from his office heads security on one of the boats."

"Is it possible to schedule another one of these next week?" Laura asked, yawning.

"Not easy, but possible," Blake said. "What do you have in mind?"

"Interstate 20," Laura replied. "If you could iron out all the wrinkles on that detail, we could hit both I-10 and I-20 on the same night."

Blake and Robert nodded. This was the way it ought to be, something cooking all the time.

"Think about the airports and the manpower you need," Laura said to Robert, sliding out of the bunk seat. A trooper was waiting to drive her north. "When you figure out how much money I have to scrape up, do me a favor and break it to me gently."

■ ■ ■ ■

"I don't care for any banana pudding, thank you," Laura said, pushing aside the small white dish with its lump of something jiggly and yellowish.

Luncheon speeches were not her favorite. There was only so much rubbery chicken a person should eat as far as she was concerned. Laura only agreed to keep doing them because the Governor and Vic insisted. The more she was seen, the better accepted she would be, which was good for Carver—and good for Laura, too.

But when she was invited to a far corner of the state, the expense often outweighed the benefits. She was forced to waste the better part of a day traveling unless she flew in one of the Patrol planes or was driven by a trooper so that she could work in the car. But both of those created a grander entrance than she liked. She decided to offset time wasted on this trip with a tour of the Gulf Air Surveillance center.

Laura made polite conversation with the club member assigned to introduce her until the program began. While the program chairman rattled through the particulars from her resumé, Laura scanned the crowd, searching for the most disgruntled-looking member to be her focus during her remarks. If he came up to thank her afterward, she figured she'd won. If he avoided her, she'd lost. Since she started keeping score, she was ten and six.

She was better known and better accepted on the Gulf Coast because the recent interstate roadblock had been so successful in catching drunk drivers. Nevertheless, those still awake after the meal appeared mildly interested, with a dash of contempt for her audacity in having a "man's" job. Her speech about the dramatic increase in drug trafficking flowed well. Thirty minutes later, questions and answers began, starting with the standard ones about why truckers don't get stopped, and why troopers speed when there's not an emergency.

The man she'd picked out spoke up, his tone bitter. "Mrs. Owen, I don't believe there's as much drug trafficking as you say there is."

"Believe me," Laura answered, upbeat but forceful, "there is and I'll prove it if I have the chance. If we get funding for more troopers and better equipment, I'll put the extra manpower on the road working narcotics. And I can practically promise that they'll be collecting drugs and drug money in record amounts. This is like fishing in a stocked pond. You put out enough lines, you'll get bites. We just don't have enough lines out. Maybe never will, but we're going to try."

"Are you using all this to run for office?" her detractor shot back.

"No, sir, I'm doing my job the best way I know how," Laura said, and paused, considering whether to play the tragedy card, one she rarely showed. The guy was such a jerk, he deserved it.

"There was some talk about me running for office immediately after I was appointed, but I didn't start those rumors nor did I encourage them. And now, after my husband was killed in a car wreck—by a doped-up kid, I might add—I'm focusing on getting my life together. One way I'm doing that is working as hard as I can."

The man asked no more questions. When the meeting adjourned, he left without shaking her hand, but half the others apologized profusely for his rudeness and thanked her repeatedly for speaking.

As soon as she cut free, she headed for the U.S. Customs Service offices, right on the water, next to the Coast Guard Station near the port docks. Turning off the highway, she passed row after row of containers recently unloaded from huge cargo boats and destined for cities in the South and Midwest. More tractor trailers were pulling in, unloading their freight containers, then waiting to take on new loads and head out.

Directed east along the pier she found Ted Campbell standing outside the Gulf Air Surveillance Center, a small, low building, its roof jammed with antennae. He was smoking a cigarette and chatting with a Coast Guard officer. As she approached, Ted pointed toward a parking space marked Reserved, Officer in Charge.

"Sure I won't get towed?" Laura asked as she locked the car.

"Absolutely not," Ted replied. "It's the Captain's space and he's in New Orleans."

"I appreciate your arranging a tour."

"Love to do it," Ted answered. "We don't get to brag very often because we can't tell people what we really do."

The lights were so low inside that it took a while for their eyes to adjust. There were three consoles, each with several screens, a keyboard, and control switches. With recent budget cuts, their operating funds had been slashed and only one console was in use. An operator wearing a headset was monitoring a radar screen and updating a computer database. Audio from the air traffic control tower at the Air Force base came in constantly.

Ted pointed to one screen. "When we're 'up,' we have complete coverage of all planes. If anything suspicious comes in and we can't get adequate identification, we can follow it in Blackhawk helicopters. The operator..." Ted motioned to a petite woman with a deadly serious expression on her face, "is in constant contact with air traffic control at the airfield."

"Can someone beat the system?"

"Of course. Not too long ago an identified plane flew in with an unidentified one flying just below it, but on radar they looked like only one plane. We caught it only because the idiots flew right over us and someone was outside having a smoke."

Laura looked at another screen. "And how many boats are out there?"

"On any given day there are upward of seven thousand vessels in the Gulf."

"So searching small private boats is impossible?" Laura asked.

"Not impossible, but it's like looking for a needle in a haystack and time consuming as hell," Ted replied. "Not unlike searching all those shipping containers you passed on the way in. Very unproductive."

"That's what we thought about searching cars," Laura said. "But now that we've been at it awhile, it's become much less hit and miss."

"That's different," Ted said. "Cars are relatively small, there are windows, and a driver to question."

"Same for boats—maybe no windows—but someone's in charge," Laura said. "Would you consider doing surprise inspections every once in a while?"

"I guess the Coast Guard could, but only if there's time in between normal operations, and there's not much of that these days. What type of boats are you thinking about? Fishing boats?"

"Anything big enough to cross the Gulf," Laura said. "The point is for the word to get out that you're looking. Who knows, maybe you'll get lucky. But at the very least, you can scare a few."

10

Alex didn't want to spend his entire vacation sailing, so he took a commercial flight to Belize City. Since he had his pilot's license and instrument rating, Alex rented a plane, and he and Tom island-hopped during the day, then Alex disappeared each evening with the handsome young woman from the village. Tom thought it was absurd to go so far for sex, but Alex wasn't taking any chances of damaging his pristine reputation by catting around in Jackson.

On the last morning, while Alex slept, Hector and Tom loaded a thousand kilos. Though Tom had wanted a test sail with five hundred before he increased the weight, he'd sailed *Next* enough to know how steady and fast she was. Doubling the load cut in half the total number of trips he'd have to make, so Tom capitulated to Hector's entreaties to take more. Underway, Tom barely noticed the difference. *Next* was a stellar performer.

On their second night at sea, the Gulf was completely calm and they were moving steadily north under power, finishing their wine on the deck under the stars. The sliver of a moon had set long before, and in the clear air, millions of stars twinkled.

"By now you might be a father," Alex said. "What's it feel like?"

Tom shook his head. "It wasn't my idea. None of it was my idea."

"You made out pretty well though," Alex said.

"How so?" Tom asked. "My otherwise perfect life just ended for dirty diapers and expensive tuition payments."

"You got this boat for starters."

"Small consolation," Tom said, "I tried all spring and summer to adjust, but I'm not the marriage type. I want to close the door and be alone. I want my own house, my own schedule. Full-time companionship wasn't something I was looking for or needed." He waved his hand, shoving the whole topic out to sea. "While we're talking about headaches, how's the campaign?"

"Okay. It's much too early to know anything."

"Any opposition?" Tom asked.

"Laura Owen," Alex replied.

"What? I can't believe that. Ann would have said something."

"Owen's not talking about it, just acting the part."

"Surely you're not serious. This is Mississippi we're talking about. We don't cotton to 'uppity women,'" said Tom, with a little extra drawl.

"I'm serious as a heart attack. She's on the road all the time, making speeches, throwing up roadblocks, and collecting illegal drugs. It never ends. I'm sick to death of Little Miss Trooper."

"I'm surprised she'd do something like that so soon after Semmes died," Tom said. "I don't know what you can make out of that, but there oughta be something there."

"Well, she's about to find out how tough playing hardball can be," Alex answered.

"What's she doing with narcotics?" Tom asked, as innocently as possible. "I thought the State Patrol just handed out speeding tickets."

"Haven't you been reading the paper or watching the news? She's turned them all into narcotics agents. They're working dope all the time."

"You always told me you were head of the task force for the state," Tom said.

"I still am," Alex boasted. "But she's not federal so she doesn't pay any attention to my game plan. I'm making it my business to know what's going on, but it's a struggle sometimes."

"Like, what's going down right now?"

"Not much," Alex said. "Half the feds are on summer family vacations. She just finished a huge surprise roadblock on Interstate 10—unbelievable publicity. Caught several couriers."

"How much of a problem can she be?" Tom asked. "Isn't she limited to the interstates?"

"And state roads," Alex said. "But if you're in my shoes, trying to mount a publicity campaign as the man tough on drugs and crime, she's a real pain in the butt, believe me. She hogs the limelight every chance she gets. And don't forget, she's got five hundred guys doing her bidding."

"Don't you have agents running all over the place?"

"Wish I did. There's only a handful of DEA agents in the state, and FBI guys don't usually work drugs—at least not straight out." Alex laid his head back on a pillow. "I don't want to talk about it anymore. It gives me a headache just thinking about her."

"Maybe she'll get tarred with some lethal rumor like that guy who ran so strong for attorney general and cratered at the end. You ought to be able to plant that seed in some devious mind."

"Now that's an interesting thought," Alex said. "I'll get my brain trust working on it."

They listened to the water slapping against the hull and the smooth rhythm of the diesel engine.

Alex spoke up. "I'm starting on a new house. I assume I can get another round of materials at your bargain-basement prices?"

Tom looked up at the moon and smiled. He'd been giving Alex better-than-wholesale prices, charging half of the costs against another job where similar materials were called for—and keeping careful track of everything Alex got through him.

"Sure. Send me a list of what you need. It shouldn't be a problem. How much have you made on this little building venture of yours?"

"With your prices, about two-hundred-thousand dollars over five years."

"Nice little sidebar," Tom said. "Very nice."

▪ ▪ ▪ ▪

Ann was sitting up, looking quite fit for having just delivered a screaming eight-pound, ten-ounce baby boy, two weeks premature. Her hospital room was filled with flowers, mostly from the Hilmans and their friends. Laura held Jesse Ruthven Hilman, inspecting his wrinkly little body.

"Keep a diary, Ann. You'll forget what this little guy was like."

"Did you keep one?"

"Of course not, that's why I'm telling you to," Laura said. "The best I did was to take pictures with a camera that put the date on each print." She laid Jesse on her outstretched legs and stroked his silky skin. "I'm glad you've decided to stay home with him right from the start."

"I wish you had," Ann said.

"I do, too, Especially when Will was three or so—that's when it got really fun," Laura said.

"Everyone says I've got a lifetime to work, but they grow up in a flash," Ann added. "Why don't you quit now? At least you'd get to enjoy a few of the early years."

"Can't really," Laura said. "I mean I could, but to have enough for all the things we do—school, the trips to Florida, college—I'd have to sell the house and move to a smaller place. Semmes had life insurance, but not that much." Laura ran her fingers up the bottom of Jesse's feet and watched his toes curl, smiling at him. "Besides, I need the office right now. I'm crazy enough as it is—not having the work would put me over the edge."

"Should I worry about you?" Ann asked.

"No, I don't think so. It's actually getting a little better." Laura paused, smiling and cooing at Jesse. "I wish Tom could have been here. Semmes always said Will's birth was the most amazing event of his life."

Laura laid Jesse back in the bassinet and Ann immediately got out of bed to check on him, pulling the bassinet closer to her bed.

"This wouldn't have interested Tom even if he'd been here."

"Ann, give him a break," Laura pleaded. "He didn't arrange for a storm, and he surely didn't know you'd be early."

"Yeah, but he didn't need to take a trip so close to my due date. He should've flown wherever he had to go, not sailed. As the time's gotten nearer, he's gotten farther away."

"That's not so abnormal. Think about what you've looked like lately." Laura held her hands out from her stomach, smiling.

"But, Laura, this is the only thing he's ever done without Daddy's help. You'd think he'd be proud of his child. Instead, he's making it clear that we're interrupting his schedule—whatever that might be."

"He's a solo sailor, Ann. Semmes needed to be alone, too. I'm sure it'll change when he sees Jesse."

"Stop defending him, for God's sake," Ann said, shifting her gaze angrily out the window. After a moment, she turned back. "Do you still miss Semmes terribly?"

"Every day and every night," said Laura thoughtfully. "But lately, I can't remember things. Can't remember how it felt when he kissed me." She paused, staring out the window. "I don't think I could have gone on, though, if it had been Will who died that night."

"Do you ever do anything except work and be a Mom? I mean, going out to dinner, or something?"

Laura shook her head. "Invitations haven't exactly been pouring in. If it weren't for you, I wouldn't have any social life at all."

They both watched Jesse, who was staring with his unfocusing eyes at the light and dark.

"And that probably won't change any time soon," Laura said. "Who would dare ask the head of the State Patrol for a date?"

■ ■ ■ ■

Laura's secretary, Deborah, brought in the day's stack of mail as well as some call sheets and waited, scheduling book in hand, on the other side of Laura's desk. The clutter was discouraging even to her.

"Do I have anything today that you know of?" Laura asked, putting her pen down and looking up from the letter she was drafting.

"Only a meeting with the family of that woman who committed suicide up in Woodley. They're coming in at two."

"Tell me again what that's about," Laura asked.

"They want you to override the medical examiner's suicide determination and substitute accidental death."

"Is there a lot of insurance money at issue?"

"None, if I remember correctly."

"Is the Doc coming, too?"

"I told him to be here fifteen minutes early."

"Good," Laura said glancing back at her letter. "Is there a file?"

"Yes." Deborah scanned the piles. "It's here somewhere, I added it to the In Box a couple of days ago."

"Oh, Lord," Laura said, leaning forward to leaf through a stack while Deborah attacked the box on the other end of the big desk.

"Here it is, Commissioner. Other than this, today's clear. Tomorrow's a bear though."

"Well, try and keep today open." Laura swept her hand over the papers. "I've got to get some of this done."

"I'll do what I can."

Already writing again, Laura murmured, "thanks" just before the door closed.

Aside from Will, in her loneliness, the Patrol had become Laura's life, sucking her into all its problems and activities. The atmosphere at headquarters had changed—for the better, or at least that's what she'd heard. The fifth floor was no longer off-limits—employees and troopers of every rank felt freer to stop by and talk, giving Laura more walking around information than her predecessors had ever had. She was the complete opposite of one commissioner who was successfully kept in the dark his entire tenure by a chief of patrol who vigilantly filtered all information flowing in and out, while doing exactly as he pleased. Laura stayed in touch with people all over the department, in and out of Jackson. They needed a standard bearer and she needed a focus, so it was simple to bury herself in work.

But it was never easy—she knew she would always be a mixed blessing. Some, with red-nosed Bill Kenner leading the pack, absolutely loathed the idea of a woman in the commissioner's chair. Even those charmed by Laura's energy and interest, never forgot her permanent, unalterable disability—she was a woman in the quintessential man's job. And she was beholden to the one organization in the state more male-dominated than the Patrol, the Legislature.

When the telephone buzzed, she hit the speakerphone button to answer.

"Commissioner?" said the switchboard operator, sounding a little anxious. For a split second, Laura thought it might be another nasty call from Mr. Mystery and she reached for the recorder.

"Two staff people from the Senate are here and they want to see you, if possible," the operator explained.

"Send them on up, then when they're in the elevators, call me back and tell me more." Laura turned off the radio and watched the traffic stream past, wondering what was up. The phone rang again.

"They said they were from the Oversight Committee," the switchboard operator said. "Very serious people."

"Thanks," Laura answered.

Minutes later, Deborah ushered in a man and a woman, both in their twenties dressed in crisp business clothes, carrying briefcases.

"Thank you for meeting with us on such an impromptu basis," said the young man.

"Certainly." At Laura's motion, they sat in the leather armchairs in front of her desk. "What can I do for you?"

Sitting back, his briefcase still poised on his knees, the man kept the lead. "We've been asked to review the last six months of expenditures for drug operations."

"Background for budget hearings?"

He hesitated a second, then said, "Yes."

"I'm ready to provide whatever you need," Laura said. "When do you want to start?"

Clicking open his briefcase and taking out a yellow legal pad, the man looked at Laura, forcing a smile. "How about right now?"

Laura hid her surprise well and leaned toward her brown appointment book, looking over the day's schedule. "Certainly, consider my calendar cleared for the rest of the morning. Should I ask the comptroller to join us?"

"That would be very helpful," he said. "We have a few questions for you until he gets here."

Two hours later, when they left to set up temporary offices in the comptroller's suite, Laura sat back, exhausted and angry at their attitude. She picked up the phone and called Vic.

"How's the Patrol?" Vic asked, sounding genuinely glad to hear from her. "We haven't seen much of you lately."

"Things were fine until today," Laura said. "I just had a visit from two Senate investigators. The guy grilled me for two hours about our drug interdiction program. They've gone down to set up shop in the Comptroller's office. Do you know what's going on?"

"Nothing involving you that I know of, other than the usual budget hearings."

Laura pulled out her Legislative Directory and browsed through the pictures. "Is Bramlett still chairman of Oversight?"

"No, Gabriel Collel took over last week," Vic said. "Could you have a problem in the Delta?"

"Not that I know of, but Collel's hated me ever since I questioned his travel expenses when I was at the State Auditor's office."

"Maybe he figures this is his chance to get back at you."

"It's great to have enemies like Collel," Laura said.

"Life would be boring without them. Anything to worry about?"

"Not that I know of, at least not that's my fault. We've got the controls on expenditures airtight compared to what they used to be. This place was a mess when I got here," Laura said. "I've told you that."

"Maybe that's it," Vic offered.

"Doubt it," Laura said. "They don't seem to be looking back that far."

11

At dawn, an unmarked dark green van dropped Robert Stone and two troopers at the driveway of a trailer sitting fifty yards back from the road. The van dropped two other troopers a few hundred yards further on, then it disappeared down the narrow road into the Johnson County woods.

All five men were dressed in camouflage clothing. It wasn't customary, in fact, it was down right foolish for a colonel to do a bust. But a steady diet of paperwork and office management, wasn't Robert's cup of tea. Since he'd been working on this case himself, he decided to lead the foray—foolish or not. Leaning up against the embankment, they pulled their weapons from their holsters and checked the clips. Getting thumbs-up from everyone, Robert crawled onto the driveway toward a dirty brown Ford pickup and the trailer beyond it. After a few yards, he signaled for the others to follow. One man whistled like a catbird to the two guys down the road and everyone headed over the embankment.

Crouching as low as possible, they eased forward silently. Robert signaled one group to head left, the other right, as he continued toward the front door. Just as the first group reached the rear corner of the trailer, their quarry, a drug dealer, stepped quietly out of the back door. He was of medium height, thin but rangy, wearing jeans and a shirt that looked like they'd been slept in for a week. Seeing the trooper, he took off into the woods.

"Stop, police," the trooper yelled, rising to follow him. "He's running!"

The trooper faltered over a tree root, lunging ahead until he regained his balance.

"Which way?" Robert yelled as he and the other trooper came around the trailer.

"North. Down the ravine."

The drug dealer barged through dense undergrowth, sliding down an embankment into a deep ravine, his arms out to keep his balance. Robert fired a shot into the air above him, repeating, "Stop, police," as often as he could while running. As the dealer reached the bottom, he moved directly up the gully, the soft earth slowing him down. Three frightened deer raced up the ravine just ahead of him, then bounded effortlessly up the side.

Looking back over his shoulder, the drug dealer saw one of the troopers gaining on him. He speeded up but then tripped and fell forward. As he was trying to get up, the closest trooper made a diving tackle for his legs.

The man kicked furiously, smashing the trooper's face with the heel of his boot. In pain, the trooper loosened his grip on the dealer's right leg but just as their quarry pulled free, Robert's hand slammed down on the dealer's shoulder, pushing his face back into the dirt and leaves.

"Are you Henry Wibbon?" Robert growled.

"Yeah," the man said. "What's it to ya?"

"You're under arrest."

The other trooper caught up and jerked the dealer's arms around his back and handcuffed him while he rattled off his constitutional rights. Robert looked at the injured trooper's face. Beneath the dirt was a cut deep enough to require stitches. He keyed his portable radio and told the van to come back for a run to the hospital. Then he called the substation and asked them to send a patrol car to take the dope dealer.

Two of the troopers kept watch on the drug dealer outside the trailer, while Robert and a third man, equipped with a video camera, went in. The drug dealer's eyes closed, wincing as if waiting for something to explode.

From inside, Robert whistled, then reappeared at the doorway. "Well, well, well, what do we have here? Is this a take-out operation or do you deliver?"

"I'm not sayin' nothin' till I talk to my lawyer," the man said, spitting into the dirt.

"Well, my man," Robert said, "you're going to need one, bad."

From the trailer came another victory yell.

"Start filming," Robert called out, "but don't touch anything."

Robert turned back to the drug dealer. "Yes, you're gonna need one, real bad. Unless of course, you want to help us."

The dealer remained silent, staring ahead.

"Have it your way." Raising his voice, Robert shouted toward the trailer. "Don't you think that pile weighs enough for ten to thirty?"

"Easy," the trooper yelled. "We need the lab out here. Get someone to call from the van."

A patrol car pulled up and a huge uniformed trooper stepped out. "Mornin', Colonel. Out awful early aren't you?"

"Got to stay in shape. Thanks for stoppin' by," Robert said, looking at the drug dealer again. "Last chance. Next time the deal won't be so good."

The man stood silent.

"Take him in," Robert said. "I'll get someone over there to do the paperwork as soon as they finish up at the hospital." Robert turned back to the drug dealer. "Oh, yeah, that reminds me, assault on an officer adds, ummm, how many more years?"

"Minimum ten," the nearest trooper answered.

"Ten more," Robert said. "You just think of that."

The drug dealer still didn't flinch, and Robert pushed him toward the uniformed trooper. "He's all yours."

Not more than twenty minutes after the suspect departed for jail, Major Bill Kenner, driving his sea-blue unmarked LTD, roared up in front of the trailer, slamming his door as he got out. Robert looked out the window cautiously and seeing Kenner, came out quickly. Kenner ignored the fact that Robert outranked him, and was up in Robert's face immediately.

"What the hell do you think you're doing pulling my trooper off the road?" Kenner said. "You got your own damn people."

Robert remained calm. "I had an injured man. I needed someone to take the suspect into the jail." Robert folded his arms across his chest. "What's your problem?"

"What's my problem?" Kenner snarled. "First, why didn't I know this was going down in my division? Second, I'm sick of losing guys to special details, particularly vengeance missions for the Commissioner."

One of the troopers came to the door to watch, his camera in his hand.

"First, Major," Robert said, getting close enough to fill Kenner's entire field of vision. "I didn't tell you because it wasn't any of your damn business. Second, if I hadn't had an injured man, we would have taken the prisoner in ourselves. Now, I have a question for you."

Kenner's stare wavered. Beginning to feel uncomfortable, he glanced at the trooper in the doorway.

"Why are you here?" Robert said, moving slightly to get Kenner's complete attention again. "In your big flashy car when we're trying so hard to make it look like business as usual and catch whoever's coming to pick up the three kilos of cocaine that dirtbag has inside? Why, I ask you?"

Kenner looked toward the trailer nervously.

"And what does the Commissioner have to do with anything?" Robert continued.

Kenner looked past Robert to the other trooper again, hating the satisfied smirk on the man's face. Without a word, Kenner turned on his heel, got back in his car and left, gravel flying in the drive.

■ ■ ■ ■

"Damn, damn, damn," Laura muttered as she flipped through the pile directly in front of her, looking for an earlier draft of the report she was working on. The disarray had reached the point where Laura couldn't find things, she shifted papers from one pile to another, not disposing of anything. Correspondence, markups of bills, draft responses to the senate investigators, budget projections, and documents from a civil lawsuit alleging a trooper had been abusive at one of the roadblocks—it was all hopelessly mixed up together.

Hearing a knock at her door, Laura looked up, hoping for a reason to stop. Blake opened the door and took a couple of steps inside.

"Hey, Blake," Laura said.

"Okay to disturb you?" he asked. "Your phones are forwarded so I couldn't call."

"Absolutely, I need a break."

She swiveled around to turn off the radio and when she swung back, she saw Blake staring at the mass of papers.

"People's desks allegedly reflect their minds—I hope you aren't alarmed," Laura apologized. "I'm making headway, believe it or not."

Blake looked skeptical. "Want some good news?"

"Always. I'm sick of responding to senate auditors, they're driving me loony. In addition to this," Laura tossed a six-page letter his way, "they stopped by late yesterday and asked for a list of all recording devices and where they're located."

"I know. Eddie told me this morning."

"What's the deal?"

Blake shook his head. "Hell if I know."

Laura sat back in her chair. "So, tell me some news."

"Last week, Robert stopped by the penitentiary and paid another visit to the driver of the car in your wreck. He'd been assigned to the prison drug rehab unit right after sentencing on the manslaughter and drug charges, and his treatment program is almost up. So now he's headed into the prison general population. Well, seems he's found the Lord and is willing to bare his soul, in exchange, of course, for reassignment to a community work center."

"What'd you promise him?"

"Nothing. He's started talking, but he's got a lot more to tell us before he gets any favors. He named the guy he bought his dope from, some redneck lowlife who Robert arrested this morning."

A satisfied look spread across Laura's face. "Did the redneck, as you call him, have anything to say?"

"Not yet, but he will. Only a matter of time, given what he's facing. The idiot had nearly three kilos on hand in his trailer—that's ten to thirty right there. He kicked one of Robert's men bad enough to require a dozen stitches, so there's another ten."

Laura's eyes widened. "Did you find anything besides the dope?"

"All kinds of stuff," Blake said. "We're still sifting through it. An address book, southern United States maps with routes marked out."

"What did the maps show?"

"Routes avoiding the interstates."

"Then why don't we work them?"

"Where would you start? They're everywhere. Besides, while this guy might be on the back roads, there are plenty still on the interstates, the blocks have shown that."

Both of them were silent. Laura turned to gaze at the traffic and then swiveled back toward Blake. Slouching down in his chair, he was staring at the giant state road map on the easel next to her desk. They both started to speak at once. Blake deferred.

"Let's block as many state roads as possible, all on the same day," Laura said.

"And block all the interstates at the same time?"

"Hadn't thought of that," Laura said. "Is that possible?"

"With planning—maybe."

"Then plan away," Laura said. "It'll give you and Robert something new to scheme about."

Blake nodded, a smile on his face. "Next up, your mystery caller."

"Know something?"

"Yes and no," Blake said. "He's clearly messing with his voice, and there might be more than one person involved."

"What about the phone numbers?"

"All phone booths."

"Where?"

"All over, but usually at malls here, in Greenville, and in Oxford. A couple of booths south of here, one in New Orleans, and one call from Memphis."

"A busy man," Laura said.

"I figure he's decided on making one call a week while he's on the road doing something else. Since locating him is really the only hope— unless someone just happens to recognize the voice—I don't know if we'll track him down."

"Something else?"

"Did you know that Alex Markham has been the incorporator of several businesses?"

"So you've started checking him out?"

"Yeah, I decided I definitely needed to know the guy a little better since he seems to like you so much."

Blake sat forward, leaning on the edge of her desk, and handed Laura a paper. "Don't you know a Tom Hilman?"

"I do. Remember when I went to Ocean Springs for Memorial Day?"

NEXT TO LAST CHANCE ▪ 141

"Blake nodded.

"I stayed at his house—his wife's a close friend of mine."

"He's the principal in all these companies that Markham helped incorporate. Hilman Development, Hilman Enterprises, Hilman Investments."

"I'm not surprised. Tom is Alex's closest friend—best man at his wedding where I was his wife's matron of honor. Can you believe that? It's one big incestuous group of people: my college roommate marries my worst enemy's best friend."

"Cozy."

"Too cozy," Laura said. "The days after Semmes' death were straight out of *The Big Chill*."

Blake didn't pick up the reference.

"Sorry, forgot you don't go to movies. I interrupted. Go on."

"When Alex became U.S. Attorney, he dropped off all boards and commissions."

"Had to, I'm sure. Main Justice would have required it."

"But he has a tremendous investment income—more than fifty thousand a year, plus his salary."

"How'd you get that?" Laura asked. "I thought tax records weren't available."

"They aren't, officially. Don't ask my sources. We're still working on where the money comes from."

Blake looked back at his notes. "Last but not least, Markham's father registered the Better Government Fund with the Secretary of State."

"You know Alex can't raise money for a campaign and keep his job."

"I know," Blake said. "But when all is said and done, I'd bet anything it'll all go to his campaign."

Laura shook her head in disgust, put her glasses back on, and looked at the work on her desk as if she had no choice but to get started again. Blake took that opportunity to leave. He was nearly at the door when she spoke. He turned and saw her staring at a photo of Will.

"Do me a favor, Blake. Talk to Corrections and make damn sure that driver, whatever his name was, spends a lot of time in the general population."

"Already did that."

■ ■ ■ ■

The phone rang next to Carolyn Hilman's face as she lay in bed. She reached for it immediately, looking at the clock as she did.

"Hello?" she asked, not quite awake.

"Mother, come over here," begged Tom. "Jesse's lying on a blanket on the floor, purple with rage, screaming his lungs out."

"It's two-thirty in the morning, Tom," Carolyn said.

"Who's on the phone?" Stephen Hilman murmured from the other side of the bed.

"I can't deal with this baby," Tom said angrily.

"Where's Ann?"

"Sick. Some virus. Been throwing up all day. The maid stayed late and got him to bed. But now he's awake again and I can't do anything with him."

"Have you given him a bottle?" Carolyn asked.

"Yes," Tom hissed. "He wouldn't take it from me."

"I'll be right there," Carolyn said. "Won't take me more then ten minutes."

Tom moved Jesse and his blanket into the television room—farther away from the bedrooms. The baby quit screaming for a minute, surprised by the change, and then as soon as the doors were closed, let out another wail. In the kitchen, Tom opened a beer and had polished off most of it when his mother knocked at the side door.

"Your father had many a night like this with you," Carolyn said, putting her things on the counter and heading toward the screaming. "Never did get the hang of it. Bring me the bottle, will you?"

Carolyn had Jesse cuddled in her arms when Tom appeared. Jesse spit the bottle away just as he had with Tom. She took off the nipple and tasted it.

"Sour," was all his mother said, rising from her chair and moving toward the kitchen.

"I'm outta here," Tom said.

"Where are you going?"

"Out," Tom growled. "I'm not cut out for this." The door banged shut behind him.

▪▪▪▪

Prison trustees dressed in white jackets and black pants served lunch in the formal dining room at the Mansion, a rather tasty meal now that the Governor and his wife were off their fat-free, low-salt regimen. Laura had been asked to stay after the morning dog and pony show where agency heads had made their pitches for priority in the Governor's legislative agenda.

She'd painted a compelling picture for trying again to make sweeping changes in the criminal justice system. The Governor used these sessions, with all their words, charts, and synopses, to confirm and strengthen what he and Vic had already decided. Laura both loved and loathed the politics of it. Nothing was straightforward, everything was contorted by timing, sound bites, bargains, and jockeying—fascinating but repulsive in its raw manipulation.

Carver couldn't take on every battle, he had to make hard choices. But whenever the discussion turned to the Governor's image vis-à-vis certain voter groups, and the impact pushing this or that legislation would have on his popularity, Laura wanted to scream. As ambitious as she was, calculations like these gave her pause. She doubted she'd be able to operate in her own self-interest as her primary motivating factor, and that was clearly what it took to be a successful politician.

"The crime bill won't be easy to pass, Governor," Laura said between bites. "As it's presently crafted, the punishment measures are Draconian. I designed it with plenty of room to back off."

"Can we count on law enforcement to back it?" Carver asked.

"Maybe," Laura looked at Vic. "It depends what you do for them."

"What do you mean?" Carver asked. "Isn't the bill enough?"

"Every cop wants bad guys locked up forever, but they've also got children to feed and they don't make diddly, excuse the vernacular, being cops. You've got to fund their pay bill, and it's got to be you, Governor, not me, who pushes it or they'll never believe you support them," Laura said. "I've already got a record with them. They may not like me but they can't deny I'm on their side."

"How much will it cost?"

"Two thousand for every officer who takes the continuing training," Laura said, pausing to calculate. "Seven million, at least."

The Governor looked at Vic, who was shaking his head. "We don't have a funding source," Vic said adamantly.

"Is this negotiable?" Carver asked.

"I don't think so," Laura said. "They'd work to defeat the crime bill to get those funds."

"I want some sort of crime bill," Carver said to Vic. "We've got to make the show, even if it fails."

The Governor turned back to Laura. "It would help enormously if the drug war was raging throughout the legislative session."

"Vic and I have already talked about it. We've got a two-week interdiction operation planned that kicks off shortly. It casts a very broad net."

"What are you calling it?" Carver asked.

"Calling what?" Laura said.

"The operation," Carver said. "The press always likes a name."

"The Blitz," Laura answered.

"Good name—has some war connotations," Carver said. "I like it."

"We'll see what we catch. But I'll wager my salary, it'll be a success."

"Maybe it'll balance what Collel's planning for you," Carver said.

"Have you heard something, sir?" Laura asked.

"Nothing specific, except he's acting very smug, and your name seems to come up several times in every conversation," Carver said. "It's clear he's not one of your fans."

"He and a passel of others," Laura said.

"You've got support from all around the state," Vic interjected.

"I know that, but by my latest count, my detractors have more arrows in their quivers.

12

"I realize I was speeding, officer," the driver of the red BMW said as a trooper approached.

"Could I see your license, sir?" the State Patrol corporal, K-88, asked. His eyes wandered over every visible surface in and out of the car as he stood there. This was the second night the smuggling apprehension teams had been out, as part of The Blitz. An informal competition on who could recover the most money or drugs was hot among the fifty-six troopers, all of whom had recently completed training in smuggling techniques. They'd already made hundreds of traffic stops.

"How fast was I going?" the driver asked as he handed over his license.

"Eighty-two in a sixty-five, sir. Where are you headed?"

"Florida."

The K-88 perked up. "Must be important to be going that fast. Business or pleasure?"

"Pleasure. My first vacation in months."

"K-88," the radio squawked.

The corporal pulled up his portable. "Go ahead," he said, looking down at the license as he listened.

"Edward-Boy-Mary-3-2-8 is registered to Russell Burrows, 2440 Spencer Street, Biloxi. Tag is current, no violations."

"Thank you."

He looked back at the driver, closing up his ticket book. The ten minutes it would take to write the ticket could be better spent stopping someone else.

"Slow it down, Mr. Burrows," the corporal said. "Make sure you get there to enjoy it."

The driver stared back in disbelief at getting off. "I will," he stammered. "I promise."

The police radio crackled again. K-88 waved the driver away and walked back to his car, listening.

"K-79, Gulfport," another trooper called over the radio.

"Go ahead, K-79," the operator replied.

"I need a check on Texas, Adam-John-David-9-4-9-6."

"Ten-four," the operator said.

"K-88, K-79," the radio crackled an instant later.

"Go ahead 88."

"Whatcha got?"

"Two guys speeding." K-79's radar had locked in on a speeder at 72 miles per hour. Since he was driving an unmarked Camaro, K-79 didn't think the driver had noticed him. "Where are you?"

"Mile marker 39 westbound."

"You should be seeing them soon. Dark blue Ford pickup. Tool box. I'm at 43 Eastbound just behind them."

"I'll find ya."

K-79 switched on the dashboard blue light and a second later, in the rearview mirror, he saw K-88's lights swinging around on the median grass behind him, waiting for a break in the traffic to cross the three lanes of cars. The pickup slowed down, pulling onto the shoulder.

"Gulfport, K-79."

"Go ahead."

"Texas, Adam-John-David-9-4-9-6 comes back to an '89 Ford pickup, red in color, registered to Blaine Coyle, 828 Via Lobos, Port Arthur, Texas. Tag expired last December."

"Thank you, ma'am," K-79 said, making a note of the name.

K-79 walked slowly to the cab, checking the truck bed as he approached. The paint job looked quite new—shiny and hard—except on the rim of the truck bed near the tool box where it had been scratched repeatedly.

"Can I see your license, sir," K-79 asked the driver, a young man with dark hair and eyes.

"Was I speeding?" he asked.

"Seventy-three in a sixty-five," K-79 said.

"Pretty strict," the young man mumbled, stretching to pull his wallet out of his back pocket.

K-88 had reached the scene and parked with his bar lights flashing.

He approached the passenger's side. The passenger, a portly man in his forties, with a well-established mustache and a three-day-old beard, rolled down his window and waited for K-88 to speak. When K-88 remained silent, the man asked, "Is there something wrong, officer?"

"Speeding, I believe," K-88 said.

The driver handed his license to K-79. Michael Teunens, 604 Belmont Avenue, Port Arthur, TX. K-79 pulled out his radio and called in the information for a records check.

"Could I see your registration?"

The driver reached across to the glove compartment. Both K-79 and K-88 moved back a couple of steps, keeping the glove box in view and unsnapping their holsters as a precaution. The driver pulled out a plastic case—one of those wallets with the car dealer's name splashed across it in gold—and picked out one of the slips of paper stuffed in the pocket.

K-79 looked it over. It matched the information he'd already gotten. He checked the license again.

"Who is this Blaine Coyle?"

"A friend of mine," the driver said.

"Why are you driving his truck?"

"He moved and I'm helping him—driving the truck."

"Did you know the tag was expired?"

"No, sir," the driver answered.

"And the color's different from the registration."

"I don't know about that. He's had this awhile and it's always been this color."

"Would you step out of the truck, please?" K-79 asked, nodding to K-88.

K-88 waited until the driver was in the patrol car and leaned toward the passenger. "So where are you two headed?"

The passenger rubbed his beard, before answering, "Atlanta."

"Your friend move there?"

"Ah," the passenger hesitated, "Yes."

"So where are you headed?" K-79 said, once they were in his car and he was writing out the ticket.

"Tallahassee," the driver answered.

"Is that where your friend moved to?"

"Yes, sir," the driver said, extremely deferential in tone. "I wish you'd reconsider the speeding ticket, officer. I haven't had a ticket in a long while."

"Wait here a minute."

The two troopers met in between the two cars. "My guy says they're going to Atlanta," K-88 said.

"Mine says Tallahassee."

"Did you see the scratches near the tool box?"

K-79 nodded. "It's been moved around a lot."

"Think you can get a consent to search?"

K-79 nodded again. "The kid's nervous. I think he'll sign."

▪▪▪▪

Three days into The Blitz, Tom was watching the six o'clock evening news in his office, a Budweiser in one hand while his other explored the smooth, stockinged thigh of his secretary, Ginger Silven, a very pretty blonde in her early twenties. These evening "work" sessions had been increasing of late as Tom found any excuse at all not to be home. Fortuitously, Ann and Jesse had left that morning, a spur-of-the-moment visit to her sister in Oregon.

Tom had a trip to Belize scheduled for a few weeks from then but he jumped at this opportunity and called Hector about moving a load while Ann was gone. Hector was eager to accommodate him. They had lost nearly fifty kilos to cops over the past week, and his distributors, greedy for more, wanted to keep the flow going. Tom was leaving at dawn.

Disengaging his hand from Ginger's leg, he sat up straight, set down his beer and, taking a plastic baggie of powder from his pocket, tapped out a small amount on the glass tabletop, and began mincing four lines of cocaine with a razor blade. Using a tightly rolled dollar bill, he snorted a line up one nostril then handed the bill to Ginger, who snorted both of her lines.

The television footage showed large amounts of narcotics being pulled from an airplane as Tim Cropley commented on the recent criminal case. "United States Attorney Alex Markham convicted two major players in the narcotics trade today."

The footage switched to Cropley's stand-up interview of Alex at the federal courthouse. Behind Alex, two men were being led away in handcuffs. Ginger gave the rolled bill back to Tom and he snorted his other line.

"Will this be an effective move?" Cropley inquired.

"I certainly hope so," Alex replied. "Taking out key figures is the only way to end drug trafficking. Seizing drugs can be an excellent tool, but without convicting the main suppliers, seizures are no more than interruptions in the flow." Alex closed his comments with his I-mean-business look.

The cameras switched to Cropley's coanchor. "In a related matter, troopers stopped a motorist near Hopkins on a routine speeding violation last night, and found fifty pounds of cocaine in a hidden compartment underneath the toolbox mounted on the rear of a truck. The driver and his passenger are in jail awaiting arraignment."

Tom suddenly stood up and started pacing about his office nervously. "Hopkins is a two-bit town near the Coast. The goddamn cops are everywhere." Tom ran his hands through his hair, agitated. "They'll be doing 'routine' house inspections if we let them."

"This stuff's making you paranoid, Honey," said Ginger, using her sexiest voice to distract him. "You're imagining things."

Tom turned her way and plopped back down on the couch. "Well, I guess I'm not imagining you, that's for sure. Too bad you get seasick, we could have had a great week on my boat."

▪▪▪▪

The Blitz was in its last hour, a success by every measurement. The number of arrests and the amounts of narcotics and currency seized were startling, even to seasoned veterans of the drug war. Sealing off the state with parallel roadblocks on every interstate had worked like a charm, and the teams had snatched up felons at every location. At two in the morning, in the I-20 rest area, just over the Mississippi River from Louisiana, troopers were checking the last truck.

The taillights on the trailer weren't working, a violation that gave them authority to do a full-safety inspection. The driver was a white guy in his early twenties, decently dressed, though by his accent and speech, not very well educated. Everyone was tired, and they were going to let him go with only a warning, when Zorro, a Black Labrador narcotics dog, became excited when he was walked by the truck on a lead.

Disgruntled by the delay, the driver reluctantly unlocked the back door, revealing a three-foot-high load of fifty-pound bags of onions. Zorro's handler stood by the front end of the trailer, holding a metal reflecting plate for the trooper to test the outside length of the trailer with her laser measuring device. Vaulting up into the trailer, the trooper pointed the laser gun at the back wall, checked the reading, then glanced skeptically at the driver.

"Your interior wall's about two and a half feet into the trailer," she said. "What's the deal?"

"I dunno, ma'am," the man answered, kicking some gravel with his boot toe, then rearing back, his hands across his chest. "This isn't my trailer. I was gonna have to deadhead back East when I got this job. Hooked her up and never opened the lock till now."

The trooper began shifting bags of onions to make her way to the back wall, but when she threw one on the pile, another slid down to block her path. Exasperated, she turned to the driver. "Well, you need to unload."

"I cain't unload this thang."

"Have it your way," the trooper said. "The dog'll happily climb over. Your choice."

"Well, that dog better not damage anythang," the driver said.

The trooper peered around the end of the trailer. "Bring Zorro up here, will ya?"

"Wait a minute," the driver began.

"Change your mind?"

The driver looked at the trailer, then the dog, and then at the trooper, towering over all of them, her hands on her gun belt.

"I don't care," the man said, walking a few feet away and dropping down onto the curb.

Several feet from the back of the truck, the handler took off Zorro's lead and in one leap, the dog was in the trailer. Zorro scrambled over the onions and pawed madly at the back wall, hind legs sliding down among the bags with every move, steadily barking. The trooper nodded to the handler, and on command, Zorro scrambled back over the bags, jumped out, and sat patiently while his lead was reattached.

"I think you have a problem here, sir," she said.

■ ■ ■ ■

By 5:30 A.M., the tractor-trailer rig was in the shop at headquarters. Despite the fact that neither had slept in twenty-four hours, Blake and Robert were right in the middle of everything, the prospect of solving the puzzle giving them a second wind. The onions had been unloaded into the Patrol moving van, and a swarm of people were busy figuring out how the front wall of the rig was fastened to the frame. Cutting it out was an absolute last resort. No self-respecting trooper ever admitted not being clever enough to figure how some sleaze-bag dope dealer had hidden his stuff. That—and the possibility of hidden explosives—kept them trying.

The driver, who claimed to know absolutely nothing about the load, watched silently, a trooper at his side. The fake wall was heavily laminated fiberglass that looked like the front of the truck. The cargo ties were the same as the ones on the side walls, but the rivets weren't holding the wall in place, something else was. But even with the power to the trailer cut off, the wall still wouldn't budge.

"Could it have been dropped in from the roof?" Blake asked. "I just read about some rig where they'd peeled back the roof and slid the panel down a track."

"Doubt it," Robert said. "It's curved at its edges so it wouldn't slide. I bet this thing has got electro-magnets holding it, like the security doors in the main building. Probably running off of a car battery on the other side. There has to be a switch somewhere—we just can't see it."

Robert looked at a communications technician standing nearby. "Find us a compass and some tape will ya?"

Two other troopers started through the cab again, looking for anything that could be a switch, while two more searched the underside of the trailer with flashlights. Blake moved the compass over every square inch of the fiberglass wall to find the magnets while Robert followed behind him, inspecting the surface for irregularities on the surface that might hide a switch.

It didn't take long. The magnetic fields were strong enough that withing minutes he'd marked five points with tape where the compass had moved—one in each corner, and one in the middle. Robert had found a tiny circle, not more than a quarter-inch in diameter, very cleverly hidden with some sort of bonding material. He carefully scratched off the covering of a tiny audio jack, the same size as a standard set of Walkman headphones.

"Are there any headsets in the cab? Ones with a small jack?" Robert called from the end of the trailer.

"Yeah," a trooper called back. "New ones, still in the box."

"Bring 'em back here, will ya?"

Robert, with the jack poised in his hand, started to insert it when Blake said, "I wouldn't do that if I were you."

Robert stopped immediately.

"They did a skillful job here," Blake said. "What if these skillful people also wired the thing to explode if it's not opened up correctly?"

"Not likely—their own people could make a mistake if it was too fancy," Robert said. "But I guess we oughta get away from the building and rig up an extension."

They moved the trailer to the far end of the back lot, tying ropes to the fake cargo ties. Using a hundred foot extension, Robert was about to do the honors again when a young trooper arrived in full riot gear—the closest they had to bomb removal gear.

"I'll do it, sir," he said. When everyone was out of the way, the trooper inserted the jack without any trouble and they tugged on the ropes. The wall moved.

Packed in as tight as possible were hundreds of kilo packages of white powder. Blake secured the area, organized the inventorying and then sent a trooper hurrying down the hill to the crime lab with a sample for testing. Robert took the driver off for questioning, and Blake called Laura.

▪ ▪ ▪ ▪

On his way to make morning coffee, Tim Cropley flicked on the police scanner. It locked into the Jackson Police Department chatter about a wreck on the interstate and the traffic tie-up. Then silence, while the receiver jumped to another channel.

"Biggest bust in the history of the state, I heard," came a different voice.

Cropley locked the channel in, then looked at the frequency, checking it against the list Alex had given him. It was the State Patrol car-to-car channel.

"Yeah, and wouldn't you know a female trooper would get the credit."

"No, no, no. The pooch gets this one. C-81 was going to give up. The dog tipped them off."

"Well, if A-Adam has anything to do with it, wanna bet C-81 gets the credit?"

The voices crackled. "You're breaking up. Catch you at coffee."

Cropley hit scan again and the frequency switched to State Patrol headquarters channel. It was silent. The scanner moved on again.

Cropley smiled. He was a face, a good-looking, smooth-talking, ambitious, face. A couple of years before, Alex Markham had given Cropley a tip on a DEA drug bust to see what he'd do. Cropley instinctively knew how to play that game—the report aired with Alex's name and photo as a prominent part of the story. So Alex fed Cropley more, and since then, they'd exchanged countless bits of information, often about Laura Owen and her maneuvers. Cropley picked up the phone and punched in a number from memory.

"Good morning, Alex, this is Cropley. Hope I didn't wake you."

"No, just about to head out actually," Alex said. "What's up?"

"I just picked up some patrol chatter on the scanner. Something about the biggest bust in history. A female trooper—C-81, I think—was involved."

"News to me," Alex said. "They've been throwing those roadblocks up for days now, but I thought it was over last night."

"Well, sounds like they caught a big one on the last truck."

"Thanks for the tip," Alex said. "I'll beep you when I learn something."

"Think about trying to break something yourself," Cropley said. "I can see an avalanche of Laura Owen stories coming."

▪ ▪ ▪ ▪

Still scribbling figures and facts on her notes, Laura stepped off the elevator into the lobby. Since early morning the phones and faxes had been ringing constantly with requests for interviews and information about The Blitz. A press conference was the only logical way to handle the inundation.

The Senate Oversight investigator came out of the other elevator a moment later and caught Laura before she went through the front doors.

"Commissioner..."

"Good afternoon," Laura said, working up a polite smile. "Coming to the press conference?"

"No, I've got lots to do upstairs."

"But this is what your audit is all about," Laura said. "Drug interdiction."

"Thanks, but I'll pass on the hype," the man said. "Could you ask accounting to release travel records?"

"For every employee?" Laura asked.

"No, actually, I only want yours."

Laura forced herself not to scowl at him. "Of course."

"And the Patrol flight logs."

"Of course. Is this about something in particular?" Laura asked.

"Just doing my job," he smirked.

"Refresh my memory," Laura said. "Just what is it you do?"

The investigator smiled confidently. "I protect the taxpayers' money, Ms. Owen. You should remember something about that."

"Well, by contrast, we protect the taxpayers. I dare say what we do here is useful. Good afternoon."

A small podium had been erected next to the eighteen-wheeler, with a large state map on the other side. Inside the trailer, stacked against the left wall, were bales of hay and white boxes to display as graphically as possible the amount of narcotics seized during The Blitz. Electric lights had been rigged to illuminate not only the hay and boxes, but the false panel. TV cameras scanned the scene as a trooper demonstrated how the panel operated.

Every news agency—radio, television, and print—was present, and Tim Cropley was standing front and center as Laura confidently approached the podium. If the Senate investigator had timed his confrontation to throw her off her stride, he missed his mark completely. Her anger only intensified her delivery.

"This morning, we concluded The Blitz as we've called this operation," Laura said. "For two weeks, troopers have been stopping smugglers all over the state. Last night, with the help of local sheriffs and deputies, we capped off the efforts with a simultaneous roadblock of every interstate. The results are frightening.

"Over the three-week period, we confiscated fifteen hundred thirty kilos of cocaine, six hundred pounds of marijuana, and more than two-hundred-and-fifty-thousand dollars. We also arrested eighty-seven felons, three hundred drunk drivers, and issued more than two thousand misdemeanor citations.

"The message is clear. This state is a landing strip for Central and South American drug operations. It's a highway for narcotics, and it's filled with their criminal activity. Let there be no mistake about it: In Mississippi we don't like criminals, we don't like narcotics, and to the best of my ability, I'll see that we show them no mercy. We intend to make it harder and harder for dopers to operate in this state."

"Ms. Owen, is smuggling increasing?" a reporter asked.

"Not necessarily, but enforcement interdiction is," Laura said.

Cropley stepped forward. "Haven't highway deaths soared while you've concentrated on smuggling? Aren't you ignoring your duties?"

"No, Mr. Cropley, I'm not." Laura's impatience with him showed. "Highway deaths have not soared—in fact, they've declined. Seeing troopers on the road—even working drugs—makes people behave."

He put his hand up for a follow-up question but Laura ignored him and motioned to the woman behind him.

13

Unlike the understaffed and underfunded Gulf Coast Surveillance Center, the Security Room of the Gulf Goddess Casino was throbbing with activity around the clock. All four walls were covered with TV monitors. Two operators wearing headsets sat at consoles, each with three separate monitors, a bank of switches, zoom controls for the camera lenses, and built-in video recorders. Every square inch of the casino could be monitored and filmed. Floor walkers and pit bosses radioed messages alerting operators to significant action so they could record big payoffs and heavy betting.

The security operators also warned floor people about suspicious things they had noticed. The zoom lenses on the money cages could get in so close that the serial numbers on currency were clearly readable. From the floor, with so many cameras with wide-angled lenses, it was impossible to tell what was being watched at any particular moment.

Olivia Alvarez, director of surveillance for the Goddess, had quit the FBI after she realized all the headquarters hype about fairness and equal opportunity was just that, hype. It would be a total long shot for her to get promoted to any significant level. When casinos started popping up, she began applying for positions, perfectly qualified for their needs. In addition to her background, Olivia just happened to present exactly the image owners wanted—tall, slender, but commanding. She'd had plenty of offers.

Much to Olivia's liking, surveillance reported directly to the owners, not to the general manager. The owners wanted surveillance watching the general manager as well as all the other employees. And, of course, the general manager tried to keep track of surveillance. The owners sat back, the beneficiaries of rampant paranoia.

Olivia took her job very seriously, watching out for more than the routine stealing that plagued all the boats. Back in the summer, when the

FBI agent on the Coast, Chris Salkin, brought her three Gulf Goddess checks picked up at an interstate roadblock, her antennae went up. The checks were all under ten thousand dollars, and all issued the same night to the same guy.

Not surprisingly, there weren't any incidents listed in the operator's logs for that night. Most of the time, the surveillance operators watched the cages for stealing and didn't pay attention to much else. Olivia went back through the check registers to pinpoint transactions then watched the corresponding videotapes. It had taken weeks to put it all together, but she was certain she'd found something significant.

Olivia called Salkin back. Even though she'd left the Bureau in disgust, once an agent, always an agent, and Chris was young enough not to be steeped in the old FBI ways. He was a decent sort, nowhere near as arrogant as some agents could be. To Salkin's disappointment, he hadn't worked many cases on the boats—most illegal activity in the casinos was state stuff, not federal. So he jumped at the mention of money laundering—that was something right up his alley.

As they watched the monitors on the cages, Olivia provided the running commentary.

"Now here's a guy, he's a regular high roller poker player, and he's been at it all day, cashing out at $9,568, just under the $10,000 currency reporting floor. He's in here once a month or so. He probably arrived with five or six thousand and he's made three or four more—a pretty decent return, I'd say."

"I take it that's standard practice, cashing out under the floor?"

Olivia nodded. "Happens all day long, and although I don't like it, there's nothing illegal about it. What I'm worried about though, is people coming in with a lot of cash, not playing much—if at all—and then leaving with a check."

"You think that's happening?" Chris said.

"I know so."

"What have you done about it?"

"All I've done so far is watch and tighten controls a little," Olivia said. "I'm keeping a database of the checks issued, and I've set up a procedure so that if a person cashes out, asking for a check more than once a week, the cage teller must get the general manager's okay on the check request."

She slipped another videotape in and pointed to a monitor. "Now, watch this collection of transactions that I've spliced together. These all took place last month. This fellow comes in with bundles of cash and buys big chips. We see him playing the slots for a while, but he never touches the chips. An hour or two later, he cashes out with the same teller, taking a check with him. A couple of days later, same guy, same routine, same teller. He's just washing his money."

"Did the teller get the manager's okay?"

"No, and this guy only comes in when that teller is here. On the rare occasions when he's come and the teller hasn't been working, whoever was on duty has gotten permission from the manager, and the guy has left with a check. They've all been deposited to a local bank account."

"What else do you know about the teller?" Chris asked.

"Not much. He had a clean background, but that really doesn't mean anything. That's why I called you. Think you could check him out?"

"It would be a pleasure."

▪ ▪ ▪ ▪

"Is Robert in there?" Laura asked the fifth floor receptionist, looking toward Robert's door, which stood nearly closed.

"He was five minutes ago," she said.

"Is someone with him?"

"Don't think so, Commissioner, I'd just knock."

Laura didn't see Robert immediately. He wasn't at his desk, but his loafers and socks were on the floor. As she opened the door slightly, his legs came into view and Laura saw he was bent over in a peculiar way, so she knocked.

"Yes?" Robert asked, his voice strangely thick.

"Are you busy?" Laura asked, hesitant to proceed further.

"Come on in," Robert said. "I'm at the end of my five minute relaxation series."

Robert's hands were on the floor, several feet in front of his bare feet and his body was arched, completing a triangle with the floor.

"I'll be done in about thirty seconds," he said, panting slightly. "This stretches my hamstrings, arms, everything."

"Is this something you do for running?"

"It's a yoga pose," Robert said. When his watch beeped, he stood up, very carefully. "Great relaxation technique. You oughta try it."

"How long have you been doing it?"

"Ten, twelve years probably. Rachel turned me on to it," Robert said, picking up his shoes and socks, and sitting down. "She took it up when we were trying to have kids. She was totally stressed out at the University Medical Center, and went to visit her sister in Los Angeles. Came back with a new diet and yoga to deal with the stress. Five minutes in the afternoon gives me a second wind, every day."

"I could use something, that's for sure," said Laura, positioning her long, full skirt so she could lean back modestly with her feet pushing against the rim of the desk. Then waving a microcassette tape, she added, "I've listened to this over and over but it rings no bells. I racked my brain all last night and I still can't place it."

She flipped the cassette toward him.

"When did it come in?" Robert asked, pulling out his own recorder/ tape player.

"Last night."

"Did you call the phone company?"

"Right away," Laura said.

"Did Blake give you the low-down on the locations of the earlier calls?" Robert asked.

Laura nodded. "That Memphis call, was it from a white or black section of the city?"

"Neither. Stuckey's near the interstate," Robert said. "They've all been from shopping centers, truck stops—busy places. I'll get someone to map them out for you. We think he's white, but as much as he screws up his voice, no one's sure."

"Well," Laura said, "I think you're right. See if you agree after you listen to this one."

Robert punched on the tape.

"'Hello?'" Laura said.

"'Halloween's coming,'" the caller said. "'Better watch who you trick and who you treat."

"'Who is this?'" Laura demanded.

"'For me to know and you to guess,'" the man rasped.

"That's all he said."

"It's clearer than some," Robert said, rewinding the tape to listen again. "But I sure don't recognize it."

"Isn't there some equipment that analyzes voices?"

"In *James Bond* movies maybe, but not in the real world."

"Well, he doesn't scare me anymore," Laura said, "Now it's annoying me more than anything."

"I don't want you to get lulled into a false sense of security," Robert said.

"I won't," Laura said, "I assure you."

She took her feet off the desk and stood to leave. "So does Rachel give yoga lessons?"

"I can ask her," Robert said.

"Don't do it quite yet," Laura said, shying away now that she'd thought about what she'd asked. "Exercise is a big step."

"I've got a great book I can loan you. It's got beginner's work-outs, great pictures, easy to follow."

"That's more my style," Laura said.

■■■■

On a crisp October afternoon several weeks later, Alex stood at the edge of the seventeenth green of the Capitol Country Club watching Senator Gabriel Collel putt. Ever since they'd met that day at Dinsmor, Alex had more actively cultivated his friendship. Collel always seemed happy to accept his invitations to play golf, and Capitol had a prettier and much better maintained course than his own club in the Delta. They settled into a pattern of playing every month and usually resisted bringing a third person along so they'd be free to scheme about politics. Collel scheduled Senate committee meetings for the morning with a working lunch, then met Alex at the club for their game, collecting per diem and travel expenses for the trip.

Collel sank his putt easily. "What's Owen really like? She seems like a pit bull to me."

"I've known her a long time," Alex said, stepping up for his shot. "Since first semester in college, if you can imagine."

Alex lined up his ball. It wasn't a long or difficult shot, but he didn't want to miss. "On the outside she is a pit bull, but..." a sneer spread across his face, "she's a marshmallow inside. I think her husband's death scraped several inches off her elephant hide. It doesn't take much to rattle her these days." Alex made his putt and pulled his ball out of the cup, swallowing the urge for a little victory gesture.

"Is she still planning on running?" Collel asked as they headed toward the eighteenth tee.

"That's the sixty-four thousand dollar question," Alex said.

"Actually, it's a million-dollar question," Collel quipped. "You'd save at least that much without a hotly contested primary."

"She's not soliciting money, at least not that I've heard," Alex said. "But that wouldn't really be proper considering how recently her husband died and how early it is."

"Vic Regis, who I've got to assume is talking for Carver, is pushing her behind the scenes, talking up her abilities and accomplishments every chance he gets."

"I'm so sick of hearing about The Blitz," Alex added.

Collel looked puzzled by his remark.

"You know, the narcotics sweep last month—roadblocks everywhere. Big load of dope in an eighteen-wheeler."

"Oh, yes," said Collel. "Quite a fuss."

Collel stepped out to tee off first. "Carver's only touting her glories because she's his commitment to women. He does it with his black appointees, too."

"As far as I can tell, there are only two things she cares about," Alex said. "Her son, Will, and the State Patrol."

Collel looked at Alex. "Well, your father and I were raised in the same school of politics. Neither of us believes in taking anything for granted. I'll handle the Patrol. In fact, I've already started."

Alex looked intrigued.

"I spent the morning in a closed-door session with the Oversight Committee staff," Collel said, "sharpening my knives for Owen's budget hearing next week."

Collel teed off and drove his ball straight down the fairway. As he stepped away, he added, "But I must give the devil her due, this won't be easy. From what they said this morning, she's playing it pretty safe—not the complete disaster everyone expected. But she's being totally bull-headed about not fixing tickets, and it's cost her a lot of friends."

Alex teed up, taking three practice swings before settling in for his shot. His ball landed in the rough, not far from where Collel's ball lay.

"But I've got my sources," Collel continued. "They'll turn up something."

Collel made certain the communication channels were always open so if and when Laura did falter, he'd find out about it immediately. Having been in the Legislature for so many years, he knew every trooper in the Delta, or someone in the trooper's family. Until recently, sheer size and personal recommendations had meant more in the trooper selection process than brains and values. Bill Kenner was walking proof of that. As befitted a beneficiary of Collel's influence, Kenner kept Collel informed about internal Patrol matters. In return, Collel had made certain that Kenner rose through the ranks—a testament to Collel's clout.

Alex smiled. "With the matter in your able hands, I'm not worried in the least."

■ ■ ■ ■

Laura couldn't get warm. She'd been reading to Will as he was going to sleep, and had to stop to get an extra blanket to keep from shivering. Once he closed his eyes, she took the blanket and hurried into the living room to turn up the gas logs and pull her huge oversized reading chair closer to the warmth.

After a few minutes, she ventured out from under the blanket and went to the kitchen to make a cup of chamomile tea with honey. Glancing at the calendar as she passed, she froze, staring at the date.

October 23. Semmes' birthday.

She'd forgotten it.

She took a deep breath, and then another, closing her eyes to get a grip. She was not going to let herself dissolve into tears again. She was tired of crying.

Laura poured a small glass of bourbon instead of waiting for the tea and took a sip immediately. As it slipped down her throat, she felt the tiny but instant prickling of release everywhere in her body, right up to the top of her skull.

She turned off all the lights in the house, and settled back into her chair to watch the flames licking the logs.

"Why me, dammit," she whimpered. "What did I ever do to deserve this loneliness?"

Will called out and Laura leapt to her feet, moving quickly to his door.

In the flickering night light, she could see that he wasn't awake, just babbling in his dreams, a smile on his face.

She sat in the rocking chair where she read to him every night, and watched him. His smile came and went with whatever visions were spinning in his head.

Who will this little boy be when he grows up? Like Semmes, if he's lucky.

She stood up, taking one last look, her eyes glistening.

God help him if he's a weeping, pitiful thing like his mother.

She went back to the fire and her blanket. Another sip of the bourbon and she put the glass down.

This is ridiculous. This must stop. "I can't spend my life like this," she said out loud.

She was only thirty-eight, with at least as many years stretching out before her. But the future was a complete blank. Everything she'd ever imagined had been erased. Except Will.

She shut her eyes to try and summon a vision. Any vision.

She imagined sitting in her office. She liked it, she liked being there.

But that couldn't last forever.

She jumped up to get the magnetic grocery pad from the kitchen, bundled back up in her chair and started a list.

— Open up a law office.

She'd never made any money at it before. If Semmes hadn't supported her, she would have been bankrupt. Not a real option.

— Join a firm.

It depended on which one. Some of them were pretty stuffy and boring. But Hamrick, Bruser, and Stein might hire her—just for her connections.

— Stay at the Patrol.

It was safe, but it might last only another year. Would the next Governor keep her on?

— Political office.

Run for Governor like Vic was always suggesting. Everybody seemed to think it was a done deal anyway. But campaigning would be tough and asking for money would be worse. And it would be hard on Will.

— Lobbying for some cause.

Those legislators wouldn't like her any better probably.

— Teach at the law school.

Good hours. Might be an answer.

— Go back to school.

To do what? Medicine?

— Quit.

There wouldn't be enough money.

But at least there were options. She went back down the list to mark the things that interested her.

— Stay at the Patrol.

— Political office.

— Teach at the law school.

Then she closed her eyes and switched to thinking about where she wanted to live when she was old.

— By the ocean. Or at least a lake, but not Jackson.

That would take money. She'd have to keep working. Quitting wasn't an option. She crossed out that entry.

She slashed through "Open up a law office" and "Go back to school."

She looked up at the Atmos clock on the mantle, endlessly spinning back and forth, powered only by changes in humidity. It was nearly eleven.

A hot shower to get really warm, that's what she needed.

She had to get some sleep. There was work and Will.

14

Tom sailed peacefully toward the U.S. coast, smoking and listening to music. *Next* had handled beautifully from the first sail, taking full advantage of every breeze. When there was a good wind, she skimmed across the water, making excellent time. Hector had begged him to take fifteen hundred kilos, five hundred more than his last load. But Tom had refused, not wanting to lose any of the boat's agility, particularly when he was sailing alone.

A speck on the western horizon grew steadily larger, remarkable only because an early cold spell had cut the number of pleasure boats Tom usually encountered in the Gulf. He trained his binoculars on the approaching vessel. It was moving directly eastward, heading straight for him at top speed. After a few moments, he recognized the flags of a Coast Guard patrol boat. He took one last drag on his cigarette and flicked the butt into the ocean.

"Goddamn, goddamn."

With all the loads he'd moved, he'd been so careful that he'd never had a close call, and that was by design. He worked only for Hector, he quizzed Alex regularly for information, and he only delivered to the hangar. If the Coast Guard were looking for him on a routine matter, they would have tried the radio but they hadn't. This must be something else.

He reached into a storage bin near his feet and, leaning out of sight, pulled out a 9mm automatic and checked the clip. He'd never had occasion to use the thing except for killing a shark near Cuba, but whenever he was near cocaine he kept the gun with him. He put it in the right-hand pocket of his windbreaker and reached in again for the hand grenade Hector had given him and put that in his left pocket. Rather than risk spending a moment in jail, he planned to blow everything to smithereens—himself with it—if necessary.

When the launch drew closer, the air horn sounded and they announced that they were the U.S. Coast Guard. Tom waved, motioning to them to come alongside. When he let the mainsail luff, *Next* stalled in the water. The launch driver cut the engine, and as they drifted toward the boat, Tom stood in his cockpit, holding the wheel. A lieutenant came to the side, a clipboard in hand, all business, ready to write.

"Where are you bound?"

"Ocean Springs, Mississippi," Tom answered.

"Your name, occupation, and address, sir?"

"Tom Hilman, vice president Hilman Air, 214 Mims Circle, Jackson, MS."

"Ship's name?"

"*Next to Last Chance,* Ocean Springs."

"Where did you sail from?"

"Belize," Tom said. "What's this about, Captain?"

"Lieutenant, actually. Routine safety inspections of boats coming in from international waters. May we board?"

"Come ahead."

A seaman swung down onto the deck, then jumped into the cockpit and started looking around. He lifted up cushions and looked in the hatches, counting life preservers, Tom assumed. Tom watched the seaman as closely as possible, holding himself back from blocking the doorway to the cabin.

"I need to check your radios, sir."

Tom had no choice but to let him below. "Sure. Right above the table." He stayed nervously in the cockpit, his hand fingering the grenade. Hector had rigged it with a very short fuse so that the grenade would explode nearly instantly.

"Is this something new, Lieutenant?" Tom asked. "I've made these trips often and no one has ever waved at me, much less inspected."

The Coast Guard radio started squawking in the background. A petty officer approached the Lieutenant.

"With the flood of all these boat people, new policies come down every day."

The officer interrupted them. "Lieutenant, sir, operations wants us to head east immediately. They have a small craft with ten people and children on board."

The Lieutenant nodded and turned back to Tom.

"Sorry to bother you, Mr. Hilman." He called to the seaman, "Smith, we've got to get underway."

"Nice boat, sir," the seaman said as he passed Tom and pulled himself back to the launch. "Bet she handles like a dream."

"She does."

"Have a safe trip home, Mr. Hilman. My apologies again," the Lieutenant added.

Tom waved and sat back down, shaking.

▪▪▪▪

All the way into port and then north to Jackson, Tom mulled over his situation. He could quit right then even though he was short of his financial goal. Or he could take one more load, maybe a double load although that might be pushing *Next*'s capacity. Or given that the odds of being searched more than once in one year were very slim indeed, he could blow off this incident as an aberration and continue with the two scheduled loads.

But he couldn't stop worrying. By Hattiesburg, he was brimming with both anger and fear, all mixed up, uncertain about which one he should be feeling. When he reached Jackson, he'd decided two things— he wasn't going to quit short of his goal, and it was time to play his Alex card.

Alex opened his front door with a flourish, glad to see him. "Man, am I sorry I couldn't make the trip."

"Pretty exciting, actually," Tom said.

"Great winds?"

"Yes and no," Tom said. "I got searched by the Coast Guard."

"What?"

Tom's anger, pent up for too long, exploded with Alex's question. "They said it was some sort of routine safety inspection, but that's bullshit. It's never happened in all the times I've come into U.S. waters. It's some part of your goddamn war on drugs. Where does it end? Next they'll be inspecting my house because I make international phone calls."

"Calm down," Alex said. "Why's this such a big deal?"

Tom looked him square in the eyes. "Because there were a thousand kilos of cocaine in the boat, that's why."

Alex's mouth formed the question "What?" but no sound came out.

Still fierce, Tom growled, "And you're gonna make sure it doesn't happen again between now and March."

Alex looked at him in disbelief. "Get one thing straight, Tom, I'm not about to get involved with drug smuggling."

Tom smiled slyly. "Wanna bet?"

"What are you talking about?" Alex said. "I'm the United States Attorney, I prosecute drug couriers, I don't help them out."

"But I'm different."

"You may be my friend, but friendship goes only so far."

"I call it mutually assured discretion," Tom said.

"What's so damn mutual about it?" Alex answered. "You've got nothin' on me."

"Oh, yes, I do."

"What, that business with your father's truck?" Alex scoffed.

"Uh-huh." Tom wandered into the kitchen and got himself a beer from the refrigerator.

"That was over fifteen years ago," Alex protested.

"And the guy you killed is still dead," Tom replied.

Alex watched him chug some beer, grasping for a reply. "Sorry man, no witnesses except yourself."

"You need to pay more attention to details, Alex."

"Like what?"

"Like the beer can covered with your prints that was left lying next to the body."

Alex stared at Tom, incredulous. Fingerprint evidence had never occurred to him.

"I've never forgotten that night," Tom said. "Never forgotten that kid's face, and never forgotten your pushing his body away like he was some kind of roadkill. All the way back to Jackson, and for months and months after that, I couldn't stop replaying the scene—like a damn videotape in slow motion. Every image, every movement."

"Jesus, Tom, why did you make such a big deal out of it?" Alex said, "It was a damn accident, for Christ's sake."

"You probably never even read the papers to find out who the guy was."

Alex shook his head.

"Well, he was a Vietnam vet, decorated for bravery, had three little children, and was working two jobs to feed them."

"It was an accident."

"Yeah, but you didn't own up to what you'd done."

"We didn't own up," said Alex, bitterly emphasizing the *we*. "So what are you going to do? Testify against me?"

"Don't need to," Tom said. "I'm sure your fingerprints are on file as a result of your job. I just have to point the way."

Hatred, or something akin to it, filled Alex's eyes. Then it suddenly transformed into confidence. "Bullshit. The case file was thrown out years ago."

Tom had no earthly idea if the file was still around, the possibility that unsolved cases would be destroyed hadn't crossed his mind.

"I don't think so," was all Tom could muster.

Alex gave him a go-to-hell smile, but it faded as Tom pulled a small tape recorder out of his pocket and flipped it on to hear Alex's voice, loud and distinct. "You ought to run drugs. It's a very profitable business, and if you did it right, it wouldn't be that risky."

"You asshole," Alex growled.

Tom pulled an envelope from his pocket and started flipping through a series of stills from the videotape showing Alex at the helm with the black bag on the deck of *Last Chance,* as well as some choice photos of Alex with his lovely Belize companion—all date-stamped. "My largesse with regard to your father's Better Government Fund, and my deeper-than-normal discounts for your building materials on these house renovations, ought to add quite a lot to the story. Not to mention that you were an incorporator of Hilman Development where I've parked all the cash."

"You said that was a real estate deal."

"It was, until something better came along."

Alex was seething, much to Tom's delight.

"Mutually assured discretion, my man," Tom said, "mutually assured discretion."

"So how many goddamn trips are you going to make?"

"Depends. Two tops, maybe only one."

"How long have you been doing this?"

"I agreed to ten trips. But when I got the bigger boat I was able to double up my loads. So far, I've made four runs, two with you aboard."

"You bastard," Alex growled. "Why not quit now? Too damn greedy?"

"That's for me to know," Tom answered. "Let's just say, by February, I'm history. I'll sail away, and you can either choose to visit or forget me."

Frantically, Alex sized up where he stood. "Is 'mutually assured discretion' all I get out of this?"

"Why?"

Alex rocked back on his heels, his hands folded tightly across his chest, ready to make a better deal. "Maybe you could help make my bargain with the devil a little more palatable."

"What do you want?" Tom asked.

"Laura Owen," Alex said. "I need her out of my life—scared, disgraced, anything."

"Let me think about it," Tom said. "I can probably come up with something."

■ ■ ■ ■

The week before Thanksgiving, the Senate Appropriations Committee met in a large, grand room, that had formerly housed the State Supreme Court. The most senior senators sat in high-backed chairs behind the bench with Senator Gabriel Collel at the chairman's right hand. The junior members were gathered around additional tables in front. Off to the side, with easy access to the legislators, sat the staffers, including the Oversight Committee investigators.

Laura, flanked by Blake and Robert, was addressing the committee from the witness table. The audience was filled with reporters, troopers, and a few spectators.

"In the few months since we began narcotics interdiction, we have accomplished startling results, but it has not been without tremendous effort and troopers' working scores of extra hours each month. We have 502 troopers now and we desperately need to bring the Patrol to its full strength of 581. But if we aren't given more positions for troopers, then we must have enough money for overtime to adequately compensate these men and women for their extra work as well as for the outstanding job they're doing under very dangerous circumstances."

Senator Collel interrupted Laura's testimony, pointing at her and speaking in a sarcastic drawl. "And you're taking full credit for every bit of their success aren't you, Madame Commissioner?"

Laura returned Collel's glare. "No, sir. I don't take credit for anything other than setting the course and finding the tools they need. I've publicized what the Patrol does with every breath. It's the only way that citizens can..."

"Spare me, please, I've heard your spiel." Collel picked up some papers and looked at them over his reading glasses. "Let's talk about expenditures. As you no doubt know," he smiled, "our auditors have compiled information on your operations. Tell me about how you purchased your narcotics dogs."

"We used funds seized from smugglers."

"And how much have you taken from smugglers, Madame Commissioner?"

"More than fifteen hundred kilos of cocaine ...."

"Not narcotics, Mrs. Owen, money. How much money did you seize?"

"You have to remember that seizing funds is inextricably intertwined with seizing narcotics. Some days we get the guy on his way to a deal and sometimes we get him coming back..."

Collel interrupted. "Answer my question, please. How much money?"

"I am trying to tell you, sir." Laura's voice was flat and direct. "More than eight-hundred-thousand dollars to date, though not all of that has been awarded to us. All forfeitures are handled by the United States Attorney, and we file reports on all expenditures."

"Do you have Legislative authorization to spend these funds?"

Several of the troopers in the audience shifted nervously in their seats. This was the first time they'd witnessed the sort of scrutiny Laura was under, and they were appalled.

Laura hesitated. "Ahh, yes, sir...." She looked down at her notebook. "Under the federal guidelines for the asset forfeiture program..."

"I don't give a damn about federal guidelines," Collel interrupted.

"You can seize all you want, but you can't spend a dime of it unless we authorize it." He looked at his colleagues, confident and expansive. "This is nothing more than a Robin Hood slush fund to finance your own very high-profile publicity campaign."

Robert and Blake stared in disbelief at Collel.

"No, sir, you are mistaken," Laura said. "Every cent spent to date has gone for equipment and narcotics interdiction operations."

"Madame, I'm not mistaken. For instance, you've purchased more than one-hundred-fifty-thousand dollars worth of electronic equipment."

"Yes, our old communications system was built in the Dark Ages, and we needed to bring it into the twentieth century as fast as possible. With budgeted funds and seized funds, we're not asking for a budget increase in that category this year..."

"Well, if everything's for the troopers, why have six telephone tape recorders been purchased for your home and your offices?" Collel sneered.

Laura could feel crimson flush her face, ashamed that her reaction was so obvious. "I've had a series of threatening phone calls, and we're attempting to identify the caller."

"Who else do you record?"

"I would never record normal calls."

Collel spat back, "That's not what I've heard, Mrs. Owen. Your troopers are taping all the citizens they stop, and now you're taping everyone who calls your office or your home."

"I object, sir. Troopers tape their stops to defend themselves from accusations of misconduct. There have already been a number of instances where those recordings proved the officer had explicit permission to search a vehicle. To infer something underhanded is not only ridiculous but cruel. You ask these people to do dangerous work, yet you won't allow them to protect themselves with something as harmless as a tape recorder."

"Tape recorders are hardly harmless, Madame." He turned to address the rest of the committee. "I have no further questions at this time, but Mr. Chairman, I call for more in-depth investigation before this committee goes any further with this particular appropriation."

"I second that motion," said one of the other senators, smiling at

Collel as he spoke.

The Chairman, caught completely off guard and disturbed by the turn the hearing had taken, looked at Laura.

"This Committee will stand in recess. Commissioner, please remain available to provide additional information.

"Of course, sir. I'm always ready to cooperate."

■ ■ ■ ■

In the hallway, reporters besieged Laura. Tim Cropley moved in first. "Do you record conversations with senators and representatives?"

Paying no attention to the rolling TV cameras, Laura glared at him. "I'm trying to catch someone who's threatening me. Don't I have a right to protect myself?"

"So you do record calls," Cropley said. "Are there any controls over your slush fund?"

Laura stifled her irritation as best possible. "It's not a slush fund. All seized funds have been plowed back into narcotics smuggling interdiction efforts."

"Except for recording devices," Cropley reminded her.

Laura turned and walked away from him. The other reporters were left empty-handed, angry that Cropley had monopolized the time.

■ ■ ■ ■

"I want to catch the 6:00 P.M. news and see what's carried out of all that blather we listened to," Blake said.

"What's their problem with her?" Robert asked, picking up the pace as they walked across the State Capitol parking lot to his car. The soft glow through the glass ceilings of the two legislative chambers illuminated the outline of the building against the dark blue evening sky.

"She told us she'd jumped on Collel once about travel expenses when she was at the State Auditor's office. What goes around, comes around, I guess."

"You think that's it?" Robert asked.

"As petty as people can be, it might not be anything more than that."

"But this is hurting the Patrol," Robert said, cranking the engine. "Collel's always been a supporter."

"When he gets his way, and his tickets get fixed."

Robert shook his head. There was nothing more to say.

"Pitiful, isn't it," Blake said.

"Two can play the game," Robert said.

"How, without pissing them off more than they are?" Blake asked. "You forget, our pay raises are on their chopping block."

"We can't leave her out there to twist in the wind," Robert said.

"I know we can't," Blake answered. "But it beats me how to fight back this time. And I've given it a lot of thought, believe me."

"Now that's saying something—Blake Coleman, stumped."

▪ ▪ ▪ ▪

The lights were out in the waiting area of the Governor's office in the Capitol and the door was locked, but on the chance that Vic was working late, Laura let herself in the side door. Every office was deserted, but stopping at a telephone, she saw one line lit up.

She punched in another button and dialed her house.

"I'm running late tonight, Mom," Laura said. "I hate that you've come to visit and I'm stuck at work."

"Well, you're not the only one I came to see. This little boy grows two inches every time I see him."

"How's Will doing?"

"Fine. Why don't I take him to Piccadilly for dinner and you don't worry about rushing home," Charlotte Hemeter said.

"It would help a lot."

"Is something wrong?"

"You can watch the news and see it. I had a bit of a confrontation over my budget today."

"Don't worry about Will. We'll be fine."

"I'll try to get home by 7:30. He needs a bath."

"I can get that started."

"Thanks, Mom."

The light went out on Vic's line just as she hung up. A moment later, she heard a door open at the other end of the maze of little offices and cubicles creatively squeezed into the space allotted for the Governor.

"Hello?" Vic called.

"It's me, Laura," she said, moving toward his office.

Vic stood at his door, his white shirt wrinkled after a long day, sleeves rolled up, and his tie loose and slightly askew. He smiled. "Come on in.

How'd it go with the press after the hearing?"

"You were there?"

"For the hearing, yes. I had to get back and catch Carver before he left for the Mansion."

"Cropley came after me."

"Not unexpected."

"What's the deal with Collel?"

"He's from the old school—the really old school—so he doesn't like your appointment much."

"It seems like more than that."

"Could it be the audit stuff?"

"I know, 'Payback is hell.' "

"You got it," Vic said, totally matter of fact. "He also goes way back with Ford Markham—way back."

"Ahh, that's the smell I caught, Alex is in this somewhere. How do I handle this? Is he going to block my appropriation because I'm doing my job?"

"He's going to try, but I don't think he'll get the votes."

"What do I do?"

"I'd talk to the chairman. And I'd keep working. Keep doing your job."

Laura looked bewildered.

"You're not going to let this guy run your life, are you?"

"I think I'm too tired to fight," Laura said. "I'm giving this the best shot I have. Legislators harass me, Senate investigators harass me, the press hounds me, some phone booth creep gets his jollies calling me and threatening Will. When will it end?"

"When you fight back."

"With what?"

"You're the one with an army at her command. Use it."

Laura started in again. "I never had a chance, never got the honeymoon agency heads usually get. This all started the first day. Even when Semmes died, did I get a break? No. Not on your life. It's almost as though I was penalized for going on, those bastards. But this takes the cake."

"Now is not the time to give up. I can't picture you, of all people, walking out and saying, 'Hey, guys, you win. It's too tough for a lady.' "

"I haven't mentioned being a woman once in this conversation."

"Maybe you should have. It's what's bothering everybody. You're getting this crap heaped on you because you didn't fail like they thought you would. I know it can wear you down, but damn, Laura, don't surrender. Declare war."

"Easy for you to say."

"Easy for you to do." Vic looked up at the clock. "Where's Will?"

"My mother's here for the night. They're dining at Picadilly, I believe."

"Can I buy you dinner?"

"Probably not tonight," Laura said. "It's been a long day."

"You still need to eat. We can talk."

Laura still hesitated.

"Or we can agree not to talk about this."

She smiled. "Sounds great."

Hal and Mal's was more crowded than usual, but there were two seats at the far end of the bar. When the bartender saw Vic, he nodded his bushy red hair, surveying the patrons to see if anyone was paying attention to the hockey game that was on the television, and pointed the remote at the set to switch the channel to the news.

"I take it you're a regular?" Laura asked as they swung onto the bar stools.

"Beats what I'd cook for myself. And I can eat here at the bar without being the lonely single guy at a table for two."

The national news was winding down and local news was next.

"A bottle of Anchor Steam?" the bartender asked Vic.

"You got some in?"

"Arrived this afternoon."

Vic turned to Laura. "What would you like? If it's beer, I recommend this microbrewery I found."

"I'll try anything once," she said. "And I know what I want to eat: a shrimp po'boy, no fries."

"Gumbo and salad for me," Vic said.

The commercial highlighting the upcoming local news had the bold headline "State Patrol Budget Under Attack" splashed across the screen behind the news commentator.

"Jeez, it must be a slow news day," Laura said, shaking her head.

"You're just great copy. I'm telling you, the world of politics is ready for Laura Owen."

"But I don't think I want to anymore."

"Never? Or just not now?"

"Definitely not now."

The first story was about a four-alarm fire in an apartment building. But the second was Cropley's story on Laura's hearing.

"In a heated debate in the State Senate today, Commissioner of Public Safety Laura Owen denied that recording equipment recently purchased with proceeds from drug investigations and installed at her home and in her office, was being used to secretly record phone calls with legislators and citizens. The Commissioner also denied any improper use of the slush fund accumulated from drug arrests."

The film cut to the interview outside the Senate. Laura's hostility was evident.

"Do you record conversations with senators and representatives?"

"I'm trying to catch someone who's threatening me. Don't I have a right to protect myself?"

"So you do record calls. Are there any controls over your slush fund?"

"It's not a slush fund. All seized funds have been plowed back into narcotics smuggling interdiction efforts."

"Except for recording devices."

The camera followed Laura as she abruptly walked away then switched back to Cropley. "This matter is far from settled, but it looks as though the actions of Commissioner Owen may severely threaten the State Patrol budget. There will be more on this in the weeks to come. I'm Tim Cropley."

Laura shook her head, her eyes closed.

"That was a pretty cheap shot," the bartender said. "I think I'll tell that little butt a thing or two when he comes in here next time."

"Change the channel, will you?" Vic asked. "Let's see if anyone else carried it."

The other stations were still reporting the fires and a shooting.

"I wouldn't lose any customers over this one," Vic said to the bartender. "It's a one-day story."

"I'm glad someone's so upbeat," Laura said. "I thought I looked like hell."

"No, you looked angry, and everyone will think that was the right response to such idiotic questions. Which it was."

Laura took a sip of beer and put the bottle down. "Think so?"

"I know so. Now stay angry and get even."

Laura looked at him quizzically. She'd never thought of Vic as vengeful. It added a new and intriguing dimension.

Vic put his arm around her shoulders and drew her closer. "Trust me. I've been in these trenches longer than you. It's pure Darwin—survival of the fittest."

She didn't pull away. Vic had been a friend a long time and she'd received a lot of similar hugs, but this one was especially nice. Just what the doctor ordered.

▪▪▪▪

When Blake got to Laura's office the next morning, the comptroller was just leaving. He smiled at Blake in passing. "I think it's your lucky day, Chief."

"What's that supposed to mean?"

He smiled again. "She's on a tear, and whenever that happens you always get to spend money."

Robert was already sitting in front of Laura's desk. There were several neat piles of paper on the floor beside her chair, and he could actually see the top of her desk.

"You've been busy," Blake remarked as he took the other seat.

"I've needed to clear out all this clutter for a long time. Yesterday helped give me a little focus."

"That Cropley creep was pretty bad," Robert observed.

"Maybe he did me a favor. Unintentionally, of course."

"How so?"

"I'm hoping Mr. Mystery watched the news and knows I'm recording him. Maybe he'll stop calling."

"We won't be able to catch him if that happens."

"I doubt we will anyway. Besides, those people are all talk and no action. Isn't that what you said?"

"Yes, but..."

"We've got bigger fish to fry."

"Such as?" Blake asked.

"First, I need to know who's feeding Collel information. Who in here owes him?"

"He's been buddy-buddy with the State Patrol for years, as long as I can remember."

"But someone may owe him more than others. Get somebody you trust to go through the personnel files. Start with headquarters people. I want to know if Collel has written letters of commendation, letters of recommendation. Anything."

"I'll handle that," Robert offered.

"And for the good news, I just went over the budget again and there are still some seized drug funds remaining. Plus, we'll have a larger than expected surplus in the salary category. With less than two months before the legislative session begins, I want to blow every dime we can scrounge on more interdiction operations. Keep as many teams working extra hours as we can afford."

"Do you think that's wise after yesterday?" Blake asked. "I mean, Collel was pretty clear that you can't spend the seized funds without their authority."

"That's what he says. But I don't read the law that way, and until someone formally orders me to stop, I'm going to keep on going."

"We can handle that," Blake said.

"Where can you get the most bang for the buck?" Laura asked Robert.

"On the Gulf Coast—working Interstate 10."

"No doubt about it," Blake agreed.

"Then have at it," Laura said. "I want Collel to eat his words before this is over."

Both men got up to leave.

"Just find the slimeball who's helping our esteemed Senator Collel. Please."

15

At three months, Jesse Hilman was the epitome of a healthy baby. He weighed nearly twenty pounds from a steady diet of breast milk, rice cereal, and recently, fruits and vegetables. Besides rolling over, trying to sit up, and discovering his toes, Jesse's most impressive feat was periodically sleeping for six or seven hours a night.

Ann had long since given up the possibility of regaining a normal life, but one night of sleep had given her a glimmer of hope. Her relationship with Tom was in a shambles. He found every excuse to be away, and when he was home, he seemed totally uninterested in her or Jesse. As a result, Jesse shied away from Tom, which only exacerbated the situation.

But Ann continued to try as hard as she could, hoping Tom's moodiness was temporary. That night, she'd cooked his favorite foods—grilled pork tenderloins with roasted new potatoes—no last minute carryout. Then she'd set the table with candles and their best china, and straightened up the house as much as possible—a daunting task given the myriad of toys and baby equipment she'd accumulated.

Tom called at the last minute to say he was taking a client to dinner. She tried not to sound too disappointed because the last thing he needed was for her to be a nag.

Jesse had fallen asleep by 9:30, so Ann took the opportunity for a long hot soak in the tub, a rare pleasure since Jesse's birth. She was in bed watching the 10:00 P.M. news when she heard the back door open.

"Hi, Sweetie," Ann called out as cheerily as possible.

"Hi," Tom answered, taking off his suit coat as he entered their bedroom, his eyes on the television screen.

Ann smelled liquor on his breath as he passed her side of the bed.

"In other news tonight," the television commentator said, "Commissioner of Public Safety Laura Owen announced that the State

Patrol's increased efforts to catch drug couriers were paying off."

The camera switched to Laura, standing near a patrol car. Cars were streaming by on the interstate in the background. "Our campaign is making a difference," she said emphatically. "We've stopped three shipments this week alone. And we're going to stay out here, working as hard as we can, as long as it takes.'"

"She makes it sound like she's the one doing all the work," Tom said, disgustedly. "Someone will scare her off sooner or later."

"What do you mean by that?"

"You'll see."

"See what?

"Those drug guys don't mess around. And I doubt they'll let a little witch like her get in their way for long."

"What are you saying?"

"That she's playing with the big boys and she ought to know better." He reached over to turn off the set.

"Please leave it on," Ann asked.

"What's there to see?" Tom asked in a surly tone.

"The rest of the news."

Tom vanished into the bathroom. When the sports came on, Ann picked up the remote and flicked it off.

Tom reappeared immediately. "Turn it back on. I wanna hear the scores."

Ann obediently punched the remote.

"Jesse nearly fell out of the grocery cart today. I think he was reaching for the bananas," Ann said.

Tom didn't respond.

"And I put on his sneakers and let him wander around the driveway in his walker."

"What?" Tom asked, without turning away from the television.

"I said, Jesse nearly fell out of the grocery cart."

"Oh," said Tom, still distracted by the sports scores.

"Glad you're so interested," Ann mumbled and turned off her reading light, settling in to sleep.

At the end of the sports, Tom turned off the television and rolled into his side of the bed. His hand reached out for her breasts.

"Not tonight, Tom, you've had too much to drink."

He mimicked back in a singsong, " 'Not tonight Tom, you've had too much to drink.' That's what you always say," he growled, turning her toward him roughly.

"It's always been true lately," said Ann, squirming away.

"That's a lie."

"No, it's not, Tom, and you know it."

"What's the use of being married?"

"I ask myself the same thing," Ann replied. "You're never here. You hardly know your son."

"Well, the little brat always cries when I hold him."

"Try being sweet. He's not one of your employees, you know."

Tom pulled her back toward him again. He still stank of bourbon.

"I said, not tonight."

"And I don't care," Tom hissed, straddling her body.

Ann put both hands on his chest and shoved him away as hard as she could, leaping from the bed. He lunged for her, catching her nightgown and ripping it as she jerked out of his reach.

"Goddamn you," she said in a deadly voice as she stared down at the torn cloth. "Stay away from me when you're like this."

"Don't you dare walk out of here," Tom snarled.

"Watch me."

Before he could get to his feet, Ann disappeared into Jesse's room and locked the door behind her. Tom rattled the handle and banged loudly, yelling, "Goddammit, Ann, come out of there."

Jesse woke up and started wailing.

"Go away until you're sober," Ann called out, heading for the terrified baby.

"Enjoy sleeping on the floor," Tom snarled.

Ann sat by the door listening for a long time. When the front door slammed and she heard Tom's car pull out of the driveway, she retrieved enough pillows and blankets to make a comfortable bed on the floor of Jesse's room.

▪▪▪▪

Laura partially awoke from a deep sleep, vaguely on edge. In a moment, her head was clear enough to realize that the next door neighbor's dogs were barking furiously. Aside from the tick of the clock and Will's breathing, there were no strange noises within the house.

But the dogs kept barking.

Now wide awake, Laura slipped out of bed to look around. Will's legs were drawn up close in a fetal position to keep warm since he'd kicked off the sheets and blankets. She tucked the covers back around him, looking out his window at the front yard. Nothing stirred.

In the kitchen, she got a glass of water, then looked out each window in the living room. There was no moon to light the driveway, but she still didn't detect any movement.

Maybe it was just some raccoons.

Back in bed, with an additional quilt pulled up, Laura turned on the bedside light and picked up the mystery she was halfway through. Lately, she'd been doing most of her reading in the middle of the night. Exhaustion made her drop immediately off to sleep, only to awaken three or four hours later, restless. Sleeping alone didn't seem to be her cup of tea.

A few pages into the chapter, dogs from farther down the street started barking, too. Laura hopped out of bed and went quickly to the front windows but no lights broke the darkness.

When the barking finally subsided, she went back to bed, tossing and turning for at least an hour before she dropped off to sleep again.

▪ ▪ ▪ ▪

"Why do I have to go to school?" Will asked for the fifth time that morning.

"To learn," Laura answered, brushing her hair. "And, it's the law. Everyone has to, I had to, your cousins have to."

"But it's not fun, Momma," Will whined.

"That's not what you say at the end of the day. You always say, 'I had a fun day.'"

"But I won't have one today,"

"I'm not going to argue with you anymore, Will Owen. Brush your teeth, find your book bag, and meet me at the door."

Will frowned at her.

"And use toothpaste," Laura added.

Heading out through the garage, Will stretched to punch the automatic door opener and then walked past Laura's own car, a four-wheel-drive Jeep Cherokee, the riding lawn mower, three bicycles, a fishing boat, generator, and endless amounts of gardening equipment that filled the space a second car would occupy. Her state car, an Oldsmobile Bonneville, was parked outside.

Laura fished out her keys and locked the house while Will, suddenly in a hurry to get to school, stood fidgeting by the patrol car door. Laura unlocked the car, threw her briefcase in the back and settled in, cranking the engine while they put on seat belts. The police radio lit up and began squawking immediately. Will went rummaging through her purse to find the control unit to close the garage door as Laura put the car in reverse. They hadn't moved five feet when there was a loud bang and the car shook.

"Get out!" Laura yelled to Will, cutting off the engine and opening her door.

Will obeyed instantly, unbuckling his belt and scrambling across the seat to her. They raced away from the car, not stopping until they were halfway across the lawn.

Will huddled next to her, silent with fear. She reached around to hug him, his little arms holding her tight. Car trouble wasn't one of their strong suits.

As the smoke and dust cleared, Laura uncoiled Will's arms. "Stay here, sweetheart," she said, stroking his smooth cheek softly.

She walked cautiously toward the car and knelt down to look under it. All she could see was jagged edges of metal.

"What happened, Mom?" Will called out.

"I don't know," Laura said slowly, suspecting more than ordinary car trouble. "Let's go inside and I'll call the office. They'll be able to fix it."

Will nodded, but tears were running down his face. "Momma, I wish Daddy was here."

With a tired sigh, Laura said, "I do, too, Will, I do, too. He could make all this better, I just know it."

By the time they reached the back door, Will's tears had dried up. "Do I have to go to school?"

Laura looked at his hope-filled face. "Yes, young man, you do."

▪ ▪ ▪ ▪

The mechanic who was sent to pick up the car, saw the scraps of metal on the ground below it and had the good sense not to touch anything. Crime scene technicians were called to the scene, but until they could get underneath, it was nearly impossible to look for prints.

By 11:00 that morning, Laura finished her meeting and made it to the office. Her state car was up on a rack in the shop where a lab technician and a mechanic were carefully inspecting the chassis. Catherine Britton, Director of the Crime Lab, was talking to Blake when Laura walked up. Seeing Catherine, and then noticing the technicians, Laura knew it meant trouble.

"No accident," Blake said. "Someone fastened a nearly de-powdered hand grenade to the pan of the car and hooked the pin to the drive shaft so when you moved, it exploded."

Laura shook her head slowly.

"They didn't intend to hurt you because they'd emptied out most of the powder," Blake added.

"Maybe, maybe not," Laura said. "Couldn't it have been a dud?"

"I don't think so," Blake said. "They left a calling card taped to the axle. You'd never have gotten it if the grenade had done much more damage."

"Three ounces of cocaine," Catherine interjected. A small woman, no bigger than Laura, but every inch a scientist, Catherine knew almost as much about the drug industry from looking through her microscopes and testing equipment as Blake and Robert did working the streets. "High quality stuff. Hardly cut, only a little strychnine added. It came from the source, not from way down the pipeline."

"Jesus, someone really doesn't like our roadblocks," Laura said. "Can you get fingerprints on something like this?"

Catherine shook her head. "So far, nothing."

"Did you hear anything last night?"

"No," Laura said. "Wait—the neighbor's dogs were barking around two-thirty or so. It woke me up."

Blake pulled an index card out from his shirt pocket. "What's your neighbor's name? Maybe they saw a car."

Lost in thought, Laura didn't answer immediately, staring at the rip in the pan. "Mitchell. Alan Mitchell. They live directly west of me—we share a driveway for a ways."

She bit on her lower lip, looking at the car. "So what this means is that while Will and I were sleeping, some creep sneaked into the yard, planted some narcotics, and messed with my car. Maybe it's the same creep who's watching Will."

"Let me check with the neighbors," said Blake.

"I didn't sign up for crap like this, Blake," Laura said bitterly. "Some days I think I've had enough."

Blake and Catherine looked stricken as Laura walked away. Blake hurried to catch up to her. "Look, you've taken more grief in six months than most people get in a lifetime," Blake said. "But don't give up, please. Eddie's already out at your house looking into the security system."

"Alarms won't solve this, Blake," Laura said. "No one thinks I belong here, and I don't want myself or my son to be a target anymore."

"I can't blame you." Blake was shaking his head. "I can't blame you one bit. But speaking for most of the Patrol, you do belong here. I couldn't have said that four months ago, but I can now."

"Thanks, but I'm not sure that's enough. Even if every trooper were thrilled, I've still got those jerks at the Legislature to contend with—as well as whoever did this."

"Promise me you'll think about this very carefully before you do anything," Blake pleaded. "You've invested a lot already and I wouldn't want you to throw it all away in a moment of panic."

Laura stared back as icily as she'd ever looked at him. "Particularly not when it would mean that you might lose your job, too."

The remark cut Blake to the quick. Though Laura had sized the situation up correctly, this was one time Blake hadn't spoken out of self-interest. He answered quietly, with deference. "You're right, as always. But I'm sorry if you thought I was speaking strictly from my own perspective. I wasn't, I assure you."

Laura instantly regretted her tacky remark—Blake had never done anything to deserve such a rebuke, far from it.

"I'm sorry I jumped on you," Laura said. She looked at her car up on the rack, where Catherine and a technician were still inspecting the damage. "I promise I'll think about it. But don't count on my staying. It's been a tough row to hoe, and it doesn't seem to be getting any easier."

■ ■ ■ ■

Laura hadn't eaten a third of her lunch even though the vegetable special at Walker's was a favorite. Food wasn't the least bit appealing at that moment. But nothing had dampened Vic's appetite—he devoured every scrap on his plate, cleaned out the bread and muffin basket, and was eyeing what she'd left on her plate when the waitress came to clear the table.

"Coffee?"

"Please, ma'am," Vic said.

"For me, too. With cream," Laura added, mustering a little smile. She turned back to Vic. "So, I took your advice and fought back. That hasn't worked too well. Now what the hell do I do?"

The waitress returned with the coffee, which gave Vic a few extra seconds before he had to respond. He'd worked with Laura long enough to know that if he let her get something out of her system, the storm would probably blow away entirely. This time might be different, but it was worth a try. He needed her to stay where she was and she needed to be there, though she wouldn't admit it at the moment.

"I agree it's getting a little rough."

"A little rough!" Laura gasped. "Will was in the car for Christ's sake."

"But don't lose sight of the fact that the grenade was rigged to be harmless."

"Isn't that some kind of contradiction in terms—harmless grenade?"

"But harmless it was," Vic said. "What happened to the fighter I've always known?"

Laura looked up from her coffee. "She fought and she's losing, that's what."

"No, no, no. You're not listening—you haven't lost. Your problem is you've won."

"Get real, Vic. You just don't want the embodiment of Carver's commitment to women to go down the toilet."

"Okay, all cards on the table. You're great for him, a real bright line on the record with women, with corruption, with narcotics. But it's not like you haven't gotten anything out of this for yourself."

"Oh, I've got plenty all right—enemies, car bombs, bad press, micromanagement by the legislature. What is it with you people? I'm the governor's magnet for the women's vote. I'm Blake Coleman's meal ticket. What's in this for me?"

"Give me a break, Laura," Vic said. "You know goddamn well that you're not just a tool. You're winning. What do you want me to do? Hire cheerleaders to wake you up every morning so you can feel good?"

Laura didn't react visibly.

"The good ol' boys are running in circles," Vic said. "You're their worst nightmare. You're not one of them, but that hasn't stopped you, hasn't even slowed you down. They thought—I heard 'em, some said it right to my face, Carver's, too—that the Patrol would eat you for breakfast and that would be the end of it. But the Patrol didn't. Not only did you survive, but you're doing well, most of the Patrol likes you. Think how those legislators feel. Some of them are half brain dead, probably never had an original thought, and they're being outmaneuvered by a woman, of all things."

"So I just keep on being target practice?"

Vic shook his head. "Target's the wrong concept—just keep on pushing, keep on fighting."

Laura put her elbows on the table to support her chin, bowing her head slightly, and closing her eyes. She yearned for Semmes' warm, strong hug, the single sensation that hadn't dimmed with time. In that safety, she'd always known what to do.

She had a child to protect from someone she couldn't see. And who, for that matter, was going to protect her?

If she left now, she'd never be bothered again by media sleazes, legislators, or their investigators.

But those people were meddlesome and petty, not dangerous.

The crazies—the criminal types who had wandered into the crosshairs of her audit investigations or encountered her since she'd been commissioner—they were different.

If she left the Patrol, she'd be completely on her own. No panic button with a small army standing by on the other end.

There really wasn't any choice.

"Is it going to get better?" she asked, opening her eyes.

Vic reached across the table and grasped her elbow gently.

His touch, even so slight a one, felt so soothing.

"Not right away, but you're going to prevail," Vic said quietly, but confidently. "I can feel that."

"Glad someone can," Laura said, smiling as she brought her hand down to squeeze his arm.

▪ ▪ ▪ ▪

Instead of going out the front door where reporters were standing ready with microphones and cameras, Laura crossed over to the old building and slipped out the side door, close to her Cherokee. She had started the engine before they noticed her. The group moved toward her car, crowding around her door.

"Commissioner, we understand your patrol car was tampered with," a young reporter queried.

"Where did you get that information?" Laura asked.

The reporter kept the microphone trained at Laura's face, not replying.

"It looks that way," Laura finally said, too indignant with what had happened to her to be coy. "A grenade was attached underneath my car, rigged to blow up when the car moved. I have no idea who did it or why. I'm just glad my son, who was with me at the time, wasn't hurt. We'll issue a statement when we have more information."

With his camera rolling, Tim Cropley pushed in to ask, "Did you arrange this as a publicity stunt?"

Completely taken aback by his question, then shaking her head in disbelief, Laura simply rolled up the electric window of her car and drove off. As she rounded the drive, out of sight of the reporters, she started screaming in anger, so loud it startled her.

▪ ▪ ▪ ▪

"I'm gonna miss our date night, Rach," Robert said.

"What's it this time?" Rachel Stone said, pulling off the scarf she'd just tied around her neck.

"Did you catch the news?"

"About the grenade?" Rachel said.

"Yeah," Robert answered.

"You know who did it?"

"Not a clue, except it was a cocaine dealer. Problem is, it kinda shook her up."

"I'd be surprised if it hadn't," Rachel said.

"And if she quits," Robert said. "Blake's out of a job."

"Not to mention you," Rachel pointed out.

"Right. Which is why we're regrouping, so to speak."

"While you ride around having a beer?"

"Now, Baby," said Robert, feigning indignation.

"I'll see you when I see you. Be quiet when you come in."

■ ■ ■

Laura intentionally did not turn on the evening news. Much as she wanted to see the coverage, she couldn't risk having Will see the story, so she'd asked Blake to tape it. Will seemed relatively unfazed by the whole event. He'd been tearing around the playground at afterschool care, without a worry in the world. His only question had been, "Are you going to get a new car?"

She did decide to serve the easiest of his favorite meals—twice-baked potatoes, chicken, corn, and yeast rolls. And cake for desert. Everything freezer to microwave except the cake—and that was out of a box. Weary as she was, she found fixing this "home-cooked" meal was a cinch.

As she stood at the front door calling Will to come in for supper, her mother drove up the driveway. Will raced in front of her on his bike, pedaling as fast as he could go, his face all smiles.

"You didn't need to come all the way up here," Laura said after she'd kissed her mother's cheek and gotten an extra warm hug.

"Of course I needed to come. I was out on the course when you left your message. I don't intend for you to stay here by yourself tonight, and I've got nothing to do in the morning."

"Grandmom, watch how fast I can go," yelled Will, shooting past them, back down the driveway.

"Mother, I can handle this," Laura said. "I'm getting an alarm system installed. We'll be fine."

"I'm relieved to hear that," Charlotte Hemeter said, watching her grandson. "He sure is getting big. Seems like he's grown a couple of inches since I last saw him."

"Probably has."

Laura's mother opened the back door of her car and started handing out packages for Laura to carry. "Now, I've brought some fresh fruit and muffins for breakfast."

Laura looked in one of the bags and found a new box of Legos. "What's this?"

"Just a little present for Will."

When it was all said and done, having her mother there that night was a tremendous help. The phone rang off the hook as soon as the evening news was broadcast and Laura was able to field most of the calls while her mother got Will into the tub for a desperately needed bath. There wasn't a word about the car incident when she kissed him good night.

"Are you reconsidering this job?" Charlotte asked as her daughter settled into the big chair in front of the fire.

"I have been all afternoon and evening. Vic doesn't want me to give up. He gave me a pep talk at lunch."

"But what do you want?"

"I don't know. I love the job. Honestly. Everything about it—I love the issues, the people, the opportunities. But I hate the opposition I'm dealing with. They're wearing me down."

"Don't let them," Charlotte said. "Where has all your spunk gone? You were the little girl who never let her big brothers get the best of her. I've been on the receiving end of those spirited defenses a time or two. I know all about it."

Laura looked at her mother, surprised. "I've assumed you would've wanted me to quit. Too dangerous."

Her mother shook her head. "If you like your work, then stick with it."

Laura smiled but didn't say anything.

"My greatest regret is that your father didn't spend his life at the farm. He loved it. He was never happier than when he was there."

"Then why did you move?"

"Money, mostly. But the money never made up for what he lost along the way."

"But this is a matter of safety. Will's safety."

"You're probably the safest two people in the state at the moment," said Charlotte, walking to the window and looking out at the road. "If I'm not mistaken, our sitter has arrived."

"What?"

"There's a patrol car parked at the end of the driveway."

"Courtesy of Blake Coleman, I bet."

"I wouldn't be too quick to give this up, dear."

▪ ▪ ▪ ▪

Robert and Blake had eaten their Back Yard Burgers in the Patrol repair shop while they inspected and reinspected the damage to Laura's car, hashing out the possibilities. Finding a perpetrator seemed remote, at best. They left for a long overdue road-beer.

There was nothing extraordinary about the grenade—standard military issue, available from hundreds of sources. And there was nothing extraordinary about the cocaine. That it was cut with strychnine was a clue, but only if some more turned up cut the same way and they could positively connect the two.

Blake was driving so Robert hopped out at a stop 'n steal on State Street to get a six pack of beer—Lites, much to Blake's chagrin. They'd wandered around for nearly two hours—up Highway 49 to Flora, southwest on 22 to Edwards, down a county road to Learned, and back through Raymond to Jackson—retelling old war stories, boldly embellishing their own roles in various cases, and talking about the office. There hadn't been time to kick back like this in months.

"Find any traces of Senator Collel in the personnel files?" Blake asked.

Robert took another sip of beer, nodding his head. "He's everywhere. Letters of commendation right and left."

"Anyone stick out?"

"I had them make a list of every time he was mentioned—name of the trooper, date, and whether it was a recommendation, commendation, or complaint. There are five or six guys who have multiple entries."

"You remember who?" Blake asked.

"Vincent up in the northeast, Melville in the Delta, Fletcher in Natchez, someone from the Coast..."

"Ladner?"

"No, none of the Ladners. I just can't remember."

"Sounds like he's got someone in every corner of the state. Anyone from headquarters?"

Robert nodded, "Kenner. Collel's all over him like white on rice."

"Kenner," Blake mused. "What sort of things were in there?"

"Several bullshit commendations when Kenner went out of his way to be helpful...."

"Ass-kisser."

"Exactly," Robert said. "And there's a letter of recommendation from Collel about nearly every promotion Kenner's gone for."

"Interesting. He's got the access to feed Collel plenty of information and he needs her gone so he can have one last chance to advance. Kenner could be our man."

"Wouldn't that be pitiful," Robert said with a shake of his head. "We need to keep an eye on him or get him out of town."

"I'll think on it but off the top, I don't know where I could I send him that wouldn't look trumped up."

"How about some training thing? He's applied for the FBI Academy again."

"Out of the question," Blake said quickly. "Even if it does get him out of town, I'm not wasting that FBI slot on someone like him. I may not like some of the jerks they hire but you can't beat the schools they put on."

"Well, you're the boss. I leave it to you."

"I think I'll suggest we issue a weapon to her. What do you think?"

"She ought to agree now. I don't think it'll take much convincing," Robert said. "I'm going out to the range tomorrow. Want me to see what's in stock?"

"Why don't you do that—something smaller. A good snub-nose."

16

"Where do you want the trailer, Chief?" the maintenance supervisor asked.

"What trailer?"

"A thirty-foot house trailer—it's on its way."

"I don't know anything about a house trailer."

"I think it's a forfeiture. That's what Colonel Stone said."

"Forfeiture?" Blake still looked puzzled. He punched in Robert's extension.

"Stone, here."

"What's this about a house trailer?"

"That redneck dope dealer we busted—we got the trailer free for the hauling."

A look of recognition spread across Blake's face. "Oh, yeah, I remember now. It's arriving shortly."

"Didn't we decide to put it out back for storage?" Robert asked.

"Yup, thanks."

"Hey," Robert added quickly. "We want to go through it one more time. Just in case."

"Right," said Blake and hung up. "Get them to put it back behind Communications," he said to the supervisor. "After Robert's guys go through it, the work crew can clean it up, paint it. And look at ripping out that carpet—it was pretty nasty if I remember correctly."

"Sure thing."

■ ■ ■ ■

The doorbell rang and Alex hurried to answer it. He swung it open to find Tom with three invoices in his hand.

"For the last load of your building materials," Tom said. "They delivered everything this afternoon."

"Since when do executives deliver the mail?" Alex asked.

"Only on high-priority jobs," Tom said.

Alex took the papers, but didn't invite him in.

"So, still pissed," Tom said from the doorway. "I hoped my mission would have cooled your anger a little."

"That little firecracker? It didn't work. She'd be a full-fledged martyr if the press hadn't been so hard on her."

"But I bet she's scared. Inside, she's real scared."

"Maybe, maybe not."

Alex scrawled his signature across the papers and shoved them back.

"Then learn a lesson from me," Tom suggested, speaking as evenly as he could.

"What do you mean by that?"

"The beer can's still in the police file for the hit-and-run," he bluffed.

Alex's angry look faded considerably. "How do you know that for sure?"

"For me to know," Tom said with a cocky grin. "It scares the shit out of you, though, doesn't it?"

Alex didn't move.

"I suggest you put that trick in your repertoire. Maybe it'll even the score between us."

▪ ▪ ▪ ▪

When Tom entered the Ocean Springs inlet, there weren't any cars at the Yacht Club, something that had never happened before. He pulled out his binoculars and looked everywhere for Hector, but there was no sign of him or his car.

All the way to his dock, he considered his options. Calling Hector was out. Most likely it was nothing, something unexpected had detained him. But, then again, Hector would have called on the cellular if it was just a matter of being late. Tying down *Next,* he went into the house, and on the chance that Hector had risked it, checked the answering machine. Nothing. He called his office in Jackson for messages. Hector hadn't called there. He dialed Ann.

"Hi, I just got in," Tom said, as cheerily as he could muster.

"Did you have a good sail?" Ann asked. Jesse was screaming in the background.

"Great."

"And Jesse had a wonderful first Thanksgiving with your parents."

"Sorry I missed it," Tom replied, still trying to sound interested.

"When will we see you?"

"I'll probably get back up there tomorrow unless there are jobs I need to check down here," Tom said, giving himself plenty of room to maneuver. "Any messages?"

"No. Not much new around here except that Jesse's getting a tooth."

"Great."

"Your enthusiasm is overwhelming," Ann said curtly.

"Let's not get started, Ann, I'm tired."

"Sorry. See you whenever."

Tom hung up. Where the hell could Hector be?

One thing for sure, he wasn't going to keep a thousand kilos of cocaine at his house, nor could he risk going to the hangar without Hector's all clear. He picked up the yellow pages and called rental storage places looking for an immediately available unit large enough to back in with the van and close the door. Most were closed for the holidays, but he finally found one, donned his wig, and headed into town.

Within the hour he'd paid cash for a month's rent at SHORE U KEYP IT and was unloading the boat. By late that night, the cocaine was safely in the storage unit, and he fell asleep exhausted.

■ ■ ■ ■

Around eight the next morning, Hector rang the doorbell. When Tom didn't answer, he walked around the outside of the house, calling for him.

"Where the hell were you?" Tom asked as he let Hector in.

"First I couldn't get out of Belize on time, then the plane couldn't land in New Orleans so we went onto Houston. Had to drive over."

"Why are you coming here, to my house?"

"You didn't answer the phone, and I didn't have a choice. Everything's screwed up. The couriers are already lined up and waiting to get their stuff. Where's the load?"

"At a rented storage place. You can go get it yourself if you want."

"Jesus, that's much too dangerous—too many people around."

"I didn't have any choice under the circumstances. I sure as hell wasn't keeping it anywhere near me."

"Sorry. I never intended this to happen."

"Forget it. I can get it to the hangar tonight."

"Not now?"

"No. Later this evening at the earliest. You'll have it after dark. You'll only be delayed a day."

"Good. I can get it on the road by dawn."

■■■■

Shortly after 6:00 A.M., Trooper K-79, a member of the drug interdiction team, was parked on the median of I-10, in an unmarked car with his radar gun aimed behind him at the westbound traffic. He was hungry for a stop that yielded results. The teams had been working every day for weeks, and everyone else had racked up pretty good stats. He loved the work, loved the overtime pay, but he also wanted some arrests—good ones.

Dawn was but a sliver of red at the eastern horizon, in an otherwise midnight blue sky. He locked in on the next set of headlights coming his way and the readout showed the car was going 82 in a 70 zone. As the car came into view, K-79 keyed his mike. "Got a customer. A guy driving a brand-new Monte Carlo."

"I'm several miles back," said K-88. "It'll take me a few minutes to reach you."

"Whenever."

"I'm at mile marker five eastbound, if you need me," came another voice, K-70. "K-93's getting gas."

K-79 turned on his dashboard and rear deck blue lights and pulled onto the highway, accelerating to catch up with the Chevy. When he was close enough to see the license plate, he switched to the substation channel and keyed his mike.

"K-79, Gulfport."

The Monte Carlo was slowing down, pulling onto the shoulder.

"Go ahead," the operator answered.

"I need a check on Texas, Robert-Henry-Sam-8-5-8-8. White Chevy Monte Carlo. Late model. I have him stopped at westbound mile marker sixteen."

He opened his door, snatching up the long steel flashlight mounted at the base of the driver's seat as he stepped out. K-88 still wasn't in sight.

He wiggled inside his clothes to reposition his bullet-proof vest more comfortably.

The driver was shifting in his seat as if he was getting his license out. The window slid down with electric smoothness.

K-79 approached the car cautiously and was standing slightly behind the driver. "Could I see your license, sir?" the trooper asked.

"I'm sorry if I was speeding. I'm ready to be home, Officer," the driver called out, intentionally never showing his face.

"I know the feeling, sir."

K-79 shifted his powerful flashlight to his right hand to illuminate the backseat area better.

Nothing to see. No luggage.

He stepped closer to the driver with the flashlight still in his right hand. His portable radio crackled.

"Gulfport, K-79. Texas, Robert-Henry-Sam-8-5-8-8 comes back to Avis Rent A Car."

K-79 reached for his radio with his left hand, taking his eyes off the driver for a moment. He could see K-88's blue lights out of the corner of his eye, pulling in behind his patrol car.

The driver looked in the rearview mirror at the new set of blue lights, jabbed an automatic pistol out of the window, aimed at the trooper and fired, just as K-79 twisted away from him.

The trooper was hurled away from the car with the impact and the driver stomped on the accelerator, gravel and shells spinning under his tires.

K-88 was grabbing his own flashlight when he heard the shot and saw K-79 fall. He lurched out of his seat, drew his gun, and fired repeatedly at the escaping car, only hitting the left taillight. Then he ran to   K-79, pulling out his radio.

"Officer down! K-79's down. Get an ambulance out here. Hurry."

The Monte Carlo roared out of sight.

"Ambulance is on the way, K-88. Do you need more help?"

"No, not here, but get someone after him," K-88 called back. "I shot out the left rear taillight. White Chevy Monte Carlo. He's moving pretty fast."

"This is K-70. I'm watching the westbound traffic. He couldn't have reached where I am yet. Try to raise K-93. He checked out for gas."

"This is K-93."

"Be on the lookout for a white Monte Carlo, with left rear taillight missing. The driver shot K-79 at mile marker sixteen."

K-70 keyed his mike. "He might have taken Highway 603."

"That's where I am," K-93 said. "Haven't seen him."

"And you won't," yelled K-70, "cuz here he comes like a bat outta hell."

"Where are you?"

"Mile marker twelve and I'm pulling out behind him now."

"I'm coming," K-93 said.

"Gulfport—notify Louisiana that we're headed their way," said K-70. "Get every man you can find up on this road. And tell Bay Saint Louis to block their exit."

"This is K-King," said the captain of the district. "I'll be at mile marker eight before he gets there."

"We're both behind him now," K-93 said. "But he's not slowing down."

Four truckers up ahead heard the CB radio traffic and knew the Monte Carlo was coming up behind them. They formed into a rolling road-block, running side by side and one behind the other, so the Monte Carlo couldn't pass them. As they slowed down, the driver shot around the first pair on the right shoulder, careened back onto the road in between the two sets of trucks and passed the front pair on the left median.

K-93, with K-70 catching up behind him, raced down the right shoulder, the truckers pulling left to give them room. They were side by side again when they caught up with him. K-King pulled in front, trying to box him in. The Monte Carlo rammed into the back of K-King who fell back, sideswiping the car in return three or four times. But the last time, the Monte Carlo swung into K-King so hard that the patrol car shot completely off the highway. K-88 and K-70 were still on his tail, and K-King spun in the grass and pulled back in behind them.

The upcoming exit had a long ramp, and the three patrol cars surrounded the Monte Carlo to trap him. The car shot across the dividing island, fishtailed in the intersection and pulled left sharply. He headed under the interstate and swung left up the eastbound entrance ramp with all three State Patrol cars on his tail.

K-93 pulled out to the left of the Monte Carlo with K-70 and K-King right behind him, keeping up but easing off the pressure. At the rest area, the Monte Carlo had no choice except to exit, shooting off the interstate at the last minute. K-70 stayed behind the Monte Carlo as it wove in between the cars and trucks scattered throughout. K-93 and K-King stayed on the interstate, doing at least 110 mph, to block the Monte Carlo up ahead at the exit from the rest area.

K-93 pulled off first and his car spun to a stop, with the nose three or four feet into the roadway. K-King squealed to a stop a couple of hundred feet farther on and jumped out, drawing his weapon, ready.

The Monte Carlo hit K-93, tearing the bumper of the patrol car off its struts and flipping it into the air. But the driver didn't stop, he kept right on going, swerving up on the grass strip to avoid K-King.

K-King shot repeatedly at the driver as he passed, missing him, but catching the left front tire. It deflated instantly, the rim of the wheel dug into the blacktop. As its rear end spun out, K-93 caught up and hit the Monte Carlo broadside, the steel bumper struts of the patrol car peeling open the Monte Carlo like a tin can.

K-King yanked the driver out and pinned him to the ground with his automatic at his head, shaking with rage.

"Did I kill that cop?" the driver rasped.

▪▪▪▪

Laura was outside the family's waiting room at intensive care, staring out the window while she waited for the latest update on K-79 who was still in surgery. The bullet had shattered his humerus, severed a branch of the brachial artery, ricocheted into his body under his arm where there was no Kevlar vest to protect him, ripped through his right lung, and lodged near his spine. He'd lost a tremendous amount of blood and his lung had collapsed. There was no word yet about the extent of spinal damage, if any.

As always, there was an immediate rush from the law enforcement community to support a fallen officer—the one moment when every difference of opinion, every bit of rivalry was set aside. Tragedies were close to home for all of them.

The room was filled to overflowing. Not only was the trooper's family there—parents, siblings, cousins, as well as his girlfriend and her family—but several members of the troop, their spouses, sheriff's deputies, city policemen, along with neighbors, his mother's pastor, and several friends from her church.

Maybe this drug busting was getting out of hand, Laura thought. Maybe she should back off.

"Commissioner?" Blake said softly by her side.

His voice jolted her back to the waiting room.

"What'd you find out?"

"Not much," Blake said, shaking his head. "Robert's talking to the driver now but the guy doesn't know anything—he's just a courier. Never deals with anyone face-to-face. We had a case with the same set-up when we did Operation Saturation."

"The motel thing?"

"That's it. The guy gets a call, goes to a motel. He waits, the keys are slid under the door with directions and traveling money. He drops the car off on the other end, gets his money under the door, and goes home."

"Where'd he pick up this load?"

"Pascagoula. Heading to Texas. Rental car. Fifty pounds of coke in the trunk."

"Can you go ahead and deliver?"

"Not with the wreck. We alerted Texas about the drop-off point. I don't know what they can do now that the media's all over this. I doubt anyone will show."

"What about the rental car?"

"We're working on that now. And I've sent a sample of the cocaine to the lab to analyze."

Laura turned back to the window. "Do you think we ought to back off?" she asked quietly.

"Hell, no."

"Didn't the cost just get a little too high?"

"It's always been this high—and always will be. We can't let this cloud our objective."

"Pretty hard-boiled."

"Ask any of the men in that room. They'll suit up tomorrow and go after the bad guys."

"But what about their families?"

"They've learned to live with it. It goes with the territory."

A doctor in surgical scrubs came through the doors and looked around the room, bewildered by the crowd. Blake stepped toward him immediately, identified himself, and then escorted him to the trooper's mother. K-79's girlfriend pushed through to stand next to her.

"Your son will be okay," he said quickly. "He's a lucky man."

The mother collapsed in the girlfriend's arms, both of them smiling and weeping at the same time.

"He's lost a lot of blood, but there's no damage to the spine. We haven't fixed his arm yet—we needed to stabilize everything else first."

"Thank God," his mother said, recovering enough to throw her arms around the doctor and kiss him. "You saved him, thank God."

■ ■ ■ ■

A week before Christmas, the fifth floor elevator doors closed on Bill Kenner, standing alone, briefcase firmly in hand, jacket collar already turned up against the cold, gearing up to forge across the cavernous ground floor of headquarters to the front doors and his car. At each floor of the descent, the doors opened to distinct but distant sounds of Christmas carols, and one or two employees, some with small children in tow, entered. At the ground floor he stepped out into all the noise and commotion of the party.

"Kenner," called Jimmie Anderson. "Going to get your children?"

Kenner shook a disapproving head as he scanned the crowded room. "They're at a church program, couldn't get them here."

"Couldn't or wouldn't, Kenner?" Jimmie said.

"This isn't appropriate, Colonel. You know my feeling about this," Kenner snapped.

" 'Will's party,'" Jimmie said. "Isn't that what you call it?"

"I didn't think that one up, but it fits."

"It's Christmas, for God's sake," Jimmie said. "Why don't you lighten up?" Anderson looked down at the small boy pulling at his hand. "Little Jim, shake hands with the Major, maybe you can make him smile."

Jimmie's grandson looked up at Kenner's forbidding face and didn't move. Neither did Kenner.

"Go ahead, son, he won't bite," Jimmie said.

Little Jim obediently stuck out his hand. Kenner nodded stiffly as he took the small hand in his, but his face didn't move a muscle.

"Can't you give her a break?" Jimmie asked. "There's no state money being spent here."

"Except time and equipment," Kenner said. "These people should be working."

"Negative," Jimmie said. "The roads are covered, everyone here is on days off or after hours. They weren't ordered to come—they came on their own."

Kenner adjusted his collar to move away.

"You ought to be cheering for her with all she's trying to do," Jimmie said. "No commissioner that I can remember has been harassed for doing the job like she has."

"If she can't stand the heat, then she ought to get out of the kitchen."

"She's standing the heat—and mighty well I might add." Jimmie looked him square in the eye. "That's what's teeing you off so much, isn't it?"

"Attention, all children. Attention!" a commanding voice boomed over the public address system. "Santa Claus has been spotted approaching headquarters. I repeat, Santa Claus has been spotted."

With screams of delight, the children rushed to the windows as Santa, escorted by two troopers, all three riding brand new Harley Davidson patrol motorcycles, lights flashing, sirens blaring, roared up the driveway, around the parking lot, and parked smack in front of the doors. Before he was through the double doors, the kids were swarming around Santa, pulling on every bit of him to find out if he was real. Kenner barged through the crowd and was gone.

With a profusion of "Ho, Ho, Hos," he made his way to a big chair and sat down. An overgrown elf lined up the anxious children, while parents and troopers stood in front to take pictures. Will was near the head of the line, having raced over as soon as Santa arrived. Laura waved at him and backed away, camera ready.

At six, Will had concluded that Laura was indeed the tooth fairy, but he wasn't so certain about Santa Claus. How could he be real, Will asked, if Santa couldn't bring his father back? But careful, like his father, he hedged his bets and made sure his request was registered. For weeks, he'd refused to tell her what he wanted, saying that if Santa was real, he'd bring the right present.

An older civilian female employee approached Laura. "Commissioner, I want to thank you. This department's never done anything for the children or the families—particularly not for the civilians."

"Don't thank me," Laura said. "The committee did all the work. I just twisted a few arms to come up with the money. For the life of me, I don't know why there hasn't been a party before."

"Because the place had been run by men, that's why," said another civilian joining them.

"But everybody needs to celebrate," said Laura, "and even men have kids."

"In the eleven years I've worked here," the first woman remarked, "my child has never seen what I do. Until today. I can't thank you enough."

A loud whistle made Laura look up. Will had just climbed up onto Santa's lap and Santa was angling him toward Laura for a photograph.

"And what do you want for Christmas?" Santa said.

Will saw Laura coming nearer so he leaned close to Santa's ear and whispered, "A golden retriever puppy."

Santa winked at Laura.

"Do you know what Santa wants for Christmas?" Santa asked Will in a voice loud enough for everyone to hear.

Will shook his head, mystified.

"Santa wants all the troopers to get big Christmas bonuses, Ho, Ho, Ho."

Nervous laughter erupted all around.

"And more new patrol cars, Ho, Ho, Ho."

Laura stepped up to Santa's chair, smiling broadly. "Okay, Will, it's time for someone else to talk to Santa."

"And more portable radios, Ho, Ho, Ho." Then Santa leaned closer to Will and lowered his voice, "Be sweet to your mom."

■ ■ ■ ■

"It was a lot easier workin' here before this bunch took over," one of the maintenance crew called out from the living room of the redneck's trailer they'd parked at the rear of Communications. He jerked back on his crowbar and pulled up a corner of the grungy carpet.

There was no answer from the bedroom where his partner was paint-ing the cheap brown paneling white, brightening the dingy space con-siderably.

"I mean, these people'll work you to death," the crew member called out, louder than before. He got a better grip on the material and pulled back as hard as he could, losing his balance as the carpet ripped away from the flooring with a satisfying series of pops.

"And I bet you just hate that pay raise they got you, too," came a deep voice from the front doorway.

The crew member blanched at the entrance of his boss. He didn't turn around, just pulled up harder on the carpet. There was another series of pops as it pulled away from the other wall.

"You know what I mean," the crew member protested.

The maintenance director stepped back outside as the crew member moved toward him with the end of the carpet. "All I know is that a lotta things that needed fixing around here have gotten fixed or replaced. And why it couldn't have happened sooner I don't know."

Ground-in dirt and dust from the carpet flew into the air around them as the man tugged it away.

"Mercy, what a pigsty this was," said the boss. "How do people live like this?"

They dragged the carpet out the door and toward the pile of scraps from the bedroom and hall. As the last corner pulled away, it caught on a thin strip of paneling near the door and pulled the panel away from the wall.

Papers that had been wedged behind, scattered on the floor.

"What's this?" the maintenance director asked.

"I don't know," the crew member replied. "Musta been under the carpet. Looks like names and phone numbers. Dates. Lists of some-thing."

"Better save that for Colonel Stone. It might mean something to him."

▪ ▪ ▪ ▪

James Stinley headed the list on the papers from the redneck's trailer. He wasn't hard to find. The woman who answered his phone said he was out of town delivering late Christmas presents, due back that night or in the morning. Robert said he'd call back later.

"If you're on his rounds this month," the woman volunteered, "he should be getting to you soon."

Robert's jaw dropped at his luck.

"I haven't been a regular, but I'm interested."

"Then call back tomorrow," said the woman and hung up.

"Unbelievable," Robert said. "She practically sold it over the phone."

"Maybe you got his business line."

"I guess so. Now we've got to get to him before he hands everything out."

▪ ▪ ▪ ▪

Blake paced the radio room while he waited for a response to his criminal history query. When the information finally rattled off the teletype machine, he hurried to the criminal interview rooms on the third floor. As soon as Blake caught Robert's eye, he waved the papers in victory.

The room was police plain, with a table in the center and six chairs. Robert, in a suit and tacky holiday tie, stood squarely at the end of the table, his arms folded tightly across his chest. Another investigator leaned back against the wall. Both were watching James Stinley who was in his late twenties, slick-backed dark ponytail, well built, and dressed in an expensive suede leather coat and jeans. For a man in as much trouble as he was, Robert thought Stinley was remarkably cool, seemingly uninterested, exhibiting no nervousness at all.

"Blake, glad you could join us," said Robert, jamming his hands in his pockets and rocking back on his heels. "Maybe you can talk some sense into Mr. Stinley here. He thinks possession with intent to distribute is no biggie. Mr. Stinley, meet Colonel Blake Coleman, Chief of the Patrol."

Stinley nodded but didn't speak.

Blake and Robert began conversing as though Stinley wasn't in the room, a dance they'd choreographed over the years.

"You know, Robert," Blake said. "He's probably right, being the first offense and all, plus it's crowded down at the jail. Yessir, mighty crowded. They won't bother to lock up a guy with only one offense."

Robert nodded.

"His attorney might be able to get him a deal," Blake said. "Drop it down to plain possession or something."

"Think so?" Robert said.

"Sure, first offense and all," Blake said. "But now, if it was the second or third offense, things might be different. Second or third, he might lose that sports car outside, do fifteen to thirty Delta time—hot, no air conditioning."

Stinley began paying more attention, watching Blake all the while.

"Yup. No TV either." Blake looked at Robert and the investigator. "You did know that, guys, didn't you? The Legislature passed a law. No TV for cons. Man, those days get long."

"You're kidding," Robert said. "Jesus, I'd hate to be in Parchman Penitentiary with all those..." Robert leaned into Stinley's face, "big, mean, sons-o-bitches wit' nothin' to do all day long." Robert pulled back and looked at Blake again. "Goddamn. No single cells, hardly any guards. But Stinley probably won't have to mess with that—first offense and all."

Stinley changed his position, his eyes riveted on the papers Blake was using to punctuate everything he said with a gentle slap on his hand. Blake looked directly back at him. "You said you were from south of Memphis, didn't you, Mr. Stinley? I used to work up there. Ran up on a white guy dealing small time to the Ole Miss boys. He got caught, little stuff. Name kinda like yours."

Blake paused as he looked at his papers for the first time. "Jim Staley. Know him?"

Stinley, very still, didn't take his eyes off Blake as he slowly shook his head no.

Blake got closer to him and inspected Stinley's face. "Kinda looked like you, too. Never forget a face—names get kinda fuzzy, but I never forget a face." Blake backed away from him. "With this new federal law, if Staley were to get caught again, those other two little charges would make him a three-time loser. Three times and you're out, isn't that what our President said, Robert?"

Stinley tensed up.

"Wrong, Blake—we're talking state court here, not federal."

Stinley relaxed a moment.

"State court, three times and you get thirty at Parchman, no parole," Robert said. "How old will he be when he gets out? Sixty-five?"

Stinley lowered his head slightly, his elbows on the table.

They all sat there in silence a moment.

"Nasty guys at Parchman Penitentiary," Robert said. "Big, black..."

Stinley put his hands up. "What can you do for me if I cooperate?"

"Whatcha have to cooperate with?" Blake asked.

"My supplier," Stinley mumbled.

"What was that? I couldn't hear you."

"My supplier. I'll give you my supplier."

Blake smiled. "We can try to keep you out of Parchman. Of course, we can't promise you anything, but this DA has never turned down our recommendation."

Stinley leaned back and looked at each of them very slowly, all of them locked in piercing stares.

Nice, neat deals like this were such a rarity that Robert and Blake felt blessed.

"The next shipment is supposed to be coming in the end of January. But I never know exactly until it's delivered. I'm supposed to get twenty-five kilos, which is almost double my normal amount. It gets to me by one of the standard delivery services—though usually it's Action Express that brings it."

"Then what."

"Then I make my distributions, collect my cash, and the main man comes to my house five days later for his money."

"What's his name?"

"Hector Rodriguez. He'll be expecting ten-thousand dollars per kilo. You got that much?"

"We will by then." Blake and Robert smiled at each other. Stinley looked sick.

■ ■ ■ ■

While the investigator did the paperwork, Blake and Robert headed out to their cars.

Blake looked down the hill toward the crime lab and the morgue. Lights were on everywhere. "What's going on in there tonight?"

"Holiday psychotics," Robert said. "The doc had to autopsy a baby.

Allegedly accidental. The mother said *it* died when *it* fell from the crib."

"Fell from the crib?" Blake said.

Robert nodded. "The sheriff didn't like her calling her baby *it*. He came down to help this afternoon."

Robert unlocked his car and was getting in. "Look, I'll call Logan about this thing and get them going on the flash money."

"Hold up," Blake said over the top of his car. "I like Logan fine, but I don't want the feds in on this one unless we've got no choice. This is our business—not theirs. Besides, can you imagine the amount of paper they'd have to write to take Rodriguez down?"

"I don't want them either, Blake, but how are we going to pull this off? You're talking about a lot of money and a lot of people."

"Who says you need an entire army to take down one damn doper?"

"What's your plan?"

"The way I see it, we keep Stinley under surveillance—get him a new girlfriend, someone who hasn't worked around here, say, MaryAnn Tolliver. She looks his type. MaryAnn hangs out with him as much as possible. And when she can't be there, we send in someone else, say, Julia St. Clair, or one of the guys. Watch him like a hawk. Put the van out there. We wire the house."

"But that's a whole month keeping a guy on ice."

"What's a month? We've both done cases undercover for a lot longer than that. Anyway, when the cocaine comes, Stinley takes some trips here and there, just like he always does. But he doesn't deliver. We sit tight until Rodriguez calls for his money. Get a couple of people in the house, and others around it. If Rodriguez will go for MaryAnn's being there, great. If not, she leaves, no problem. Stinley hands Rodriguez the bucks, we tape the whole thing, and arrest him."

"Where are we going to get the flash?"

"We've got forfeitures in the bank, haven't we? They'll loan us the money against those. I'm sure the Commissioner knows the bank president."

"We can't get her involved. This is a little close to the bone for that, don't you think?"

"Maybe. Let's let her decide. Once she hears what's happened, I bet she volunteers. Hop in."

"Now?"

"What better time? She's probably home alone, and God knows she doesn't need that, not at Christmas."

■ ■ ■ ■

Lights flooded the entire back side of Laura's house as Blake and Robert drove up. Pulling up their collars in the cold, they both looked around at the very well-lit area, a result of Eddie's design for the alarm system.

"Kind of overdid it, didn't we?" Robert asked.

"An extra kilowatt here and there never hurt anything," Blake answered.

As they rounded the corner, more dazzling lights came on, flooding the entire front yard.

"Okay, I get to tell her," Blake said.

Robert pulled on Blake's arm and turned him so they were face-to-face. "Cuz you're chief, right?"

"Rank does have its privileges."

"It was my score and you know it."

"Whadda ya mean?" Blake said. "I remembered him. You were striking out."

"Striking out!" Robert said. "My black face up in his white one is what did it."

"Hey, I thought of the 'no TV' line."

"Maybe y'all ought to argue in here where it's warmer," Laura called from the front door.

They turned, sheepish. "Good evening, Commissioner," said Blake. Robert smiled.

"Evening," Laura said, holding open the door. "And to what do I owe this pleasure?"

"We were riding around, tired of holiday parties and decided you needed company."

"And we have news about all your favorite people."

"Well, let me take your coats. I assume you can stay long enough to drink a beer?"

"Of course, it's time to celebrate." Blake headed for the sofa and plopped down as though he'd been on his feet all day. In the corner of the living room stood an enormous Christmas tree, at least ten feet tall, covered with strings of popcorn, twinkling lights, and dozens of ornaments. The dining table was Lego-land central. Laura had been reading, curled up in a huge chair near the fire.

"High test or unleaded?" Laura asked.

"High test for me—Robert?"

"Unleaded."

"Wimp," Blake scoffed.

"Just keeping my trim figure," Robert said, patting his tight stomach, "unlike some people."

Laura inspected Robert's tie with the Day-Glo Christmas trees as she handed him his beer. "Nice, very nice."

She sat back in her chair, tucking her legs underneath her. For someone with so much authority, sitting there in blue jeans and a sweatshirt, she looked young and vulnerable.

Blake looked over at the Virginia pine. "Pretty tree."

"Thanks. We got it from the tree farm up at Pocahontas—had to hire a guy to get it in the stand."

"You shoulda called someone at headquarters..."

"Right. I can hear Collel now. 'And Commissioner, exactly who put up your Christmas tree?'"

"Betcha Will likes it," Robert said.

"He doesn't want to take it down."

"Does he believe?"

"I think so," Laura said.

"What did Santa Claus bring besides Legos?" Blake asked.

"Well, magical person that he is, Santa knew that Mom had found a puppy that isn't quite old enough to leave its mother, so Santa brought the dog bed, collar, leash, food dishes, and a whole pile of bones."

Robert smiled. "I remember my first dog. I was seven and we didn't need a dog bed, he slept with me."

"Well, that's probably what'll happen with this pup when she arrives in six weeks. Tell me, gentlemen, what are we celebrating?"

Blake smiled. "In jail, his plans for New Year celebrations completely ruined, is one James Stinley who sold dope to the redneck, who sold it to the car driver."

"Yes," said Laura, somberly delighted. "I knew you could do it."

Robert interrupted Blake. "But the best news is that the next most main man, one Hector Rodriguez, is coming soon and Stinley volunteered to arrange a meeting for us."

Laura raised her glass to toast them.

Robert was opening his mouth to continue, when Blake cut him off. "Today, I'm visiting with a friend from the Coast Guard who tells me that Washington ordered them to stop searching small private boats unless refugees were on board."

"What's the deal?"

Robert picked it up. "Apparently Senator Markham called the Coast Guard, very upset about some search they'd done."

Blake finished Robert's explanation. "The Coast Guard checked their records. They'd only searched a few dozen boats, but one happened to belong to Alex's and your friend, Tom Hilman."

"Well, well, well," Laura said softly, staring at the twinkling tree lights. "Alex's fingerprints are all over that move, aren't they."

Blake and Robert sat back and sipped their beers, silent.

"Do you need help from the feds to pick up Rodriguez?" Laura asked.

Blake acted very matter of fact. "With something this big, they would expect to bring him in."

"Why? They have something we don't?"

"Not really, but they've got manpower, fancy equipment—plenty of cash for the buy. We'll need big-time flash money."

"How much?"

"Probably a quarter million."

Laura whistled, impressed, but already scheming. "How much do we have in forfeitures?"

"Three hundred thousand, give or take, but it hasn't been awarded yet. You don't think the bank would loan it to us against the seizure account, would they?"

"Maybe, maybe not. Could you get by with less?"

"Possibly. But I don't want to screw up the deal."

"I'll talk to the president of the bank, if that would help."

Blake took a satisfied sip of beer, not daring to smile at Robert.

"What about manpower?" Laura asked. "Do you have to get extra folks from the feds?"

Robert spoke up. "These round-the-clock deals eat up manpower. It would be a stretch, but we could do it with just Patrol people if we detailed some TAC team members, special ops people, and a few investigators."

"But how do you keep this quiet?"

"We'd have to be real careful about who we choose."

"Be careful, then."

17

Even though the New Year had arrived, Tom and Ann's living room was still filled with Christmas. The tree in the corner was shedding its needles something fierce, doodads and decorations were everywhere. All over the coffee table and scattered around a blanket stretching into the walkway were Jesse's new toys. Most of the house was dark as Tom, well on his way to drunkenness, watched the news.

Increasingly nervous since the Coast Guard search that had prompted him to involve Alex—an impetuous act Tom deeply regretted now—the screw-up with Rodriguez really hacked him off. He'd been toying with calling it quits and leaving altogether. But the Cayman account was still short of his goal.

All evening long he'd been thinking about how much money he'd pissed away. Money seemed to vanish around Ann, and the baby was a black hole for cash. After polishing off several beers, Tom was certain of only one thing: the time to unload Ann and the kid had arrived.

How to get the ball rolling was the issue. He'd thought about telling her he was leaving to take up with his secretary, Ginger. But that could get complicated, and he wasn't interested in keeping Ginger part of his life any longer than necessary.

Still photos of Laura and Alex filled the TV screen. Tom picked up the remote and punched up the volume.

"United States Attorney Alex Markham and Commissioner of Public Safety Laura Owen seem locked in a battle over who's in charge of the war against drugs in Mississippi.

Footage of Alex leaving the federal courthouse rolled. Behind him, walking out jubilantly, were three scruffy drug dealer types, their hands raised in victory. When they saw Alex, they shook them in anger.

Tim Cropley's voice could be heard in the background. "Mr. Markham was forced to let three major drug dealers go free."

The camera switched to a stand-up interview of Alex, who looked angry and frustrated as he spoke. "Ms. Owen directed the narcotics agents to move too quickly, and the arrests were fatally flawed. It's a tough loss for the citizens."

Switching to a freeze-frame of the victorious waves of the drug dealers, Cropley added in voice-over, "Commissioner Owen was not available for comment."

Tom, talking to the TV, changed the channel to an action movie. "Goddamn politics. Jesus H. Christ. Serves her right anyway." He headed for the kitchen to get another beer, crushing the empty can.

Tom opened the refrigerator, muttering as he moved baby food and lite beers to get to the Budweisers, "There's no goddamn space for real beer." Loud gunshots could be heard from the television.

As he walked back into the living room, Tom tripped over a pile of Jesse's toys. Regaining his balance, he punted the plastic Duplo structure across the room where it broke against the wall, falling with a terrible clatter.

Ann awoke, her eyes open but confused. She reached for the clock on her night table. From the living room she heard Tom shout.

"Ann!"

She sat up, half-mad and half-scared, in the dark room. It was after 10:00 P.M., the television was blaring, and Jesse was crying. Throwing off the covers, she stumbled out of bed, waking up more with each step, and headed into the hallway as another series of clatters erupted. By the time she got to the living room, Duplos, wooden blocks, pieces of broken plastic and bits of decorations were scattered everywhere. Tom was eyeing the Christmas tree. He glared at her.

"Clean up this goddamned mess."

Ann went directly to the television and turned it down. "Keep your voice down. Jesse's crying but maybe he'll go back to sleep."

"I won't lower my voice. And it's too damn bad if he's crying. I've had enough of friggin' Santa Claus for a goddamn lifetime."

"Laura and Will were here for dinner. We waited for you...."

Tom mimicked her in a singsong voice. "'Laura and Will were here.'...Clean this mess up now. Jesus, there's crap every goddamned where. There isn't even a place to put my beer."

Ann watched in disbelief as Tom swept the contents of the coffee table onto the floor, sat back in the easy chair and put his feet up. He pointed to the floor area around the table. "Clean it up." He turned his gaze back to the television.

"Are those the only words in your vocabulary?" Ann asked as she started for the hall. "This can wait until tomorrow."

Tom jumped up and grabbed her arm. "No, it can't. Do it now." Tom shoved her at the toys and pushed her face down toward the floor. "I nearly broke my damned neck. Clean it up now."

Ann started to gather the toys into a pile. "What's wrong? This isn't about toys or too many Christmas decorations. You've hardly been here during the holidays."

"Well that doesn't make me any less sick of toys, and you and Little Miss Commissioner and the baby and all this crap that is suddenly everywhere in my life."

Tom tossed his empty beer can onto Ann's collection. She dropped everything and started toward the hall again.

"I'll do this when you're sober."

Tom got up, stepped toward her, and hit her hard across the face. Ann staggered back, clutching her right jaw. "You hit me, you animal," she said, stunned. "I told you that if you ever..."

"Well, you just got your wish. Get out of my house. Now."

Ann hurried past him, staying as far away from him as possible, cradling her jaw as she went. "Just stay out of my way long enough for me to leave."

■ ■ ■ ■

Shortly before midnight, Ann drove up to Laura's house and lights came on everywhere. When Laura reached her, Ann was half inside the backseat of her dark blue BMW, unbuckling Jesse's carrier, her face turned so that the bruises didn't show.

"Are you sure it's okay if I stay with you for a while?" Ann asked.

"Of course you can. You know there's plenty of room. Will'll love it."

When Ann pulled her head out of the car with Jesse in her arms, Laura saw her face and gasped. "Oh, Ann, what did he do to you? Is anything broken?"

"I don't think so. I started to go to the emergency room, but then I decided to get Jesse settled first. I'll see a doctor tomorrow if I have to. I do need ice on it though."

Laura picked up two suitcases and the diaper bag, and they all headed inside, out of the cold night.

As Ann got Jesse down in the guest room, Laura dumped a tray of ice cubes into the sink and wrapped the pieces in a washcloth.

"Jesse never woke up," said Ann, wincing as she put the ice on her jaw. "Thanks for taking us in."

"I wouldn't let you go anywhere else."

"Where's a glass? I need a drink."

"How about brandy?"

"Anything alcoholic. You pick it."

Laura poured some brandy and slid it toward Ann. Holding the ice on her cheek with one hand, Ann gulped down the whole shot as if she did it every day. Laura poured another and they headed toward the couch.

"The creep, he just exploded over nothing," Ann said. "Too many toys, too many decorations, crap like that. He's been weird lately. Maybe he's always been weird, I don't know. One day decent, even playing with Jesse. The next minute, we're dirt. He was gone half of Christmas, but he has the gall to complain about how I celebrated."

Ann took another swallow. "At first, I thought it was just the baby, but even a baby wouldn't make someone crazy. He will never, ever hit me again."

"Is it business?"

"Maybe, I don't know. He doesn't tell me anything. It's like living with a damn wall. And he's hardly ever home. I think he's been trying to leave since the day of the wedding. He's kept his distance—I think he's been doing it with everyone all his life."

Laura came back with the bottle and Ann poured another shot. "From the bank statements I've seen, money's coming in right and left. Every day they have another contract, and most of the time it's a casino, so they're getting their money up front. I push him to go sailing because it usually calms him down. But lately, he's come back worse than ever."

Laura looked at Ann's bruise. "Is this the first time he's hit you?"

"This hard, yes," Ann admitted. "He's shoved me around when he was drunk before, but not like this."

"What about counseling?"

Ann laughed so hard she winced with pain. "Are you kidding? Tom would never admit anything was wrong. Even if it was, it wouldn't be his fault. I got pregnant, I forced us to get married. No. He'd never go. I'm not going back there, ever. What if he went off like this with Jesse? I don't trust him. Deep down inside of him, something's really rotten."

"Ann, you can't be serious."

"I am. He's sick, I know it. I never told you this, but the day after that bomb went off under your car..."

"It was a grenade."

"Whatever. Tom was watching the news about it. He wasn't surprised or sad or angry. I'd swear he smiled. Just a small, but knowing, smile, and he wiped it off as soon as he realized I'd seen it. But it was there. I saw it. He's sick."

Laura looked truly shocked. "You think Tom had something to do with the grenade?"

"I don't know, but he wasn't surprised," Ann said. "I've thought about this hundreds of times and I should have told you, I guess."

"I understand," Laura said.

"We had a fight and I locked myself in Jesse's room. He left the house and was out half the night. I remember that night very clearly."

■ ■ ■ ■

Driving in to the office, Laura was mad at the world. The ever-dreaded Legislature was convening. The Governor's elderly mother had died an agonizing death from cancer, and Carver had been incommunicado for two days. Now Ann's problems were shifting to her. The New Year was not starting out well, to say the least.

To ice it all, a brand-new Cadillac passed her on the way to work, driven by a woman holding a toddler in her lap—sure death or at least substantial internal injuries to the toddler if the woman was thrown forward. Laura picked up the radio, called in the car tag and asked them to get the owner's information sent up to her office. Mississippi's toothless seat-belt law—a violation but no fine—was passed reluctantly after years of lobbying, so Laura waged her own private war. She sent drivers like this woman, one of her letters describing the pounds-per-square-inch thrust that would be applied to the child during a wreck, when crushed between the driver and the wheel. It probably didn't do any good, but it made Laura feel like she was trying.

She went directly to Blake's office where Robert was drinking a cup of coffee.

Laura barged past the door. "Got a minute?"

Seeing the all-business-no-bullshit look on her face, they both paid attention. "Shoot."

"Ann Hilman—Tom Hilman's wife, Alex's good friend—is at the doctor's getting her jaw fixed. Tom nearly broke it last night when he was drunk. She needs her statement taken and some pictures of her bruises. At this point, she doesn't want to file charges. She just wants a divorce."

Robert answered. "No problemo. I'll send Quinn if the Governor can spare him. If not, we'll find someone reliable. Where can we find her?"

"She'll probably be back at my house within an hour or two. She's going to stay with me for a while."

Laura stared out the window at the early morning traffic. "Something else. Ann said Tom smiled when he heard about the grenade blowing up under my car. Said he'd been out late the night it was planted. That he wasn't surprised at all when he heard the news. She won't say it in so many words, but she thinks he knows about it."

Blake and Robert exchanged surprised looks. "Why?"

"That I don't know," Laura said.

"Have you done something to him?"

"Not that I know of," Laura said. "Ann has always been a close friend of mine. Maybe he doesn't like the advice I've been giving her."

"That's not much reason to put a grenade on someone's car and a bag of dope."

"You know all I know," Laura said.

"I've got a little something to add," said Blake, clearing his throat. "The annual filing for Senator Markham's Better Government Fund shows that the Senator's been busy raising money but, catch this, Tom Hilman is the big bucks. Twenty grand so far. And, you'll just love the next part. The only person who has gotten any money from the fund is

Senator Collel. He got five thousand."

"Ooooh," Laura said. "All my favorite slimeballs in one place."

"We'll get on all this," Robert said. "Pronto."

▪▪▪▪

Laura stepped off the elevator and approached the receptionist sitting behind a dark cherry desk. Large brass letters spelling "Hilman Air" filled the wall behind her.

"I'm Laura Owen and I need to see Tom Hilman. I don't have an appointment, but it's very important."

"Does he know you?"

"Yes, he knows me."

The receptionist picked up a phone and dialed. "Ginger, there's a Ms. Owen here to see Mr. Hilman. Yes. Okay."

She turned to Laura. "He can see you in just a moment. His office is down the hall to your right. There's a waiting area outside his door."

"Thanks."

Tom opened his door as Laura approached. She smiled at the secretary at the desk right outside Tom's door. The woman looked Laura over very closely. Tom didn't introduce them. "Hold my calls, Ginger," he snapped.

He motioned Laura into his office and closed the door. Laura waited until he suggested which chair she should take and then sat down.

"I assume she went running to you?"

"She did. And she's staying with me. I'm here to deliver messages."

"Like what?"

"Her injuries are being documented, and she'll press assault charges if you go near her or Jesse ever again. She has a lawyer and wants a divorce."

"She's got it."

"She's going to pack her stuff over the next several days and doesn't want you around."

"I'll make that easy. I'll go down to the Coast for the week. Be gone by this evening. Anything else?"

Laura hesitated, and Tom immediately jumped up, opening the door to end the meeting.

"Don't you even care about Jesse?"

"Not really," Tom said. "The kid was her idea, not mine. I'll pay what I'm obligated to pay, but that's all."

"I know from experience," Laura said as she walked through the door, "that some day you'll change your..."

Ginger was still at her desk.

"Cut the crap, Laura, I don't want your advice. I don't want anything to do with you or her or Jesse. Need I be clearer?"

Looking straight back at him, Laura spoke in as calm voice as she could muster. "Hardly. But remember Tom, Ann isn't by herself anymore. If you ever touch her or Jesse again, you'll have to deal with me. Need I be clearer?"

Laura walked past him through the door and then turned back. "It was nice meeting you, Ms.?..."

"Silven, Ginger Silven."

"You work for a prince of a fellow," Laura said and strode away.

Tom looked at Ginger. "That sounded like she threatened me, wouldn't you say?" He headed back into his office, then stopped. "Get Alex Markham on the phone for me, will ya?"

▪ ▪ ▪ ▪

"Want to bury the hatchet on a short sail in the Gulf?"

Alex was surprised and immediately pissed by Tom's call. It was a delicate dance the two of them were doing these days. He wasn't about to be lured in deeper, but Alex also couldn't afford to offend Tom if he ever planned to wriggle out of his hold. Civility was clearly the better part of safety.

"Wish I could, man, but I'm covered up here. When are you leaving?"

"As soon as I can get my stuff packed. Ann and I have split, and I just told Little Ms. Commissioner that I'd be out of the house while Ann moved her things."

"What does Laura have to do with this?"

"She showed up here to tell me Ann was staying at her place. She damn near threatened me if I went near Ann again. Sounded like a goddamn trooper—so high and mighty, it made me want to retch."

"What was the threat about?"

"I knocked Ann down. Too drunk to know what I was doing. We haven't gotten on from the start, and I guess I was fed up. She's already gotten a divorce lawyer."

"Too bad you gave her so much ammunition. That one swipe probably doubled the alimony she'll be awarded."

"What's done is done," Tom said. " Laura wanted to make sure I knew she'd get the whole damn Patrol on my butt if I touched Ann again. As if I'd want to."

"Cool off Tom, you do need a sail."

"Damn right."

"Wish I could. But like I said, I can't get away right now."

"Well, probably best. I wouldn't be much of a companion anyway."

▪ ▪ ▪ ▪

Boxes were all over the house and Ann was packing objects, books, toys, and equipment in a totally haphazard way. Heading down the hall toward the bedroom, she passed Tom's home office door, his private domain. He rarely let anyone else in, not even her. Though he'd relied on her accounting background for business matters before they'd married, he'd never let her handle their personal finances, aside from the household checkbook.

Entering his office, she went immediately to the computer and flipped it on. After a few moments, the screen message asked for a password. She started typing combinations of names and places—HILMANAIR, JESSE, ANN, RUTHVEN but was having no luck. Then she tried LAST CHANCE and the screen cleared.

"It would be his damn boat."

She worked for a few moments bringing up file lists to see what was there, careful not to open anything. Besides engineering programs and a couple of games, the entire hard drive was data in various financial software programs. Rummaging through the desk, she found two full boxes of formatted diskettes and started backing up the whole drive, packing some things while it downloaded, and returning to change the diskette from time to time. When she was done, she flipped off the computer, closed the door, and dropped the diskettes in one of her packing boxes.

▪ ▪ ▪ ▪

Laura eased past Ann's stuff in her garage and came through the kitchen, depositing her briefcase by the couch. Ann was sipping a beer while she and Will entertained Jesse on the floor.

"Momma," Will yelled, running across the room for a hug.

"How's my boy?"

"Fine," Will said, snuggling his face into her coat. "How many more days until we get the puppy?"

"Twenty-nine, I think. I'll have to check the calendar." She looked at Ann's exhausted face. "Looks like you've been busy."

"Packing all day long, but I'm nearly finished. Sorry about the mess."

"Don't worry about that. It doesn't bother me."

Having Ann around was actually turning out to be a great help. She was good company and they'd quickly re-established some of the rhythms of their roommate years. Ann was able to handle the shopping, do some of the chauffeuring for Will, and best of all, get dinner underway each night. She was drinking too many beers, but so far that was limited to nighttime, and Laura wasn't going to comment. Everyone has their own way of dealing with stress.

Ann pulled out the diskettes. "How much space do you have on your hard drive?"

"I should have plenty. We upgraded to this mega-mega hard drive last year to hold all Semmes' design programs, but his partner cleaned those off months ago. What do you need?"

"I copied Tom's financial files. He keeps track of money better than anything except his boats. I want to look at them, but I've got to load them somewhere. Mind if I use your computer?"

"Heavens no, go right ahead," Laura said. "Let me change my clothes and I'll get dinner on the table."

Loading took the better part of an hour, shuttling between the computer and the children. When it was finally finished, Ann opened the program and checked the list of accounts.

"Holy smokes!" Ann said. "Laura! Come look at this."

"Something interesting?" Laura asked, appearing behind her in ratty blue jeans and sweatshirt, pot in hand.

"I didn't know about all this, look." Ann pointed to the screen. "There's more than just Hilman Air. There's Hilman Enterprises, Hilman Investments, Hilman Development."

"Alex was an incorporator on those."

"How'd you know that?"

"He's been trying his damnedest to slow me down. We came across it when we were doing a little checking."

Ann opened a Hilman Development Company file and ran a comparison profit and loss report. "Hilman Development must be making money. Look at last year's numbers over this year."

Laura whistled. "And Tom's never said anything? Did you sign a prenuptial agreement?"

"Nope, and since we haven't filed joint taxes yet, I had no idea." Jesse wailed in the background. Ann looked away from the screen and started to get up.

Laura put her hand on her shoulder. "Stay here and keep working. I'll worry about feeding the kids."

"Thanks," Ann said, already typing. She watched the screen, her eyes widening with each new report.

"This jerk is gonna pay," she muttered.

▪ ▪ ▪ ▪

Needing time to sort through case files on a trial set for the next week, Alex arrived at the office early. A morning news program was on and he half-heartedly listened while signing correspondence and initialing case reports.

One of the national networks was starting off the year with a series on the drug problem, and the day's topic was law enforcement's predicament. As he picked up another letter to read, he heard Laura's voice from the television. She was standing on the front steps of headquarters near the memorial statue to slain officers, looking very serious.

"There is no more dedicated, hardworking group of people in the country today than the officers of the State Patrol. But if the legal system can't handle their cases, and the penitentiaries can't lock away the criminals they catch, there's not much point in asking them to risk their lives."

With a backdrop of the list of officers killed in the line of duty, the commentator then ran through the statistics from The Blitz, and posed the question, "What's to account for these amazing results?" The camera switched to Lt. Colonel Jimmie Anderson, in uniform, speaking in his deep, soft southern accent.

"Commissioner Owen told us to come up with a war plan and she'd find the tools we needed to carry it out. We did and she did. It's that simple. If they're out there to be caught, we'll keep on catching 'em."

Another report began and the tape switched to open warfare on a Los Angeles street. Markham's private phone line rang.

"Alex, did you see that piece?" Senator Markham bellowed over the phone from his Washington office.

"Good morning, sir," Alex replied. "I did."

"What a softball report," the Senator said. "Why didn't they interview you? Can't you do something about her?"

"She's had every break in the world, sir. But her luck has to run out."

"You damn well better not leave this to luck, Alex."

"No, sir, I won't," Alex said.

"What can you do?"

"I was thinking about just that when you called."

"Well don't just think, son, do something," the Senator said, hanging up abruptly.

"Bitch," Alex said to himself. "Six years of shitty trials, champion of the little man..."

A tap on the door interrupted his muttering. Hal poked his head in. "At it awful early, aren't you?"

Almost shaking from the anger he'd built up, Alex snapped back, "Lots to do before the trial starts on Thursday."

Recognizing that Alex was in no mood for chitchat, Hal backed out. "Well, I saw your car in the garage when I came in and just wanted to say good morning. Catch you later."

Alex got a grip on himself. "I'm sorry. I was teed off at a national news story featuring Owen and her band of merry men."

"Yeah, I saw it downstairs."

"What's the deal, Hal?" Alex said. "Why didn't they talk to me? I've been doing this a lot longer than she has. How can she just whip in here and monopolize everything?"

"All I can figure is she's a new face, and a very different one, and it attracts attention. And she doesn't make mistakes."

"Goddammit, Hal, are you suggesting I make mistakes? I've been working my butt off for four goddamn years."

"Alex, I didn't mean it that way. Your record's great, too. Calm down and let's think about this thing."

"If I'm going to run for Governor, I can't be behind the goddamn curve," Alex said, now pacing behind his desk. "I've got to be out front, looking like a winner. And I am a winner, but nobody cares, they're all busy watching that little cunt."

Hal was stunned by the outburst and stood there silent.

Alex ran his hand through his dark hair, revving up again. "By God, the name Markham stands for power, for service, for accomplishment. My record as a U.S. Attorney is one of the best in the country. She's been meddling in my life for too long. Nothing but a pain-in-the-ass Goody Two-shoes. She's a novice, a nobody."

"Don't forget the First Families bit."

Alex scowled. "Her people might have been here a long time, but they haven't done anything worth remembering, haven't had one damn ounce of responsibility. Christ, what are things coming to if people like her get to make the decisions? And we're in real trouble if a woman represents this state to the nation. With my father in Washington, and me as governor, we could really deliver great things, more than she could ever think about bringing home."

He stopped his harangue and then looked straight at Hal. "And if you want to be commissioner anytime soon, you'd better help me win."

Hal locked into Alex's stare. He'd thought vaguely about his own possibilities if Alex were elected, but this was the first time Alex had raised it so directly. Commissioner Easterbrook. Sounded good.

"Let's blow off some steam at the range and then talk about it," Hal suggested. "You're overdue for qualification, remember?"

■ ■ ■ ■

Laura was parking behind the classroom building when Robert jogged up in winter track clothes and his Saints cap. He stopped, bent over, panting as he talked.

"You qualifying?" Robert asked.

"I have a gun issued to me, don't I?"

"I don't think commissioners have ever bothered before."

"I wouldn't know, but I'm not planning to be the exception to the new firearms policy," Laura said. "Imagine those headlines."

Laura hadn't ever carried a weapon—even when she was practicing criminal law—and breaking with tradition, she'd refused to have one issued to her when she became commissioner. The giant rechargeable flashlight installed in her car was about as menacing a weapon as she cared to have around. Even the phone calls from Mr. Mystery—which seemed to have stopped—hadn't really rattled her, given the nonaggressive profiles of those types. But the grenade under her car put her over the edge. At Blake's next entreaty, she agreed to keep a revolver in her briefcase.

"Before I forget," said Laura, reaching for the list of account numbers Ann had printed out, "could you find out where these are from? My good friend Tom seems to have accumulated lots of money."

"I'll try," Robert said, glancing over the paper before folding it away in his pocket.

Blake had revised the general order on firearms qualifications, tightening up substantially on the skill requirements. The danger posed by a lack of stiff standards had come keenly into focus when a cop somewhere up in the Northeast killed an innocent bystander. The family of the victim had a field day when they discovered that his department had never required regular qualifications. Blake was bringing troopers in, class by class, so the old guys were kept separate from the younger officers. This last session was reserved for troopers in administration, civilians carrying a weapon, and anybody who'd missed their scheduled session.

Blake, Robert, Laura, Jimmie Anderson, and Bill Kenner, plus thirty-five others, were ready. An instructor sat in the center tower issuing signals over a loudspeaker so that every position at the outdoor range could hear his orders. Kenner intentionally chose to shoot right next to Laura.

"I'll show the little lady a thing or two about shooting," Kenner confided to the trooper next to him.

After putting up their targets, everyone returned to the seven yard line and waited for the all clear. They fired six rounds, reloaded, and fired again within twenty seconds. Nearly everyone was within the eight ring, but a few, including Kenner, had perfect tens.

Laura's score—six nines and six eights—came as a complete surprise, particularly to Kenner. Everyone had assumed that her reluctance to carry a weapon was a function of not being able to shoot. Kenner still managed a swagger as he moved back to the fifteen yard line.

Six rounds, no reloading this time. The scores reversed: Laura had four tens and two nines; Kenner had all nines. A buzz began among the spectators, and two female troopers were grinning broadly. At the twenty-five yard line, everyone fired six rounds kneeling, reloaded, six rounds from the left of the barricade set at each station, reloaded, and the last six from the right. Laura shot more tens than nines, with one in the target's x-ring. Kenner did the same.

Lieutenant Mickey Travis, the range officer, ambled over, his back to Kenner. "Commissioner, is there something I don't know about you?"

"You mean about my shooting?"

"For starters," Mickey said, smiling.

"We had a rifle range in our attic," Laura answered. "Dad was the scout master for Troop 45, and my brothers were both marksmen. I practiced all the time."

Mickey put his head back, laughing. "Can you make this last series?"

"Probably. For some reason, I've always been better at a slight distance. Six rounds, no reloading, right?"

Out of the corner of her eye, Laura saw Alex and Hal appear from the parking lot and stop to watch the round. At the all clear, everyone fired. Both Laura and Kenner had a mixture of nines and tens. The two female troopers did a high five. Kenner didn't even stay to score his target.

"Laura, what a surprise," Alex said.

"Hello, Alex, Hal." Laura's tone was cool, slightly acidic. "Welcome to the range. It's qualifying day."

Alex and Hal both nodded to Laura and the others as they passed by with their ammo pails and targets. The Pistol Team—national and world champions for several years straight—had stepped up and immediately began practicing their perfection.

"I guess we should have checked first," Alex said, looking at the six men who were shooting. "I figured it wouldn't be crowded."

Mickey, always drumming up business, encouraged Alex and Hal to stay. "Have some coffee, Mr. Markham, watch the team. They're getting ready for the Police Revolver Championships. They'll be done in a few."

Alex watched Laura and Blake at the coffeepot as Laura took a cup off the stack and filled it, measuring in plenty of creamer. "We've got time, don't we, Hal?" Alex said, "Let's join them."

"Who taught you to shoot?" Blake asked Laura as she stirred her coffee.

"My dad, I guess. But mostly I taught myself. Lucky for me, it's like riding a bicycle and you never forget, because I haven't shot in years."

Everyone chatted while round after round hit bull's-eyes. After a few minutes, Laura put her empty cup down on the outside window ledge. She'd done her best to ignore Alex, but finally she couldn't resist.

"Why'd you stop the Coast Guard from searching boats?" Laura asked.

Her question was completely unexpected, but Alex mustered haughty indignation. Blake, Robert, and Mickey, all sensing the storm that was brewing, eased away. Hal stayed.

"I didn't," Alex said.

"Oh, don't give me that. They searched Tom's boat, he told you, you told your father, your father called the Coast Guard and—presto bingo— no more searches."

"Aren't you out of your jurisdiction?" Alex shot back. "I don't recall the high seas being part of the highway system."

"At least I'm trying, Alex. That's more than I can say for you," Laura said, turning away. After three steps, she stopped and looked back to Alex. "Next time, make your move a little less transparent."

When Laura had joined the others, Alex smoothly dropped his cup into Laura's empty one, and gingerly held both by the rim of his cup, the upper one.

"I'm outta here," Laura said to the men. "See ya back at the ranch."

Laura nodded to Hal as she passed. Alex was watching the team with an oddly contented look on his face and didn't make eye-contact.

18

C-96, a Trooper First Class from the Jackson District, turned onto McGovern Road to head home, his Saturday shift over until 5:00 P.M. the next evening. He came up behind a dark blue BMW with a woman driving, and as he followed her, he realized she was weaving, slightly but continually. "Damn. Right at the end of the day," he muttered.

City streets weren't in his jurisdiction except when a violation occurred right before his eyes. He picked up the radio mike to call in the tag and then stopped.

"I don't have a goddamn hour for you, lady."

C-96 was considering what to do when the BMW sailed through a red light and made his decision for him. Traffic had filled in the intersection, so he watched where the car went. As soon as he could move forward safely, he turned on his lights and siren and caught up with it.

Driving with the music up loud, crying, and singing along to "Stand by Your Man," beer in hand and three empties on the floor behind her was Ann Hilman. Just as she started to belt out another verse, she looked in the mirror and saw the blue lights. She wiped her face, sat up straighter, turned down the music, put on her seat belt, and pulled over, placing the bottle of beer behind her feet, out of sight. Then she grabbed her purse and peeled off a breath mint, popping it in before getting her wallet out.

C-96 picked up his ticket book and got out, hoping the woman didn't appear drunk, or if she did, that she lived nearby and he could take her home and be done with it. As he approached her window, C-96 noticed the empties. It was getting harder to solve without a ticket.

"May I see your license, ma'am?"

Ann offered him her wallet.

"Just the license, please," C-96 said.

Ann fumbled around trying to get the license out of its plastic compartment. All the while, the trooper watched her. When she finally handed it to him, she looked up. "Is something wrong, officer?"

"You ran a red light and you were weaving."

As he read the address, his heart sank. Ann Ruthven Hilman, 214 Mims Circle, Jackson. She lived on the other side of town.

"Is this your current address, ma'am?"

"No sir, officer, I'm staying with a friend on Middlefield Road."

There was hope again. Middlefield Road was closer, not more than five minutes away.

"Would you step out, ma'am?"

"Certainly."

C-96 opened the door and as Ann got out, she knocked over the beer bottle. He reached for the bottle and placed it on the roof of the car.

"Ma'am, do you know about the open container law?"

"No, I don't, officer."

"You can't have an open alcoholic beverage in a car. Come back to the patrol car, please."

Ann walked unsteadily to the rear passenger door of his car. Normally, he put violators in the front, but after a drunk tossed his cookies all over the seat, he decided he'd rather have that happen in the back. He pulled out his ticket book and started writing.

"Officer, I can explain everything. My friend..."

"You'll have a chance, ma'am. What's your address on Middlefield?"

"Five-three-three Middlefield Road."

The address rang a bell but he wasn't sure why. Looking up at her in the rearview mirror, he asked, "What's your friend's name?"

"Laura Owen."

C-96 turned around to look directly at her. "Commissioner Owen?" Ann nodded.

"Why didn't you tell me sooner?" Without another thought, he wrote "VOID" across the ticket.

"Let's get your things out of the car, Mrs. Hilman," the trooper said. "Lock it up and I'll take you home. You can pick the car up later."

"Thank you, officer. I really appreciate this."

That Saturday afternoon was particularly busy. Laura had taken Jesse for the day so Ann could have a break. He'd had his nap, an afternoon snack, and was now contentedly sitting on a blanket in the middle of the room, chewing on his hand and drooling everywhere. Tchaikovsky's "Peter and the Wolf" filled the living room and Will skipped around, busily building a block tower. Laura had every square inch of counter space covered with cans, vegetables, and utensils, cooking quarts of pasta sauce for the freezer.

Will was the first to see the trooper coming up the walk. He raced to open the door, ever fascinated with troopers and policemen. Standing next to C-96, Ann was tiny, and today, looked totally forlorn.

"Commissioner, I stopped Mrs. Hilman on McGovern Road weaving pretty bad. She had an open beer and several empties. Sailed through a red light."

Ann stepped inside. "I'm so sorry, Laura, I just got so depressed. I never went shopping. I've been driving around for hours."

"It'll be all right, Ann," Laura said, patting her friend's shoulder. "Go see Jesse. Let me find out about your car."

As they walked toward the patrol car, the radio squawked in the background.

"Where's her BMW?" Laura asked.

"A couple of miles north of here on McGovern, left side of the road." The trooper opened his door. "Can I give you a ride?"

"No, we'll get it later. Thanks anyway."

Laura watched him drive away, wondering how to deal with Ann. When she turned back to the house, Ann was at the picture window, looking utterly miserable and ashamed.

▪▪▪▪

The Chairman of the Senate Appropriations Committee for the Mississippi Legislature insisted that all committee members be present for the formal budget hearing on any major agency. This was when budgets got fine-tuned—everyone could put in their two cents and no one could gripe later. Laura brought all her departmental directors with her so that any questions she couldn't handle could be answered right then and there.

Laura got through her opening statement without interruption but that was it. Collel had whipped each committee member into a different frenzy about some aspect of her operations so that with every new topic, she was confronted with pointed questions.

When they came to traffic enforcement, Collel took over himself. He asked her to recite statistics about every type of ticket and the dispositions, focusing on drunk driving where she had placed the most emphasis.

"Commissioner," Collel said sharply, "in all your speeches, why do you continually harp on your ridiculous assertion that legislators are the worst offenders on fixing tickets?"

"From my first day, I have forbidden ticket fixing. It was rampant but I've never singled out legislators...."

"Don't get on your high horse with me," the senator interrupted. "You've turned every legislator who ever asked for help with a constituent into a crook, haven't you, Madame?"

"I'm doing my job the best way I know how—straight up. Ticket fixing may be as old as the hills, but it's a rich or powerful man's game, completely unfair. I believe in impartial application of the law."

The troopers were mystified about where the senator was headed. Cutting out ticket fixing had indeed raised a real stink since it was long considered a perk of legislative office. But the legislators all knew it was wrong, and they'd all lived by a code of silence. No one anticipated such a blunt attack, virtually admitting the practice.

Laura never took her eyes off Senator Collel. The Oversight Committee investigator passed a pink copy of a traffic ticket to him. Robert and Blake exchanged nervous glances.

"Commissioner, aren't you a bit like the pot calling the kettle black?" With a flourish, he put on his reading glasses and intentionally took his time looking over the pink paper. "Didn't one of your troopers bring a woman to your house just this past week who had been driving and drinking?"

Laura turned crimson, but kept her eyes on Collel. "Yes, sir. A friend is staying at my house and a trooper brought her home."

"Drunk, wasn't she," Collel said. "Didn't you ask him to tear up her ticket?"

"I did not. The officer had voided the ticket before he got to my house last Saturday. Two days later, when I discovered that he hadn't ticketed her, I asked him to do so."

"Convenient. The real story is you fixed a ticket one day, realized your mistake, and corrected it."

Laura's frustration and anger appeared to be confusion at first, but she quickly got her bearings and answered. "I repeat, I did not know the officer had not issued the ticket until two days later. I will bring him here to testify about the entire matter, if necessary."

"A commissioner can 'correct' things, can't she?" the senator added, unmistakably snide. "That's all I have, Mr. Chairman."

"Mr. Chairman, I respectfully request that if the budget of the Patrol rests in any way on this one false accusation, I have the opportunity to rebut these charges."

The Chairman was obviously irritated with the bickering. "You'll get your chance, Mrs. Owen, let's continue to the next topic."

Collel sat back with a satisfied smile.

A full hour and a half later, the hearing adjourned and Senator Collel went directly out into the hallway where Tim Cropley stood ready to tape his statement. When Laura walked out a moment later, in front of the phalanx of Patrol personnel, reporters rushed forward calling for her. Lights and cameras went on and Laura handled several serious budget questions in quick succession.

Then Cropley barged in, "How many tickets have you fixed, Commissioner?"

"I have never fixed a ticket, Mr. Cropley. Never." Her patience was exhausted by this point. "If you'll excuse me, I have an appointment with the Governor."

Laura stepped past the reporters, and Blake and Robert followed. Cropley's cameraman was still filming.

"Are you going to tell him about the ticket you fixed?"

Laura didn't look back but Blake stopped. "Didn't you hear her? She didn't fix a ticket," Blake said, teeth clenched.

"Were you the one who warned her that she'd made a mistake?" Cropley asked.

If Robert hadn't grabbed Blake's arm, Blake might have hit the reporter. "You're putting words into her mouth, and mine," Blake snarled.

Cropley smirked as he wound up the cord for his microphone and put it away.

"Why didn't you mention it?" Blake asked when he and Robert were finally alone with Laura in the waiting room outside the Governor's Capitol office. They'd left Bill Kenner and Jimmie Anderson outside.

"It wasn't a big deal," Laura said, "at least I didn't think it was at the time. I can't go running down the hall every time something happens."

"We're never too busy," Blake said. "You're not bothering us."

"I don't know how you take that stuff," Robert said, shaking his head. "You couldn't pay me enough to have your job."

The door to the Governor's office opened and Carver's secretary stepped out with a pile of letters in her arms and signaled to Laura.

Laura turned back to Robert to respond. "Well, if legislators were the only idiots I had to deal with, it might be okay." She paused as she picked up her briefcase, looking through the glass doors at Bill Kenner.

"But you tell me," Laura said, "who told them about that stop? It sure wasn't C-96. I made him issue the ticket. He was mortified when he realized the implications of what he had done. And I don't think it was his captain—he seemed just as concerned."

She took a couple of steps toward the Governor's door. "Ask yourselves who did that to you?" Laura said. "Because it's your pay raise that'll die in committee just because one jerk doesn't like a woman telling him what to do." She disappeared inside.

The men headed for Kenner.

Governor Carver was signing stacks of certificates at the far end of the room. His official office was at the Capitol, but since he much preferred working at the Mansion, it was reserved for ceremonial functions. However, during the Legislative session, he moved his base of operations to the Capitol, so he'd always be on hand to comment on legislation as well as to twist arms when votes were close. It was a spectacular room, perhaps the most impressive part of the Capitol renovation, because over the years, its beauty had not just been tarnished, but completely hidden. Few people had even remembered the vaulted ceiling or fireplaces and carvings that had been covered up by a drop ceiling and cheap paneling.

Vic entered from the side door behind Carver's desk as Laura took a seat in one of the straight, hard chairs, allegedly original to the room. Impossibly uncomfortable, they were nevertheless useful when the staff was whistling legislators in and out for conferences. If the Governor wanted a person to stay and chat, he directed them to the armchairs in front of one of the two fireplaces. But since he didn't move from where he was this time, Laura figured he hadn't called her in to commiserate.

He stopped writing for a moment but didn't put his pen down. "What's this about ticket fixing?"

"Ann Hilman. A friend of mine and Vic's. She left her husband Tom, vice president of Hilman Air—I think you know his father, Stephen Hilman. Anyway, Ann left Tom when he nearly broke her jaw. She's staying with me. Tied one on last weekend. A trooper stopped her and brought her back to my house. I didn't ask about a ticket at the time, I figured he'd issued one. Found out later he hadn't."

The Governor picked up another stack of certificates not saying anything. His silence was uncomfortable.

"I should have asked him about it right then," Laura said. "It was two days before I realized what had happened, I made him issue one then."

"How did Collel find out?"

"My guess is Major Bill Kenner. He hates my guts. He's not the only one, but he's at headquarters and had access to the ticket books."

"Transfer him somewhere," Carver said.

"I can't do that, Governor," Laura said.

"Your predecessor certainly did," Carver said. "He wouldn't allow somebody to whipsaw him."

"Perhaps *can't* was the wrong word," Laura said. "I won't. I don't operate that way."

"Well, then make it a one-day story, dammit, get all the facts out fast, even if it hurts your friend. You're on the block now. Actually, we're both on the block, and she's put us there."

Vic looked at his watch. In a voice much calmer than Carver's he added, "It's too late for the six o'clock news. Do it tomorrow, early."

"Would y'all like some good news? Laura asked, awkwardly, wishing she were somewhere else.

"Always," Vic said, hoping to change Carver's mood.

"We think we have a break that will get us inside a huge narcotics operation."

"When will this happen?" Vic asked.

"Not until the end of the month, unfortunately."

"That is unfortunate," Vic said. "Tomorrow or the next day might have been very nice timing."

The Governor showed remarkably little interest. He was still signing papers when she walked out. Vic stayed behind with Carver.

■ ■ ■ ■

By 5:52 P.M. it was dark and the headquarters lot was almost empty. Laura raced to the fifth floor, almost running into a janitor as she rounded the corner to get to her office.

"Sorry, wasn't looking," Laura muttered and kept on moving.

She opened her door, flicked on the lights, gathered up the remote control, and fell back in her chair to watch.

Because of a dearth of gruesome accidents or murders, Channel 4 had led with a piece about Legislative action.

"The deadline for the Senate subcommittee vote on the increase to the State Patrol budget is tomorrow. In other..."

Laura switched to Channel 2. Cropley was doing a stand up at the Capitol. "Commissioner Laura Owen made her pitch for the largest budget increase in the history of the State Patrol today, citing the war on drugs as the chief reason for her request. But Ms. Owen faces stiff opposition from senators who questioned her squeaky-clean image, accusing her of fixing a drunk driving charge for a close friend."

Laura stood up and started pacing. The camera switched to the interview with Collel.

"What can you tell me about this ticket fixing?"

"Mrs. Owen told a trooper to fix a ticket. I have the proof right here." Collel held up a copy of a ticket and the camera closed in. "The people deserve straight answers from Mrs. Owen. She lied about this ticket, and I think she's lied about her budget needs. Her estimated costs are riddled with padding so that she can wage a personal publicity campaign."

The film switched to old footage shot when Laura was questioned about the grenade planted on her car. Cropley's microphone was pushed aside as Laura rolled up the window and drove off. "Commissioner

Owen denies that she has fixed a ticket. She's often refused to answer difficult questions, and her refusal to be forthright today may have scuttled chances for the Patrol to get the resources it needs. This is Tim..."

"You bastard," Laura muttered as she picked up a book and hurled it over the TV at the wall above a bookcase. The book fell, knocking over several others on top of the bookcase, all of which slid toward others, and everything fell to the floor.

A moment later, one of the cleaning crew opened the door, hesitantly. "Are you okay, Commissioner?"

She looked up, still seething, and started jamming papers in her briefcase. "I'm okay." Unfortunately the outburst hadn't been cathartic enough. "Sorry to frighten you. Some books fell." She paused again. "Thanks for asking. By the way, I'll be out of here in just a minute. Should I leave the door unlocked?"

"Sure, I was headed in here just as you came in."

Disgusted with herself for losing control, Laura closed her door and left. Then she saw Bill Kenner headed to the elevator, her anger erupting anew. "Wait up, Major Kenner—I want to talk to you."

"Yes, ma'am?" His smile was more tentative than when she'd seen him after the hearing.

By the time she reached him, Blake and Robert had appeared from the other side of the floor. " Blake, Robert, I need you in on this," she ordered.

Laura looked at Kenner. "Remember my pledge—I'll do what I promise?"

The major nodded.

"Well, listen up," Laura said. "Here's a promise. I've been very patient, but no more. If you've done what I think you have, you've managed to jeopardize everything including the pay raise—your own pay raise. Tomorrow morning..." Laura looked right at Blake, "the Chief will begin investigating how Collel got a copy of C-96's voided ticket and why he didn't get the whole story. And when Blake's through, he'll put the report and charges on my desk. I'll wait until after the news has circulated that there won't be a pay raise and why, then I'll select the officers to hear the case. Since you're in his chain of command, I want you to be interviewed first."

Laura was pleased with Kenner's discomfort, the desired effect. "Sleep well, Kenner, pleasant dreams." She got in the waiting elevator and as the door closed, she wriggled her fingers in a wave.

"Well," Blake said, looking at Kenner, "how does eight o'clock sound?"

Kenner nodded.

Robert had punched the down button after the doors closed for Laura. The other elevator opened and Blake and Robert stepped in.

"Coming?"

Kenner shook his head. "I remembered some things I need to do."

"Can't imagine what," Blake muttered.

Robert stopped the door from closing and looked out at Kenner. "Say, how much more time do you have before retirement?" He waved goodbye, mimicking Laura's wriggling fingers.

The doors closed, leaving Kenner alone.

▪ ▪ ▪ ▪

At 8:05 the next morning, coffee in hand, Tom Hilman was leafing through a stack of mail and message slips, when his father stormed in, unannounced, with the newspaper in his hand, shaking. On the front page was a story about the ticket fixing episode, disclosing Ann's name and the fact that she was separated from her husband, giving Tom's name and business. Though the facts confirmed Laura's version of the events, the paper hadn't been able to resist mentioning, apropos of nothing, that commissioners could indeed "correct" their own mistakes.

"Why in God's name didn't you tell me about this?" Stephen Hilman bellowed.

"Because I didn't know about it."

"Don't you even communicate with her?" his father asked.

"No, only through our lawyers."

"Ann left a message with us last night but we were out and it was too late to return the call when we got in," Stephen said.

"She was probably going to tell you even though she didn't call me."

"Can't you do anything right?" Stephen said. "You marry a lovely girl, you have a beautiful baby boy, and then you throw it all away in a fit. Only an ignorant, undisciplined idiot would hit a woman."

He didn't back away from his father's stare but neither did he know exactly what to say. Stephen, sensing Tom's confusion, jabbed again.

"The only thing you have any talent for that I can see is sailing—and you do that all by yourself so you won't need to cooperate with anyone."

This pushed Tom over the edge. "No, sir, you're wrong. I've made this company bigger and stronger than you ever could have. But you don't have the character to acknowledge that because you've spent your whole damn life blaming me for my brother's accidental death—something I didn't want or cause—measuring me against some invisible, unattainable standard. Well, you can take your whole damn life and shove it."

His father was flabbergasted. After a long silence, he spoke up in a deep, calm voice, "You ungrateful bastard," and left.

Tom picked up his briefcase, stuffed the stack of papers inside and swinging his suit coat over his shoulder, headed out the door. He had no idea what his father would do next.

He stormed past Ginger, paying her no more heed than he gave any other employee. "I'm leaving for the Caribbean this afternoon. Be back next week."

19

FBI Special Agent Chris Salkin walked into Olivia Alvarez's office at the Gulf Goddess Casino, looking glum. "Did you think I'd forgotten about you?"

"I'd been wondering. But I'm well acquainted with the Bureau and its careful pace."

"Unfortunately, I've got only good things to say about the teller you're so concerned about. He keeps his nose clean, current on all his payments, got a nice wife and two children. He probably shouldn't be buying the house he's in, the payments are a little steep, but he's making it. However, I have developed some information about the people getting the checks. A few are small time drug peddlers and the like, who have been in or out of jail at one time or another. One guy is a contractor."

"Well, he did something yesterday that was really unusual and that's why I called you. Check out this tape."

She turned on a monitor in the corner and pressed the start button on the video player. The tape was already cued. "This guy comes in..."

"Who is he?"

"One of the regulars—he's gotten checks before so he's on that list I gave you—he comes in at 7:20 A.M., real slow time. My guy is the only teller on. He hands over some cash, all hundred dollar bills. The teller counts it—eighty-nine hundred dollars. I'll fast forward a little. Then they talk for a moment, the teller makes a phone call, hands the phone to the customer, he talks a minute, then the teller takes the phone back, nods, and then hangs up. Now, here, he doesn't give him chips, doesn't pass go, just converts it straight to a check."

"I think you can talk to him now," the agent said.

"Want to be there?" Olivia asked.

■■■■

The teller's wife stayed behind in the kitchen, listening to every word

Chris Salkin and Olivia Alvarez said to her husband. She looked around her at the new marble countertop and the big double-door refrigerator—Christmas presents from her husband—her skin prickling at an awkward silence from the dining room where the three of them were sitting. From her place in the shadows, she could see them looking at her husband, and he looking back, paralyzed by something—fear she supposed—unable to say anything.

"What's your explanation," Chris Salkin repeated.

His wife caught her husband's eye and with one slow blink, let him know that no matter what happened, they'd be fine.

He nodded back, smiling meekly. Olivia turned and saw her then looked quickly back at the teller.

"Schaeffer gave me a list of people for whom I could write Casino checks without getting his permission each time—all under the reporting limits," the teller said.

"What was in this for you?"

"Bonuses," the man replied. "That's all."

"How'd you do it?"

"They'd come in and get chips from any teller, hang around for a while and then cash out with me. This last time, was different though. No one was at the other cages and the man was in a hurry. He insisted I take the money and write the check directly. I called Schaeffer and he told me to go ahead. Just that once."

"How many people did you do this for?"

"Six or seven. I can go get the list—it's in my cash drawer."

"Why should I believe this is Schaeffer's deal and not your own for a percentage of the money?"

The teller smiled. "Because I tape recorded the conversation the day Schaeffer gave me the list."

Neither Olivia nor Salkin showed their glee.

"So you knew something was wrong from the start?" Olivia asked.

He nodded his head, slowly. "I needed the extra money. And since the extra money came in my paycheck—not under the table—taxes paid, everything, I figured the problem was Schaeffer's, not mine."

"It's not quite so tidy as all that, but we'll see what we can do to help you."

▪ ▪ ▪

Friday morning, Olivia learned that Schaeffer was leaving for Las Vegas on Saturday and called Salkin hoping he could interview Schaeffer that afternoon during her weekly meeting with him.

Immediately after Salkin introduced himself, Schaeffer insisted that his lawyer be present. It was an hour before his lawyer could get there.

Salkin, Olivia, and a second agent sat on one side of a table in the conference room, with Schaeffer and his lawyer on the other. They hadn't let Schaeffer out of their sight, and the armpits of his bright green sport coat were soaking with sweat.

"Your teller was no dummy," Salkin said. "Not only was the list in your handwriting, but that little tape-recording seals it."

The lawyer stopped Schaeffer from saying anything.

"We've done a little research on the people you were helping—drug peddlers and petty criminals mostly."

"My client didn't know their business," his lawyer said.

"I don't think that matters," Salkin growled. "Do you?"

"It certainly does."

"Well," Salkin said, leaning back, fully at ease with his position, "this last little move, changing cash directly to a check, is what killed you. It's called money laundering and the federal government has always had an interest in that sort of criminal activity."

Schaeffer rolled his chair back and talked to his lawyer privately. After a few moments, they returned to the table.

"My client would like to cooperate," the lawyer said.

"How?" Salkin asked, not moving from his spot.

"He has some information that will be available in just a few hours. Are you interested in a deal?"

"It depends on what you're offering."

"How about if one of those people on the list is delivering some cocaine tonight?"

"Interesting," Salkin said. "How much is he bringing?"

The lawyer consulted with Schaeffer again and then looked at Salkin. "He's brought Cleve as much as a pound in the past."

"Now that might be worth something," Salkin answered.

■ ■ ■ ■

They didn't have much time to get ready. While Salkin called Jackson to get permission for the video and tape recordings from the Special Agent in Charge, they wired Schaeffer's office, hiding a camera behind his desk that could film nearly the entire room. They also placed bugs sensitive enough to pick up whispers in several spots. Salkin was worried that nervous as Schaeffer was, he'd blow it even though all he had to do was chitchat until the cocaine was handed over. He made Schaeffer change into a dark-colored suit coat.

The power could go on the minute approval came through. The suspect's name didn't ring any particular bells with the SAC when he called back. He tried to reach Alex Markham, but Alex hadn't responded to his calls. Since technically the FBI SAC didn't need Alex's permission, he told Salkin to go ahead and he'd keep trying to find Alex.

When Tom Hilman arrived around 8:30, the Security Guard at the front door alerted everyone that he was on his way up. Schaeffer warmly welcomed Tom as he always did, and moments later, they were sipping drinks in the sitting area. Tom seemed exhausted.

"Long day?"

"Momentous day. I sold my first sailboat and had to get it ready for the new owners."

Tom put a small bag of cocaine on the table. Schaeffer picked it up and walked to the safe.

"This isn't much," Cleve said. "I'll need more."

"Sorry, no more."

"Why?"

"Bad for your health."

"A pity, my high rollers do enjoy the perks of playing here. I don't think anyone else serves a complimentary line or two. Is something wrong?"

"No," Tom said. "Just cleaning up my act."

"Well, I certainly appreciate what you've done," Schaeffer said. "Do you know someone who might be interested in continuing in your place?"

"No idea." Refusing to be drawn into Schaeffer's questions, he changed the subject. "Two more boats filed for bankruptcy. What's the deal?"

"Did they owe you money?" Schaeffer asked.

"Not too much, but I doubt I'll ever see any of it."

The men chatted on for ten minutes more before Tom stood up to leave, chugging down the last swallow of his drink.

The double doors opened and Salkin and his assistant entered, their credentials out. Olivia stepped in behind them.

"Thomas Hilman?" Salkin said.

Tom nodded.

"I'm Chris Salkin, special agent for the FBI. You're under arrest for delivery of a controlled substance. Please put your drink down and your hands in the air. Remain standing."

Tom watched a cold sweat break out on Schaeffer's face. "You prick," Tom muttered.

They patted Tom down, handcuffing him behind his back as Salkin read him his rights.

"I want to talk to Alex Markham," Tom said. "I'm not saying a word to anyone until then."

▪▪▪▪

Tom paced around the conference room of the FBI offices in the Gulfport Federal Building, chain-smoking, while Salkin and another agent leaned back in their chairs, watching him and explaining, over and over, what he was up against. Tom listened to everything they said, but true to his word, said nothing in response. He was angry and scared, and for the longest time, he couldn't get a handle on the angles of the situation or how to think about his options. When the door opened and Alex entered, relief spread through him but only for a second. From the look on his face, Alex been fuming all the way from Hattiesburg where Salkin had tracked him down.

Salkin jumped up. "Good evening, sir."

"Hey, Tom," Alex said, glancing quickly at him and then riveting his attention on the agent. "Salkin, what's this all about? Tom's an old friend of mine."

"Sorry to bring you all the way down here, Mr. Markham. Mr. Hilman has been supplying the manager of the Gulf Goddess with cocaine since it opened a year ago. I'm trying to get him to help himself out. He said he wouldn't say a word to anyone until he'd spoken with you."

"Is this true, Tom?"

Tom looked from Salkin and to Alex. "Could we talk privately? Is that allowed?"

Alex looked back at the agents who both shrugged their shoulders. He addressed Tom. "Well, it's not standard procedure, but since I won't be handling this matter in any way..." Alex looked at Salkin. "Give us a minute. Maybe I can explain things to Tom."

The agent walked out. Alex and Tom sat close together at the end of the table.

"You've got to help me, Alex," Tom said. "What do I tell them?"

"You stupid son of a bitch," Alex said. "What have you said so far?"

"Absolutely nothing."

"Good. Then this is what you say until we have time to think this through. Tell them a story about bringing in a pound or two from Belize. Tell them the supplier sometimes comes to the U.S. and you can arrange to introduce them. Don't use real names. Be very careful because they'll try and trip you up if you say anything inconsistent. Agree to cooperate. They'll charge you, print you, and let you go. Not enough manpower to tail you for long. Stay out of circulation for a couple of days and don't call anyone—definitely not your supplier. Rent a car and come to my house on Monday. I'll be out of town all this weekend on a deal that can't be canceled. Then we'll figure something out."

Alex reached in his back pocket and pulled out his wallet, getting out a card and writing an address and phone number on the back. He was bearing down so hard he nearly bent the tip of the pen.

"I don't know what happened, and I don't want to know, but I can't believe you were so goddamn dumb." He handed Tom the card. "Here's the number and street address for the new house. Call me from phone booths only. If I'm home, I'll answer it."

"I appreciate this, Alex."

"You damn well better." Alex got up, went to the door, and yelled down the hall, "Salkin."

Salkin and the other agent appeared from around the corner.

"Tom's ready to talk. As you can understand, I can't be involved, but I've explained the process. He'll cooperate, I'm certain." Alex looked back at Tom, disgust spreading across his face. "Good luck."

As Alex walked away, he realized his jaw was so tight his teeth hurt. Completely distracted by his anger, he was stopped outside Jackson by a trooper for doing 85 mph in a 55 mph zone. He hadn't paid any attention to his speed until the blue light came on. The trooper let him go with a warning.

▪ ▪ ▪ ▪

Late that night, the doors of the courthouse opened to the quiet streets and heavy air, a thick reminder of the long, hot summer to come. Tom walked quickly to his Jaguar, slamming his hand on the roof with such rage that the sound echoed off the wall of the building. Yanking open the door and getting in, he sat a moment, shaking his head. Finally, he cranked the engine and drove off. A nondescript compact car followed him.

▪ ▪ ▪ ▪

Master Sergeant MaryAnn Tolliver was on duty at the home of James Stinley, when a fifty-five-pound box arrived by Fast Action Express having been shipped late Friday evening from Pascagoula. She watched the drug dealer sign for the shipment, then she called Robert and told him the party was on for that night. By the next evening, the entire house had been wired for video and sound. Stinley left Sunday morning accompanied by his new girlfriend, MaryAnn, to make his rounds.

All they had to do was wait.

▪ ▪ ▪ ▪

Early Monday morning, Tom phoned Alex before he left for work. Keeping the call short, Alex suggested Tom stop by after eight that evening. As soon as he got to the office, Alex called Hal in, and with just the right amount of disgust in his voice, unloaded his hostility toward Tom for dragging him into the arrest. He managed to get a full report from Hal without arousing any suspicions.

Shortly after seven that evening, Alex was in his kitchen finishing cleaning his .38 snub-nosed revolver when his father called, having just gotten back to Dinsmor from a meeting of the Delta Conference where citizenship awards had been presented to area residents. Laura had been the featured speaker at the conference.

"She was good, son," Senator Markham said. "That was the first time

I'd seen her in person. Sounded so damn sincere. How does she do it?"

Alex put the gun in the pocket of his sweatpants and paced the kitchen of his new house, cradling the phone against his shoulder, thinking about Laura and Tom.

"I don't know, sir."

"Did you see the Crime Forum responses?"

"Yes, unfortunately. I can't understand how my performance rating has plummeted. So far I've been winning my cases, not losing."

"Maybe the responders are comparing you to her?"

"She has a whole damn army to do her work."

"Perhaps that's it," the Senator mused. "She appears so squeaky-clean. Is it possible that she's not as wholesome as she looks?"

Alex didn't answer immediately, frustrated, as always, with his inability to mar Laura's pristine reputation. "Maybe."

"There aren't any skeletons in your closet, are there?"

Alex hesitated, which alarmed the Senator.

"Son, did you hear my question?"

"Well, I'm not a virgin, sir."

"I should hope not. If it's heterosexual, and nothing too kinky, you're fine."

"Then I'm fine."

The Senator sighed, relieved. "Well, son, while it's not quite time to panic, you can't let her take over the spotlight like she's doing. You can't let up on the pressure."

"She's bound to screw up. I've seen all the sides of her over the years and she's far from perfect."

"But I'm counting on you, and so are some very generous friends of mine. Don't let this slip through our fingers, dammit. I've worked too hard."

Alex looked at the clock and started pacing again. "Senator, I've got to go."

"Keep working on her, son," the Senator said. "You can do it, I've got confidence in you."

"Thank you, sir. I'll be in touch."

Alex stared across the empty living room, focusing on one of Bill Dunlap's paintings from his dead deer carcass phase. He went out to his car and dialed Laura's listed number on his carphone, covered the mouth-piece with cloth, and was ready to add a thick twang to his words when Ann answered.

"Is Laura there?" Alex asked, adding two extra syllables to the phrase.

"No, she won't be back until later this evening," Ann said, hitting the record button. "Is this someone from the Patrol?"

"Just a friend."

A silver Lincoln Town Car drove in and parked in Alex's driveway. Wearing a turtleneck sweater for the cool evening, Tom looked a little haggard. He checked the cars passing by on the street and headed up the walkway to the front door, not noticing a pile of building debris until he'd walked through it. He attempted to wipe his running shoes on the concrete walk since there wasn't a doormat. Some forgettable rock music played in the background, drowning out the doorbell.

After Tom rang a few more times, Alex finally answered, inordinately cheerful. "How's it going?"

"Okay, considering," Tom said. "What are you so happy about?"

Alex shrugged, a silly smile on his face.

Decorating was still in progress and building materials were stacked around the foyer. Painter's cloths covered part of the floor. The living room walls had been finished in a creamy beige, and Alex had grouped several paintings on each of two walls. Otherwise the room was empty.

"Very nice," Tom said, looking around.

"Anyone know you're here?"

"Nope," Tom said. "Rented the car late this afternoon and haven't been home since. They tailed me from the time I left the courthouse until shortly after I got to Jackson, but then they disappeared. I drove all over before coming here, just to make certain. Except for being fol-lowed at first, it went like you said it would."

"So what deal did they cut you?"

"I agreed to set up my supplier, but I told them his name was Raoul and it isn't. I didn't tell them how big an operator he was or how much I was moving."

"Did you mention my name?"

"Of course not." Tom paused. "At least, not yet."

"What do you mean by not yet?"

"If you don't help me, then mutually assured discretion ends. All I want is to walk off into the sunset, without any cops tailing me. But I can't give them my source. This is a first offense, small amount of dope. If I have to pay a fine or spend some time on probation, I can handle that. But nothing major and no one touches my money. Now do your stuff and get me out of this or I'll take you down with me."

"And then I get the boat videotape, the tape-recordings, and all the stills?"

"Exactly. They're locked up tight where only I can get them."

"Aren't you prepared."

"An Eagle Scout to the end."

Alex patted him on the shoulder. "You want a beer?"

"Sure."

Alex went into the kitchen, opened the refrigerator, and pulled out two cans of beer, watching Tom the entire time. Tom had just turned away from him, and was slowly running his hand up the side of his head through his hair, frustrated and fatigued. Alex pulled the gun from his pocket, quickly stepped back into the foyer, raised it to Tom's head and fired through his brain, grazing the edge of Tom's right hand. Blood and brain tissue splattered in a wide arc across the foyer wall and into the living room.

Tom staggered for a second then gripped the corner between the foyer and the living room with both hands, desperately holding on. He leaned against the wall for a moment trying but unable to speak. Then his lifeless weight dragged him down. His dead eyes stared up at Alex as a pools of blood spread from his head and hand.

Alex watched him for a moment to make certain there was no more movement then went back to the kitchen. He put the gun down on the counter, pulled a pair of nylon examination gloves from a drawer and put them on, grabbed one of the painter's cloths from the foyer floor and rolled Tom's body onto it. He examined the corner of the wall—blood had splattered everywhere, there were smears from Tom's hand wound, and looking closer, Alex noticed several places where Tom's fingernails had scraped the paint.

He searched Tom's pockets for the rental car keys. He found not only those keys but Tom's house and car keys and a small baggie of cocaine. Keeping both sets of keys, he stuffed the baggie back in Tom's pocket. He dragged the body into kitchen where he stopped at the sink, ripped off a paper towel, wet it and wiped off the bottoms of Tom's shoes. He examined Tom's hands and pulled out a small paring knife. Putting a paper towel under the hands, he quickly pared under Tom's fingernails.

After throwing the towel in the trash, Alex dragged the body down three steps, Tom's head klunking on each step, and stopped at the door to the garage. As he started to touch the doorknob, he stopped, turned back into the kitchen, peeling off the dirty gloves and throwing them away, and pulled on another pair. Then he returned to the garage and closed the house door before he hit the garage door opener. He moved his office car out and backed the rental car in, closing the garage door behind him. He dragged the body over the doorsill and down the last step.

When he lifted the body out of the cloths, Tom's head fell toward Alex's shoulder, blood dripping on Alex's shirt. Alex dropped the torso into the trunk with a thud and then pushed it as far back as he could, lifting up the hips and legs, and bending them to get everything in. As he slammed the trunk, Tom's eyes were still on him. Alex took the painter's'cloth and stuffed it in a large plastic trashbag and took the bag into the kitchen with him.

He changed gloves again, and cleaned the gun, placing it in a kitchen drawer. From under the sink, he got a plastic bucket, sponge and cleanser. After sopping up the blood and brain tissue as best he could, he sprinkled cleanser everywhere and scrubbed the stains on the floor and walls until he couldn't find any more traces. He took another painter's cloth from a stack in the corner of the foyer and spread it over the area. The sponge, towels, gloves, and kitchen trash all went into the trash bag.

Alex hunted everywhere for the bullet and finally found it in the wall about three inches from the edge of the Dunlap painting. He lifted the canvas down and headed back to the kitchen for an awl. He was about to get hold of the bullet when he shifted his weight forward slightly, pushing the bullet all the way through. He heard it drop into the space between the living room and bedroom walls.

"Goddammit," Alex cursed.

It couldn't be retrieved without removing the whole section of wall. But he needed to get the body out of the house as fast as possible. Alex settled for repositioning the painting to cover the hole—he'd fix the spot later somehow.

Throwing the awl into the kitchen tool drawer, Alex changed into dark running clothes and added his bloodstained sweats to the plastic trash bag. He tossed the bag into the garage then went back to the kitchen. From behind some sauce bottles in the cabinet next to the range, he extracted a baggie containing a styrofoam cup. Putting on a new pair of gloves, and holding the cup by its edge, Alex headed to the garage, locking the house and setting the alarm. He placed the cup under the front seat of the rental car, stashed the trash bag in the trunk of his Cadillac to throw away later, got in Tom's rental car, and drove off.

On a stretch of Laurel Street not far from the entrance to a vest pocket park, the streetlights were burned out and it was dark. Alex parked in the darkest spot, moved the driver's seat forward as far as he could, got out, and locked the doors. Stuffing the gloves in his pocket, he jogged home in the darkness.

Three hours later, several blocks from Tom's house, Alex parked and walked up Mims Circle. There were no cars on the street. He ran past the house to the next intersection and turned back. Approaching quickly, he darted in Tom's driveway and disappeared behind the house, pulling on his gloves.

Having been there often, he knew the alarm didn't work. But out of caution, he opened the door then stepped back out and hid in the bushes, watching in case a silent alarm had been activated. After twenty minutes, when neither the police nor the neighborhood patrol showed up, he went back in. He turned on the lights but stayed away from the windows. The house was a mess except for Tom's office. With the file cabinet keys in hand, he searched drawer after drawer until he found the incriminating videos, the recordings, and the photos.

20

A very chilly ground fog hovered over the Laurel Street park early Wednesday morning. The garbage truck, on its weekly rounds, moved down the street and pulled up next to the rental car that was blocking easy access to the large, dark green garbage can in the park. Three stray dogs were nosing around the rear of the car.

When the young black man hopped down from his perch at the back corner of the truck, the dogs growled at him. He ignored the strays at first, but when he got closer to the trunk, they snarled louder to keep him away. He backed off and yelled to the driver.

"Must be something dead. It stinks around here."

Stepping back, the young man got down on his knees but saw nothing under the car. A morning runner slowed down but catching a whiff of the smell, sped up again, shaking his head. One of the dogs jumped at the trunk again.

Leaning out of his window, the driver yelled, "It's in the trunk, whatever it is. Forget the pail. We'll get it next time. I'll call Dispatch."

The young man looked around a bit more, then jumped on the back, whistled, and the truck rumbled off to the next house, the driver talking on the radio.

■ ■ ■ ■

Police cars flanked the rental car. The two cops had waited for the Hertz people to get there with a key, but after half an hour they decided to pick the lock and pop the truck open. As the lid flew up, the stench became much stronger and the policemen backed off, turning away from the sight of the greenish, bloating face.

"Shit! Why did this have to happen on my shift?" groaned the first officer.

A light blue minivan pulled up half a block away at the entrance of the park and a woman got out, looking back at the police officers as she opened the sliding side door. She began to unbuckle the first of three children, all in car seats.

"Oh, Jesus," the second officer said.

"Go tell her the park is closed, will ya?" the first officer said, pulling out his portable radio to call downtown.

▪ ▪ ▪ ▪

Catherine Britton was in the serology section at the Crime Lab talking with architects from the building commission about installing new fume hoods when a lieutenant from the Jackson Police Department's homicide unit called asking if the Lab could cover a crime scene.

"Everyone I got is working the triple last night at the motel," said the JPD lieutenant. "We're breaking some new record on homicides, and bodies are stacking up for autopsy. Could you handle a case for us that's right in your neighborhood?"

"Just the scene or do you want the Patrol to investigate?" Catherine asked.

"I really need both. But at this point, I've got to get the body out of there. It's in the trunk of a car, near a neighborhood park, and I'm told it's not a pretty sight."

"No problem. If you would, call Robert Stone about investigating."

"Fine," said the lieutenant.

"Where do I send the paperwork?" Catherine asked.

"Stay in touch with me."

Catherine turned back to the architects. "Duty calls. Anything more you need from me, or can the technicians handle your questions?"

"Go ahead, we've got almost everything."

▪ ▪ ▪ ▪

By the time Robert arrived, the normally quiet neighborhood park looked like a set for a TV cop series. The two police cars covered the ends of the two-block area, prohibiting general access. An ambulance was waiting to take the body to the morgue for autopsy. Two marked crime lab vehicles, the medical examiner's four-wheel drive, and several unmarked investigative cars were parked away from the rental car. A television news truck, having picked up a tip from their scanner, was just pulling up. Bright yellow crime scene tape sealed off the area, holding back a small collection of neighbors and mothers with strollers full of young children headed for the park.

Analysts and investigators walked carefully around, some with sketch pads, some with cameras recording as many details of the scene as possible before the car was removed. The medical examiner finished his on-site investigation and conferred with Catherine about moving the body out. The crime scene people had collected all they could and motioned Catherine to go ahead as they continued discussing the scene, gesturing here and there.

Robert went straight to Catherine, watching over her shoulder as they struggled to get the body out of the trunk. "Why are we working this?" he asked.

"The police are covered up. Jackson homicide called, desperate for help."

"What's the deal?"

"Dead, gunshot wound to the head. Been here one or two days—got a chance to cook yesterday. Thomas Hilman, 214 Mims Circle."

"You're kidding," Robert said.

"Know him?"

"God almighty, his ex-wife lives with the Commissioner."

"Holy cow," Catherine muttered.

■ ■ ■ ■

Laura was leaning against the second floor railing of the Capitol Rotunda talking to one of the younger new legislators from the Gulf Coast about the crime bill when her beeper went off. She looked down at the readout to find the emergency signal.

"Could you excuse me for a minute?" Laura asked. "This is one of those run-don't-walk calls."

"No problem. You've got my vote in any case. I'll see what I can do with a few of my colleagues."

"Thanks very much for your help."

She hustled into the Governor's office looking for the first free telephone to return Blake's call. Listening to the details, she sank into a chair, stunned.

"I'll track down the Hilmans and Ann," Laura said. "Make sure Alex gets the word. For once, I ought to be compassionate."

■ ■ ■ ■

When the elevator doors opened at the fifth floor, Deborah called out without even looking up from her typing, "Everyone's in the conference room, Commissioner."

"Who's everyone?"

"Colonel Coleman, Colonel Stone, Ms. Britton, a nice guy from the Jackson Police, and two FBI guys—no small-talk-types."

Hal Easterbrook and another FBI agent Laura had never met, were fixing their cups of coffee, ignoring the Jackson Police investigator standing near them. Catherine, Robert, and Blake were deep in conversation a few feet away.

"I'm Laura Owen," she said, stepping up to the police officer.

"JPD Homicide, ma'am. I appreciate your people helping out today— we're overloaded downtown."

"That's what we're here for," Laura said.

"Good afternoon, Hal," Laura said. "I know this isn't your normal beat, but Tom was such a good friend of Alex's."

"We appreciated your calling," Hal said. "Turns out this really is our territory—Hilman was arrested last Friday for selling cocaine. He was out on bond after he'd agreed to set up a meeting with his supplier."

Hal swung his hand toward the other agent. "Commissioner, this is Walter McNee, a new agent in our office who specializes in homicide."

McNee was about six feet tall, dark hair, and light blue eyes, 45 or so, and in FBI good shape. He shook Laura's outstretched hand as she looked at Robert and Blake who were just as shocked by the news as she was. "Tom Hilman was dealing?"

Hal answered. "He only admitted bringing in small amounts in from Belize. He was supplying the manager of the Gulf Goddess Casino in exchange for laundering some cash from time to time. That's how he got caught. The director of surveillance for the Gulf Goddess Casino had called us in on the laundering business. But from what the manager said, he thought Hilman was moving in a lot more. We tailed him after he was released to make certain he went home, but we didn't have the personnel to stay on him after that."

Blake stepped closer to Hal to get his attention. "And of course, you didn't call us—the manpower specialists, did you?"

"No," Hal said abruptly, as if he'd never deign to ask for the Patrol's help. He turned to Laura. "I understand from Alex that Hilman was getting a divorce. What's the status of that?"

"Why don't we all sit down," Laura suggested. As she pulled up a chair and settled in, she continued. "The Hilmans' divorce was messy—in fact, Ann's living with me. Remember the great ticket fixing debacle? A trooper drove someone to my house?"

"I read about that," Walter said.

"That was Ann Hilman."

Walter looked at Catherine. "What kind of evidence do you have so far?"

"Looks like he was shot at close range—less than twelve inches. The medical examiner thought the body'd been in the trunk about for one, maybe two days."

"We're canvassing the neighborhood for people who saw the car," Robert interjected. "It's not unusual, apparently, for cars to be parked there."

Catherine nodded and continued. "It was hot and sunny Tuesday—warmer than usual for February—and the trees around there don't have any leaves on them to block the sun, so the body had a chance to really cook. The garbage people noticed the smell this morning. Doc's doing the postmortem now."

"What about prints?"

"There are prints all over the car, as you would expect with a rental. But there are also a lot of smudged ones. The killer was probably wearing gloves. A styrofoam cup up under the driver's seat had a couple of latent prints of value that weren't Hilman's, and some gunpowder residue. And we're preparing the photos to overnight to Washington. We can't do the search here—still aren't online with the automated fingerprint system."

"We'll make sure the Lab speeds up this one," Hal said, in his usual officious tone. "You might be able to fax the photos if they're clear enough." Turning to Laura, he asked sharply, "What else can you tell me about his wife?"

"Ann left Tom after he nearly broke her jaw one night during the holidays. She and the baby have been staying with me ever since. Divorce negotiations have been rough. He didn't want to pay a dime over minimum child support even though he's got gazillions."

Hal kept looking at Laura, not saying anything.

"Ann didn't do it, if that's what you're thinking. She's been at my house every night, taking care of her son and mine. On Monday night she was at Tom's parents, with both kids because I was getting back late. I've been on a round of speeches."

Robert spoke up. "Our investigators on the Gulf Coast are already at Hilman's Ocean Springs house and searching the boat. I should be hearing from them in an hour or two. And I'll be heading over to his house here after this breaks up."

Hal turned his attention from Robert to Blake. "We'd like to handle this. Hilman's supplier may have found out he'd been picked up and set up the hit."

Laura tightened her lips in resignation, nodding to Blake to agree. He looked over at the lieutenant then addressed Hal. "It's not really our case, Hal. This was inside the city—JPD Homicide called us in."

Hal looked at the police officer for the first time.

The lieutenant threw up his hands. "Hey, I don't even have time to be here, much less get ticky about who's going to handle it. You guys decide—whatever you do is fine by me."

"Actually, it would be a good idea for you to handle it, Hal," Laura said. "Considering how bent out of shape the press got about my involvement in Ann's traffic ticket, they'd have a field day if I investigated her husband's murder."

Catherine leaned forward. "We're already working on the fibers from the scene. I assume you want us to continue?"

Hal looked at Walter who shrugged. "No point in disturbing your work. Just report everything directly to us." Then Hal turned to Robert, and barked out orders. "We'll handle the Jackson house search. Send us your report on the Coast visit."

Finally, he turned to Laura. "Where can we find Mrs. Hilman?"

"I just left her at Tom's parents' in Northwoods—Stephen Hilman on Mockingbird Lane. I suspect she's still there. They've got a lot of decisions to make all of a sudden."

▪ ▪ ▪ ▪

Shortly after four that afternoon, Laura walked into Catherine's office to find Blake and Robert. Everyone looked tense. "Any results?"

"A few."

Laura took a seat next to Robert on the couch.

"Hilman was shot probably Monday night, maybe Tuesday morning, from six to ten inches away. His hand got in the way of the bullet and from the position of the two and the angles, Doc figures Hilman was standing or sitting, not lying down. It was probably a .38 caliber or so— no way to tell exactly. The tread of his shoes had particles of building materials in them, so we suppose that he'd recently been at a construction site."

"He was a heating and air-conditioning contractor."

"Under normal circumstances debris might be meaningless, but in this case, someone wiped his shoes off—not sure why they didn't just take the shoes off entirely. Anyway they missed some particles in between the treads. We're still analyzing these, but so far we've identified one— mahogany. We're working on the others." Catherine stopped and consulted her papers again.

"Someone had cleaned his fingernails, but missed two particles of colored material embedded deep under two of the nails. Microscopic size."

"Can you identify them?"

"The fragments are so small that we haven't done any tests, just looked at them under a low-power microscope. Probably paint, but it could be something else. We'll only be able to do one, maybe two tests, so until we know what we're looking for, I'm holding off."

Blake spoke up. "Only someone who knew what to do would clean the nails. I doubt if the killer does this for a living though, the bad guys usually chop off the fingertips and throw them away. This guy didn't do that—maybe intentionally."

Robert turned to Laura. "He had a baggie of cocaine in his pocket. It matched the stuff that arrived in your little explosive present, and was similar to what we found at the redneck's trailer. High-grade, cut with strychnine."

"Are you saying this proves Tom planted that grenade?"

"Well, given his arrest on the Coast, he was into cocaine, though how deep we still don't know. Maybe it was significant, maybe your campaigns were cutting into his business. He knew you, and he thought he knew how to get to you."

"So Ann might have been right."

"I think she was right—the same kind of grenade turned up in the search of his boat. How many people know about Ann's suspicion?"

"I've only told you two. I doubt if Ann would have talked about that to anyone. Why?"

"Because when we reported all these results to Hal—the medical examiner's findings and lab results—he was more interested in the cocaine analysis than anything. Has he called you?"

"Not that I know of. He was interviewing Ann at three o'clock. She..." Laura stopped, aghast, and looked at Blake. "You don't think they consider me a suspect because of the grenade and the cocaine, do you?"

"No—I can't imagine they'd waste their time like that."

"What about the prints?"

"No answers yet. Washington's got the faxes and the pictures were good enough to start the search. We're preparing the prints from the Coast house at the lab down there. Hal's doing the ones from the house here. He assured us it has top priority. They'll get the hard copies in the morning."

"Anything else?"

Blake picked up a plastic evidence bag. "Alex Markham's card was in Hilman's wallet."

Laura's curiosity was aroused. "Can I see it?"

Blake handed her the packet containing a standard Department of Justice card. She flipped it over and seeing the handwriting on the back, reached for a pad and pen and wrote the information down. "Robert, what about those account numbers I gave you last month?"

"One's Swiss and the others are all Caymans, but none of the banks will give me any information."

"Well, maybe now that he's dead and also a drug dealer, they'll help out. We've at least gotta know who the signatories are."

"Where did you get those numbers?"

"Ann copied Tom's financial files when she was packing up."

"Well, the FBI's probably got them by now."

"Why?"

"They've finished searching the house."

"How do you know that?"

"I assigned someone to watch the place."

"I'll get the details from Ann tonight." Laura looked at her watch. "Jeez, I gotta get Will. How about we meet here tomorrow morning at nine."

"I should have all the fiber evidence by then, maybe even the prints," said Catherine.

"Call me if anything comes up."

▪ ▪ ▪ ▪

As Ann came in through the garage with Jesse sound asleep on her shoulder, Laura stopped scrubbing a pan and turned off the tap so he wouldn't wake up. She reappeared a few moments later, and sank onto a stool across from Laura.

"I'm numb. Can't even think."

"I know the feeling," Laura said.

"Is Will asleep?"

"Went out like a light. Did you eat? I brought some extra barbecue from Chimneyville."

"No, thanks. Funeral food started showing up at Stephen and Caroline's about mid-afternoon. But I'd give anything for a beer."

"Sure." Laura turned and got a Lite from the refrigerator. "How are they doing?"

"In shock about Tom's death, and mortified about the drug dealing. Caroline wanted to keep Jesse with her tonight to take her mind off everything, but I didn't think that was such a good idea. I'll drop him off in the morning."

"Did you decide about the funeral?

"Tomorrow at four o'clock—St. Philip's, private burial, three-hour visitation after lunch."

"What happened with the FBI?"

"I'm sure glad you and Stephen made me take a lawyer with me. You would have thought I was a suspect from the questions they asked."

"Like what?"

"All about our relationship, the times he hit me, what I thought about him, every step I took Monday night down to how many pages of *Salamandastron* I read to Will. Then they started on sailing and acted like I must have been in on the drug dealing since I knew how to handle a boat. My lawyer cut them off several times."

"Bastards. What did they find when they searched the house?"

"The place was a pit. They looked around for quite a while. Took an address book, financial information, and the computer."

Laura finished filling the coffeemaker for the next morning, and they moved to the living room. After taking a big swallow of beer, Ann leaned back and sighed.

"So how do you feel?" asked Laura.

"Sad, I'm surprised to say. But I feel sorry for Tom. His life was a lot more complicated than I ever knew. I wish I'd been able to draw him out—maybe I could have stopped him if I'd known."

"Don't do that to yourself, Ann. He was in this long before he hooked up with you."

"I still can't figure out why he was selling dope."

"Money."

Ann sat forward. "But he had money."

"It was all Daddy's. You were the one who pointed that out. He wanted his own—a lot of it, and fast."

Ann laid her head back and sipped her beer. "But so what? It was still just money."

"So, I don't know. Money corrupts."

"No, it's power that corrupts."

"Same thing."

21

Laura, dressed in a dark suit for the funeral service in the afternoon, went straight to the crime lab when she got to headquarters that morning. Running her access card through the reader, the lock buzzed and she pushed the door open.

Catherine jumped when she saw Laura at her door. Her usually tightly braided hair was loose and frazzled. Blake wasn't in much better shape. He clearly hadn't been home to shave—the five o'clock shadow made an already stern face, grim. Robert buried his face in a report.

"Didn't you go home?" Laura asked, dropping her briefcase by the door and sliding into a chair.

"About five-thirty this morning," Catherine volunteered. "Grabbed a shower and clean clothes."

"What's the matter?" She looked at Blake who was watching her closely. "Did someone else die?"

Catherine cleared her throat. "The FBI identified two of the latent fingerprints on the cup."

"So..." Laura said.

"So," Catherine said, looking to Robert or Blake to bail her out, "they're yours. And there's gun powder residue on the cup."

"What!" Laura's eyes shot open as big as saucers. "That's impossible."

"Two joint prints and a partial haven't been identified yet," Catherine went on. "They aren't in the FBI files, civil or criminal. Yours were there from the eighties. Did you work for the courts?"

Laura nodded, still stunned. "I clerked for two federal judges."

"We've started to manually search Mississippi cards that aren't in the FBI's computer," Catherine added.

Laura rubbed her forehead, growing more tense.

Robert spoke up. "If we identify the other print, we may have the killer or maybe prove the cup was planted."

"But how did someone get a cup with my prints on it?"

"Maybe out of the garbage," Robert said, "you leave a river of coffee cups behind you."

"Didn't someone say the cup had gunpowder residue on it?" Laura asked.

"Yup," Robert said, "the shooter would have left it on the cup."

"How long will a manual search take?" Laura asked.

"Days," Robert said. "There are thousands of cards that aren't even indexed—if it's even on file."

"Monday, Monday...where was I?" Laura said.

"You were in Greenwood," said Blake, speaking up for the first time since she'd entered the room. He continued to look straight at her. "You didn't get home until after ten."

Laura's eyes narrowed. "How'd you know that?"

"Radio logs," Blake said.

Laura and Blake locked stares for a long, painful ten seconds, neither one glancing away. Blake had already investigated every move she'd made that night. Robert and Catherine watched them, not moving a muscle.

"You don't think I did it, do you?" Laura finally said.

After another long moment, a tiny smile eased Blake's long stern face. "Nah. It's not your style."

"You wouldn't need to get that close to kill someone," Robert added, breathing again.

Laura closed her eyes, then exhaled. It rattled her all the way to her soul to think that Blake or Robert had ever suspected her, even for a few hours. Looking back at them, she smiled meekly. "Thanks for the vote of confidence."

Blake seemed equally relieved. "We were just talking about the cup when you came in. Tell me, where do you drink coffee from plain styrofoam cups?"

"Here. Restaurants, I suppose." Laura paused, thinking. "But mainly here."

"That's what I thought," Blake said. "Catherine, why don't you concentrate the search on Patrol personnel."

Robert piped up. "And eliminate people who have been in the service.

They'd be in the civilian FBI files. I'll give you everyone I can spare who knows anything about prints."

"Good thought."

"Does the FBI know about my prints?"

"Of course. Washington responded to them, not us."

"Jesus, I'm surprised they haven't called me."

"Haven't had time—we just got the results ten minutes ago. Hal did ask what caliber gun was issued to you."

Laura shook her head, closing her eyes again for long moment— as if to push away the entire matter. Then she reached for her briefcase and pulled out her gun.

"Here, take this," Laura said, handing it to Blake.

"No...," Blake began to protest.

"I insist," Laura said. "Never should have had it issued to me in the first place." Then she looked intently at Catherine. "What about the fibers?"

"So far mahogany, plaster, cement. Stuff that's used at every construction site where Hilman Air is working."

Catherine's phone rang. She answered it and then punched down the hold button, handing the phone to Laura.

"Let me guess. Hal."

Catherine nodded.

"Hello, Hal." She shook her head as she listened. "Yes, I can come down. I'll be there within the hour."

As she hung up, Blake looked at her quizzically. "Are you going alone?"

"I am."

"What's that old saying? Only a fool has himself for a lawyer."

"I think it wouldn't be too slick to make my first appearance with a lawyer already in tow. Sends the wrong signal, don't you think?"

"I wouldn't worry about signals at this point."

"You may be right. But I didn't do it, and I'm not going to act like I'm worried about their questions."

▪▪▪▪

Bullet-proof glass protected the receptionists from people entering the waiting area at the Jackson FBI offices. Laura flipped through old

Newsweek magazines, waiting for Hal. When he finally appeared, he was all business, steering Laura to a conference room where Walter was waiting.

"An official interview, I see."

"Just standard questions, Ms. Owen," Hal said brusquely.

Walter stood up as she entered. "Good morning, Commissioner."

"Hello, Mr. McNee."

Laura sat in the chair at the end with Hal and Walter to the same side so that one could watch her while the other asked questions.

"How long had you known Tom Hilman?"

"Since my first year of college."

"Was he a friend?"

"An acquaintance would be more accurate. Our social patterns didn't cross much until he married Ann. Even so, he really wasn't a person I considered a friend."

For an hour, although it seemed much longer to Laura, they probed her relationship with Ann and Tom. "Did you suspect Hilman of planting the grenade under your car?"

"Not until Ann mentioned her fears. But even then, I had nothing else to go on," Laura said. "I found out about the cocaine match the same time you did. I guess it makes sense, but it still could have been someone else, someone he sold cocaine to. They'd have the same quality stuff unless it was cut in between."

Hal and Walter remained silent.

"But the grenade sort of makes it certain it was him, wouldn't you say, gentlemen?"

Neither nodded, although Laura detected an ounce of empathy from McNee before he resumed his questioning. "Hilman's secretary, Ginger Silven, says you threatened to kill Tom."

"Say what?" Laura looked at Walter and then at Hal, then Walter again. Neither of them spoke.

"We had a very heated conversation, but I never said I'd kill him," Laura answered. "I probably said something about an eye for an eye. I went to Tom's office after he'd taken that swipe at Ann to tell him I'd documented what he'd done to her. I've got the report if you want it. I warned him not to get near her again."

"You're very close to Mrs. Hilman, aren't you, Ms. Owen?"

"I've known her since college—we were roommates."

"But you're very good friends." Walter couldn't see Hal's expression, but he winced at Hal's tone of voice.

"Obviously. What are you implying, Hal?"

"Nothing, nothing. Did you know about her settlement negotiations?"

"Yes."

"And that she'd do better with a lump-sum payment—something as large as his insurance proceeds?"

Laura glanced at Walter. He seemed uncomfortable with the direction Hal was going. She focused back on Hal. "I take it, I need a lawyer."

Neither man responded.

"Your silence speaks volumes."

"I'm sorry, Commissioner," Hal said. "I'm very sorry."

"I'll just bet you are."

■ ■ ■ ■

Vic sat in an armchair, remaining calm in the face of Laura's fury as she summarized Hal's line of questioning. Ever since she'd told them about the fingerprints, the staff had been debating with the Governor about what they should do. Carver had insisted on her resignation, but Vic convinced him that resigning would only bolster the suspicions of her guilt. And while she might never serve as commissioner again, the Governor shouldn't be adding his signature to her death warrant. They'd settled on temporarily removing her from office until her and Ann's names were cleared, and then they'd consider the long term.

"They acted like we were a couple of dykes knocking off Tom for his money!"

"I'm sure they did that to get your dander up."

"Well, by God, it worked. Jesus Christ, what kind of sick people live in this state?"

"Eating our young seems to be a sport," Vic said, his voice solicitous. "Listen, Laura, we can reconsider if you think you can hang on."

"No, the Governor doesn't have any choice. This has crippled me— I ought to just resign."

"Resignation says too much. We don't want to send that signal.

Removing you temporarily is more than enough."

"Alex is already gloating—I can feel it."

"Forget Markham. Think about yourself. Find out who the hell did it and find out fast. I assume you're talking to a lawyer?"

"I'm due at his office in about ten minutes," Laura said, getting up.

Vic stood up, too, and gave her a vaguely distant but friendly hug. "The Governor will do everything he can to soften the announcement."

"I take it he doesn't want me there."

"No."

"And I notice he's not here now."

"You know he doesn't dish out bad news. That's my job."

"Well, thank him for me," she said, heading for the door.

"Why don't you go out the side door while we've got everyone in the waiting room?" Vic said, redirecting her toward the other end of his office.

"Thanks, I'll stay in touch."

As she stepped away, Vic caught her hand and gave it a gentle squeeze. "Laura...be careful. Whoever's doing this, doesn't give a damn about anything or anyone."

■ ■ ■ ■

Alex practiced his putting as he listened to Hal and Walter. He looked up after his stroke. "Hope you don't mind, but there's a golf tournament this Sunday as part of the U.S. Attorney's convention. Pebble Beach, no less."

"When do you leave?"

"The conference doesn't start until Monday afternoon, but I'd been planning on spending the weekend out there. They've got eighteen-hole practice rounds scheduled for Saturday afternoon. I'll decide tomorrow whether I can go on or whether I need to wait. Wish this could be wrapped up before then."

"The way it's going, not a chance—if it's ever solved."

Alex lined up another shot. "Did you hear that Governor Carver removed Owen from office?"

"I'm not at all surprised." Hal seemed pleased. "He'd take an enormous amount of heat if he left her there with this dark a cloud in her sky."

"So, Owen threatened Tom and there's a witness?"

Walter spoke up. "Ms. Silven says that Owen said, 'I'll kill you if you get near Ann.' "

Alex stroked a ball. "Is she credible?"

"Yup," Hal said, nodding. Walter made no assertion at all, just kept watching Alex. "Though, if I had to bet," Hal continued, "I'd guess Hilman was screwing her on the side. It also sounds like Owen and Ann Hilman had something going, too."

"Like what?"

"They were very close," Hal said. "Very close."

Alex looked up, surprised. "You think they're lesbians?"

Walter interrupted. "I want you to know that I don't agree with that inference at all. There's nothing to support it, nothing."

"Okay, okay," Alex said, gesturing as if he were settling a fight. "Let's get on with solid evidence. Hal?"

Hal looked at his notes. "The only prints identified so far are Owen's on the cup. There was also gunpowder residue, and a partial print that hasn't been matched."

Alex stopped putting, but didn't look up. Hal added, "It's not in the federal files—criminal or civilian."

With this, Alex relaxed and hit his next ball.

"The crime lab's searching state files now. Might take days, if it's even there."

Alex pulled two more balls into line and stepped into position.

"The lab reported this morning that the cocaine on Tom Hilman's body matched the cocaine planted in the Commissioner's car when the grenade exploded. And there was a grenade, exact same type as the one on Owen's car, found in Tom's boat. Ann Hilman told us she'd suspected her husband of planting the grenade, and she'd told Owen about her suspicion not long before the murder. Hilman might have been angry about Owen's antidrug campaign and decided to scare her off. And if Owen believed Tom had tried to kill her, she might have decided to get revenge."

Alex stroked his ball, leaning to help it in. The ball stopped short. He looked up at Walter. "Do you believe she did it?"

"Her kid was in the car with her," Walter said, then he paused a moment. "I don't know. She's real tough. I wouldn't want to cross her myself."

"She does know her way around guns," Hal added, "and the one issued to her is a .38 snub-nose."

"But remember," Walter interjected, "the medical examiner doesn't know the precise caliber —no bullet."

"She's got access to an entire arsenal—every caliber ever created."

Alex lined up another ball. "Have you read Owen her rights, Walter?"

"Not yet. The cup could've been planted. And the cocaine in Hilman's pocket could have been a plant, too, for that matter. We don't have enough to bring her in."

Alex looked up at Hal. "What do you think?"

"I'd have to agree with Walter, we don't have enough..." Hal hesitated, "yet. Mrs. Hilman had the big motive. A million in insurance benefits when Tom died. It would have been a lot better than fighting with an ex for your money every month."

"Ann doesn't have, never did have, the kind of guts it takes to do something like that," said Alex. "But Laura does. She can be mean when she wants to be. Even if they aren't lesbians, the two of them were good enough friends to have pulled off something like this." He looked at Hal. "Any other evidence?"

Alex pulled another ball toward him with his putter, then bent over it, concentrating on his shot.

"The crime lab found particles of construction materials in the tread of his shoes, but given that Hilman was a subcontractor on a lot of buildings, it could have come from anywhere," Hal said. "His secretary is providing a list of sites where he'd been working."

Alex took a slow, deliberate practice swing.

"His fingernails had been cleaned, but the killer left some microscopic particles under two of them."

Alex's jaw tightened, but he didn't change his stance.

Hal continued. "It could be paint, but they don't know yet. As small as the fragments are, they won't do tests until they have some idea what they're looking for because they'll only have one shot."

Alex got ready to hit the ball. "What else?"

"Did you know your business card was in his wallet?" Walter said, and watched Alex miss his putt completely.

Alex kept his head down and lined up another ball, talking all the while. "I gave him my new number the night he was arrested in Gulfport in case he got nervous about what he was doing. By the way, what did he offer to do?"

Hal seemed completely satisfied with the explanation and launched into the details. "He agreed to set up his Belize connection, some guy named Raoul. He said he'd moved small amounts of cocaine for the last year. Schaeffer got some in exchange for laundering cash from time to time."

"I had no idea," said Alex without a hint of deception. "Just goes to show, you may never really know someone. Even a longtime buddy. We used to sail together. Best friend I had," Alex said, shaking his head with regret. "Anything else?"

"Not at this time. We have no idea when we'll get a break. The fingerprint search may clear her, but it could take days."

Walter watched Alex as he leaned his putter back in the corner, straightened his tie, and smoothed back his hair. "I'm leaving for the funeral. I'll check back in after five this evening."

Hal and Walter, heading for their offices, followed Alex out. When they reached the reception area, Tim Cropley was waiting with a cameraman.

"Mr. Markham, can we get an update on the Hilman murder investigation?"

"We have no details to report, but we'll be certain to let you know if there are any new developments."

"Isn't it true that Laura Owen's fingerprints were found at the scene?"

Walter shot a hot look at Hal, who just shrugged in response.

"I can't comment on the evidence," said Alex, giving the camera his serious look.

"Is Ms. Owen a suspect?"

"*Suspect* is the wrong word at this point."

"Do you have any comment about the Governor's decision to remove Ms. Owen from office?"

"I think it was a wise move," Alex said. "While Ms. Owen is a very capable person, she obviously has many other things on her mind at this time, and couldn't be expected to meet all the demands of her position effectively. Now please excuse me."

■■■■

Ann was still in her black dress, holding Jesse on her hip, while she warmed up his dinner in the microwave. He chewed a cracker contentedly, dropping wet crumbs all down her front.

Laura was leaning over the counter, rubbing her forehead as she talked on the phone.

"No, Mom, I don't need you to come up here tonight. I know you're worried, but it wouldn't be helpful."

"But Laura, I want to do something for you," Charlotte pleaded.

Laura closed her eyes and shook her head while she listened.

"You can help me by staying in Natchez. Will's taken care of tonight—he's at his best friend's house down the street, having a ball, I'm sure. I don't want him to miss school tomorrow."

"What about tomorrow night?"

"Let's talk about that tomorrow," Laura said. She looked at the Patrol tape recorder that had been hooked into her phones when the crank phone calls began. She pressed the rewind button, then turned her attention back to the phone and her mother. "You never know what could happen in twenty-four hours."

"Are you certain?"

"Absolutely. Stay right where you are and read a book."

"If you insist," Charlotte said. "Will you call tomorrow?"

"I'll call. I love you, Mom."

"I love you, too."

Hanging up, Laura looked at Ann. "Did you record any phone calls?"

"No, I don't think so." Ann dropped a serving dish on the counter that had gotten too hot. She shook her fingers in pain. "Wait! You did get a call on Monday. I had come back because I'd forgotten Jesse's pacifier. The phone was ringing when I walked in. The man had an odd voice and I hit the record button."

They rewound the tape and listened. "'Just a friend,'" was all that was on the tape. Neither recognized the caller.

Laura pulled a new tape out of the cabinet, inserted it, and put the recording in her briefcase. She rubbed her eyes. "What in hell's name are we going to do?"

"I feel as though all I bring you is bad luck."

"Listen," Laura said. "You didn't do it, and neither did I. But some bastard, probably the same person that's been doing the rest of this shit to me, did kill him, and some damn way I've got to find him. But I haven't got a clue how."

▪▪▪▪

Hector Rodriguez was drinking a beer and watching a basketball game from one of the easy chairs positioned for maximum viewing of the giant TV screen in James Stinley's house. The shades were drawn. Stinley came back in the room with a briefcase. He dropped it on the table between them, shoving aside the beer bottles and the remains of a bag of chips.

"Did you move the furniture around?"

Stinley hesitated at the unexpected question. "Oh, yeah, too much glare when I was watching something in the daytime. I got one of those new little dishes that has hundreds of channels. I can watch some kind of game from somewhere in the world around the clock if I want. Even Yugoslavian badminton and croquet tournaments from France or somewhere."

"Hum." Hector opened the case, looked briefly at the stacks of money, closed it and set it beside his chair.

Stinley picked up the last handful of chips. "What happened this time? I had people climbing the walls for something to snort."

"Bad storms. But we've got a much bigger problem than delays now. My main man won't be transporting for us anymore. And I don't have anyone lined up to take his place."

"What happened?"

"Died last week," said Hector, not taking his eyes off the game. "Jesus, did you see that toss?"

"Do you think you'll find someone? I got good customers, and I sure don't want to lose them. It's been bad enough with the cops breathing down our necks like they have."

"A thousand kilos is a lot to move." Hector leaned back, his hands locked behind his head. "The thing about this guy was that no one would ever have suspected him. Very quiet, hardly any risk. He'll be very hard to replace."

Two criminal investigators walked in from the hallway, guns drawn, aimed right at Hector. The front door opened and Robert stepped in. Hector moved for his gun.

"Don't even think about it, Rodriguez."

■ ■ ■ ■

"Tom Hilman moved your cocaine for you?" Robert asked. He was sitting across from Hector in the dining room. "He was found murdered yesterday."

Hector's lips were tightly closed as if he wouldn't answer, then they parted. "I know."

"Your hit?"

He shook his head vigorously. "No way. I needed him alive, not dead."

Robert stared at him, not saying anything.

"Do you honestly think I'd be in this country if I'd known he'd been arrested? I found out about the murder in the paper. I should have left immediately, but I couldn't go back until my business was finished."

"Why not?"

"I'm not saying anything more until my attorney gets here."

■ ■ ■ ■

Laura and Ann were staring into the fire, each with a glass of wine, though Laura had barely touched hers and Ann was polishing off her second. Their uneasy quiet was broken by the phone ringing.

"I hated to call you, but I can't get out there right now," said Blake.

"What is it?"

"We picked up Hector Rodriguez tonight—Stinley's supplier."

"Jeez, I'd forgotten all about that. How'd it go?"

"Perfect. But guess who moved his stuff into the United States."

Ann had turned and was watching her, listening to Laura's end of the conversation.

"Not Tom?"

"You got it," Blake said.

"My God." Laura was stunned, caught completely off guard. "What did he say?"

"Not too much—just confirmed what Tom had been doing. We're

going to talk to him again in the morning when his lawyer arrives."

"Call me if there's more I need to know."

Laura walked slowly back to the couch.

Worry creased Ann's brow. "What was it this time? What else has Tom done?"

Laura shook her head slowly. "I'd asked Robert and Blake to work their way up the chain of narcotics suppliers from the kid who killed Semmes. It just landed in Tom's lap."

"Oh, Laura," Ann moaned. "How do I say I'm sorry?"

"You don't need to—it's not like you had anything to do with it." Laura watched the fire a little longer. "I never thought I wouldn't want to know until just now."

Ann watched her friend's face transform from near emotional collapse to anger. She didn't dare speak.

"Who were Tom's friends?" Laura asked.

"Didn't have many besides Alex. He knew lots of people, but he had no friends. Kept very much to himself as though he was scared to let out something."

"Did he see much of Alex?"

"They went on several long sails earlier in the year and Alex came to dinner regularly during the spring, right after the wedding. Then it slowed down. And Tom was gone a lot, too. After Jesse was born, I hardly ever saw Alex. Babies made them both nervous."

"What did they talk about? Business?"

"Politics, mostly, and lately, building."

Laura stared at her. "What about building?"

"Alex was always buying houses and renovating them, then buying another and doing it again. He's been working on one this past year— always pissed off about how much materials cost. Tom was supplying stuff wholesale."

Both were quiet for a moment, then Ann continued, "They used to laugh about how much cheaper builders and laborers were when you

"Did he move in?"

Ann shrugged her shoulders. "I haven't heard from him in so long, I don't know. From what I gathered, he really gutted the place and started you paid cash."

over. I don't think he'd moved when I was still with Tom or we would have been invited over."

Laura wandered into the kitchen and got a box of gingersnaps from the cupboard and started eating, staring off into space.

Ann waved her hand in front of Laura's eyes. "Earth to Laura...."

"Where was the house?" Laura asked.

"Somewhere over in Woodland Hills. I never saw it actually."

Jesse began crying and Ann jumped up, heading down the hallway to settle him.

"Can I look at Tom's financial files?"

"Of course you can," said Ann, disappearing into the guest room to see to the baby.

■ ■ ■

Long after Ann had fallen asleep with Jesse in her arms, Laura was frantically searching Tom's files, racing down the lists of transactions randomly with no idea what she was looking for. Near midnight, tears of exhaustion, anger, and fear suddenly came spilling out as if some militantly guarded floodgate deep within her had collapsed. She'd never given the least thought to being this close to the other side of the law. And she'd certainly never felt this abandoned. Every nerve ending in her body was raw.

"Why did you go away and leave me alone like this?" Laura whispered bitterly into the darkness.

She gathered up a quilt and went outside, settling into the hammock hung from the pergola that extended from the house over one side of the terrace. Bare grapevines were tangled around the lattice work over her head. The air was very cold. And the full moon high in the blue-black sky had washed everything in an eerie pale gray light. Although the details were fuzzy, the outlines of the trees, the fence, and the gardening shed were sharp.

Laura rocked slowly, one foot on the flagstone floor, staring at the shadows. She found herself longing for a cigarette even though she'd quit fourteen years before. She closed her eyes and recalled from her last inspection of the penitentiary, the frightening sound of steel clanging against steel, and the ominous, unforgettable *clank* of many automatic locks bolting into place simultaneously.

Her eyes shot back open and she shivered, terrified.

Goddammit, how can this be happening?

She hunched into the quilt, drawing her feet up to her body and wrapping her arms more tightly about her.

Questions raced around in her head, crowding out every other thought or sensation.

Who was out there? Who was trying to get her?

What did they want from her?

Why her?

Her mouth grew drier as the fear grew stronger. She licked her lips, and rubbed her forehead over and over until it ached.

How could she undo all this without Semmes to help sort it all out? Oh, Semmes...

She closed her eyes again and forced herself to visualize her husband.

Semmes was running toward her on the driveway, holding onto the back of Will's bike seat as their little son wobbled from side to side. Then the front wheel straightened up, Semmes let go of the seat, and Will pedaled the rest of the way on his own. Triumph burst across both of their faces.

It made Laura smile. She opened her eyes and took a deep breath. Then another. The cold, fresh air seemed to help.

As her head cleared, she realized that her toes were numb with the cold. She pulled the quilt around her again and went back in.

Laura filled the coffeemaker, and while the coffee dripped into the pot, she ran through a series of six quick stretches from the book Robert had given her. Then she headed back to the computer.

Starting from the date of the earliest entry, she reconstructed Tom's life through his money. Whether it was a waste of time or not, it was the only thing she could think of doing, and she had to do something, anything. Semmes would expect her to keep fighting—for herself and for everything she'd managed to accomplish.

■ ■ ■ ■

It was close to two in the morning when Rachel Stone undressed as silently as possible in the corner of their darkened bedroom.

Robert opened his eyes just as she stepped, naked, through the door into the bathroom. He heard the shower start, and if he'd had an ounce more energy in him, he would have followed, and made love to her in the steam and pouring water. He closed his eyes and drifted back to sleep.

"Everything okay at the hospital?" Robert whispered in the darkness as she slipped between the covers.

"Mothers and babies are fine," said Rachel, moving across their king-size bed to snuggle up against his broad muscular back. "But I'm sorry if I woke you."

"You didn't," Robert lied, gathering her arm close around his chest and maneuvering himself into as tight a fit with his wife's sleek body as he could manage. "I wasn't sleeping very soundly if I was asleep at all. Too much to think about."

Rachel planted soft kisses all over Robert's back. "So how come you're not sleeping?"

"I don't know where to start," Robert said.

Rachel knew he wouldn't talk unless she prodded him, and he wouldn't sleep at all unless he talked.

"Give me number one on the list."

"The Commissioner may not make it."

"But she didn't murder that man, did she?"

"No," said Robert.

Rachel could feel he hadn't a doubt about this.

"But someone's been very cleverly throwing suspicion her way," Robert said. "I feel for her. And for Blake. His neck is on the line."

"And what about yours?"

Robert didn't answer.

"You know, Sweetie, there is life after the Patrol, if worse comes to worse," Rachel said. "You just haven't had time to notice."

"I know that," Robert said, still sounding unconvinced—the ugly specter of living off his wife's money rearing its head again. "Thing is, I don't want a new life. I like the one I've got."

"Well then, I suspect you'll get to keep it," Rachel replied, attempting to soothe away her husband's unspoken fears.

"It's not looking too good."

"Why?"

"Whoever did it knows his way around. He didn't make many mistakes and we haven't had any lucky breaks."

"Don't forget, she'll be untouchable if you and Blake pull her through—I mean, when you pull her through."

Robert turned and enveloped Rachel in his arms, pulling her toward him. "You're probably right as usual," he said, nibbling softly on her ear. "Let's just hope we find the killer real soon." Then he lost himself in a long, slow, passionate kiss with his wife, remembering what a lucky man he was to be sharing a life with her.

22

Hal and Walter were waiting outside Alex's door when he arrived.

"What's the progress report?" Alex asked, noticeably more chipper than the day before.

"I think you ought to stick around another day or so," Hal said.

"Why?"

"There's no evidence pointing anywhere except to Owen. She had the motive—Tom had tried to blow up her car with her and her kid in it. No one can vouch for her whereabouts in the middle of the night when he died. And she had access to plenty of guns that could have been the murder weapon."

"I wouldn't put it quite so solidly," Walter interrupted, "but there isn't anyone else on the horizon."

"We just got reports on Hilman's bank accounts that we found on the computer. Most were in the Cayman Islands. Nothing remarkable, no joint owners or beneficiaries. We've frozen them while they research the individual transactions."

"I've been thinking this over and over," said Alex. "I never thought Tom had the balls to do something like this."

"I'd hate for you to be at a golf tournament if something breaks," Hal said, "particularly since you were his friend."

"You're probably right. I'll get a backup reservation for Saturday just in case."

■ ■ ■ ■

Blake and Robert came up the front walk, and seeing Laura wave through the picture window, opened the door to a rich coffee aroma. She was on the phone.

"Mom, I've thought about it and it would really help if you could take Will to Natchez with you for the weekend."

Blake and Robert stood just inside the door, looking a little ill-at-ease. Laura rolled her eyes, exasperated with how long the call was taking.

Charlotte didn't seem convinced. "I could stay there and cook supper for you."

"No, it would be best if I didn't have to worry about anyone else for the night. There's a lot to do."

"Then I'll pick Will up at school. What time do I have to be there?"

"Two-twenty."

"Do you want me to stop by before or after to get his things?"

"Why don't you come by here around two, get his suitcase, and then pick him up."

She started tapping her fingers on the counter.

"That's fine. Are you sure there's nothing else I can do?"

"No, ma'am," Laura answered. "Mom, some guys from the Patrol are here, I've got to go."

"Love you, Laura."

"I love you, too."

"I called your brothers last night to tell them what was happening."

"Mom, I'll talk to you later."

"Okay."

Laura hung up and tried hard to smile, but her eyes were so puffy from lack of sleep that upturned lips didn't change the total picture much. "So what do you know good this morning?"

"Not much more than yesterday," said Blake with a shrug.

"How're things at the office?"

"Everyone's stunned," Robert said. "Thank God, Bill Kenner retired and isn't around to beat the drums. Although I bet he's been steady on the phone talking to people."

"Who's running the place?"

"It's on automatic pilot," Blake answered.

"This is one helluva damn time for automatic pilot," Laura growled.

"Well, would you rather have me worrying about the budget?" Blake growled back, his voice deeper and more stern than she'd ever heard.

She took a deep breath. "Sorry. I'm just a little tense. Coffee?"

"Sure. Where's Mrs. Hilman?"

"Ann's over at her house. She's moving back in although it will take her a day or two."

While Blake stirred in some milk, Robert took over. "Commissioner, we've gotta start from the beginning again."

"I don't know what I can dredge up that you don't already know," Laura said.

"We'll see," Robert answered. "Relax and take yourself back to that night."

Blake put his coffee down on the table and pulled some index cards and a pen from his shirt pocket. "I know when you left Greenwood, and I know you called Jackson about a guy weaving on 49 south of Yazoo at about 9:55 P.M.," Blake said. "After that nothing."

"I for one am glad you've gotten so chatty on the airwaves, Commissioner," said Robert, smiling.

"What did you do next?" Blake continued.

Laura was pacing in front of the window. "I drove home."

"Did you stop anywhere?" Blake asked.

Laura thought for a moment, shaking her head, disgusted with her inability to remember that night. Then she stopped and turned to Robert, waving her hands in delight. "Gas. I got gas at the High Street Texaco."

"Did you talk to anyone?"

She shook her head. "Unfortunately not."

"Credit card or cash?"

"Credit card. And it was at the pump—that's why I go there—you don't have to go in the store."

"Do you have the receipt?"

"Think so." She started toward her office and stopped. "No. It went out with the trash on Thursday. I entered it in the computer that night and tossed it. Trash was picked up yesterday."

"Was it your personal card or the state card?"

"Personal. I've been buying every other tank of gas in case someone objects to my dropping off Will at school and running other errands."

"What's your credit card number?" Robert asked. "We'll get Texaco to give us a copy. Maybe it registers the time of day."

Laura went to the shelf in the kitchen where she kept her keys and wallet. "Here's my MasterCard," she said, handing it to Robert.

"Then what?" Blake said.

"I came home. Ann had both children at the Hilmans' for the night. Will loves it over there—they have a heated indoor pool. So with Will gone, I worked half the night. I wasn't going in the next morning since I planned on leaving for Hattiesburg straight from here."

"What did you do?"

"Taxes."

"This early?"

"They're a nightmare this year. I've got the estate to deal with as well as the regular stuff. I can't go to the accountant until I have everything in the computer, and I hadn't updated in months. I started with the easy ones—the savings accounts, then I did the estate account, and then my personal account."

"No one here, right?"

"Unfortunately not." Laura had returned to her track in front of the window. Blake got up and started pacing behind the couch.

Robert looked at the two of them. "Would one of you sit down? Or at least get on the same beat? You're driving me crazy."

Blake stopped and looked up at Laura. "Just how do you do it?"

"Do what?"

"Update the computer."

"I make all the entries, reconcile each statement, and bring it up to date."

"Do you call the bank?"

Laura's face brightened. "Yes, yes, yes. I called the bank at the end. One of the reasons I work at night is because I never have trouble getting into the system at that hour. I probably called around two in the morning."

"What did you inquire about?"

"Last thing I do when I finish balancing is to call the bank and check the current balance on each account and see if there are transactions I haven't recorded."

"Then what."

"I went to bed after 2:00 A.M."

"How do you know that?"

"Because *Jazz After Hours* had come on before I finished. It starts at two in the morning, and I don't normally have the music on at that hour."

"Sleep well?"

"As good as ever, which is never very good. But I slept. Got up around 8:00 A.M. Called the office and got messages, checked on the budget with accounting. Returned some calls from here and left for Hattiesburg around ten."

"So from the time you got gas until you arrived in Hattiesburg, no one saw you. But you did talk to people, and you called the bank. How can you prove what you did that night?"

"Jesus Christ, I have no damn idea." Laura bit all the way across the nail on her middle finger as she concentrated. "My computer files! It logs the date and time whenever they're updated. I haven't used some of those files since then—it'll show the time I was working," she said, getting up. "Hold on—I'll print out the list for you."

As she disappeared into her office, Robert called out, "If only we could narrow down the time of death to Monday night."

"Why can't you?" Laura hollered back.

"Body was in the trunk, which was relatively airtight," Robert said. He and Blake wandered down the hall toward her office and stood in the door. "At least, tight enough not to have flies. If you have maggots, you can figure out how long the insects have been alive. But no maggots here."

"And no other way to tell?"

Blake shook his head. "Unfortunately, this is the real world, not Perry Mason. If we knew what he'd been doing—what he ate, what he..." He stopped and looked at Robert. "What about stomach contents? What did the doc say?"

Robert sifted through papers for the autopsy report. "'Stomach contents normal' is all he said. He didn't do an analysis."

"Shit," Blake said. "How could we have missed it?"

Robert stuck his hand out to reassure him. "Don't panic, my man. Toxicology usually gets the contents anyway. I don't have their results here."

Blake hurried to the kitchen phone, dialed Catherine, and continued to talk down the hall while they paged her. "Jesus, Robert, we've got to get to Hilman's house before they clean up the kitchen."

Robert looked to Laura. "How can I reach Mrs. Hilman?

"She left here to go to their house," Laura said, pulling a paper out of her printer. "But she had to drop the baby off at her mother-in-law's first—972-3459."

"Is there another phone, Commissioner?"

"Use this line," Laura said, punching down a button next to a glowing light of Blake's line. She handed Robert the handset.

Laura took the pages she'd printed, and went back to the living room. She stared out the window at the cardinals landing on the bird feeder. The warm weather had disappeared as quickly as it had arrived—she needed to put more food out.

"Catherine, you're brilliant," Blake said. "I'll call you later." Blake turned to Laura with the first smile she had seen in two days and then grinned at Robert who was walking in from the office. "Catherine had already thought of it. He'd just eaten—hardly digested. Chinese food."

"More good news," Robert called out. "Mrs. Hilman hasn't even gone over there yet. She said she'd meet us. Let's pray he ate at home and didn't make it from scratch."

"Carryout. I'd bet my life on it," said Laura, looking a little more cheerful. "But that's not much of a bet right now, is it?"

Seeing rays of hope cross her face, Blake hated to bring her down. "You do know that even if we find out where he got the food, we can't be sure when he ate it."

"I know that. But doesn't it stand to reason that you wouldn't buy food and then let it sit around?"

"Reason doesn't always make it right, especially not since they invented microwaves."

"Here's the times I logged off on each financial file," Laura said, handing the papers to Blake. "I hope it helps."

They gathered up their things to go. "We'll tell you what we find—we're going to see Hector Rodriguez later this morning."

"Does Hal know about Rodriguez yet?"

"Nope," Robert said. "And I'm not telling him till we've had a chance to talk to him first."

They were almost to Blake's car when Laura caught up with them and handed over the tape of the telephone call. "I don't know what you can do with this, but this person called Monday night around quarter of eight. Ann had just come back to the house to get some things and answered the phone. There's only a snatch of it."

"Did you call the phone company?"

"Not at the time. But I let them know about it this morning."

"We'll listen to it, but it's a real long shot. Maybe they can trace it."

■ ■ ■ ■

Hector Rodriguez was in a single cell with no view at the Hinds County jail. Though there would certainly be a batch of federal charges laid on him, Blake and Robert hadn't let the feds in on the bust, or on Hector's comments about Hilman. They were seriously out of bounds on this since Hal had formally taken over the Hilman homicide investigation. But they chanced it anyway.

Off the main visitor's area were small private meeting rooms that also didn't have any windows. Hector's attorney from New Orleans was a young, very straight, expensive suit type. He'd arrived at the jail around ten o'clock that morning, and after hearing about Hilman's murder, had convinced Rodriguez that cooperating was in his best interests.

"Rodriguez," Robert began, "Delta Airlines just confirmed your story about arriving on Tuesday morning, so you're off the hook as far as pulling the trigger. But you could still help us."

"And what do I get in return?"

"Don't know yet," Blake chimed in. "Can't tell till I know what you know."

"Try me."

"Tell us about Tom Hilman."

"Like what?"

"How did he operate? Did he have friends? Did he ever say anything about being scared or pursued? Anything, everything. Start from when you first met him."

"This deal between him and me was as uncomplicated as could be. We loaded his sailboat. I wired money into accounts in the Cayman Islands. He moved the cocaine to the hangar in Pascagoula. He never saw anyone else during the whole transaction that I know of. Didn't want to."

"Did he sail alone?"

"Not always. But he loaded the boat alone. That was his one rule: No one saw him load or unload except me and my lookout."

"How often was he in Belize?"

"He sailed all around the Caribbean, and he was in Belize several times just for fun. He was planning to move there."

"Where would he stay?"

"He rented a house from me in Monkey River. That's how I got to know him. We were friends for a year before this started up."

Robert looked at Blake. "Why don't you get your good friend Logan over at DEA to have someone in Belize search the rental house. I assume that's okay with you, Mr. Rodriguez."

Hector looked at his attorney and then nodded. Blake got up and headed for the door. "Keep going. I'll see what Logan's people can do." He left the room at a trot.

"So who visited Tom when he was in Belize?"

"Women," Hector said.

"Anyone else?" Robert asked.

"A friend named Alex."

Robert looked up, his interest greatly aroused. "Alex who?"

"Markham."

"He's the United States Attorney," Robert said.

"I know."

Robert stared at him, incredulous. "Didn't that make you nervous?"

"Yes and no. I didn't know it at first. But when I found out, I figured the advantages outweighed the disadvantages."

"How so?"

"If Tom ever got caught, he had two plans. If he was on the boat with all the cocaine, he'd blow himself and it up."

"How?"

"He asked me for a grenade—which I gave him."

"We found it when we searched on Wednesday afternoon. What if he wasn't on the boat?"

"Then he was certain Alex would be able to cut him a good deal."

"Why so certain?"

"Never said exactly," Hector answered. "Tom said they'd been through it all together and Alex would never let him down. I always figured he had something on him. He asked me to take videos of the two of them when they came into Ocean Springs, just in case their friendship wasn't enough. But those tapes wouldn't have been worth much without something else."

"Did Alex sail with him often?"

"Twice that I know of when Tom had a load on board."

"Have you ever talked with Alex?"

"I've met him, but that's it," Hector said. "Tom wanted to keep him out of it. He was a trump card only."

Robert looked up as Blake came back in the room.

"I got through to Logan—he'll do it," Blake said. "He's very interested in talking to you, Mr. Rodriguez."

Robert turned his attention back to Rodriguez. "Did you give him more than one grenade?"

Blake's eye's lit up at the question and he sat down closer to Rodriguez.

"No. Well, I take that back. I had two, but we used one to practice on."

Blake interrupted. "Practice?"

"Yeah. I showed him how they worked, how to load it—stuff like that."

"What happened to the practice one?"

"I don't know. I guess he kept it, too."

■ ■ ■ ■

Hot water cascaded over Laura's head and shoulders as she leaned against the wall of the shower, soaking in the steam and thinking. She'd been standing there for nearly half a tank of hot water and hadn't come up with any new ideas.

Fingerprints.

Where on God's earth had they gotten her fingerprints?

A plain Styrofoam cup.

Not Dunkin' Donuts—theirs aren't plain. And Cups has a logo on theirs, too.

The coffeepot on the fifth floor? Secretaries, troopers, maintenance—everyone has access to the trash.

But how would someone have known it was her cup?

Her office. That's the only place someone could be sure.

But could they be sure? Blake, Robert—lots of people come in with their coffee.

Where else had she been that she'd had access to a coffeepot?

Laura turned up the hot water.

Plain white Styrofoam cups. In those plastic packs. Double stacks in each bag.

The Legislature. Patrol substations. Will's school PTA meetings. Communications. The Crime Lab. The pistol range.

The water turned suddenly colder. The tank was empty.

Laura gasped but not at the chilly water. "That's it! That must be it."

23

Laura let them in, looking a little more focused than she had earlier, but still bleary-eyed from staring at the computer screen and reading legal opinions.

Blake and Robert immediately began relating all the details of their talks with Rodriguez, and Alex's sudden appearance on the scene.

Laura looked at them carefully. "I've been thinking about that cup with my prints. Has anyone had luck with the partial?"

"Nothing. A complete dead end."

"There was gunpowder residue on the cup, correct?"

"Yes. Primer residue—barium, antimony, lead—from a person who'd shot a gun. It probably wasn't an automatic since they discharge less residue."

"How much residue?"

"I don't know, just residue."

"Well, what if the residue came from my hand at the time I fired a gun?"

"What are you getting at?"

"The only time I've shot my gun, any gun for that matter in the last few years, is when I qualified. So the cup may have come from the range."

"I hate to burst your bubble, but the residue could have come from the unidentified other person who held the cup."

"Maybe. But let's assume it was from my hand. Remember, I shot my revolver at least fifty times that day. I would have been covered with residue. Who could have picked up my cup and known it was mine? Who was out there that day?"

"All of us. Bill Kenner."

"No, he left. Remember, he didn't even score his target he was so pissed off. Keep thinking," Laura said. "Tell me when you give up."

"I give up..." Blake responded, annoyed. "This is no time for games."

"I don't," Robert said. "Alex Markham and Hal Easterbrook were there."

"Bingo," said Laura.

Blake's eyes narrowed. "Do you think Markham murdered Hilman?"

"Beginning to. Think about it. Very neat crime. Right here in Jackson. The killer knew a lot about forensic evidence."

"Jesus Christ, how do we handle Alex as a suspect? There's not a shred of physical evidence pointing to him."

"Maybe, maybe not. Alex has just renovated a house in Woodland Hills. Maybe the fiber evidence would match his materials."

Blake relaxed, trying to absorb all the details Laura was shooting at him. "Tell me more."

Laura repeated everything she'd learned from Ann about Tom and Alex's conversations and Alex's renovations.

"But if Tom was getting him materials, the fibers will match up with other sites, too."

"But didn't Catherine also get paint?"

"She got colored material," Blake said. "She started on the analyses this morning. She'll have both by nightfall. There's so little, she'll have only one shot."

"Why would there be paint under his fingernails?" Laura asked.

"He was around paint all the time," said Blake. "He works at construction sites, for God's sake."

Laura leapt at the assertion. "A guy has just been popped by the feds for cocaine and he's painting?"

"You could be right," Robert piped up. "But we can't prove it— Markham could have killed him anywhere."

She met Robert's question. "Do you honestly think Mr. In-Charge would meet Tom, a recently arrested drug smuggler, at any place where he did not have complete control over the situation?"

Blake and Robert were clearly impressed with her theory. The possibility that it was Markham was still a shock.

"I need to get in there," Laura said.

They shook their heads, almost in unison.

"Without a warrant, no way," Blake said flatly.

"And we don't have a chance in hell of getting a warrant," Robert added.

"You can't search, but I can," Laura said.

Blake's hands slipped down to his hips in defiance. "What do you mean?"

"I mean I'm not the commissioner right now. I'm a private citizen. No bar against my being in there."

"Bull," Blake said immediately. "You're temporarily suspended, that's all."

"That's good enough," Laura said.

"No, ma'am," Robert said adamantly. "You're talking about a formality. A court would see right through that."

"It's enough, I tell you," Laura insisted. "I've been reading cases all day long."

"Okay, suppose it is legal," Robert said. "How do you plan to do it? Walk up and ring the bell?"

"Maybe the workmen will let me in."

"What workmen?" Blake asked.

"The ones who are swarming all over the place as we speak."

"How do you know that?"

"I drove by after I dropped off Will at school this morning," Laura said.

"How'd you happen to do that?"

"Ann told me that Alex was remodeling a house. I just thought I'd check it out."

"No dice," Blake said, adamant. "Too dangerous."

"Why?"

"Because if you're right, Markham is a killer," Robert answered. "And he'll know you're on to him."

"And if I don't go, I'll get to do his time for him."

"You aren't going to do any time," said Blake, shaking his head emphatically.

"What makes you so damn sure? By my calculations, there are more than three hours unaccounted for before I called the bank—assuming I can prove I made the call..."

"Correction..." Blake interrupted, "two hours, fifty minutes based on the time on your computer files."

"Thank you..." Laura said, impatient with the interruption, "and more than five hours unaccounted for after I called the bank. I'm very familiar with handguns, and my fingerprints were present at the scene. So I had motive, ability, and opportunity. If I were prosecuting, I could get a conviction."

"But you aren't—you're defending," Blake said. "And I'd bet on you any day."

"Thanks, but my butt's never been in this kind of a crack, and I don't intend to leave it strictly up to the legal system. Now, since I always wear my pager—you haven't disconnected the number yet, have you?"

They shook their heads.

"Then I assume someone will warn me if anyone unexpected arrives while I'm in there."

In the instant she'd given them, Robert and Blake tried to sort out all the implications of what Laura was proposing. Blake spoke first. "Someone will..." he paused, giving Robert a knowing look, "but, of course, since Patrol involvement might taint something, we never knew about your plans, did we?"

"What plans?" Robert responded, smiling first at Blake then Laura.

"Jesus Christ," Blake said as soon as the car doors closed. "Is she right about the legality of the thing?"

"I have no damn idea, but I doubt we could talk her out of it."

They both sunk into silence on the way back to headquarters, each sorting out the mess they found themselves in.

"I can't believe we were so blind about that cup," Blake finally said.

"No time to cry about that now."

"Right," Blake said. "We gotta put a tail on Markham."

"Already done," Robert said. "I got someone on it when I called into the office on the hard line from her house just now."

"My, aren't we on the ball today," said Blake.

"Getting on the ball would be more accurate."

"Next, we gotta tell the FBI about Rodriguez. Those guys'll hit us with withholding evidence if we don't."

"Why don't I visit with Hal and Walter while you watch the

Commissioner's tail," Robert said.

For just a moment, Blake smiled. "You forget, Lt. Colonel Stone, I'm the acting commissioner now. Pity we didn't have time to drink a beer to my promotion. But I don't think it'll last for long, do you?"

Robert chuckled, turning north onto the interstate. "Hardly. Like I said, I'll talk to Hal and Walter. You take care of her."

"See if you can get to Walter by himself. Hal makes me nervous. And don't tell them we knew about Hilman last night. It doesn't help us, and I doubt they'll probe deep enough to find out."

"Agreed."

"And be a diplomat. Consider the size of the turd Hal's about to step in."

A broad, perfect Cheshire cat smile spread across Robert's face. "If she's right, I'll start working on the warrant."

■ ■ ■ ■

Laura met her mother in the driveway with Will's suitcase in hand. Charlotte looked more worried than Laura had ever seen her—even in the days after her father's stroke before he died. Laura put her arms around her mother and gave her a hug.

"I think I know who did it," Laura said quietly, "but we don't know if we can prove it or not."

"Who?"

"Can't tell you yet. But I'm pretty sure of it—I can feel it in my bones."

"Why's this happening to you?"

"It'll make some sense—but not a lot—when you know all the facts."

"Are you okay?" her mother asked.

"I'm going to be. Thanks for helping with Will."

"Are you sure it wouldn't be better for me to take care of him here? I brought my things along just in case."

"No. I think this'll be a long day and a longer night." Laura kissed her mother again. "I've gotta go."

■ ■ ■ ■

Hal was out of the office, but Walter had the time to see Robert. He seemed edgy, wasn't wearing a coat, and his tie was loosened—very unlike what they'd seen when the case began. Robert figured something was bothering him big time.

"Thanks for seeing me right away," Robert said, shaking hands with Walter.

"Sure." They reached Walter's tiny federal-size cubicle and sat down. Walter immediately leaned back, his hands behind his head, but doing a poor job of looking carefree. "What can I do for you?"

"We arrested a Belize national named Hector Rodriguez last night. Seems he supplied a whole bunch of dopers. And his stuff came in to Ocean Springs on Tom Hilman's sailboat."

The front legs of Walter's chair hit the floor as he sat up straight. "You're shittin' me."

"Nope." Robert filled him in on the details leading up to the arrest. "We couldn't talk to him until this morning when his lawyer got up here from New Orleans. He's over in the county jail right now. He says he didn't have anything to do with Hilman's murder. I believe him. His passport says he cleared Customs in New Orleans after the killing occurred. The airlines confirm his story."

"What did he say about Hilman?"

"Are you ready for this?"

Walter nodded.

"First thing is Alex Markham was with Hilman on some of his Belize runs."

"What!?" Walter cried in a hoarse whisper.

"And there's more," said Robert. "Rodriguez said Hilman was certain Markham would bail him out if he ever got caught. But to be certain, Hilman had Rodriguez video Markham on the boat. Told Rodriguez it was part of his extra insurance if Markham ever hesitated."

Walter was silent. Robert thought he detected a flash of relief before panic spread across the agent's face.

"What are you suggesting?" Walter demanded. "That Markham killed Hilman?"

Robert remained impassive.

"Be careful what you're thinking, Stone, this is the United States Attorney you're talking about."

"And it's the Commissioner of Public Safety you're talking about."

"Former commissioner."

"No. Temporarily suspended commissioner," Robert corrected. "I don't know who got your pants all wadded up about her, but you're wasting your time."

"Why? Is there something you know that I don't?"

Robert responded with total confidence. "In a couple more hours, we'll be able to prove it couldn't have been her."

"What are you withholding?"

"Nothing. We're just following up all the same leads you've got at your disposal."

"Jesus, I can't believe this."

"Go talk to Rodriguez yourself. I'm sure there's a batch of federal charges you can dream up to file right after ours."

▪▪▪▪

Walter was pacing by the time Hal finally stepped off the elevator.

"What's the damn emergency?"

"Hector Rodriguez—alias Raoul, Tom Hilman's supplier—is in the Hinds County jail. Robert Stone arrested him last night in connection with a dope deal they've been working."

"Why are we just hearing about it now?"

"He wouldn't talk until his lawyer got up here today—some suit from New Orleans. Robert convinced them that cooperation was a smart move in light of the homicide. They agreed."

"Okay, it's a good lead, but what are you so lathered up about?"

Walter recounted all that Robert had reported about Markham.

Hal's face darkened. "Don't kid with me, McNee."

"I'm not." Walter smiled, almost a smirk. "And for once in this case, I'm glad you're in charge, cuz the senior man would certainly be the best one to handle questioning the boss."

24

Ann and Laura circled the block in Laura's Cherokee. A small dark blue Toyota pickup with Construction, Inc. emblazoned on its side, had pulled into Alex's driveway and its driver, a man in pressed khaki pants, was entering the house through the garage.

"Ready?"

"Are you sure this isn't illegal?"

She hesitated only a fraction of a second. "Absolutely. But even if it was illegal, we have to get in there. Correction, I have to get in there."

Laura and Ann parked behind the pickup, looking around as they got out. Laura slung a large black leather bag that held her camera equipment over her shoulder, and they were headed to the front door when a workman came down the walk.

"Have you seen Mr. Markham?" Laura asked with seeming innocence. "We were supposed to meet him this afternoon to look around the house at the remodeling and decorating."

"He didn't say anything about it to us. We're working overtime to get everything done before he leaves for California."

"California? Alex didn't mention leaving, but I guess that explains why he wanted us to come by today."

The khaki-pants man came out of the front door. Laura spoke a little louder. "Ann is about to hire builders to remodel her house, and Alex has been raving about your work."

The man approached them. "Did I hear you say you have remodeling work?"

"Yes, we're friends of Alex's. This is Ann and I'm Laura. Alex has had nothing but praise for your work, so I asked him for a tour. Must have gotten our signals crossed."

"I suppose you could look around anyway. I don't think Mr. Markham would mind." The builder looked at Laura. "You look awfully familiar to me."

"I don't live too far away," Laura said quickly.

"That's probably it. We do a lot of work around in this neighborhood."

Ann interrupted, diverting him. "I can see why Alex is so pleased. These windows—are they real casements?"

The builder nodded, and Ann guided him down the walk toward the front of the house, talking constantly. Laura tagged along behind, looking at the ground. There was building debris everywhere and a pile of scraps lay not far from the front door.

The man began expounding about the job, clearly proud of his work. "The slate roof—you know it never wears out—gives the house such a classy look. The wooden shingles, coordinated colors, deep red brick."

"It all works so well together," Ann said. "Mind if we take a sample or two?"

"Have all you want. Markham wants the place completely cleaned up today. In fact, the landscape people are supposed to be here now."

The builder gestured toward the front of the house, rattling on about the new roof and the skylights. Ann pointed to the front door as Laura rummaged through the pile for scraps.

"Built that myself."

"Just beautiful," Ann said. "You should be proud."

The man's chest puffed out a bit as he showed them into the foyer, a large room, illuminated by a skylight.

"This is simply gorgeous. Laura, look at how open and airy it is." Not waiting for an answer, Ann turned to the builder. "Who was the architect?"

"Bennett Essman. Great guy to work with if you haven't already hired someone. He's coming to inspect shortly."

Color flooded up Laura's neck toward her face. Bennett Essman had been a good friend of Semmes.

"I don't believe I've ever heard of him, have you Laura?"

Laura did her best to act nonchalant. "You'll recognize his face. And I know you've seen some of the houses he's done. That sky blue house on Gillespie—glass heat chimney on the top." Laura had regained her composure and nodded to Ann to keep going. With luck they'd be out of there before the architect arrived.

The foyer and living room were absolutely bare of furniture, the wood floors beyond the slate entry area were glistening from having been stained and sealed very recently. Four painters were putting second coats on the walls.

The builder directed them into the kitchen, pointing out the mahogany cabinets. A newspaper with pictures of Ann, Laura, and Tom lay open on the counter.

Laura barged past them, stopping right at the newspaper, declaring expansively, "Now this is a kitchen I could handle, Ann." She leaned on the counter as she spread her arms, obscuring the paper from the man's view.

"Well, the difference is this is custom-built, right on the premises. Don't usually like dark wood in a kitchen but that's what Mr. Markham wanted—mahogany. We had to darkened it a bit with stain to give it this shiny ebony appearance."

The builder pulled out a drawer to demonstrate its smooth action and was headed toward where Laura was standing when Ann piped up.

"The dark wood is probably a 'guy thing.' Terrific storage, don't you think, Laura? But I really love this foyer. What kind of tile is this?"

Ann and the builder walked out and Laura folded the paper, shoving it back on the counter, then followed them into the foyer.

Laura called out. "Do you do your own flooring, sheetrock, and painting, or do you sub that out?"

"My own crews. The painters had finished the foyer and the living room..." The man's arm swept toward the living room, which was being painted a deep shade of blue. "But Mr. Markham changed his mind about the colors earlier this week. The painters had to come back anyway. A dresser or something had fallen over and crushed a whole piece of wallboard in a bedroom and it had to be replaced and repainted."

Laura pointed to a solarium off the living room that was filled with furniture and artwork. "I guess I didn't realize Alex had moved in."

"He had to move out of his old house before we were finished, so the furniture was put in there. We'd planned to move it in by today, but when the floors had to be re-sanded, and the walls repainted, we got behind."

"Why re-sanded?"

"Something spilled on Monday before we'd sealed it. Right about here actually." The builder moved to the corner where the foyer and living room walls met. "Mr. Markham made a mess cleaning it up. Men really do need women..." He stopped abruptly realizing his faux pas.

Ann waved her hand reassuringly. "I know what you mean. My husband would pour boiling water on a carpet stain, certain he was doing the right thing. Can you show me the bedrooms and the bathrooms? Laura may like kitchens, but I love bathrooms."

The builder and Ann walked past the painters and into the bedroom area, but Laura lingered in the living room and spoke to the painter nearest the foyer while she inspected the wall more carefully.

"Pretty drastic color, wouldn't you say?" Laura looked closely at three indentations near the corner about four feet off the ground.

"I wouldn't have my house this dark," one painter said. "But that's why there's chocolate and vanilla."

"What color did it used to be?" Laura's beeper went off and she looked down to see the emergency signal.

"Nice creamy beige in here. The foyer was always dark green. We're just putting a fresh coat on it. Messed up both walls right at this corner. Had the paintings hung and everything. Looked perfect by my book."

Laura stepped up and had just placed her hand over the ridges when the front door opened and Bennett Essman stepped in, looking around at the workmanship as he walked.

"Laura. What are you doing here?"

"Hey, Ben. I've been checking out the great work y'all have done. My friend..." Laura motioned to Ann who was coming from the hallway with the builder. "Ann is hoping to do some work on her own house."

"What did I hear about you last night?" Essman asked.

"Just politics," Laura said. "Big messy case, but it'll all straighten out."

Laura's beeper went off again. "We gotta go, Ann. Ben, good to see you." She looked at the builder. "And thank you, sir."

The builder had dug out his wallet and handed Ann a business card. "Let me come and give you a bid when you're ready. We can do a good job for you."

Ann smiled at him. "I'll keep you in mind. Thanks for the tour."

Laura hurried down the path to her car with Ann trailing behind her. She didn't recognize any of the vehicles passing on the street and felt more relieved when they were out of the driveway and headed away.

The radio crackled and Blake's voice filled the air. "Pull over at the next corner and wait."

Laura looked in her rearview mirror but saw only a white panel truck. When she'd parked, the panel truck pulled up behind her and Blake stepped out.

"Thanks for the warnings, Blake."

"I didn't page you," he said, feigning innocence. Blake looked past her to Ann. "Hello, Mrs. Hilman."

"Hello, Blake," said Ann, leaning across. "Please call me Ann."

Laura handed him some wood and shingle samples. "Here are the scraps I picked up—I think this is the mahogany."

"Thanks. I got a piece of it and some other things myself from the Dumpster."

"The foyer and living room walls are being repainted now. If the color from the left hand was green and the right hand was beige, I know how it happened. They had to re-sand the floors because Alex made a mess cleaning something up that had spilled right at the corner between the rooms on Monday."

Blake grinned. "You just got yourself off the hook."

Laura breathed deeply, as though it were the first time in days. "Let's hope so."

"I happen to know so," Blake said confidently. "What you just said conforms with what I got from the lab just a minute ago. They tested the fingernail scrapings—both paint—dark on the left, light on the right. Now, I've got to figure out how to get samples legally."

"The trash?"

"It didn't look like any paint cans were in the Dumpster but I couldn't dig down. What else did you find out?"

"First, a piece of sheetrock in the bedroom had to be replaced." She turned to Ann. "Did you notice where they were working?"

"Right in the corner near the door to the porch."

Laura turned back to Blake. "That would be the other side of the living room wall." She pulled a notepad from the armrest pocket and sketched out Alex's floor plan. She pointed out locations as she talked.

"This is where wallboard was replaced—directly behind the living room wall that's been repainted. And here's where I think Tom fell to the floor," said Laura, pointing to the foyer. "There are two slight ridges at the corner of the wall about four feet off the ground, right above where Alex was doing the cleaning."

"Ridges?"

"Well, *ridges* might not be the right word." She gestured in the air as if both hands were clawing to hold on to something. "It's not smooth there—as if it had been gouged out slightly. Couldn't check the other side, the paint was wet."

"I'll get all this back to the lab."

"And the man who called..." Laura added, "maybe it was Alex, screwing up his voice."

"We'll have to figure out how to check that."

"By the way, the workman said Alex is going to California tomorrow."

"Damn, we've got to hustle then. Where are you headed now?"

"I need to talk to Vic."

"Are you sure? Couldn't you wait until we've got the evidence?"

"He needs to know in case this explodes on me."

"I don't think he should tell the Governor," Blake said.

"I'll make certain he doesn't. What about you?"

"I'm thinking of getting some advice from Logan Cummins."

"Why Logan?"

"He knows how the feds think and operate better than I do," Blake said. "We might need you there."

"Do you think that's a good idea?"

"If I set it up right. Keep your beeper on."

"Always. When are you going to tell the FBI about the paint?"

"Don't know. Robert's laying the groundwork with them now. I don't trust those guys not to blow it. Particularly Hal."

"Hal's a jerk, but Walter McNee might be okay," Laura said. "Maybe even honorable."

"Don't go too far," Blake said.

"You still have a tail on Alex?"

"Yup. He's at the office. There's someone on each door and at the garage."

▪ ▪ ▪ ▪

Blake picked up the mike for the hi-band investigator's radio. "A-1— B-Boy."

"B-Boy," Robert answered. "Go ahead."

"Bingo."

"Well, well, well. Meet me at the lab."

"Will do."

▪ ▪ ▪ ▪

The guard at the Mansion stepped out of his little kiosk to look more closely at Laura.

"Oh, it's you, Commissioner. I didn't recognize the car. Will you be long?"

"I don't think so. Why?"

"Big party tonight. Go ahead and park in the first space where you can get out."

Laura hurried up to the side door. The urns were filled with freshly planted azaleas. Sandy Quinn held the door for her.

"Good afternoon, Commissioner."

"Wish I still were," Laura said. "Something big happening tonight?"

"The Governor's Awards for the Arts."

"Another guest list I didn't make this year."

Sandy smiled awkwardly.

"Vic's expecting me."

"I'll let him know you're here. Why don't you wait in the conference room."

"Nicely out of sight?"

"I didn't..." Sandy began.

"Don't apologize," Laura said. "That was tacky of me, I apologize to you. Just tell him I'm here." She glanced at the new paintings hanging in the center hallway as she passed. They were a little more modern than she usually liked, but the colors were warm enough to make the shapelessness pleasant. Then she turned around. "And if the Chief calls, interrupt me. No matter what."

"Yes, ma'am."

"Any news?" Vic asked, closing the door behind him. He gave patted her shoulders affectionately as he took a seat next to her.

"Yes. We have a suspect."

"Well? Spit it out."

"You've got to promise me that what I tell you, you don't repeat. Not to the Governor, not to anyone. "

"I promise I won't repeat anything," Vic said anxiously. "Who is it?"

"Alex Markham. We think he killed Tom, at Alex's new house, Monday night."

"Jesus!" The wheels inside Vic's head began spinning.

Laura ran down the details of her visit to Alex's house. "They're trying to figure out how to get corroboration of what I found before he realizes what's happening."

"Who's they?"

"The State Patrol."

"Not the FBI?"

"Laura shook her head. "They've ignored everything we've developed so far. They're not in on this."

"But what you did taints everything, am I not mistaken?"

"I sure as hell hope not—I did some research first. They'll call it underhanded and sneaky, but they won't get unconstitutional to stick, not with the Supreme Court going the way they're headed these days. Besides, I've got the best criminal lawyer in town working for me."

"Did he know about your visit beforehand and give it his blessing?"

"Couldn't reach him, but I've talked to him since. It made him nervous, but he agreed that I'll be okay. It'll cause a stink—probably a big stink, but what else is new."

"Alex will get some hotshot defense attorney in here."

"Yes, but never underestimate how distasteful pompous politicians can be to regular old citizen jurors."

"You've been busy." Vic exhaled, raking his fingers across his hair and massaging his forehead. "Senator Markham will go berserk when Alex is arrested."

"If he's arrested..."

"This isn't a done deal?"

"Hardly, he could slip through our fingers so easily. All I'm certain of is that I can prove the paint under Tom's fingers was from Alex's house, and I can give a reasonable explanation for how my fingerprints were on that cup. I'm praying that will get me out of the line of fire. Whether we get Alex behind bars is another matter."

"Let's hope you're wrong. But either way, this'll all get blamed on us. My Lord, what a mess."

"For some reason," Laura said, "I'm not so worried now that I know I can save my own skin. And the Patrol's gotten me this far, they'll get me the rest of the way."

Vic nodded, "Good people."

"The best," Laura said with certainty.

"What are your plans when this is settled?" Vic asked.

Laura looked across the table and out the window at the Japanese magnolia that had started to bud. She thought about all the bulbs that would be blooming this spring—flowers that Semmes had planted, some he never got to enjoy.

"I want my job back if it's available."

Vic hesitated, looking peculiarly concerned. "Are you sure?"

"Absolutely. It's the only place I'll ever be safe."

"I'll have to talk to Carver—I don't know what he'll decide. He's hated every minute of the controversy that's surrounded your appointment, and it took some fancy footwork to get a temporary suspension for you rather than an outright dismissal."

"But that's not fair," Laura argued. "I've been framed."

"Fair doesn't matter in some cases," Vic said, reaching out for her hand. "You know that. You've been a lightning rod since the beginning."

"What did he expect? If I remember correctly, he asked for a take-no-prisoners war on drugs. I gave him exactly that."

"I know, Laura, believe me, I know. But it's made things very tense with the Legislature, and he's a politician, first and foremost."

Laura looked truly glum. She didn't withdraw her hand but she didn't respond to his touch, either. "See what you can do when the time comes," she said, standing up to leave. "I've got to see about saving my ass."

Vic accompanied her out. Laura gave Sandy Quinn one of her quick salutes as she passed.

Seeing the grim, all-business look on Vic's face, Sandy called out, "We're behind you, Commissioner. Every last one of us."

Laura stopped and turned back, smiling. "Thanks, Sandy."

"I'll do what I can," Vic said, as they walked to her Cherokee.

"Just remind him about all the national press coverage of my little war," Laura said.

"I will."

"And remind him his stock wasn't so hot with the Patrol before I got there. He can ask Sandy about that."

"Laura...."

She looked at Vic. "I know what you're going to say—whether the Patrol is happy or not, doesn't matter one iota to Carver."

Vic was nodding.

"And I'd be a one-day story.

Vic nodded again.

"But if he wants to keep charging ahead, building his record as tough on crime, I've been doing a bang-up job. Why switch horses?"

25

Catherine's office looked like a war room. Empty coffee cups were everywhere, a half-eaten pizza was on a side table, blowups of finger-prints were pinned to the wall, and charts of scanning electron micro-scope results lay scattered on the coffee table.

"How'd it go with our friends the Feds?" Blake asked.

"It musta made them real nervous because the jailer just called me," Robert said. "Two FBI agents blew in there about three-fifteen, all hot to see Rodriguez. Haven't heard another word."

"Good. They deserve to be nervous as much as they've pissed away this alleged investigation."

"I don't like not telling them about the forensic stuff."

"Look, it doesn't matter what the Commissioner saw. Without a legally acquired paint sample from the house, we don't have a damn thing. Hilman was Markham's friend. He could have visited him at any point during this renovation. They'd make mincemeat of us in court."

Catherine jumped in. "Well, how about sending them the analyses on the stomach contents and the food cartons? They've missed that completely. Didn't I see an interview with the Food Manchu manager somewhere?"

"Right here." Robert handed a short report to Catherine. "Kung Pao chicken, the Monday special. He had to have bought the food before eight Monday night and it was probably earlier."

Blake looked a little brighter. "Send it on. Any bets on how fast we get a call back?"

Robert smiled. "Or how pissed they'll be?"

"By the way, where's that tape recording? Could it have been Markham?"

"It didn't sound like Alex," Robert said. "And no one has voice print equipment except the CIA. The phone company's still working on the call—they're pretty sure it's cellular."

"Well, this is the FBI's investigation," Blake said, "send that on, too."

Robert was headed out the door to the fax machine.

"How about if I get Logan Cummins from DEA over here," Blake asked. "We need some federal perspective."

"It's okay by me if you trust him."

"Almost as much as I trust you. And I've got the Commissioner on standby. Logan needs to hear what she saw today, but not until he's convinced she wasn't involved."

Robert nodded. "When do you want to do this?"

"Soon as he can get here."

"Then I'll go work on the warrants," Robert said. "Let me know."

Catherine looked up from her report. "You want to do it here?"

Blake nodded.

"I assume I should be ready to do the whole song and dance," Catherine added.

"You betcha."

■ ■ ■ ■

Hal knocked on the door with Walter right behind him. He turned the handle and leaned in. "Alex, do you have a moment?"

Alex was hanging up the phone. He'd been going through a drawer in his locked cabinet, his briefcase open on the desk. "Sure, just getting some papers together for California. Thought I'd try to make the evening flight so I can get there in time to practice before the afternoon round tomorrow. What's up?"

"Stone has been working a totally separate drug case, and he arrested a guy named Hector Rodriguez last night who had been importing for the last few years. Come to find out, Hilman was moving his cocaine for him. We interviewed him an hour ago."

Alex gripped the side of the briefcase, his knuckles turning white. "Why am I just finding out about this?"

"They didn't tell us until about two this afternoon. Rodriguez wouldn't talk unless his lawyer was present. The attorney, some guy from a big New Orleans firm, didn't arrive until late this morning. Robert said that when Hilman's name came up, he came right down to brief us. But Rodriguez told us he mentioned Hilman last night right after the Patrol arrested him."

Alex's eyes flashed. "They may be the State Patrol, but that's with-holding evidence."

Hal was distinctly pleased. "My thought exactly, Alex."

"Didn't Tom give you a different name? Roberto or something?" Walter asked.

"Raoul. Could have been to protect Rodriguez."

"Must be a pretty big guy to have a New Orleans lawyer up here so fast," Hal said.

"Rodriguez said that Hilman had moved several thousand kilos for him," Walter added.

"Did you get his fingerprints?"

"Yes, sir, but they don't match the partial on the cup where we found Ms. Owen's prints."

Walter looked at his copy of his notes, then watched Alex as he spoke. "Rodriguez said Hilman claimed you'd be able to get him off."

It stopped Alex completely for a second. He looked down at his desk, shuffling some papers. "Typical. Tom Hilman has had someone bail him out, every step of his way through life," Alex said, throwing another item in his briefcase and snapping the case closed. "Did he say anything else?"

Hal took over. "Not really. Rodriguez said Hilman had a totally one-man operation. He never heard of or saw anyone else in the deal."

Walter looked at Hal, expecting him to continue, but Hal remained silent, leaving him the dirty work. "Well, that's not quite true," Walter interjected. "Rodriguez said Hilman asked him to videotape you on Hilman's boat."

Alex stared coldly at Walter. "I took a lot of trips on that boat—some of the best, most relaxed moments of my life. But I knew nothing about Tom's smuggling cocaine. You don't honestly think I'm that dumb, do you?"

He was clearly insulted by the remarks, and Hal decided to change the focus. "The stomach contents analysis shows that Hilman had re-cently eaten Chinese food. The food was purchased Monday night be-fore eight. Wasn't even digested. That may or may not eliminate Owen from suspicion. We're going to interview her again in the morning."

"You're assuming he ate right after he bought the food."

"Yes, sir, I am."

"I've seen that evidence all kinds of ways. Anything else, Hal?"

Hal shook his head. Walter raised his finger. "They've got a recording of an unidentified caller. Call came into Ms. Owen's house last Monday evening. She routinely tape-recorded calls because someone was harassing her."

Alex didn't flinch. "What's it sound like?"

"Pretty bad—muffled."

"Well, send it on to DC. I assume that's why they gave it to us, isn't it?

"Yes.

Alex checked at his watch. "Since it looks like we won't have a resolution right away, I'm going to take that 6:00 P.M. flight. Hal, could you drive me to the airport? I want someone to service my car while I'm gone."

"Sure thing. We can leave around five or so?"

"Great. And find out what the Patrol is doing, holding out on us about Hilman, will ya?"

Walter closed the door behind him and headed briskly down the hall to catch Hal, reaching him just as Hal got to his office.

"You mean you're going to let him leave?" Walter asked, incredulous.

"What basis do we have to keep him?"

"What Rodriquez said for starters—Tom Hilman was going to use Markham to get him off."

"And?" Hal demanded.

"And what? If that's true, Markham has as big a motive as Laura Owen had to do away with him. Maybe bigger."

"What motive? Some jerk is going to try to frame him? Some schmuck tries that one at least once a week. Markham is a sitting duck for every two-bit friend he ever had. Anybody can say they'll use their influence, but that doesn't mean Markham was, in fact, influenced."

"But what about the evidence the Patrol says they have to clear Owen?" Walter asked.

"When we see it, we can evaluate it. So far, I don't have squat from them. What exactly did they say they had?"

"Stone said they were just following up on leads we all had access to."

"Well, maybe if they cooperated a little more, we could get somewhere. But until then, we don't have one piece of evidence that links Markham to this crime. Nothing except the hearsay of some dirtbag dope peddler based on what his dirtbag courier told him. There's no way in hell we can hold him. Jesus, we don't have enough to arrest Owen yet and her fingerprints were at the scene."

"I've got a feeling about this," Walter said.

"Feelings," Hal sang out, mimicking a schmaltzy lounge lizard singer as he walked to his desk.

"This is serious, dammit."

"He's going to a friggin' convention of United States Attorneys, for Christ's sake," Hal said. "The place will be crawling with cops."

■ ■ ■ ■

Blake hurried into the entry area when Logan arrived.

"This must be important."

Blake nodded. "Are you willing to skate on some real thin ice with me?"

Logan looked at Blake's worried face and thought how out of character it seemed for a man who was normally so coolly confident. "Absolutely. You've done it for me hundreds of times."

"Well, I warn you, you'll break some departmental rules if you stay."

"Never bothered me before."

"Thanks, Logan."

They rounded the corner to the conference room where Catherine and Robert were waiting.

"There's no good order to this," said Blake, "so we'll just start from the top. If I forget anything..." Blake looked at Catherine and Robert, "interrupt, please."

Piece by piece, the three laid out all the information they had on Hilman's drug running, and Ann Hilman's relationship with Laura. Then they started on the homicide.

"Hilman was killed Monday night. He'd bought carryout, the Monday special at Food Manchu on State Street, some kind of pow-wow chicken dish. They don't remember any customers after seven-thirty and they always close at eight—Monday's their slowest night. The food wasn't digested, so Hilman had to be killed soon after he ate."

"But when exactly, you don't know for sure. Right?" Logan asked.

"Right. There's no evidence of a homicide at his home, so we figure he ate and then went somewhere." Blake looked at Catherine. "You cover the autopsy stuff."

"He was killed standing up or sitting, most likely," Catherine said. "The bullet grazed the side of his hand before or after—we think before—it passed through his brain, so his hand had been up near his head at the time. Probably died instantly. He weighed 212 pounds, 218 or so with his clothes and shoes on, so whoever moved him had to be strong."

"Or there was more than one person," Logan said.

"That's true," said Catherine. "We do know his body was placed in the trunk pretty quickly because there weren't any maggots breeding. Do I need to explain that?"

"I know about maggots," Logan said. "That's all I ever deal with."

Catherine smiled at Logan's remark and then continued. "The soles of his running shoes had been wiped off, but deep inside the tread on both shoes were particles of building materials. All common—mahogany, plaster, cement. His fingernails had also been cleaned after he died, but on one finger of each hand, the killer missed microscopic particles of colored materials. We knew that the left index particle was a dark color, and the right was off-white."

Blake nodded to Robert. "In the car where the body was found, there were no identifiable prints except those on a single Styrofoam cup," said Robert. "They were the Commissioner's fingerprints, plus one partial print that remains unidentified. The cup had significant amounts of gun powder residue on it. The car was left by a little park, right in the middle of Belhaven, no later than 5:30 A.M., early Tuesday morning, because at least three morning runners saw it when they passed. No one paid any attention to the car or noticed the stench until the garbage collectors came by Wednesday morning."

Logan looked impassive. "So where was the Commissioner?" he asked as he leaned forward to take notes.

Blake responded. "She was in Greenwood until 8:00 P.M., when she left a dinner meeting where she'd been the main speaker. She headed south, talking on the radio from time to time, all the way to Jackson. At 10:20 P.M. she bought gas at the High Street Texaco. She said she went home after that, and since no one else was there—Ann Hilman had both her own child as well as the Commissioner's son at her parents-in-law for the night—the Commissioner worked on her taxes. She called her bank's computer customer service line at 2:10 A.M., and stayed on the line for eight minutes, checking four different accounts."

Logan put his hand up to halt. "Does that require a password?"

"Yes," Blake replied.

"Do her computer files show when she made changes that night?"

"Yes. But when she got information from the bank at 2:10 A.M., she went back in and updated three of the four accounts again, saving those changes some time after 2:35 A.M. Except the smallest account, which she had done first. That file was saved at 11:20 P.M."

"She could have messed with the date on her computer," Logan said without looking up from his note taking.

"But not with the bank computers. She couldn't change those."

Logan nodded and signaled Blake to go on.

"Then she says she went to sleep," Blake explained. "She checked in with the office at 8:02 A.M. The secretary said she joked about leaving everything under my control and then asked to be transferred down to the comptroller's office. She talked to him about the budget hearing, and left for Hattiesburg in time to make a speech at Southern at noon. She chatted it up on the radio as usual."

"Does she own a weapon or have one issued to her?" Logan asked.

"Yes," Blake said quickly, "issued to her in December after that grenade went off under her car."

"You said the cup had residue on it," Logan asked. "Can she shoot?"

"Let's just say if she tried out for the Pistol Team, she wouldn't embarrass herself," Robert interjected. "She's best at distances."

"How often does she shoot?"

"Never," Blake said. "The only time in the last four years was when she qualified last month on January eighth."

"How'd the speech go?"

"What speech?"

"In Hattiesburg."

"Great. The Lion's Club president said they kept her thirty extra minutes because everyone had so many questions and comments, and she seemed willing to stay on."

"She didn't do it," Logan said confidently, dropping his pen on the table and leaning back.

"Why don't you think so?" Blake asked.

"There are only two hours and fifty minutes unaccounted for before the call to the bank, and five and a half hours after the call and computer work. Unless Hilman ate in the middle of the night, he died before midnight, and without an accomplice, she couldn't have killed him, moved the cars around, slept well enough to joke with the office, and then give a bang-up speech. Even if she did have an accomplice, she would have given herself a better alibi than calls to a bank computer. Besides, what kind of a person balances a checkbook in the middle of the night anyway? A compulsive, do-right type, not a killer."

Blake shook his head. "How do you explain the fingerprints?"

"Her trash. Hit man poses as member of the cleaning crew."

"I thought of that. The regulars haven't had substitutes in months. For safety's sake, I asked each one to be polygraphed—they all agreed and all passed with flying colors."

"Well, I can't explain the cup. But it was a plant, believe me."

"But why frame her?"

"When you find the killer you might know," Logan said. "Other than the prints, why are you wasting your time on her? You obviously don't believe she did it."

"Because that's who the FBI's concentrating on if you read their tea leaves and the leaks to the press."

"Screw them," Logan said. "It's somebody else and it was probably a hit."

"Glad you agree with us," Blake said. "Now we want to tell you the rest of it. Do you mind if someone else joins us?"

"Of course not," Logan said.

Blake opened the door to Catherine's office and Laura walked in carrying a load of papers, haggard but relaxed. She knew that if she'd been invited in, Logan didn't think she'd done it.

"Hi," she said, her voice husky with fatigue.

Logan stood up immediately, startled, looking from Laura to Blake. "I'm sorry for all of this, Commissioner."

"Thank you, Logan," Laura said. "For the record, I'm not commissioner right now. Just private citizen Laura Owen."

Despite what he'd said about her innocence, Logan watched Laura, wary. Blake spoke up. "We've brought him up to the time of the murder. And we were just about to start on the other part." Blake looked at Laura. "You want to do the honors?"

"No, I'll just add the color commentary."

Blake turned back to Logan. "Let's get back to this Styrofoam cup. If the gunpowder residue was from the Commissioner's hand, then the cup came from the range because the only time she fired a gun, as I said, was when she qualified. She shot fifty to sixty rounds that day using a Colt revolver. Plenty of residue."

Laura stopped Blake from continuing. She looked right at Logan, returning his stare. "The only people at the range who were around me when I drank coffee and would have known which cup was mine— besides Blake, Robert, and Mickey Travis..."

"And it wouldn't be any of us," Robert added, "even though Blake does like the ring of Commissioner Coleman."

Laura appreciated the interruption, it gave her a moment to collect her wits before she finished. "The only people around me were Hal Easterbrook and Alex Markham."

Logan sat straight up in his chair. "You're kidding me, aren't you?"

Laura shook her head slowly. "I wish I were, particularly when I consider the ramifications."

"Why were they there?"

"Happened to come out to qualify," Robert said, "Chance, pure and simple, as far as we can tell."

Blake let it sink in a moment longer then broke the silence. "We think Markham murdered Hilman and framed her," nodding toward Laura without glancing away from Logan.

"Holy shit." A puzzled look spread across Logan's face. "But why?"

"Blackmail maybe. Rodriguez told us Tom had something on Markham and planned to use it if he had to," Robert said.

"Tell me more," Logan said.

They ran through Rodriguez's comments and the latest lab results on the microscopic particles from the shoes and what Blake had taken from the Dumpster.

Catherine jumped in. "My initial report on the paint was incomplete in that I didn't identify as much as I knew about the color or which hand had which color."

"Was that on purpose?"

"Well..."

"Blake asked you to hold it back, didn't he?" Logan asked, looking at Blake.

Blake spoke up to defend himself. "I wanted to see if those Bureau guys would ever ask. They were so quick to be the experts, it really pissed me off. You would not believe how sloppy they've been."

"Yes, I would. Don't get me started, Blake."

Blake smiled.

"Did either of you tell anyone?" Logan asked.

They shook their heads. "No one," said Blake. "Well, Robert, of course, but not the Commissioner—excuse me, Ms. Owen—and no one else has noticed. Hal and Walter McNee have had plenty of time."

Laura piped up. "I've been reconstructing Tom's finances, and can't find much except a small annual entry for some little bank in a town north of here every year since he started keeping records. It may be a safe-deposit box—we'll check on Monday. He had another box, but that one's already been searched and had only the usual stuff in it. There's one file that lists building material purchases, and there seem to be corresponding payments to Hilman Air, but nothing's identified."

"That safe-deposit box may have the ticket," Logan said "Got to be something important in it to keep it up all these years. Can you get into it sooner than Monday?"

"We're working on it. Without a key it has to be drilled," Blake said.

"All we have on Alex," Laura continued, "is general information from his tax records."

"Where'd you get that?" Logan asked.

"Don't ask," Blake answered quickly, "and I won't have to lie."

"I think he files a financial disclosure form each year," Logan offered.

"He does, but secretly getting a copy from the Justice Department is another matter," Laura said. "Anyway, Tom's wife Ann told me that over the past few years, Alex has renovated a series of houses, one every other year or so. Apparently, Tom supplied him at wholesale, and they sometimes joked about how much cheaper things were when you paid cash. From his total income, it looks as though he makes a pretty profit on the houses. Or from something."

"You don't think Alex is involved with the narcotics, do you?"

"Your guess is as good as mine on that," Blake said. "We don't get any corroboration from Rodriguez on that point. I can't see him being that stupid."

"Murder isn't stupid enough?"

"Murder is desperation."

Logan looked around at them. "So, you have nothing to go on."

"Except what I saw," Laura said.

"Saw where?" Logan asked.

"At Alex's house," Laura answered.

"When?"

"I stopped by earlier this afternoon."

Logan sighed and shook his head. "You really screwed up, if you'll pardon me for being so blunt. Stopping by Markham's house will taint everything and cost you the arrest."

Laura blanched, but started talking to regain her composure. "I don't think so. I went back through my search and seizure files from when I practiced law—the cases are a little old but still good law, far as I know. My position as Commissioner was not as a sworn officer, and arguably I could have searched his house and it wouldn't have been under color of law. But as soon as the Governor relieved me of my job—and at that time, neither of us had a clue about where this was headed—I lost what little color of law I ever had."

"That's a very fine line," Logan said. "I wouldn't go to the bank with that one."

"And I never told one lie while I was there and neither did Ann."

"Ann who?"

"Ann Hilman, Tom's wife," Laura said. "She went with me.

Logan threw his head back in frustration. "Jesus Christ."

"She's the only person who's not a cop who I could trust. It may make it messier, but it's no more or less unconstitutional."

"I don't believe this."

"Wait till you hear what she found," Blake said.

Laura went to the chalkboard where the floor plan to Markham's house was sketched out.

"This is central portion of Alex's new house."

Logan watched her carefully.

"If Tom were standing right here at the corner when he was shot and fell forward, he might have gripped the walls as he dropped. He'd get green paint on the left hand and beige on the other. Blood would be all over this area. The bullet went through the brain, so let's say it hit this wall." She drew a dotted line across the living room. "The wallboard slowed it down enough so that it lodged in the plasterboard, went all the way through the board, and out the other side—or dropped in the space between the walls."

She looked at Logan to make certain he was still with her, and then continued. "There's no furniture in the living room except the paintings because the floors haven't been sealed. But the bedroom was finished and furnished. If Alex had to get the bullet out, it would look really peculiar to mess up the wallboard in the living room, so he covered that hole with bondo or something, and touched it up. Then he conveniently knocked over a dresser in the bedroom, crushed the wall right behind here, and fished out the bullet. Then he made a mess cleaning up all the blood.

"When the workmen arrive, they replace the wallboard, repaint the mess he made in the living room and foyer, re-sand and seal the floors, and presto, no evidence."

"Neat," Logan said.

"And tidy. Not a shred of evidence against him except the two paint specks he missed under Tom's fingernails."

Logan looked at each of them, shaking his head. "And you can't prove that because you tainted the search."

"Are you so certain?" Blake asked.

"I can't think of a judge who would give you a search warrant based on your evidence." Logan sat back, folding his arms across his chest, looking at the four crestfallen faces. "But let's assume the best and the Commissioner's right. You need to know where Alex was that night. But the person who would know, if anybody, is Easterbrook. And as far as I'm concerned, he's a weasel."

"What do you know about McNee?"

"Good guy. Straight shooter. But all of them—and most of all the SAC—are scared shitless of Markham and his father. No one wants to get transferred to Fargo for screwing up."

Robert's pager went off and he automatically went to the phone and punched in some numbers. "It looks like my visit and the fax did the trick," Robert said as he hung up. "Walter McNee's calling me and apparently he's pretty hot about something."

"Guess we'll have to give him the paint results and have a set-to pretty soon."

"Wait a minute," Logan interrupted. "Before you call McNee, you need to think this through. Panic would set in with any United States Attorney in this sort of spot. But Markham isn't your run-of-the-mill U.S.A. He's got a big wheel daddy holding everyone's purse strings." Logan stood up and stretched nervously. "Two seconds, maybe three, after you tell someone at the Bureau—anybody—even Hal, they'll start covering their collective asses. The SAC will call the Director. The Director will call the Attorney General. The Attorney General will call the White House. The President will call, ummm, he'll call Senator Markham directly, and if he's not home, he'll call whoever the right guy is at the Senate."

Laura, who had been pondering Tom's financial summaries, looked up. "Senate Majority Leader."

Logan nodded. "Whoever. The point is, assuming everyone's home to take the call, it could all happen within twenty-five minutes. Then the whole thing comes down on you."

"I assume that is what you would normally do?" Blake asked. "Maybe not through the FBI, but you'd call the DEA Administrator, right?"

"Right."

"But you're not going to quite yet, right?"

Everyone was looking at him. "Right," Logan said. "All I did tonight was talk about the Hilman narcotic evidence, right?" he said.

They all nodded, but silence filled the room for a long awkward moment. Laura broke the tension. "I really appreciate your coming—more than I can say."

"The least I can do—I wouldn't want to be in any of your shoes."

"So you're saying we'd better have him in custody before all that starts to happen," Blake said.

"I would," Logan said. "Maybe whatever Robert said is enough of a nudge that he'll do something stupid."

"The builder told me he's leaving tomorrow for California," Laura said.

"The warrants are ready to go," Robert added. "I've just got to find a judge."

"I'm thinkin' worst-case," Blake said. "Markham takes off while we had evidence we didn't promptly disclose and the Commissioner..." he looked at Laura, "excuse me, Ms. Owen is off the hook for murder, and on the hook for all the mistakes we made. Not to mention the rest of our butts."

"You've only made three mistakes with the FBI that I can see," said Logan. "Hedging on paint results that weren't meaningful yet, was one. Horning in on their investigation, which they do to you all the time and doesn't really count, that's two. And three is not telling them immediately about Rodriguez and Hilman."

Then he turned toward Laura. "But I still believe you did yourself in, Commissioner. I hope I'm wrong, I really do."

"At the very least, I can use the evidence to prove I didn't do it. Even if it's suppressed against Alex."

"Now that's a novel idea," Logan said. "Hadn't thought of it that way. You're probably right."

Robert leaned forward. "I think I'd better get started shopping these search warrants around before we give up on finding an judge."

"And you ought to find that builder—he's probably read the paper by now and put two and two together," Logan said. "Let's hope he didn't report your little visit to Markham."

"The architect, Ben Essman, was there, too, and he knows me," Laura said. "Doesn't know Ann, but knows me."

Robert stood up. "If you don't need me, I'll be on my way."

"What about McNee?"

"I'll return the call a little later."

The intercom rang. "It's for you, Blake," Catherine said.

Blake took the handset and listened for a moment. "Markham's on his way to the airport with at least a fifteen minute head start. The guys missed him when he left."

"I'll go out Lakeland," Robert said, moving for the door.

"I'm going with you," Laura said.

"I don't think that's such a good idea...," Robert protested.

"I don't care," Laura said. "Let's go."

"I'll be right behind you," Blake said. He turned to Catherine. "Catherine, call Walter McNee with the paint results. Tell him we're going to arrest Markham."

Blake looked at Logan. "What's Markham's office number?"

"His direct line is 959-6515. His secretary's name is Gloria but they may have already left for the day."

Blake gave Logan a salute and was out the door. Logan called after him, "Don't forget, Markham's got his pilot's license."

As he hustled to his car, Blake dialed Markham's office on his cellular phone. "Gloria, this is Blake Coleman at the Patrol. I need to speak to Alex Markham, please. It's quite important."

"He just left for California."

"Damn, this is really important. Do you think I could catch him if I had him paged at the airport?"

"You can try. He's on Delta 725. It was scheduled to depart around 6:00 P.M., but it's running late."

"Thanks.

26

Hal drove past the General Aviation offices with its tarmac full of small planes and then up the ramp, stopping at the Delta entrance. Curbside check-in was closed. Alex hopped out, opened the back door, and handed out his clubs to Hal, while he got the suitcase and briefcase.

"You don't need to wait," Alex said as they entered the terminal. "I've got a confirmed reservation."

"Sure?" Hal asked, looking over the long line.

"Absolutely. I'll call you at home in the morning to get an update and I'll plan to see you end of the week. But if something's going to break, I can come back immediately."

"Probably won't be necessary. Even though her fingerprints were there—and they remain a puzzle—I think this is coming down to a professional hit and we'll never know who did it."

"You could be right," Alex said. "All it would take to get her prints is access to her trash."

"We're already checking into that." Hal drew closer to Alex, making absolutely certain no one overheard him. "I doubt it will stick on Owen, but she'll never recover from the exposure, that's for sure."

"Hope you're right about that," Alex said, looking around to see if anyone had noticed him. "But damn, she can be a cold-blooded bitch." He moved his bags one position closer to the ticket counter. "Thanks for your help and counsel. I don't say that often enough and I should."

"Sure thing," Hal said, vaguely uneasy with Alex's sudden flattery.

They shook hands. When Hal had pulled away from the curb, Alex picked up his bags, took the escalator downstairs and approached the first cab in line.

"General Aviation," Alex said.

The driver shook his head.

"I can't carry all of this," Alex said. "I've got a bad back. I'll pay you twenty dollars."

The fellow stuck out his hand for the money.

"When we get there," Alex said.

"I'm not losin' my place in this line for a quarter mile trip without the money in advance," the man said.

Alex thrust a crumpled bill toward him. "Let's go."

▪ ▪ ▪ ▪

Robert keyed the mike for the hi-band radio. "B-Boy, B-27."

"B-27 here," the investigator answered.

"Where are you?" Robert asked.

"About three minutes from the terminal."

"Get to Delta and find out if he checked in."

"You know the flight?"

"No, and I'm just assuming it's Delta. I'll be there in a minute."

▪ ▪ ▪ ▪

"Good afternoon, Mr. Markham," said the manager of General Aviation, a tanned, athletic type. "Good to see you again. Your plane's almost ready. They're fueling it now. It's eight-one-whiskey, the blue and white Cessna 210, parked closest to the runway on the south line."

Alex forced himself to smile—the plane was supposed to be ready. "Good, I like that one. Any problems with my flight plan?"

"Nothing. Clear sailing all the way to the Bahamas."

"Great."

"Your trip sounds mighty attractive."

"It is mighty attractive."

"Need any help with the door?"

"I can get it," Alex said.

"And you'll be back by next Sunday?"

"Got to be here Monday for work, bright and early, unfortunately."

"Have a great trip."

Alex walked out onto the general aviation ramp and spotted the blue and white Cessna with N6781W on the side. He headed briskly toward it.

▪ ▪ ▪ ▪

Walter dialed Hal's cell phone from his office while he checked his ammunition.

Hal answered, "Easterbrook."

"Do you have Markham with you?"

"Dropped him off at the airport already."

"Go back and get him."

"Why?"

"Get to a pay phone if you want an explanation—but just get to him and hold him."

"For what reason?" Hal asked.

"The State Patrol is headed to the airport—if they're not already there—to make an arrest."

Hal didn't respond.

"Do you understand now?"

"I do."

Walter bolted out the door into the entryway. The receptionist waved through the bulletproof glass at him, and he stopped.

"Find the boss. Tell him the State Patrol is going to arrest Markham. I'm headed out to the airport now. Send anyone else you can find. Tell them to meet me at the main terminal."

▪ ▪ ▪ ▪

"A-1, B-Boy," Blake said as he raced down Lakeland Drive for the airport.

"B-Boy," Robert answered. "Go ahead."

"Where are you?"

"Turning in Airport Road."

"He's on Delta Flight 725," Blake said.

"He didn't check in," came another voice. "This is B-27, Chief. I just talked to the Delta people."

"He's got to be there somewhere," Blake said. "Start checking all the other flights. I'll go to General Aviation, just in case. He's got a pilot's license."

▪ ▪ ▪ ▪

"I'm sorry to bother you, sir," said the FBI office receptionist to the Special Agent in Charge, "but there's something you need to know."

"Go ahead," the SAC said from the phone on the veranda at his racquet club. "I've got a doubles match waiting for me."

"The State Patrol is headed to the airport to arrest Alex Markham for the murder of Thomas Hilman. Agent Easterbrook had just dropped Mr.

Markham off. Agent McNee's on his way out there also."

The SAC stared off across the courts, stunned.

"Sir?"

"I'm here," the SAC said. "I'm coming back in. Track down the FBI Director. I'll call him as soon as I arrive. He'll need to call the Attorney General."

▪ ▪ ▪ ▪

Robert looked in his rearview mirror to see whose blue light was behind him.

"Goddammit, it's Hal Easterbrook."

Laura turned to look back. "I'll deal with Hal," she offered. "You go on in."

As fast as they pulled up to the arrival level of the terminal, Hal was out of his car headed for Robert.

"Go on," she called out to Robert, scurrying around the end of the car and yanking on Hal's sleeve to stop him.

"Get out of my way," Hal snarled. "I want an explanation."

"The paint under Tom Hilman's fingernails," Laura said, jerking him around so that Hal had to face at her. "Those particles that the killer missed. They came from Alex's house."

That got his attention. "How do you know this?"

"From the contractor."

"And that makes Markham the killer?" Hal said.

"We'll have even more proof after we search the house."

"Let me talk to Robert."

Laura had slowed Hal down enough to let Robert get in the building unhindered. "Be my guest."

▪ ▪ ▪ ▪

"Jackson ground, Cessna eight-one-whiskey, on the general aviation ramp, taxi for takeoff," ground control said. "We're using one-six right for takeoff. Taxi out of the ramp on Charlie seven—left on Charlie, left on Bravo, right on Alpha. Contact tower, one-two-zero-point-nine, on Alpha."

"Roger, ground control," said Alex, and he repeated his instructions.

▪ ▪ ▪ ▪

Blake dashed into General Aviation, pulling out his credentials.

"Did Alex Markham rent a plane today?"

"Yes, sir. He's headed to the runway now."

"Can you stop him?"

The man shook his head.

"You've got to stop him. He's wanted for murder, and he's escaping."

The General Aviation manager was frozen with astonishment.

"You're never going to see your goddamn plane again if you don't stop him. Which runway is he headed to?"

"I think they're using one-six-right," the manager said, pointing west past the main terminal. He moved toward the phone to call the tower.

"Do what you can," Blake said, sprinting out the door.

▪ ▪ ▪ ▪

Robert was keying his portable radio when Hal appeared.

"Where are you?" Robert said.

"General Aviation," Blake said. "Markham rented a plane. He's already out there, going for the west runway. I'm going to get out there somehow."

Hal turned and bolted for the door.

Robert looked around wildly. "Not a cop in sight."

"Let's go out on the observation deck," Laura said, already running in that direction. "Maybe we can see something and direct Blake."

▪ ▪ ▪ ▪

Blake jumped in his car and backed onto the street just as a truck approached the gate on the airfield side and the chainlink rattled open. Before the truck could block him, Blake shot through the opening, careening around the vehicles in front of him, and racing onto the taxi way.

▪ ▪ ▪ ▪

Robert and Laura could see a small private plane on the crossover between the runways, turning toward the takeoff point.

"Blake," Robert shouted into his portable. "He's turned to taxi to the top of that far runway."

"I see him," Blake answered.

▪ ▪ ▪ ▪

Walter's and two other FBI cars piled into the lower level reserved parking spaces just as Hal took off in his car, heading for General Aviation. As

Hal approached the gate at the end of the terminal where the airport police and administrative personnel park, a dark sedan drove up. The driver inserted a key-card to open the gate. Hal stomped on the accelerator and jumped the curb, sweeping through the gate ahead of the Buick.

Baggage carriers were converging all around Hal in preparation for the Delta flight that was arriving. Hal swerved, narrowly missing a carrier loaded with U.S. Mail flats. As he cleared the area, he could see a Delta jet on final approach, landing gear down.

Markham would be forced to wait. There was a chance to catch him.

■ ■ ■

"Cessna eight-one-whiskey," called ground control, "switch to tower 120.9."

Alex reached forward and changed the frequency setting on his radio, then keyed his mike. "Tower, Cessna eight-one-whiskey on Alpha."

"Cessna eight-one-whiskey," the tower replied, "taxi up to and hold short of runway one-six-right. There's a Delta MD-80 on a two-mile final."

"Hold short, one-six right, eight-one-whiskey," Alex repeated back.

"Delta 1248, cleared to land," announced the tower.

"Cleared to land, Delta 1248. Wind check?" called the Delta MD-80.

"One-eight-zero at five knots," replied the tower.

Alex moved toward the threshold of the runway, pulling up to the hold-short line.

■ ■ ■

Blake saw a car, with flashing blue lights on the rear deck, cutting a diagonal swath across the grass and runways, headed for Alex.

"Robert," he called into the radio. "Who the hell is ahead of me?"

"Hal Easterbrook, I'm pretty sure."

■ ■ ■

Alex looked to his left at the sea of blue, red and white airport lights. Daylight was fading fast. As he glanced to the left at the wind sock, he noticed the pulsing blue lights of two cars, tearing toward him. The closest one was crossing the grass with the second right behind it. He reached into his briefcase and pulled out his .38 snub-nosed revolver, laying it on the seat beside him. He shoved the throttle in and headed out onto the runway.

"Cessna eight-one-whiskey, your clearance was to hold short!" said the tower insistently.

Alex kept moving.

"CESSNA EIGHT-ONE-WHISKEY, HOLD SHORT!! DELTA 1248, GO-AROUND, GO-AROUND!! AIRCRAFT ON THE RUNWAY!!"

The jet was about a half mile from the end of one-six-right, landing gear in place, 150 feet in the air, and no more than ten seconds from touching down. It was still descending as Alex finished his turn onto the runway.

"Delta 1248, going around," called the Delta pilot as he clicked off the flight director with his left thumb, shoved the throttles forward, and pulled back on yoke, calling for go-around power. The downward inertia of the MD-80 would keep it descending for several seconds, smoke pouring out of the tailpipe all the while.

Alex aligned the Cessna with the runway and firewalled the throttle.

"CESSNA EIGHT-ONE-WHISKEY!" the tower shouted, panicking at the possibility that Alex would lift off into the MD-80. "CANCEL YOUR TAKEOFF CLEARANCE!"

Alex was on the roll.

"CESSNA EIGHT-ONE-WHISKEY, DO YOU COPY? CANCEL YOUR TAKEOFF CLEARANCE!"

Alex recognized Hal as he passed the car closest to him and angrily waved him off.

Hal swung around behind the plane, caught up, and stayed side by side along the right. He rolled down his window, waving to get Alex's attention and honking the horn.

Alex saw Blake closing in from the left, heading dead for the plane. Alex opened the latch, lifted the window, and aimed his gun at Blake.

"Goddamn fool," Hal screamed, keeping his palm glued to the horn. He steered with his knees as he pulled out his 9mm pistol and fired once into the cockpit, a split second before Alex fired into Blake's windshield. Blake's car swerved away.

Hal popped off five more rounds in rapid succession and managed to spray the right side of the Cessna, punching holes in both windows and the door before piercing the cowling and nicking a fuel line. He didn't know what damage he'd done, but a thin mist was coming out around the exhaust stacks. He stopped shooting when the high-pitched whine of the still-approaching MD-80 suddenly became a deafening, screaming roar. The huge plane passed barely 75 feet above them, landing gear still down, bringing with it a tunnel of turbulence.

Alex had dropped his gun on the floor to concentrate on flying. Fifty knots, sixty, seventy—then the air speed indicator momentarily pegged as the jet blast hit him. It was all Alex could do to keep the Cessna from flipping over on its back.

"CESSNA EIGHT-ONE-WHISKEY, I REPEAT, CANCEL YOUR TAKEOFF CLEARANCE," shouted the tower.

Alex's bullet had shattered Blake's car windshield, but missed Blake. Blake fell back in behind the plane, rocking in the wake of the MD-80. He accelerated, planning to ram the plane from the back. Small tongs of fire were licking out from the space between the engine cowl and the fuselage on the underside of the plane.

As Alex desperately fought to keep control of the Cessna in the turbulent aftermath of the jet wake, he yanked the plane off the runway and banked away from Hal. The Cessna pitched up and the gas that had accumulated in the bottom of the cowling sloshed back, bursting into flame as it contacted the red-hot exhaust. The plane, streaming a trail of orange fire, climbed steeply into the air a hundred feet or so, before the fuel line broke completely, killing the engine.

Blake and Hal both slammed on their brakes, slid to a stop, and threw their doors open. They were standing half in, half out of their cars as they heard the engine sputter. The plane appeared to slide back on its tail, then it rolled off to the right, landing on the wing tip and cartwheeling over onto its left wing. The fuel tanks ripped open and exploded. The entire plane burst into flames. Fire engines could be heard screaming on the crossover.

From the observation deck, Laura and Robert watched, riveted as the darkening sky burst into color. Laura stared, shaking her head, her hands covering her mouth as if to keep away the horror. Robert saw the agony of the last days suddenly coalesce in the horrific sight. Laura leaned against him in her exhaustion and he gently put his arm around her shoulder and held her as they watched the drama come to its violent end.

27

Reporters jammed the conference room of the Governor's Mansion. When the Governor, still dressed in his tuxedo for the Arts Awards, and Laura, in a straight dark-blue dress and heels, entered, the lights went on, shutters clicked, and the TV cameras began rolling.

Catherine, Blake, and Robert stood in the back, along with an assortment of onlookers. Vic, who'd entered behind Laura, made his way down the side of the room and stood next to Blake. At the last minute, Rachel Stone slipped in the door and threaded her way through the crowd to Robert's side, ever elegant even with surgical scrubs peeking below her coat. Her hand reached out for his and she squeezed it tightly.

The Governor stepped up to a low podium set at the end of the conference table and waited until everyone had settled down and all the cameras were rolling.

"I'm announcing the reinstatement of Laura Owen as Commissioner of Public Safety effective immediately," Carver said simply, displaying little or no emotion about the decision. He turned to Laura and she stepped up to the TV microphones.

"As my first official act back on the job, I must announce the death of United States Attorney Alex Markham. He was killed while fleeing from arrest for the murder of Thomas Hilman."

There were gasps all around the room.

"Over the past few days, since the discovery of Thomas Hilman's body, the State Patrol has been working around the clock, in concert with federal authorities, to solve the murder. Evidence was developed this afternoon that conclusively linked Alex Markham to that murder.

"By that point, Markham was booked on a flight to California. He did not take the commercial flight, but instead rented a twin-engine Cessna from General Aviation. He was attempting to leave when his plane was surrounded by both FBI and State Patrol vehicles. Ignoring instructions from the control tower, Markham pulled out in front of a Delta jet to takeoff. Shots were fired to stop the plane, hitting the fuselage and breaking a fuel line. After takeoff, the engine stalled and the plane crashed, killing Mr. Markham."

Laura looked slowly around the room at all the stunned faces. The Associated Press stringer was gripping the handle of the door, ready to dash out and file his report.

"Before I take any questions, I want to give credit where credit is due. Were it not for the remarkable work of three people—Blake Coleman, Chief of Patrol; Robert Stone, Assistant Chief of Criminal Investigations; and Catherine Britton, Director of the Crime Lab, we would not have discovered the truth about Thomas Hilman's death." Laura motioned for them to come forward.

Self-consciously, the three stepped out of the crowd as the cameras spun around to film them. Laura smiled at each one and then turned back to the reporters. "A year ago, I hardly knew these three people, but today I can confidently say that, without them, I couldn't do my job. There are no finer law enforcement professionals anywhere." She stood back, applauding them, and heard the Governor's strong clapping behind her. The audience followed suit.

After the applause died down, Laura took a deep breath. "I'll take questions now."

"Ms. Owen! Commissioner!"

Tim Cropley had not raised his hand. Laura started to signal to a reporter in front but paused, looking at Cropley, quizzically. "Mr. Cropley, don't you have a question?"

He didn't respond.

She turned and pointed to an eager young woman.

▪ ▪ ▪ ▪

It was shortly before ten when Blake finally got home, but the lights were still on, and Sally ran out of the house to meet him. They stood still, wrapped in their embrace for a long time.

"I wish I could have come, but there was no one to stay with Mother."

"I knew that, I wasn't expecting you."

"Is that a new car?" Sally asked as they walked, arm in arm to the house.

"The other's in the shop," Blake said.

"Was it damaged that badly?"

"Nothing major, really. It'll take a day or two to fix." He hoped she'd never see the windshield and the place in the seat, three inches from his shoulder, where the bullet finally lodged.

"So tell me what happened," Sally insisted.

"Let's see what the news says. Then I'll tell you the real story."

▪ ▪ ▪ ▪

Alex's driveway was full of official cars and vans when the builder arrived. He parked his pickup on the street. Since he had a spare key to the house, knew how the alarm system worked, and would be able to tell them about the re-sanding and painting that had been done, they'd waited for him to arrive.

After Robert pointed out the areas where the crime scene technicians were to gather paint samples, the builder described the details of all the extra work they had done during the last week. Combining the autopsy analysis about the direction the bullet had traveled with where the wallboard had been damaged and the floor re-sanded, they were able to narrow down where the bullet would have entered the far wall. Catherine and a technician went over the area with magnifying glasses and finally found a small spot that had been carefully patched and sanded. They sent for a saber saw to cut out the portion around the patch.

Robert and Walter McNee debated removing the baseboard, and after hearing about the extent of the area defaced by Alex's cleaning job, decided to go ahead. The builder knew where nearly every nail was and skillfully pulled the baseboard back from the wall. A tiny line of blood had seeped down behind and they were able to scrape off samples. Later that evening when the house could be darkened sufficiently for luminol to phosphoresce any other blood particles, they'd come back.

Outside the house when no one else was around, Robert stopped Walter to talk. "Blake told me he's been trying to get up with Hal all weekend, but none of his calls have been returned."

"Hal's been suspended, pending the outcome of the investigation."

"But that's standard, isn't it?"

"Yeah, but Hal doesn't have many friends in the office. He's been keeping as low a profile as possible."

"I didn't get along with the guy very well either, but I've got to hand it to him. Blake says Hal probably saved his life, distracting Alex the way he did," Robert said.

"Between you and me," Walter said, "I doubt either Alex or Hal could have made their shots. But Hal did try, I'll give him that. How's the Commissioner doing?"

"This hasn't exactly been a cakewalk."

"Tell her I'm awfully sorry," Walter said. "I really disagreed with the way they were handling it."

"She knows that—it came through loud and clear."

■ ■ ■ ■

Monday afternoon was sunny and warm enough for Carolina Jasmine buds to open. Driving back from the veterinarian where Ranger had passed her first physical with flying colors, Will had fallen asleep with the little retriever lying across his leg, snoozing.

Laura pulled into her driveway, relieved that Ann's car was gone. It would be the first night in weeks that she and Will would be alone, and though once it had frightened her, this was now the way it should be. Ranger woke up but Will didn't, so she put the puppy inside a small fenced area near four Adirondack chairs on the back lawn and left Will to sleep in the backseat. She could watch him from the lawn.

As she was heading into the house, Blake and Robert drove up. Blake called over the roof of the car as he got out, "I see the puppy arrived."

"Shhhh," Laura pointed to the car and Will.

He mouthed the word, *Sorry.*

They walked quietly past the car.

"Something to drink?" Laura asked. "Coke? A beer?"

"Sure. Coke, please. It's too early for a beer. Robert?"

"Water would be fine, please, ma'am."

"I'll be right back." Laura motioned to the chairs. "We can sit over there."

When she reappeared with the drinks, Blake had Ranger out of her pen and was playing tug-of-war with a stick. Robert was leaning back, his eyes closed in the warm sun.

In between Ranger's little barks and growls wrestling with Blake, Robert brought Laura up to date. "Guess what was in the safe-deposit box."

"Money?"

"Nope," Robert said. "A To-whom-it-may-concern letter. Apparently, years ago, Tom was with Alex—actually, Alex was driving Tom's father's company truck—when they hit and killed a man. They fled the scene and never admitted it to anyone."

"We checked with the sheriff's office," Blake said, "and there was a hit and run in exactly the place Tom mentioned in the letter, same date. The file indicated there wasn't anything to go on except broken glass and a beer can but the prints on it could never be identified."

"I bet I rescued those files. Don't you remember, Blake," Robert said, opening one eye as he turned his head toward him, "When the former sheriff died and that idiot the Board of Supervisors appointed as the interim sheriff threw everything out? I'll wager that case file was in the stuff I pulled from the trash."

"Well, whatever," Blake said. "There must have been quite a ruckus about it. The victim was a bright, young, hardworking man with a family, who'd done a tour in Vietnam. Served with distinction."

"But you can't be sure that Alex was driving," Laura said.

"That's true," Robert said, his eyes closed again, soaking in the sun, "but if he was, it could explain why Alex covered Hilman on his smuggling operation. Rodriguez said Tom was certain Alex would bail him out. And the only way I can think of that happening was if Tom had some leverage over him—or Alex thought he did."

"Or he would make a lot a money," Laura said.

"Maybe, but Alex had money," said Blake. "Didn't need any more, and certainly didn't need the risk. What he wanted was to be Governor—so bad, he could taste it. And you were horning in on his limelight. And he needed to get rid of Hilman. So he kills him, frames you, and gets rid of you as a political rival forever."

"You're probably right," Laura said, stretching forward to scratch Ranger's head. "Anyway, it's over."

"We'll—actually, you'll—be feeling the repercussions from all this for a long time to come," said Blake.

"You're right about that. Carver wasn't in favor of reinstating me—he saw it as a great opportunity to move a new, less controversial person in. But Vic convinced him the sympathy for me would be strong enough to create a backlash if he didn't reinstate me."

"I gotta remember to thank Vic," Blake said.

"Sandy Quinn said it was touch and go, right up to the last minute," Robert added.

"But Carver was in a box," Laura said. "He was going to catch hell from Senator Markham and didn't need to piss off everyone else at the same time."

"You know, it's possible that Senator Markham will resign in disgrace," Robert said.

"And Carver will get his seat which is what he wants anyway," Laura said.

"The Senator's already scheming, I know that," Blake said. "He's up at his place in the Delta. People have been streaming in since he arrived last night."

"How do you know that?" Laura asked.

Blake smiled. "I never reveal..."

"Your sources," Laura finished. "Sorry, I should know better by now."

Laura looked over at Will who had awakened and was heading toward Ranger. Will looked more and more like Semmes with every passing day. "If Carver takes Markham's Senate seat, I'm history," she said quietly.

"Markham's not going to resign," Blake said.

Laura looked at him quizzically.

"He's not," Blake said. "Trust me."

"How do you know these things?" Laura said.

"A master," Robert said. "We worship at the feet of a true master."

Blake smiled broadly, displaying the long dimples that he kept hidden most of the time. It felt good.

"What they took away from you will always be lost," Robert said quietly.

Blake sipped his drink. "Death is better than either Markham or Hilman deserved."

Robert still hadn't opened his eyes. "At least you won't have to share this sun with the likes of them ever again."

Laura's eyes glistened as Will came running toward her with Ranger fast on his heels. She gathered him up on her lap and gave him a very tight hug. The puppy was jumping up to be included.

"Is something wrong, Momma?"

"Not a thing, my little man, not a thing."